Copyright 2021 for Caroline Angel

Cover design by Red Cape Graphic Design

Edited by P.J. Blakey-Novis, Red Cape Publishing

First Edition Published 2021 by Red Cape Publishing

The characters and events in this book are fictitious. Any similarities to real persons, living or dead, is coincidental and not intended by the author.

To Helen, thank you for being there for me. I treasure your support, encouragement, and love.

ORIGIN OF EVIL

Book Two

Beginnings

Caroline Angel

Chapter One
Earth
Present Day
Donald Greene

Sometimes the night is a little colder in the mountains than in the city, but Donald didn't mind. He liked the crisp, clear nights, and the stark relief of crystal cut stars spread against the black velvet of a late spring sky. Life was good, his work was going well, and if things went to plan, by this weekend he would be an engaged man.

He was pretty sure that things would go to plan.

Huffing the last of his garbage bins to the curb, Donald ran one hand through his hair and looked up at the stars. The sight of the endless sky never failed to fill him with awe. Away from the city lights there seemed to be so many more stars than was possible, a scattering of light against dark that was worth taking a few moments to admire.

Down the way a little, there was a streetlight, but it was at the far end of his quiet little cul-de-sac, and his ancient porch light barely spread its soft illumination to the front gate. Even so, when the lights crackled and went out for a second, Donald was plunged into darkness so complete he could not even see a hand before his face. He waited a moment and his lights crackled, blinked on and off again before coming back on, albeit at half the strength they were before.

He pulled his robe tighter against the chill and tiptoed hurriedly back inside, his bare feet near frozen on the cold concrete of his drive. He was worried the power would go out, and stay out this time, as it often did on the mountain. For all the joys of living out of the city, the one bugbear was how many times the power went out. Always some half-tanked asshole driving into a pole on the main highway and taking down the lines that fed this whole side of the mountain. Donald would have to get his candles and flashlights ready in case the power did go down, for sure if it cut out he would spend half the night in darkness. Fortunately, his clock radio had a battery backup so he would not be late getting up for work, but his water was fed by a tank and that needed the pump to power it. If the power didn't come back on, he'd be off to work shower-less. Not for the first time, either.

Thank God for deodorant.

He nearly made it back onto the porch before the power did go out, the hiss and crackle of the lightbulb on his porch heralded a deep blackness that would not allow him of even a hint of where the front steps may be. He'd foolishly neglected to put on shoes before making his garbage bin run, and he didn't want to crack a toe on the heavy wood steps that led up to his elevated front porch and doorway. He stuffed a hand into his robe pocket and breathed a sigh of relief when his fingers found purchase with a packet of cigarettes and a lighter. No need to scramble around in the pitch-blackness of the night, he had his own little torch of fire, courtesy of Bic. Donald pulled out the lighter and illuminated his way up the front steps until he was standing by his front door. From his vantage point he could see down into the valley, across his side of the treed mountain, all the way to the city's edge. Complete blackness greeted him most of the way - whatever had taken out the power must have blown the main substation right at the start of the highway. The lights came on from the other side of the highway, that side run by a different substation. *Well, that's just great*, he thought. *Power will probably be out most of the night, maybe right through the next day.*

Pulling out the crumpled soft pack of cigarettes, Donald let the lighter go out for a moment as he extricated one of the smokes with his teeth, lit it up, and blew a stream of unseen smoke out into the darkness. *Can't watch TV, can't get on the computer, may as well smoke for a while.*

He leaned against the wooden railing that enclosed his front porch and circled the house. It was old, but sturdy, and an oft-used place for Donald as he smoked and contemplated life's mysteries. Or tried to work out his weekly projections for work. Either way, it was his favorite spot to smoke and pass the night away. If it wasn't a weeknight, and damned cold, he may have had a beer or two while standing out there reducing his life expectancy with a couple of Camels. Just one smoke tonight, then off to bed, seeing as how there was nothing else he could do with the power out.

A snap of a twig didn't alarm him, even when it

was followed by a rustle in the undergrowth of the thickly grown shrubs that surrounded his house. Donald lived on a couple of acres on a softly sloped block on the side of the mountain, both native and non-indigenous plantings heavily grouped around the property, and they hid a multitude of small wildlife that would fossick around, especially on garbage night, hoping for a dropped scrap or a fallen treat. Donald would occasionally leave food out for the small creatures that lived on, and around, his property, he also had several tall bird feeders that were kept well stocked with seeds and nuts for the native critters. The rustling grew closer, the bushes near him whispered of their unseen occupant and Donald was sorry that there was no light to see what forest creature was gracing his presence.

Once his girlfriend agreed to be his wife, he would set about renovating this old house, bringing it up to a standard suitable for a bride and, hopefully before too long, a family. Maybe two or even three kids, running around the trees and shrubs, feeding the animals, maybe he'd get a dog and even a cat, as well. This would be a great place to bring up a family, and he knew his girlfriend loved it as much as he did. She would be thrilled with the thought of renovating the house and Donald was sure he wouldn't get much say in the new décor or even the layout of most of the rooms. He smiled to himself as he dragged deeply on his smoke. Life was good. Life was *very* good.

The bushes rustled again but this time something was different, something sounded out of place.

Donald couldn't pin down how he thought things may have changed, but suddenly gooseflesh broke out all over him, and the hairs on the back of his neck stood on end.

He turned his head to see where the noise was coming from, but the darkness was too complete, he couldn't see anything other than the softly glowing tip of his smoke, the world had been plunged into complete blackness and he was blind to anything hidden within it.

He still held the Bic in one hand but knew if he lit it up it would only make things worse, he would be able to see only his immediate surroundings. Whatever was lurking in the shrubs would still be hidden from him. He squeezed his fist tight around the Bic as the rustling grew even louder, until it stopped suddenly, somewhere in front of him, somewhere around the front steps. He hoped it wasn't a bear; though he had never seen one around here, he had heard stories. Though he was not a fearful man, the thought of a large bear in the complete darkness and chill of this late spring night was a bit more than he wanted to have to deal with. He sucked in his last lungful of smoke and flipped the butt off into the darkness, the gooseflesh on his arms still present, his senses on overdrive with a fear that sprang unheeded.

Donald pulled his robe as tight as he could around himself and turned to go inside, he would feel much safer with his door bolted tight against the unseen and certainly unfounded night fears that had taken hold of him. He didn't usually spook, at least not this easily, and he was quite ready to shake it off and climb under his goose down quilt, willing sleep to take him away from whatever night creatures were on the loose this dark evening. He tensed as the wooden decking on the porch creaked as if someone was creeping towards him, someone stealthy and almost silent, and Donald felt his heart start to beat a faster rhythm in his chest. A bear would not creep so quietly and slowly towards him, and even though he was fairly sure his imagination was beginning to run wild, he didn't desire to take any chances. Old houses creaked, it happened to this one all the time. Why he was feeling fear growing like a coiling snake in his stomach he could not explain, but it was a feeling he was not enjoying, and he was keen to put it behind him. He flicked the Bic with his thumb, the flame sputtered at first before catching, a single beacon of light against the suddenly oppressive dark.

Donald thrust his hand out in front of himself as he stepped towards his front door, then cursed as a gust of breeze blew out the small flame. He flicked the lighter again, and just for a second as it caught, he thought he saw something, some*thing*, there, near the door.

The cigarette lighter was growing hot under its extended use, but Donald held on, he did not want to lose his one bright ward against the darkness. Again, a soft breeze as flimsy as an exhaled breath extinguished his lighter and this time Donald was sure he saw something as the flame died, something tall, something dark, something *not quite human.*

His thumb flicked the lighter again and this time the flame sputtered but stayed lit. Donald felt the breath catch in his throat as the figure before him leaned forward, and he saw the face of evil up close.

Donald dropped his lighter as his bladder let go in fear. The thing before him stepped forward and Donald threw his head back, his lungs filling with air to scream, but the sound died unreleased as a hand as cold and strong as dark iron gripped his neck from behind and lifted him from his feet, dangling him in the air, his feet kicking, scrambling for purchase, but finding none.

His heart was beating an irregular staccato beat, so hard that it seemed it would burst from his chest, the strong hand around his neck growing tighter, the fingers circling his throat and cutting his air supply. The hand lifted him still higher and now forward, just a little, until Donald was face to face with the unseen thing. He could see, just faintly, a pair of glowing green eyes, eyes that were not human, that were half lidded and seemed to swirl with an evil power.

He lifted his hands to claw at the grip around his throat, his lungs now screaming for oxygen, his heart hammering its beat in panic and fear, pulsing spots of color appearing before his eyes as his vision swam. He clawed at the cold hand, the skin impervious to his nails raking against it, the grip too tight, too cruel. Surely, he would soon pass out. Still he fought, still he kicked his legs, his heart now changing its rhythm to one of an irregular pounding of impending death.

Donald kicked forward, trying to connect with the thing that held him aloft, but he missed, the arm span of this thing was too wide.

As he felt his life start to leave, his soul crying out for release, the thing leaned in and tore a chunk of his throat away with its cruel, sharp fangs. Finally, the grip loosened, dropping him to the cold wooden boards. Donald desperately gulped a breath of air as he felt the thing lean over him and suck at his gaping wound, drinking his life blood as it spilled freely from the ragged edges of his torn skin.

Mercy came too late for Donald as consciousness left him, his last thought not of his love, his future fiancé, nor of the life he had lived, but of the green glowing eyes that stared into his as it fed from his life's blood.

Across the valley and up to the highway below, the lights crackled and came back to life.

Chapter Two
Earth
Present Day
The Pinup Boys

Detective Nick Cotter stood on the low retaining wall, it gave him a better view over the garden and the street below. At six feet four inches tall he was already at an advantage over the other policemen gathered at the scene, it was only his partner, Sam Longstaff, who could out-see him. He was another three inches taller and had the eyesight of an eagle. He stepped up beside Nick and turned, looking all around. "There's clear footsteps leading up to the house."

Cotter nodded. "Yeah, the uni's already pointed that out. The grass is crushed all the way up there, but the footsteps don't lead into the woods, they turn away, then go into the house. Dog squad should be here soon, hopefully they can tell us where the trail leads."

Longstaff turned again, this time looking at the grand old house that stood high above the street. It would have been magnificent in its day, long, balustraded verandahs surrounding a wide timber porch, three stories of turn of the century elegance looking out over the suburb below. The house reminded him of those old movies about the south, of slavery and civil war. It was a beautiful house, but an aged beauty. Her once lovely paintwork now peeled and faded to gray. Her windows and dormers were dark and covered with many seasons of spider webs and dust. While not looking quite deserted, she certainly did look neglected. The gardens were weedy and overgrown, the paths almost covered in last fall's crumpled brown leaves.

"Did he live here alone?" Sam asked his partner.

Nick pulled out a little notebook from the back pocket of his jeans. "Yeah, he did. George Riley, ninety-two, wife Mildred May Riley, passed away eight years ago. No surviving children, three nieces and a nephew, all live in town. Mind you, they're in their mid to late seventies."

"Well, doesn't look like they knocked the old man off. Did they have kids? I'd say old man Riley was worth a pretty penny and some great niece or nephew may have been a bit impatient for the inheritance."

Nick frowned. "Seriously? You think a relative did this?"

Sam turned to look Nick in the eyes. Funny how they now shone with splinters of brighter green and iridescent purple through his sea-green eyes. Sam knew his own hazel-green eyes also bore the same tiny flecks of green and purple, little shards of amethyst and emerald that the ladies noticed and liked. They did not always have touches of strange color in their eyes, these detectives. It was something that happened only a few months ago. A lasting reminder of their encounter with the strange, alien woman. Both men were forever tainted, forever changed, and the changes, while subtle and slow to surface, were becoming more and more apparent. The color in their eyes, their enhanced eyesight, they also seemed to be stronger, leaner and more muscled. They were always tall, attractive men, they were dubbed 'the pinup boys' at their precinct, but now they were so much more. Try as he might, Sam could not help but worry they were becoming something that might not be quite human. Something more like the monsters they had lately been chasing...

Sam shook his head to clear his thoughts and folded his arms across his chest. "I'm going to follow a normal course of investigation so that people don't think we have gone all *X-Files* on them. I'm going to say he was murdered, then some feral dogs made a meal of the cadaver."

"And ate his heart," Nick added.

"Yeah, well, we don't know that yet, do we?"

"No, not officially," Nick agreed. "But it seems we've got a monster kill here. Strange that it was such an old guy. That's not normal in these types of kills."

Sam shrugged. "Since when have any of these kills been normal?"

"Let's check out the house." Nick turned and walked across the fresh spring grass. The soft new blades showed every footstep left on them, and from this vantage point the clear path of the suspicious tracks that led to the wood were of a man, not of a four-legged beast that ripped the chest apart of the elderly man and had eaten his warm insides.

The wooden porch creaked under the weight of the two tall detectives as they ducked under the police tape that a young, uniformed officer was unrolling and pinning around the balustrade. The house was dark, unkempt, and old on the outside, but the interior was bright and almost cheerful in its faded glory.

Floral wallpaper, while bleached pale from years of reflected sunlight, still showed large peonies and roses, pink blooms amidst satiny lemon background. The wide, long hallway led straight to a staircase, on both sides of the hall there were doors that led to the parlor, study and downstairs bedroom. The kitchen and dining room were at the back, behind the staircase, the timber floors polished and clean, the hall runner vacuumed and tidy. Sam poked his head into each room as they worked their way through the house, everything was neat, clean and old fashioned. The settees were floral and overstuffed, the heavy drapes were swagged and, though faded, were clearly of a good quality and craftsmanship. The parlor was lined with large bookcases that were crammed with leather bound volumes, the same with the study and even the dining room. The kitchen was clean, neat and surprisingly modern for such an old house; it must have been remodeled in the last few years.

There was a uniformed officer dusting the stair rails for prints. He looked up as Longstaff and Cotter approached.

"Housekeeper came twice a week, said she mostly cleaned the downstairs, upstairs was unused," the officer told the two detectives. "Mr. Riley didn't need to use anything other than the ground floor since his wife passed, so she wasn't required to maintain up there."

Nick stood on the bottom step, noting that the carpet running down the middle of the stairs was dust free.

"She only came up once a year to give it a spring clean. She was due to do that today, she searched the house for Mr. Riley, after looking through the house she checked the gardens. That's how she found him."

Sam nodded his thanks and followed Nick up the long staircase. There was a landing halfway and that must have been as far as the housekeeper cleaned each week, for once they stepped off the landing the dust was thick and white on the wine-red carpet. Sam pulled a small flashlight from his shirt pocket and aimed it at the stairs in front of them. Footprints could clearly be seen in the dust. Three sets, a larger set that probably belonged to Mr. Riley that led upwards only, and smaller sets from the maid, leading up, and then down. The third set was larger than even Mr. Riley's, and they only led down.

"Forensics already got shots of them," Nick told Sam. "It's okay to walk over them." He reached over and flicked the light switch on. Sam smiled and turned his flashlight off before proceeding up the stairs.

The next floor was dark and smelled closed. Not moldy and damp, rather it was dry and a little stale. The wallpaper here was different, a soft stripe and paisley pattern of lemon yellow and pale pink. Nick flicked a light switch and the long hallway lit up, small crystal chandeliers lined the hall and they twinkled their soft beams against the shadows. The dusty footprints followed the hallway and led up the next flight of stairs to the third floor.

Sam tried a door and found it locked. "All of the doors up here are locked," he said as he tried each one. "Who has the keys?"

Nick shrugged. "No idea. We'll have to look into that, though no tracks lead to any doors." He pointed to the third-floor landing where the tracks all overlapped. "That's weird, right? The tracks just stop here. Or start here, if you look at the really big ones."

Sam nodded. "Yeah, it's weird." He looked around but could see no doors, no hidden trapdoors, nothing to show where the second set of prints might have originated. Nick looked up towards the ceiling. Sam followed his gaze, turning his flashlight on to illuminate the faded pearl white paintwork.

"There." Sam reached up, his height allowing him to touch the ceiling without doing any more than reaching up. Nick pulled out his flashlight as Sam hooked his finger into a small, silver colored loop and pulled. A latch opened and an attic ladder slid smoothly and silently down, stopping at the dust-covered carpet. The attic was dark, nothing could be seen but a gaping maw of blackness. Both detectives immediately drew their weapons, their senses high, their stances slightly crouched, ready for attack.

Without a word, Nick led the way, climbing the angled ladder hands free, both of his hands occupied holding the flashlight and his gun. Sam let him climb a step or two before he joined his partner on the ladder, his hands mirroring Nick's.

The musty, dry odor of the attic assaulted their nostrils as they stepped into the blackness, the flashlights projecting beams of light into the void.

"Smell that?" hissed Nick as he stepped aside to let his partner access the attic.

"Yeah. What is it? Stinks of blood and piss."

Nick snorted. "I'd say it's blood and piss, then."

Moving forward, still in their crouched stance, the men fanned out a little, the beams of light illuminating cloth shrouded shapes and objects.

"Smells like an animal's been holed up here," Sam crinkled his nose in disgust. "Of course, I know what's probably what's been holed up here."

Nick nodded his head, though in the darkened attic there was no way for Sam to see him. Both men circled around a large wardrobe, the top half of it covered with a striped bed sheet.

"Nick?" called Sam in a hushed voice.

"Yeah, what?"

"How the fuck did they get this huge wardrobe through the tiny stair-hole?"

Nick shrugged but didn't answer. As he searched around the large wooden structure, he realized his friend was right, how did they get the massive wardrobe up the access hole? It was no more than four feet by three, and the wardrobe was taller than

Sam and nearly double that in width.

"You've got a point," he told Sam as they came together on the other side of the wardrobe. "I'd say there must be another entry, and if that's the case our little monster may have left by that exit."

"It would have to be a massive entrance," Sam agreed as they searched the rest of the attic. "You couldn't even pull that thing up a normal staircase. Okay, I can see a light switch. Hold on while I try it."

The overhead lights came on with a soft buzz and clink, bathing the dusty furniture and cloth covered shapes in a dim, yellow glow. Both detectives turned off their flashlights and slipped them into pockets, their guns still held high. They continued to search the attic but found nothing out of the ordinary, though both knew the thing they hunted had been there, the stench of urine attested to that with every breath they took.

Sam turned to his partner.

"Nothing," he muttered.

"There's only one hiding place left." Nick lifted his weapon higher as he faced the front of the huge timber wardrobe. Sam stood back a little, to one side, so anything that may rush from the wardrobe would not be able to take them both out in one strike. They had been partners a long time, these two, and didn't need to talk to communicate what their plan was. Sam pulled out his flashlight as they both breathed out a countdown from three to one, though silent, they were perfectly in sync. Nick pulled the door open as Sam stepped forward, flashlight shining into the wardrobe. The first thing that rushed forward to meet them was the incredible stench, it hit them like a thick, miasmic wall of foulness. Nick felt the bile rise in his throat as Sam shone the light around the interior of the hulking object, but the only thing they found inside was an old, ruined bed cover and feces. Lots and lots of feces. Sam raised his gun hand, the wrist covering his mouth, his eyes watering from the fumes.

"Dude, if we don't get outside soon, I'm going to lose my breakfast."

Nick nodded, stepping back from the offending object. "Well, it's obvious the thing was here. The footsteps led back to this house, not away, even the marks in the dust led up, none went out. So where is it?"

Sam moved even further away from the stench. "Right now, I don't care. Just get me out of here."

He backed into the wall and was surprised when it moved a little, just a little, like a door or window might if pushed. He shone his flashlight over the wall and was shocked to see that it was not a solid drywall as he first thought, instead it was a painted over glass wall. The dim overhead lights did not give any clues to the makeup of the wall earlier on, and there was no reason for the men to touch the wall.

Nick ran his hand along it until he came to a slim vertical handle. He pulled his own flashlight out and examined it before trying a little tug, hoping it would open or slide along.

"I'm thinking this is a large glass door that's been

painted over," he told Sam as he pulled again, this time the door slid to one side, letting in a tumble of bright, morning sunshine and a breath of crisp, clean air. Nick stepped onto a large balcony that jutted out from the back of the attic, the glass doors more obvious from the outside. Sam almost pushed him over in his haste to exit the foul-smelling attic space.

"Well, that answers our questions as to how the wardrobe got up there." Nick motioned to a large outdoor staircase that led down to the second level balcony. It was obvious that the balcony had not been used for some time. There were many layers of autumn leaves, plastic bags and blown in litter that covered the fairly large area, a general sense of neglect and clutter adding to the feel of abandon.

"Over here," called Sam as he pushed his way through a bank of leaves to the top of the stair. "There's footprints. I'd say we've found how our stink boy got out; the prints lead out only."

Nick nodded and followed his partner down the large wooden steps. The prints in the damped down dust that Sam referred to were spaced very far apart, only hitting every third or fourth step, as if the one leaving them ran, or leapt, all the way down. The men followed the steps to the second-floor balcony, where it seemed obvious that whoever left the footprints had vaulted over the railing instead of following the staircase to the ground floor. Both detectives leaned over the railing and looked down onto the paved area below. "That's got to be about twenty feet," Nick shook his head. "No human could make that leap without doing himself some serious damage."

Sam whistled through his teeth. "Nope, no *human.*"

The paved area was very large, stopping only about a hundred feet or so from the wooded area at the back of the property.

"Should we get the dog squad in?" Sam asked.

"Can't hurt," Nick agreed. "And it's probably the only way we can track it." He led the way down, the staircase to the ground level made an easy exit onto the paving. They examined the paving, hoping to find a spot where their perpetrator landed, but the large brick pavers held their secret. They moved around, this way and that, slowly making their way to the edge of the woods, but no clues would reveal themselves to the detectives.

Nick looked up at the woods, they were overgrown, densely thick and dark, with no obvious paths or walkways leading in or about. Just looking at them made the hairs rise on the back of his neck. His uneasiness only grew the longer he stood there, he felt as if someone, or something, was watching him. He shuddered and turned away, his partner following him to the front of the large old house.

Chapter Three
Earth
Present Day
Stinky Boy

From the woods something relaxed a little, it breathed out a quiet breath and blinked its large green eyes. It was safe, for now, but knew those who looked for him were dangerous, they were a threat, and it needed to retreat further into the woods, into the dark, to find a place to hide until the moon rose. Then it would run in the dark, run free in the night, far from here and the dangers it held.

The creature moved quietly, slowly, not just hiding from the prying eyes of men, but also avoiding the soft spears of light that found their way through the canopy of the trees. The light, while not deadly, was irritating, an annoyance that was best avoided. He knew he was a creature of the night; it was his domain, it was the time when he was released, free, able to run and roam and hunt. The smells, the sounds, the feel of the night air were intoxicating to him, and he usually ran until he was at the point of exhaustion.

When dawn's early light started to turn the sky gray, he would usually lope back to the large house, he could climb over the balconies in a couple of easy leaps and snuggle inside the unused attic. He would take his meals there, be they a small forest animal, or one of the neighborhood pets, and he could eat and sleep away the day with no worries of being disturbed. Well aware that the building was not abandoned, he kept quiet, softly sleeping the days away while the old man inhabited the living areas two floors below.

It was all going well until he was disturbed. He didn't know why the old fellow climbed the narrow steps to the attic in the cold hours before dawn, only that the man made a noise and the creature awoke with a fright. The man ran, oh, he ran fast, for an old man. The creature let him run, the thrill of the chase exciting him, opening his blood lust and making his heart race in anticipation of the kill.

He had been so careful, so very secretive up until this morning. He didn't mean to kill the man, he didn't, but the smell of fear, the scent of blood, and all rational thought left him. Not that he had many rational thoughts anymore. Not many at all.

He did have memories, and he did remember a life before this one. A life where he knew rational thoughts, feelings other than hunting and killing, desires other than a wish for blood and warm flesh. His memories we disjointed and faded a little more every day, and after eating the old man's heart this morning his memories pushed even further back, but they were still there, if distant.

He moved through the woods with a loping, uneven gait, moving from dark shadow to dark shadow, keeping the sunlight away from his thick, shaggy hide. He wore no clothes other than the ragged cuffs of his business shirt that somehow managed to survive, though the shirt they belonged to was long gone. Dirty and torn, they decorated his hairy wrists in a parody to his once human shape.

But this creature was human no more.

His face was elongated, a long, canine snout that held a black, wet nose and a mouth of cruel sharp teeth. His eyes were green, set in a black surround, and his body was covered in long, shiny black hair. No more was he a young, well-dressed businessman, recently married and soon to be father.

Now he was a creature of nightmare, a vision from a horror movie, a thing that should not exist. He was not sure how this happened. He could not really remember, maybe he had never really known. He just knew that there was not always this life, not always, there was a time before. A time when he drove a car, when he walked his dog, when he made love to his beautiful wife. But that time was gone. That time was before.

Before.

Now there was only this. This existence. This scent, this trail, this raggedy strange new life.

He moved forward, to the side, then forward again, avoiding the light but needing to get away from the house he had been living in, from the men that would hunt him and from the carcass of the man he killed. He still had enough rational thought to know that killing the man was wrong, and it would bring the wrath of men raining down upon him. He didn't care about the man he had killed, not now, though before he tore the man to shreds, he was careful to avoid hurting people, avoid killing anyone.

The taste of a warm, still beating heart had taken the last ounce of compassion from him and he no longer cared that he killed someone. He now only cared to get away, to find somewhere dark and safe to spend the day. Somewhere he could await the night, somewhere further from this place and perhaps he could hunt again. Perhaps he could find another person, another human.

Yes… *another human.*

Maybe this time he would take someone younger, someone not so very old…

Chapter Four
Earth
Present Day
No Shit, Sherlock

"Donald Greene, twenty-eight, finance director at Howard and Sterns. Report says that the girlfriend found him when he didn't turn up for work. The employer rang the girlfriend after not getting any answer on the victim's cell, and she came to his house to find him. Coroner puts the death between eight PM and midnight." The uniformed officer closed his notebook and looked up at the tall detective. The *very* tall detective. Sam nodded and turned to his partner, who was squatting next to the body.

"Not the same M.O. as our other victim." Nick used a pen to point to the gaping wound in the neck of the fallen man. Sam chewed on his lower lip and frowned.

"Why did the dogs bring us all the way here?" Nick asked as he stood and pulled off his rubber gloves.

"They have to be connected. It's no coincidence that the dogs followed a scent all the way here."

"No shit, Sherlock." Nick moved away from the other police officers, a nod of his head indicating that Sam should follow him. They made their way off the front verandah of the late Donald Greene's house and walked around to the immaculately landscaped backyard. From there a long staircase took them to the top of the garage, where Donald had built a large viewing and entertaining deck.

"Outstanding view," commented Sam.

Nick leaned on the railing and nodded towards the woods behind the boundary fence. "That's probably where our stink-boy went. We'll have to bring the dogs back to track him. But why did he come here? We've never seen a vamp and a wolf work together, or even interact with each other."

"Look, in the months we've been hunting these things, the one constant is that *there is no pattern.* Most of them were recently turned and really have no idea what they are doing. They've never joined up with any of their own species, let alone any other monster, so why do you think they are together now?"

"You don't think they're together? You think this is a coincidence?"

Sam shook his head. "No, I don't, I don't believe in coincidences. What I do think, though, is that maybe these two have been around a bit longer than the other ones we've hunted, and that maybe they are drawn to each other. Or the wolf, at least, was drawn to the vamp."

"Makes sense, like how we can tell when we're close to one of them. So, now we just have to see if they join up or not."

"You think they could join up? Really? I can't see that happening. We haven't learned much, granted, but we know the wolves are dirty, irrational creatures that just kill and eat hearts as often as they can. The vamps we've found are at least a little cleaner, but they are solitary things, they don't work with anyone or anything."

"We've never hunted one that has been turned for a long time. Stink-boy's hold up was months old. He's been tucked up there since last spring, at least."

"Why didn't we find any bodies before now?"

Nick shrugged. "I guess he was being careful. Or lucky. Maybe a bit of both. The dog squad did find a lot of animal carcasses in the woods. If you looked closely at them, I'd bet they're all missing their hearts, along with what other choice organs they like to eat."

Sam leaned against the railing and looked up the mountain. It was heavily wooded, the trees thick and close knit. Every now and then a small ribbon of smoke would punctuate the heavy green canopy, the white fingers drifting off toward the skyline. "There're houses up through there?"

"Yes, it's quite the unique bohemian lifestyle. Expensive real estate up through there." He pointed up the mountain to the streams of smoke. "But with a vamp and a wolf in the area, it might not be such a safe place to live." He looked up from his phone. "I think we need to check out all of the houses up there. Perfect place for a vampire to hide out."

"We'd better get on to that, then. Seems our little wolf hunt has led us to another creature to dispose of. You know, I never thought we'd be monster hunters."

Nick smiled at him. "I guess I didn't either. But then, we never thought we'd meet an alien, either."

Sam frowned and looked back to the woods. "Have you felt like we're being watched today?"

"Yes!" Nick agreed. "All day, since we got to the old guy's place. I can't shake the feeling that something's been watching us".

Chapter Five
Earth
Present Day
Pamela Evans, Twenty-Six

Tall trees lined the winding, pot-holed track. Small shrubs, piles of leaf matter and detritus, dampened by the heavy rains from the previous evening, cluttered the edges of the track and made walking difficult. The deputies pushed their way through to the crime scene, only a couple of yards from the little used track, but totally hidden by the dense undergrowth of the forest. The yellow police tape surrounding the crime scene was wound around the trees and bushes, flapping in the brisk autumn breeze.

The day was a cold, overcast remnant of winter, the temperature low and damp, the trees still bare, undergrowth wet. Birds didn't lend their voices to the day, and a chill in the breeze cut through the deputies' uniforms and made them shiver as they shoved fisted hands into their pockets.

Sheriff Andrew Banfield was kneeling, his back to the approaching deputies. He turned as the crunch of boots signaled company and nodded a greeting.

"Jim. Good. Did you bring the camera?"

A young deputy handed a camera to Jim before turning and throwing up in the bushes behind him.

"Watch out for evidence!" Jim cautioned as he

leaned over to see what made the young man lose his breakfast. He regretted his decision immediately.

On the ground before him were the remains of what must have once been human but were now something that could only be described as a corpse. There were bones and flesh, a half of a skull with bits of gristle, flesh and hair still clinging to it. The torso was in equal disarray, broken ribs flared open to show an empty cavity, Jim could see the spine in the gaping hole. The lower part of the torso and the legs seemed relatively undamaged, and Jim could still see the brand name on the expensive hiking boots. The feet seemed small, too small for a man.

"Is this a woman's body?" Jim asked the sheriff.

Banfield wore standard issue silicone gloves and was holding a pair of oversized tweezers that he was using to pick off the various pieces of leaves and forest floor trash and deposit them into a clear plastic envelope. He nodded.

"Yes, female, ID is in the plastic pocket, there," he tipped his head to indicate the little pile of bagged evidence. "Pamela Evans, twenty-six, from Mayfields. She filed a hiking notice on Friday, her and three companions. I need you to organize the boys to search the woods, see if there are any other bodies." Andrew stood up and closed the envelope he was holding. Jim again couldn't help but think how much taller he seemed, not just a little, but a good few inches. He was sure that Andrew had always been about the same height as himself, but now the sheriff clearly towered over him. The one time he brought it up Andrew blushed and laughed it off as ridiculous. Now, though, he wasn't so sure it was ridiculous. Same with the bright green shards of color in the sheriff's eyes. He knew they hadn't been there before. He was *sure* of it.

"Pull the hiking notice and follow up on the companions, see if they have returned home, any hits on location or credit card, the usual work up." The sheriff frowned. "Everything okay, Jim?"

"Sure, Drew, just, you know, this is a pretty gross thing. The body, I mean. What could have eaten her like that?"

The sheriff pursed his lips and looked thoughtful but didn't answer. Deputy Jim took this as his signal to instruct his fellow deputies in their search duties, and radio back to base to follow up on the hiking notice. He was unfolding a map on the bonnet of his car when he felt the hairs on the back of his neck stand up. He stiffened as the distinct feeling overcame him that *someone* was watching him. Unclipping his sidearm he turned to face whoever was spying on him.

There was no one.

Jim turned, looking this way and that, the dirt track was free of any life except his own. Still, he couldn't shake the feeling that he was being watched. Even now, he still felt the uneasy sensation that he was not alone.

"Something wrong, Jim?"

The deputy started at the sudden words and huffed an uneasy laugh into Sheriff Banfield's face. "I didn't hear you come up behind me, Drew."

Andrew nodded. "Why are you so spooked? It's not like you to let a corpse get to you. Not the first time you've seen a body eaten by scavengers."

Jim ran a hand through his hair, a self-conscious frown painting his face. "No, not the first, nor I dare say, the last time. It's just that I could... I don't know, I swear someone was watching me."

"Yeah. I felt that, too, when I first got here, and even when I was taping off the body. Couldn't find anyone, but man, that feeling..."

Jim nodded, a little relieved that he wasn't losing his mind. He turned back to the map and worked out the search quadrants with Drew, but the whole time he could not shake the feeling he was still being watched.

"Anyway, let's get back to this. So far three bodies turn up like this. Three hikers, all dead in the past two months, and their hiking partners are missing. Something's going on here and we need to find it and shut it down – yesterday."

Jim nodded at his friend's words. "I'm thinking we need help."

Drew gave him a strained smile. "I'm thinking you're right, there, Jim."

Chapter Six
Academy of Skills
Trauiss Prime
Five Years Ago
Top Adjacent

Sarah holstered her weapon and rubbed a hand across her forehead. It was a warm day, hotter than she preferred, hotter than it had been when she had arrived here. She had been training all day, running drills and taking target practice. Even though she had been training almost every day for the past five years, day in and day out, there had been no requirement to train today. Today was traditionally a day of rest, she had been told, the day before graduation was a day to reflect, unwind, and relax.

For five years she had trained so hard, so long, perhaps longer than most, in order to be chosen as a guardian. Not just any guardian, either. She wanted to be chosen as a Guardian of the Gate. It was the most prestigious position, and the most sought after in all of the guardian positions.

Sarah had not fitted in easily, the day she had passed through the Gate she remembered her great feeling of loss and sorrow, knowing that she may never see her children again. The journey from Earth to the Gate had only taken a few weeks, and she had spent that time learning about her condition, the ship she was on, and the people that served there. It had been both frightening, overwhelming and, in a strange way, comforting. They had saved her life, these Guardians, though at the cost of her never returning to that life as she knew it. She wasn't given a choice, it had been made for her, and she was truly grateful for that. She didn't know if she could have decided on this life, had she been able to choose, but now that she was here, she was glad she had survived, glad she had become so much more than what she was.

And she was so much more than the humble middle-aged office worker she had once been, alone and lonely, nothing to live for while growing old and older. It all changed for her that one fateful day when she had found the dead body of a poor girl in the park, brutally torn apart and consumed by some unknown creature. That very same creature had tracked her to her home, chasing and attacking her, she had been almost devoured by the awful thing. The Guardians had saved her that night and brought her aboard their ship, explaining that she would never be able to return home, never be mortal, never be entirely human again.

While it had been a lot to take in, she had not been the only one that the Guardians took aboard their ship. Major Ayden Jacobs and Corporal Peter Jones also joined them, and they had formed an immediate bond. Jacobs and Peter were still her closest friends and comrades, both training alongside her at the Academy of Guardianship. Jacobs had progressed much faster than her, his military experience giving him a distinct advantage. Peter, though, was different. He had also been in the military, but on a more technical side. He had moved into research and design within the first year and was thoroughly enjoying his training.

Always a smart man, coming to this new world had given him the push he needed to really use his intellect to its greatest advantage. He was much loved and appreciated by all that worked with him. Same with Jacobs, Sarah mused. She didn't know anyone that didn't like the man. He was respected and honored, and Sarah was sure that he would be chosen as a Guardian of the Gate. She just hoped she would be considered good enough to join him.

She strolled back towards the barracks, the shower block was down a level, and it was cool and quiet. Sarah stripped off and looked at herself in the mirror. No one would know she was a woman in her fifties, formerly a little overweight and completely unfit. To look at her now you'd pick her as no older than twenty-five, and she was trim, muscled and in peak condition. She didn't look quite the same as she did when she was really twenty-five, either, there were subtle changes now. Her eyes, for one. They were now green.

Everybody had green eyes here, and Sarah's had changed very quickly from her original color. Peter and Ayden's had taken a little longer, but now were the same bright, vivid green that everyone else had. She had been rather alarmed at first, all the changes were rapid, strange and new, but as time went on Sarah had come to accept her new shape, new look, and new life. Peter had compared it to a total body makeover that Hollywood stars would pay millions for. Sarah had laughed at that, but he was right. The other changes had resulted in them becoming more attractive, more flawless. Their defects had smoothed or remodeled or even disappeared, like Peter's acne scarred skin and Ayden's slightly crooked nose, they were now almost perfect.

It was a pleasant side effect.

"Hey, Sarah, you been training again?"

Sarah turned to see one of her fellow trainees, a young red haired fellow named Frank. He had been the one that had finally made Sarah feel like she could fit in here, made her feel that she could call this place home. Frank had also been a rescued person from Earth, he had arrived here before her and had not had any family to grieve, but he was a nice guy, and he did his best to make sure she fitted in and felt comfortable with everyone.

"Yeah. I just want to give myself every chance, you know?"

Frank threw her a towel and then handed her a robe from one of the many hanging from hooks on the shower block wall. "You're going for one of the top jobs here, girl. You know they wouldn't even consider you if you weren't at the top of the class."

Sarah flung the towel back to Frank and wrapped herself in the plush robe, then took Frank by the arm, leading him from the shower block. "Not really the top of the class, I'd more say top adjacent."

Frank shrugged as he pulled the door closed behind them. "I heard that some of the Guardians are going to be at the pre graduation party. Some of the guys you probably met when they brought you here. If nothing else, Sarah, it will give you a chance to catch up."

"Yeah, well, maybe I'll come. Hey Frank, can I ask you something?"

The overhead lighting highlighted his bright shaggy locks as Frank shook his head. "Anything, honey. Anything at all."

"Do you feel like you really fit in? I mean, I know it's been five years, but sometimes I feel like I'm going to wake up and find that this was all just a dream. A very vivid, weird dream, but a dream nonetheless."

Frank leaned over and plucked a quick kiss on her cheek as they walked towards their barracks. "No, honey, I don't. I put a lot of effort into turning that side of me off. This is life now. The past was the dream. You just need to do that, too. I know it's harder for you, having kids and all, but they're gone. You know that. Even if you ever got to go back to Earth you know they wouldn't recognize you now, and they've gone on with their lives. They survived. It's about time you realized that you survived, too."

"Yeah, you're right. As usual." Sarah sighed. "I could be a grandma by now."

"A hot one at that." Frank pushed open the door to the barracks. "GILF. Grandma I'd like to fuck."

Sarah took a swipe at him. "You're gross. But thanks for the compliment."

"I'll see you tonight at the pre-grad party?"

"I guess so. We need to let off a little steam after all this hard work."

Chapter Seven
Earth
Present Day
Mary, Please

Sheriff Andrew Banfield threw the report on his desk and pulled a chair out for the lady that stood before him. As she seated herself, he hung his jacket on a hook and took his place behind the desk. His office was fairly neat and tidy, there were a few files on the side, his 'in' and 'out' trays were fuller than they should be, and there was more than one newspaper folded on the bureau behind him, but all in all it looked like a workable sheriff's office.

The woman arranged herself on the overstuffed chair and smiled coyly at the sheriff. She was a very attractive woman, a vibrant red head on the verge of forty, her clothing on the lower end of designer, her make up flawless. She held a tissue in one manicured hand and dabbed at her dry eyes, feigning tears. "You've been so kind to me Sheriff, or may I call you Andrew?"

"Sheriff is fine, Mrs. Kane."

"Oh, it's Ms., but you can call me Mary. Paul and I were separated. I stopped calling myself Mrs. when we broke up."

Andrew forced a pursed lipped smile and pulled the file over and opened it. "Says here you were still living in the same house? Nothing here mentions you were separated?"

"Well, it wasn't really official yet. We'd only just started living apart."

"And, if you don't mind me asking, why did you break up with Paul?"

Mary smiled, but it was a sad smile, and her face, for a moment, looked every one of her nearly forty years. "He changed. It's hard to really put a finger on it, at first, anyway, but he changed. He became, well, withdrawn, silent, sort of, I don't know how to explain it, he just sort of disappeared."

Andrew raised his brows in query.

"Well, before he actually disappeared, that is. He just kind of faded before my eyes. He didn't talk, he stopped walking the dog, he stopped touching me. He didn't read anymore, and Paul *loved* to read, pretty much anything he put his hands on he read, but he just stopped."

"When did this all start?" Andrew prompted.

"Well, I'm not sure how this will help, but anyway, I guess it can't hurt. Paul used to walk the dog twice a day, we had a Dalmatian, and those puppies have A.D.H.D., I swear. Paul loved that damn dog. Baby replacement, I always said. Mind you, I did rather like him a lot, too. But one day Paul came home without the dog. He was covered in blood, like, soaked through to his underwear, and just said that the dog had been hit by a car. He didn't have the body, and he wasn't hurt, but he wasn't the same after that."

"When did this happen, Ms. Kane?"

"About two months ago. Pretty much from that night on he was different. At first, I put it down to him missing our dog, but it didn't stop, it just got worse. And he started eating meat."

Andrew frowned. "What's wrong with that?"

"Well, Paul was a vegan up until then. A strict vegan, you know the type, bordering on fanatical, he wouldn't touch *any* animal products at all. But in the space of a few days he started eating hamburgers, bacon, hot dogs, then, before I knew it, he was cooking up steaks, rare, bloody steaks, and wolfing those down. It was disgusting. The last time we actually spoke civilly to each other he was eating his steak raw. *Cold* and *raw!*" Mary screwed up her nose in disgust.

"Did he do anything else, any other aberrant behavior? Anything else out of the ordinary?"

As she looked down at her hands, Andrew could see Mary screw up her forehead in confusion. Finally, she looked up at the sheriff, real tears forming in her eyes. "I think he started eating animals. Live animals. I'd find bits of fur and blood on his clothes, and animals in the neighborhood were going missing. A lot of animals, you know, people's pets, dogs and cats, well, they went missing. I don't know what happened to him, Sheriff, I really don't. But I kind of hope you never find him. Not now. He really creeped me out towards the end, he really changed. He was super scary. Between you and me, I hope I never see him again. I hope you find him dead in a ditch somewhere." Mary shook her head at Andrew's shocked expression. "I know how it sounds, and I know it makes me seem completely guilty, or whatever. But you weren't there. You didn't see what he'd turned into. He was a freak, a monster, and I'm glad he's gone. I am, and I'm not sorry about that. Not even a little bit."

Drew nodded and opened the file containing the report of Paul's disappearance. "Paul hadn't been going to work anymore?"

Mary shook her head. "Not that I knew, at least, not until they rang me, but he hadn't been for over a week before he went missing."

"And he took nothing with him? No clothes, bags, nothing at all?"

Mary shook her head again. "No, nothing. Not his wallet, cell, credit cards, nothing."

Andrew nodded and turned a few more pages. He looked up at the beautiful woman in front of him and gave her a smile. "I think I have all I need here. Thank you for coming down, Ms. Kane. I appreciate it."

He stood as Mary pushed her chair back and moved sensuously to her feet. Even with her husband freshly missing she was still trying to flirt with the sheriff. Drew took her proffered hand and led her to the door.

"Please call me if you need anything or want to know anything else. You can call me anytime, you know. *Any*time."

"I appreciate that Ms. Kane."

"Mary, please."

Andrew smiled and gave a little nod before closing the door after her. He wouldn't need to call her, he didn't think he'd be talking to her again, at least not until he had taken care of Paul.

He was pretty sure Paul was the one causing all the trouble in the woods with the hikers. And so far, Paul had been able to evade all efforts to capture him. Andrew was worried that his little small-town police force would be no match for Paul Kane when and if they finally cornered him.

"I'm going to need a little help on this one," he muttered as he picked up his cell phone from the bureau behind his desk. He scrolled through the contacts list until he found what he was looking for and stabbed the number with his forefinger. As he listened to the ringtone, he felt the hairs on the back of his neck stand up. Someone was watching him. He kept the phone to one ear as he turned, very smoothly and slowly, to see who was there.

There was no one. He was still alone in his office.

Drew moved to the window and peered out through the wooden slats of the plantation shutter to see if anyone was spying on him.

He was alone. There was no one.

The call connected, though it went straight to voicemail. Drew waited for the quick spiel to finish before he left his message.

"Hey, boys, it's Andrew Banfield. Long time and all that. Say, I seem to have a little problem in my neck of the woods that you two are uniquely qualified to help me with. Please give me a yell when you're free."

Chapter Eight
Earth
Present Day
Deathly Afraid

Artu yawned and stretched, his muscles popping under the strain. He clicked his neck, first this way, then that, and then yawned again. This time his mouth opened wide, showing his very white, straight, healthy teeth. Sliding down from each side of his mouth, just above his canines, were fangs, white, long, sharp, deadly looking fangs. He shook his head and the fangs slid back into their slit in his gums.

Artu would usually sleep until the sun comfortably set beyond the horizon, but today was different. Today he was waking from troubled dreams several hours earlier than he normally would, and it bothered him. Not just the waking early, nor even the dreams. The fact that the dreams were what disturbed his sleep made him anxious, but it was the details of his dreams, and what his dreams were about, that deeply disturbed him.

Right from the start, the darkly handsome man felt a distinct connection to his fellow *changees*, the other men and women that had been infected by evil and turned into something that was no longer human. He was not sure if all of them, or if any, for that matter, felt the same connection to him that he did to them, but that mattered not to him. He felt the presence of these fellow creatures, especially the ones like him, the ones who were now vampires. He also felt a connection to the ones that were entirely different creatures, the wolves, the snakes, the air and the sea creatures. There were many, some extremely strange, some beyond description, but he felt them all, every one of them, he knew at any time where they were, what they were doing, and how they felt. In some strange way he could feel what they felt, he could taste their hunger, breathe their anger, hear their despair or their hatred.

Lately they were feeling afraid.

Deathly afraid.

Something was hunting them, these creatures, something was hunting and killing them. At times he was sure there was more than one hunter as the fear and pain of death of his fellow creatures called at him from many miles apart, and once or twice he had caught a mental image, a psychic glimpse of a man or men right before the creatures died.

He recognized the men; he had seen them before.

Quite some months ago, when he was left for dead in an old motel. Those men were there, they were with his master, his creator, and now they were hunting his kind.

They were not the cause of the fear that rippled through the supernatural creatures such as himself. He was not sure what else was hunting them, what else was killing them, but he did know that it was fearsome, frightening, and it never failed to eliminate its prey once it set out to destroy them.

This thing that was causing such fear, this thing

that was disturbing his sleep, it needed to be found, it needed to be stopped.

Artu would be the one to do that.

His name meant *One*, or *First*, and he was the strongest of all of the creatures, he was the one his master left in charge.

He would be the one to take out the thing that gave fear to the ones that should be feared. He would destroy the thing that was destroying his brethren, that was giving nightmares to the creatures of nightmare.

He would leave as soon as the sun's rays left the sky.

He would leave tonight.

Artu walked to the door of his sleeping quarters, but before he could grasp the handle, the door exploded inwards and he was overpowered within seconds by several tall men, all dressed identically in black suits and dark sunglasses.

Chapter Nine
Trauiss Prime
Academy of Skills
Five Years Ago
Five Years

Sarah found Peter as soon as she entered the party. The organizers had decided to hold it in the Guardian's reception center, a large ballroom with a parquet floor and a band area, a seated area and massive French doors that led to a large balcony. Tapestries and ornate sconces decorated the walls, and massive vases of exotic flowers were placed everywhere, their heady aroma filling the ballroom with a sweet, tropical scent.

The room was full, the graduates and their guests filled the dance floor and the tables, their shiny, casual training uniforms worn by all the graduates, their guests dressed in easy, colorful party clothes. The sound of soft music danced around the graduates and their guests as they swayed in time to the band, enjoying this last night of being trainees. The mouthwatering aroma of hors d'oeuvres caressed her senses and Sarah smiled as Peter grabbed a handful of food from a passing tray.

"Always look for you near the food!" she laughed. Peter smiled back around his full mouth as he nodded.

"I'd be the size of a house if I ate like that boy does." Ayden leaned in and shook Peter's hand, then hugged Sarah. "Big party, hey?"

Peter nodded past Ayden's back. "The big-wigs are here. Recruiters for the Gate squad."

Sarah grabbed a glass from a passing hover tray. "Frank said that the guys who brought us here should be coming tonight. Do you think they will?"

Ayden nodded. "I heard the same thing. It would be nice to see them again. It's been five years. Long time. If we are going to be accepted into the Gate squads then we might even be seconded to their battalion."

Peter shook his head. "Doubt it. They are the crème of the crop, seasoned and hardened soldiers. We're just graduates. Newbies."

"Five years of academy and training, Peter," Sarah sipped her wine. "It's not like we are complete babies."

"On this world we are," Peter replied. "To these people, five years is nothing. In the grand scheme of things, if you are immortal, five years is hardly a hiccup."

Ayden nodded before accepting a beverage for himself and Peter from another hover tray. "They don't base selection criteria on experience so much as potential and talent. I think we have those."

"If you don't get Alpha, do you have a second choice, Ayden?"

"Yeah, I think I'd like to get on the Rescues Team. I think that could be something I'd be good at. I spent a week there, last seasonal break. I wanted to know how it all worked. It's pretty awesome, the way they review history, swooping in to save the lives of people who deserve a second chance."

"You don't find it all reeks of a bit of a god complex? Deciding who gets to have a second chance? They get to come through the Gate and live forever, but they don't get asked if that's what they want." Frank looked at the three graduates, now staring at him with shocked expressions. "I find it all a bit creepy. Anyway, enough of that. I'm pretty confident you'll all be chosen for Alpha Squad."

"I'm not so confident," Sarah sighed. "I think the three of you are a shoo-in, but I don't think I have what they are looking for."

"You might be surprised," a deep voice beside her gave her a start and the trio turned to find Kyle, the First Protector of the Alpha unit. Beside him stood Michael and Luke, also members of the Alpha unit. Sarah once found the tall, muscular men intimidating, but was now used to seeing so many perfect specimens of humanity after living and training alongside these people for five years. She smiled and grabbed Kyle's hand, pumping it enthusiastically. "It is good to see you, Sarah," he told her. "It is good to see all of you."

Ayden grinned. "It's been a long time."

Michael shook his head. "Not as long as you think. We told you time was different."

"Yes, the days have thirty hours. Took a bit of getting used to," Peter nodded.

"Not just the long days." Michael ran a hand through his shoulder length hair. "The time passes differently here, through the Gate. You think we have been gone, how long?"

"Five years," Peter answered.

"Five years," echoed Michael, smiling. "It's been five weeks."

"Seriously?" Peter's eyes were wide with surprise. "Five weeks? You're kidding, right?"

Kyle nodded as Michael explained, "Through the Gate, things are different. The way time passes, for one. And there are other dimensions, other gates, where time passes even faster. Some of those pass a year for one day here."

"Great place to take holidays. A day off is a whole year's sabbatical," Luke interjected.

Ayden put his arm around Sarah's shoulders. "Five weeks since we left Earth? Why didn't anyone tell us this? Why is it a secret?"

"It is not," Luke shrugged. "Maybe it just never came up."

Kyle gave Sarah a reassuring smile. "Your family is fine. They are doing well. We have checked on your family, many times, for you. They are fine. You can be proud of them. They live to honor you, not mourn you."

Sarah nodded, her eyes glistening with unshed tears. "Thank you, that does mean so much to me." She swiped a hand across her eyes and smiled again. "So why are you here? Recruiting for the Alpha Unit?"

Kyle smiled but didn't answer. Sarah noted that he looked sad, wistful, but didn't comment on this. He took his leave of the group and walked towards other groups of graduates.

"It's the first graduation ceremony that Angie will miss out on in many centuries," Michael explained. "Kyle feels he has failed us all in not finding her. Most of all I believe he feels that he has failed himself."

"No luck at all in finding her?" Peter asked.

Luke and Michael shook their heads. Quietly they stood, all lost in their own thoughts, as the music continued around them.

Chapter Ten
Earth
Present Day
All Gone

She stood with her back to him, not more than a few hundred feet away, and he didn't think that she could see him. He was downwind, standing in the dappled shadows of a large mottled pine, the scent of the fresh air embellished with the earthy smells of the forest floor.

He had not seen her arrive, in fact, up until about ten minutes ago he was one hundred percent sure that he was alone here, no other human being should be in this part of the reserve. He had looked away for a moment as he grabbed his thermos, and when he looked back, there she was, standing in the clearing, her long, curly blonde hair waving in the slight breeze, her shirt lifting occasionally to show her tanned lower back.

His binoculars pressed against his face, he watched her, a mixture of awe and fascination coloring his features.

She seemed short, diminutive even, though there was no point of reference to judge that by.

He quietly leaned over in his fold out camp chair and picked up his camera. The lens was long, heavy, he owned the finest photographic equipment that money could buy. Thirteen years and five grants from the university allowed him the privilege of having the best of everything he needed for his wildlife studies, and he wasn't about to let this slim little girl go without at least snapping a few shots of her.

The camera was totally silent, a necessity when you photograph wildlife, even the tiniest shutter sound could send a flock of birds to wing in an instant. He sat the binoculars onto his lap and brought the camera up to his eye, unclipping the lens cover as he did so.

He could see her more clearly now, see the tumbling platinum curls were interspersed with long dreadlocks, her shirt, he presumed a button down, was too big for her, and the sleeves were torn away in what he supposed was a fashionable manner.

Her blue jeans flared out over boots, though the grass was long he could see the tan of leather as the grass waved in the early spring breeze. Her arms were brown, tanned, and he could make out a tattoo on each. It looked a bit like a flag, not quite American, perhaps a British or Australian flag. She presented a rather bohemian visage, a slim, white blonde woman, standing in a large grass clearing in the early dawn. He wondered who she was, what she was doing there, as he snapped a few frames of her as she turned a little, this way, then that, but not enough so that he could see her face. He contemplated standing and walking out to her when he caught a glimpse of something on the edge of the clearing. There was movement from the darkened forest, he couldn't quite make it out, and flipped a few switches on the camera until the picture lightened and zoomed in on the forest edge.

He gasped when he realized it was a wolf, no, there was another, and another. It was a pack of wolves, and they moved cautiously out into the light, sniffing the air, their tails raised, their ears pointed forward.

The woman was turned to face the canines, she stilled her movements as they stepped forward, slowly at first, then more intently, as they converged on her position. The largest animal, a blackish-grey giant of a thing, slowed as it approached the girl, its nose extended as it sniffed her, ears now back, sharp against its skull as it advanced in predator stance.

The girl lifted her hand for the wolf to sniff, and he did, intently, before his ears flicked up and his large pink tongue slurped the girl's palm. The wolf wagged his tail and his mouth lolled open like a pet dog. Through the camera lens he could see the wolf was happy, almost joyous, as it wagged its tail and cocked its head to one side.

Taking the cue from their leader, the other wolves rushed forward to sniff the girl, they too, wagged their tails and bounced with joy. There had to be ten or twelve of the huge beasts, but instead of attacking the woman they now bounded about like playful puppies, enjoying the clearing, obviously buoyed along by the presence of the blonde girl. She was as at ease with the pack as they were with her and she moved with them, easily, almost sensuously, her movements fluid and smooth like those of a dancer. He now caught a glimpse of her face and he felt his heart miss a beat.

She was beautiful.

The most beautiful woman he had ever laid eyes on.

Her face was perfect, her nose small, tipped, her lips full, moist and red. High cheekbones disappeared under a pair of dark sunglasses as she frolicked about with the dogs, her hair shining in the early morning sun, her shirt tossing against her lithe body and lifting now and then to give him a glimpse of her taut stomach and olive brown, smooth skin.

He remembered what he was holding and his finger found the shutter control and rested it there, letting it take a stream of shots of her dancing with the wolves. Playing, her face happy, her lips parted in a smile as she romped through the green, damp grass. The camera zoomed in on her face, her features filled the viewfinder and for a moment he forgot to breathe.

He snapped many shots, taking pictures of the wolves, of the girl, her tattoo and her clothes, her smile and her hair.

He leaned forward subconsciously, and the binoculars fell from his lap and hit the thermos, the loud clunk echoing across the clearing from his hidden position and stopping the movement of the wolves and the girl in an instant.

All heads turned to face him, and he knew he was discovered.

As one, the wolves turned and fled, streaking off into the trees faster than he knew they could move.

The girl stayed; however, her head tilted first this

way, then that, as she regarded him from afar.

He didn't think she could see him as well as he could see her, and he lifted his camera back to his face.

It had taken less than the blink of an eye for him to lift his camera, but she was gone.

In that instant she had perhaps fallen, the grass was long enough, in places, to hide her form, so he stood, sweeping the camera back and forth, but she was not there. He strode out into the clearing, looking this way and that, but she was gone.

She disappeared, though it was impossible. She could not have left the clearing that quickly. There was no way...

But she did. He looked over to the trees where the wolves had escaped but they, too, were gone, there was just him, alone in the clearing. If it were not for the crumpled grass where the group romped, it would have seemed like they had never been there in the first place.

He lifted the camera and checked the playback feed.

She was there, all the photos were good, they showed her face, her beauty, her almost alien grace.

He didn't know who she was, or where she was from, but he would never forget her.

The hairs on the back of his neck prickled and he turned, sure he was being watched.

Though he turned a full circle the surrounding forest kept its secret well, he could see no one or no *thing* watching him, but the sensation of being watched persisted. Feeling uncomfortable, he strode quickly back to his campsite, the unseen eyes following the entire way.

That evening he downloaded all of the pictures onto his computer and uploaded them to an external hard drive for extra protection. He had been doing this for way too long to not back up his work every night, he could not afford to lose a day's images if the power went out or his computer failed.

He slept restlessly that night, his dreams haunted with the images of the woman, her body moving as one with the wolves as they circled him, their breath hot and fast, their movement sinuous, sensual, hypnotizing. At one stage in his dream, just when he thought they might turn on him and tear him apart, he felt a soft touch to his brow and he fell into a deeper, restful sleep, undisturbed by any further dreams.

The next morning, he checked the pictures, but the images of the strange woman were gone.

All gone.

The pictures of the wolves remained, even those that contained images of the woman the day before, but she was gone from each shot, all traces of her were erased as if someone photoshopped each and every picture. He checked the hard drive and the camera chip, but they were all the same.

She was gone.

It was as if he imagined her, as if he dreamed her, but he hadn't, he was sure of it, she was *real*.

Wasn't she?

It was only later as he was repacking his car that he remembered the binoculars contained a memory chip as well, though small and not quite the quality of the camera, it had the ability to capture images too.

Running back inside he held his breath as he inserted the chip into the reader on the desktop computer, his fingers drumming the wooden bench impatiently as the computer read the information before filling the screen.

He ran his hands through his hair as he sunk back into the chair.

There she was.

She was real.

Her back was turned to him, and the pictures were a little grainy and the lighting was off, but there she was, she was *real*.

He scrubbed a hand over his mouth as his brows knitted confusion.

He wondered, though, *who the hell was she?*

Chapter Eleven
Trauiss Prime
Academy of Skills
Five Years Ago
You First, Peter

The day was clear and bright, warm from very early in the morning. Sarah adjusted her academy uniform, her fellow graduates all standing ready to take their place on the podium. One hundred and twenty-two graduates, all ready to receive their final certificates and their assignments for the future. She glanced over at Peter, he stood with Ayden on the edge of the group. He noticed her and winked back, smiling reassuringly.

The speeches were long but only a little boring, the officials and dignitaries impressing on the graduates and their families how important this day was, and how honored the graduates should feel to be joining such a privileged and appreciated unit.

Sarah had learned that being a Guardian was the most sought-after career, and also the most revered. The people of this world, of this dimension, knew and appreciated the Guardians and their protection of their lifestyle, and indeed, their very lives. The graduates were not just joining a military unit, they were entering a way of life.

Finally, the speeches came to an end, the dignitaries taking their seats. One by one the graduates' names were called for them to receive their certificates and placements, a ceremony that reminded Sarah of college graduations back on Earth.

She clapped as each person accepted their plaques, envelopes and scrolled certificates, cheering as Peter and then Ayden were called, then it was her turn. As she stood on the dais and looked out to the thousands of people in the tiered stadium, she felt her eyes grow hot, knowing that her family was not here, could never be here. The crowd clapped and cheered for her and she smiled and bowed low, the way she had been taught. To them, she was a hero, someone who had given up her life on Earth to come and protect theirs. She knew she had to leave her memories behind, and had vowed that today, at this graduation ceremony, she would put her family firmly in her heart and no longer wonder what might have been, had she not been attacked that fateful day.

She joined the graduates on the side of the stage in their special seating and watched the entertainment. Live music, singers, acrobats and stunts were performing for the crowd and for the officials, the celebration was long and spectacular. It was some hours before the graduates were allowed to take a break, to leave the side stage to get changed, don their party attire and finally check their future assignments.

Sarah, Peter and Ayden had arranged to meet in the foyer of their barracks to open their assignments together. Frank joined Sarah as she changed from her graduation outfit to her celebration clothes. The graduates were on official break now, they had a week off to enjoy themselves and rest and recuperate before taking on their new assignments.

"Did you find out what your assignment is yet?" Sarah asked Frank.

"No, I thought I'd open it up with you and the other guys in the foyer. Us Earthlings all stick together." He hooked his arm in hers as they walked down the long, wide marble staircase to the expansive foyer.

Peter and Ayden were waiting for them in a quiet alcove off to the side of the foyer. There were several alcoves like this, and all had been claimed by similar groups opening their assignments.

"You first, Peter," Sarah encouraged as she sat down beside Ayden. Frank sat on a chair opposite her.

Peter took the scroll from his jacket pocket, broke the intricate seal and smiled at the three eager faces watching him. He took a deep breath and unrolled the scroll, reading it quietly as the others waited for his results.

"Well?" Frank demanded. "A guy could die of old age waiting for you."

"Not on this planet." Peter looked up from his assignment and smiled.

"Let me guess. Research and development? Scientific discoveries?"

Peter nodded. "Yeah, I guess it was a foregone conclusion with me, wasn't it? Right up my alley, though, and I'll be working with everyone I've been studying with, so that's a bonus. Who's next?"

"Me!" Frank pulled out his scroll and opened it, his face giving nothing away as he read. He took a long time to read and finally Sarah threw a cushion from her sofa at him.

"Okay, okay, I get it," he laughed. "Guess mine!"

Ayden shrugged. "I have no idea, man. Maybe pilot? You outperformed nearly everybody, including the instructors, when we did flight training."

Frank's smile broadened. "Spot on. It's what I wanted, but it gets better. I'm on inner gate security. I'm a Guardian of the Gate!" He accepted the congratulations from his companions before turning to Sarah. "You next, girl. Rip it open."

Sarah had been holding her assignment in her hand and now she turned it over, almost reluctant to open it. This here, this was her future, this was what she would spend the next few millennia doing. She suddenly didn't want to open the scroll, she wanted to tuck it under her arm and run back to her room.

She rang a thumb over the wax and cracked the seal. As she read it, she felt a twist of disappointment in her stomach. Looking up from the scroll she met the eyes of her companions. "I'm on-land security," she murmured. "I didn't even make guardian."

Ayden put a comforting arm around her shoulder. "I'm sorry, Sarah, I know how much that meant to you."

"Oh, Sarah, I'm so sorry." Frank leaned forward, his face lined with concern. "You can always try again. You could, you know, in a few years."

Sarah forced a smile onto her face. "Yeah, that's right, I could. And hey, it's a really responsible position, isn't it? Looking after people who never break any rules?" She felt a betraying tear escaping down her cheek and she brushed it aside angrily. "Well, Ayden, what about you? Why don't you open yours?"

"No, it's okay, I'll open mine later."

Sarah shook her head. "No, please, open it. I insist. I'll be okay, really." Her words didn't fool her companions, but Ayden played along and opened his scroll.

"You got Guardian, didn't you?" Sarah asked him.

Ayden nodded. "I got Gate," he said in a hushed tone, and Sarah hugged him.

"What unit, Ayden?" Peter asked, leaning in to look at the scroll.

"Outer. Beta unit."

His companions gasped. This was a very high honor, Ayden Jacobs had managed to earn a position in a garrison that many had tried for, but few had succeeded in achieving. Sarah was happy for him, she really was, but she felt that twist of disappointment turn into a corkscrew.

"Hey, let's not go back to the celebrations, yeah? Let's just get drunk here?" Ayden suggested.

"Good idea," Frank agreed, pushing his red hair from his eyes. "What do you think, Sarah, just stay in? Drink till we drop?"

Sarah pushed another smile out, this time it was a little easier, and looking at the three earnest faces in front of her turned it into a genuine smile. They were good men, these three, and she was lucky to have them as her friends.

"Hell, no! Let's go party! Training is over, now our long life can begin, right?" She stood up and straightened her outfit. "Let's go, boys, let's celebrate in style!"

"Not so fast," Kyle called out as he and Michael walked over to the group. "Congratulations are in order, I presume?"

Sarah's smile faltered but she accepted the outstretched hands that were warmly offered, shaking each firmly.

Ayden, Peter and Frank were happy to share their new positions, but Sarah felt her face grow hot when the two Alpha Guardians turned to her to see what her assignment was. "I'm, uh, well…"

"She's on-land security," Peter quietly finished for her.

"We know," Kyle smiled at her. "It is what we requested. Alpha garrison get what they ask for. We also wanted Ayden, and after he finishes his six-month final training in Beta unit, accompanied by Sarah, you will both be joining us in the Alpha unit."

Sarah felt lightheaded. "What? Why? Oh my god, really?"

"We feel that we may be a little out of touch with Earth, so the two of you will be invaluable in our search for the Dahn. Michael, Luke and I will be returning to the search tomorrow, and after six months Trauiss time you two will join us there, along with some new weapons being developed that will help in the fight against the Presas."

"You think they are still after Angie?" Peter asked.

"There is no reason to believe otherwise." Kyle saluted the graduates as he and Michael took their leave.

"Okay guys, I think it's time to eat, I think they are serving the main meal now." Sarah stood and moved her chair to allow Ayden to step out of the alcove. "You coming Peter? Frank?"

"In a sec." Peter smiled up at her. "I'll let you wander around to find our table, that way I can make a beeline to the food."

Frank stayed seated, watching them go, before he turned to Peter. "I think I'll do the same, I don't feel like standing in their shadow as they tell everyone about making it to Alpha Squad."

Peter grimaced. "You too, huh?"

"I thought you were happy with your assignment?"

"I am, yeah, I really am. It's just that, I dunno…"

"I do know," Frank nodded. "I didn't make Guardian, yet I've been at the academy a year longer than you guys, and I'm the best engine matrix operator they've seen in centuries, or so they tell me."

"Why couldn't they take us after six months, too?"

Standing, Frank tucked his scroll into his jacket. "Let's go eat, looks like they've found our table."

Chapter Twelve
Earth
Present Day
White Feather

Andrew Banfield smiled as the pretty waitress placed the huge steak in front of him, the aroma of the seared meat making his mouth water. The heady scent of his food mingled with the soft, dusky smell of perfume and perspiration, the diner was full tonight and there were too many bodies pressed into a small space. Drew's sense of smell was now acute, his senses were amplified, and he now saw, felt and based everything so much more intently than before.

Before.

It was almost a reference of time for him, the now, and the before.

Before he met her.

He cut into the bloody hunk of meat with relish, each bite was something to savor, an almost sensual experience. He ate here most nights, too lazy to cook for himself and the diner, while quaint and dated, did provide a good and hearty meal. It made it easier for anyone to find him, as well, and as the local sheriff he felt it was his duty to not only support the local businesses but to keep a fairly high profile. He was well known and well-loved in this town. Being a rather handsome man, he was also much sought after by many single (and some not so single) women that lived here, but Drew promised himself years ago not to shit where he ate, metaphorically speaking.

His occasional dalliances were consistently with out-of-towers, and there was always a fresh supply of those. The town was on a major tourist route and fresh faces appeared every day.

Today was no exception.

A table of what appeared to be college girls were giggling and giving him eyelash battering smiles, blushing beauties that would quite happily drag their nails down his back in the heat of passion.

"Looks like you'll be having a late night again, boss," Jim laughed as he swung into the opposite side of the booth.

Drew shook his head as he swallowed. "Not tonight, Jim, too much work to do with this case. Besides, they're barely legal."

"Since when has that ever stopped you?"

"That's what I say to Nick all the time," Sam laughed as he slid into the booth beside Jim. Nick slipped in beside Drew as he moved over, signaling the waitress as he did.

"Jim told us you'd be here," smiled Nick as they shook hands all round. At the sight of the two tall, handsome, city detectives the table of college students became louder, their giggling and loud whispers making them stand out in the noisy diner.

"The city boys told me you'd called them in to help us out with our recent murder spree," Jim nodded to Drew. "They're having the same trouble back home, I hear."

Sam raised a brow and nodded. "We think we have a case that is connected, yes, and Drew wanted to consult and compare facts."

"Good. What's happening here isn't right, it isn't normal. Not for this town, anyway. Maybe these things happen in the big smoke, but we don't have this kind of trouble here. We only get your usual tourist crap, a murder maybe once every four or five years." Jim shook his head. "It's horrific, there's no other way to describe it."

Nick pursed his lips and nodded. "It's horrific no matter where it happens, and you are right, it shouldn't be happening here. We'll do our best to give you guys a hand and hopefully catch whatever sick fucker is doing this."

Jim's phone rang and he answered it, his words short and concise as he finished his quick conversation before pocketing the cell and shaking his head. "Well, that's it for me, boys, we've got a three-car pile-up on the interstate. No one badly hurt, but a few tempers frayed, sounds like. I'll keep you informed," he nodded at Drew as he left.

The trio ordered drinks from the hovering waitress before settling back in the booth, ignoring the flirty girls, not even turning to watch them as they left, faces downturned with disappointment.

"Good to see you two," Drew pushed his empty plate aside. "You both look like you've grown another couple of inches."

"Not just us." Nick accepted his beer from the waitress and waited for her to move on before he continued. "And it's not just height. It's build, and sight, and taste, pretty much everything, I feel like I've been supercharged."

"It's slowed down, though, I don't feel like anything is continuing to change. Maybe this is it, this is what we have become."

"What we have *become*," Drew sighed. "What is that, I wonder? I feel so different from before. I barely feel like me. I don't do the same things I used to; I don't have the same hobbies anymore. What have we *become*, boys? What the hell are we?"

Nick looked down at the table while Sam held his gaze. "Been asking ourselves the same thing, Drew. We don't have any answers. We even feel like we're connected to these things, these monsters, I don't know, like we can sense them? Have you noticed that?"

Drew nodded. "Yeah, I have, I figured that was our Angie connection, that we all have her DNA or some such thing. Mind you, the fact that I can sense anything, let alone our formerly mythical creatures, is another thing I don't give too much thought to, for fear I'll run screaming naked down main street."

"An added tourist attraction for this town," Nick smiled.

"Not one I'd want to promote," Drew smiled back, holding his coffee cup for refill as the waitress glanced warmly at his companions before moving to the next table.

"So, you've a little puppy problem lately?" Nick prompted, changing the subject.

"That I have. People have been found with their

hearts and other various internal organs torn out of them, the coroner swears it's a large wolf, based on the teeth and scratch marks." He tipped his head to one side a little. "You boys are having the same kind of problem, I hear."

"That we are, Sheriff, and while we're pretty sure it's not the same pup that's killing people, we know they're linked somehow."

"Well, my main suspect was bitten about two months ago, something must have taken a chunk out of him to turn him. Do you think it could've been your wolf boy?"

"Highly likely," Nick replied.

Sam nodded in agreement but frowned suddenly. "Do you two get the feeling like we're being watched? I've had the feeling all day."

"Yes, me too, at the crime scene today I could swear there was someone there, watching. My hackles were raised, it's disconcerting." Drew sipped his coffee. "It's not like a 'normal' feeling of being watched, either, don't you agree?"

The detectives nodded their heads in agreement. Sam opened his mouth to speak but a piercing scream cut him off as it split through the air.

As one, the three lawmen were on their feet and running to the back of the diner where the scream originated. A door was ajar, two or three people standing near it as they comforted the waitress who was sobbing, her face buried into the chest of a rather plump gentleman.

"What is it? What happened?" demanded Drew as the two detectives drew their weapons and stepped cautiously through the door.

The waitress lifted her head, her face pale with shock. "It was in there; I went in to get something and… oh my god … there it was. It was, oh lord, it was like a giant wolf thing. It snarled right at me, Drew, I could see its teeth. Oh my god," she sobbed and buried her head back into the portly man's chest.

Drew nodded at the onlookers who were quickly growing in numbers. "Please stand back, let my colleagues and I handle this. We don't want anyone getting bitten by a rabid mongrel or anything," he said as he turned to follow Sam and Nick into the darkened storeroom.

The detectives held their small standard issue flashlights up with their weapons raised high, Drew pulled the door shut and fumbled for a light switch, bathing the room in stark fluorescent light.

"Light switch. Smart thinking," Nick grunted.

"Why didn't you think of that?" Sam hissed and moved sideways, his long legs bent at the knees as he moved, his head constantly turning as he searched for the creature that startled the waitress.

"Wish I had a good comeback for that." Nick moved in the opposite direction to his partner, Drew mimicked their stance and crept towards the back of the rather large storeroom.

There were piles of boxes, beer kegs, soda bottles, various indoor and outdoor chairs and tables, umbrellas and heaters arranged in an abstract collage of disarray. Although there was an excess of clutter, there were not too many places for the creature to hide. There was really only the rear of the room, where the trash bins and large collapsed cardboard packing crates were discarded, that would seem to provide any refuge for a supernatural wolf man to cower.

Sam could feel the hairs on the back of his neck prickle and rise before the acrid scent of the creature assaulted his senses. He glanced across at Drew to see the same odor was felt by the cop, Nick was not in his sight line, but he was sure that his partner would be picking up the same clues as they were.

A low, quiet growl rolled from behind the cardboard crates signaling that the monster felt the men draw closer and Sam cocked his weapon.

"You got silver in that thing?" hissed Drew.

"Of course. You?"

"Never without it these days."

The cardboard shuddered and pushed aside a little and both men squatted low, guns ready to fire, but there was no attack.

"It's out!" called Nick from the other side of the pile of trash as he pulled the cardboard crates to one side, revealing a broken door standing ajar. "Shit of a thing is running."

The three men leapt out into the misty evening, the parking lot that backed up to the diner was well lit and there were only a few cars scattered around, not many places to hide a large werewolf. A flicker of movement in his peripheral vision whipped Sam's head to one side and Nick fired, his shot a loud report in the quiet town.

A grunt and a thud followed the gunshot and the three lawmen ran to the fallen monster, reaching the creature as it rolled towards them, long tongue lolling out between terrifyingly sharp teeth, matted, filthy grey fur covering its entire carcass. As it died, the clear blue eyes of a man stilled, the light fading from them as the wolf became a man, a dirty, naked, emaciated looking man with a scruffy beard and face of innocence.

"That's Joe Hampshire." Drew ran a hand through his hair and shook his head. "Reported missing about a month ago. I'd thought him a victim, not the perpetrator."

"He may have been a victim." Sam crouched beside the body and indicted the sunken stomach and clearly visible ribs. "This fellow hasn't fed much, if at all. I don't think this is the wolf that's been eating your locals. He's way too lean. Awesome shot, by the way," he pointed to the single heart shot that had taken down the werewolf. Nick nodded, acknowledging the compliment.

"So we're no closer to finding the thing that's killing my town's people?" Drew slung his pistol back in the holster and turned to watch the small crowd of locals spilling through the storeroom door towards them. "While I won't have a problem explaining this fellow, I will have an issue when the next victim turns up with their innards missing."

"Wait … did you feel that?" Nick asked, a frown creasing his forehead.

Sam stood up as both he and Drew frowned, their expressions an exact mirror of Nick's.

"What is that?" Drew whispered. "What the hell is that?"

A loud howl split the night air, a dangerous wolf cry that set their hair on end and their nerves tingling.

The three men ran towards the howl as it continued, the long, piercing sound emanating from the woods that edged the parking lot. The howl turned into a growl that suddenly cut short, a yelp of fear and pain followed by silence, the pounding of shoes on asphalt and the puff of labored breath the only sounds.

The three men broke through the edge of the woods and skidded to a halt at a small clearing, the ground illuminated by the nearest parking lot light.

On the ground lay a werewolf, a big, black shaggy carcass that was quickly reforming to human shape, the hair and paws disappearing, the skin and flesh reforming to that of a well-built man. The head of this man lay a few feet away from the body, the cut on the neck clean and precise as if cleaved with one clear strike.

"*Sweet baby Jesus ...*" exclaimed Nick as he drew closer to the body, his weapon at the ready.

Sheriff Banfield walked to the head, turning it a little to view the face. "This is Paul Kane," he looked back at the two detectives behind him. "Wife reported him missing after he'd been bitten by something a couple of months ago. He *was* my main suspect behind the killings."

Sam bent over and picked up something beside the torso. He held it up for his companions to see.

The overhead lights sent soft shimmers of silver along the length of a slender, opalescent, white feather.

"What the fuck?" Nick stood and frowned.

"Angie," breathed Sam. "Angie was here."

Chapter Thirteen
Trauiss Prime
Academy of Skills
Five Years Ago
Why Is It So Creepy Down Here?

"I'm heading off guys, been a big night." Ayden stood and stretched.

"Me too," Sarah added.

"And me." Peter looked down at Frank, the only one left at their table.

"Not me, this party boy has plans with a group of fellow horny graduates. Catch you guys on the morrow."

Ayden and Sarah headed back to the barracks, though they weren't housed together their rooms were close to each other.

Peter had been sleeping in the tech room accommodation, he had moved his few personal belongings there within days of acceptance at the training academy. He liked to be close to the work rooms and research labs, often helping with experiments and projects that were not part of his training. He didn't mind the solitude, most of the time, with few people actually staying in the accommodation.

Tonight the dorm was particularly quiet, a lot of the technicians were attending the party and would most likely return to their own homes afterwards.

He stopped at one of the labs to check on a couple of timed experiments, the darkness of the research rooms a little creepy, especially at this time of night. He had asked why the rooms were always kept so dark, but no one had ever explained the reason to him.

As he turned to leave, a face against the lab window nearly made him scream, until he realized it was Frank. He took a deep breath to steady himself, then pushed open the lab door.

"Dude, you looked like you were going to shit your pants!"

"Not funny, Frank. Hey, I thought you were going to stay on at the party? Couldn't find anyone up for your carnal delights?"

Frank smiled at him but didn't answer. He just turned back and looked through the lab window. "Ever wonder why it's so creepy in here? Not just the dark, but you feel it, right, it's always weirdly eerie in this part of the laboratory."

"Yeah, though I thought it was just me that felt that way, you know, because it's dim, and quiet. Everyone speaks in hushed voices."

"They say no one is allowed in here longer than two hours. Did you know that, Peter?"

"I did. I'm also not supposed to let anyone in. How did you get back here?"

Frank moved away from the window. "I don't have the same restrictions as you. I also know why it's uber creepy in here." He put his arm around Peter's shoulders as they walked towards the accommodation. "There's so much you don't know, and so much you need to learn, my boy. And I may even introduce you to a few friends of mine. Rather important friends."

"So why is it so creepy down here?"

"Because, about two hundred feet below this laboratory is another lab, a very secret lab. Then under that is a storage facility. It's absolutely ancient, been there for almost longer than our written history. The lab is where they mixed up the ingredients, the clever little experiment that made our esteemed leader, the Dahn Ah M'Rath. But what ninety-nine-point-nine percent of our citizens don't know is that they made her using bits and pieces of monsters. Bad creatures, vile, disgusting, evil things, the stuff we used to read about, and have nightmares over. Things very much like werewolves, vampires, evil aliens, and other nasty creatures. It's the stink of evil that seeps up through all the rock and ore and dulls the light and gives you the heebie-jeebie feelings. But you know what the worst bit is Peter? The very worst thing of all?"

They came to the door between the accommodation and lab and Peter placed his hand on the panel beside the door to allow him access. "Do you want to come through?"

"Nah Peter, it is very late, and I do want to get back to what's left of the party."

"So, what is it?"

"What's what?"

"What you were about to tell me. The very worst thing?"

The door lock timed out and the lock clicked closed. Frank smiled at Peter.

"The very worst thing that they house down

there is a demon. A real-life demon. A black, wretchedly cursed creature more terrifying than anything mentioned in the Bible. It's huge, something like twenty feet tall, and there may be more than one. What is truly terrifying, my boy, is that they also used that thing to make our dear Dahn. From what I am told, they pretty much made her with more demon than anything else. The god-like, eternal, all-powerful supreme ruler of the multiverse that we are trying to find and bring back is not much more than a damned demon. A fucking demon! Can you believe that? No wonder one of the side effects of this perfect life is sterility. If she was a good thing, babies would by flying out of every vagina. Instead every single person becomes sterile, for life. Even if they leave, they don't regrow their fertility. Get used to never settling down and raising a family. Never going to happen."

Peter realized his mouth was gaping open and snapped it with an audible click of teeth. He shook his head, trying to gain some clarity with all he had been told.

"Why doesn't she look like a demon? I've seen her, she's beautiful. And small, like, maybe only five foot three. Also, you don't feel any evil from her, not even the creepy feeling you get from the lab."

"Of course not. You think they could parade her around as some holy savior if she looked or felt like a demon? That's what the controls are for, Pete. To keep her looking human. They take away all the demon features and signs and make her look like something they can dress up and put on show. You know they kept her chained in a dungeon for over a thousand years? She was too dangerous to let out, it wasn't until they came up with better controls to use on her that they could release her. I know it sounds too far-fetched to be true, I felt the same way, at first. But I've seen the records, and I've seen the dungeon. There are claw marks as deep as my hand in the stone walls. She is a monster, there is nothing else to it. Why do you think they need to find her before her controls need changing? They know she will revert, and they'll have to lock her up again. That is, unless she reverts too far. Then god help us all, because nothing else will."

Chapter Fourteen
Trauiss III
The Laboratory
A Long Time Ago
These Things Are Night Creatures

The stench was the first thing that slapped you in the face as the heavy, solid metal doors slowly creaked open. A feeling of dread whooshed over the seven people that walked through the doors, they had been warned before they came that they would feel this, but the emotion was so strong they felt their hearts beat faster, their arms prickle with gooseflesh and the hairs on the backs of their necks rise.

The air seemed to grow thicker as they traversed the dark corridor to the main atrium, where, even though there were many banks of bright lights, it still held an air of darkness and foreboding.

A team of uniformed researchers bowed low as the seven entered and stood uncomfortably in the center of the large room.

"Welcome, Lords, to our humble facility," a rather portly, balding man stepped forward, his arms spread in a welcoming gesture. "I am Elund, the senior lead researcher in charge. We are honored to have your esteemed presence before us today, and we thank you for accepting our invitation to attend in person."

"Your invitation bore merit," the most senior

Lord, a tall, imposing woman, nodded at Elund. "It is all very well for us to view the files in the comfort of the palace, however we do need to assess the results in person."

"If you will follow me," Elund turned and led the party from the atrium, the stench growing as they walked into darkness. The hallway they entered contained a multitude of lights, but the darkness seemed to be an oppressing force, subduing the light and creating dark shadows and pockets, a greyness that felt as if it permeated even the very air they breathed. Hearing the nervous murmurs and fearful, shallow breathing, Elund turned and offered a reassuring smile. "Please, my Lords, do not let this overcome you. This is not real, it is an illusion our creations cannot help but emit," he turned and pointed to the unremarkable looking door at the end of the hall. "Somehow it leaks out to here like a stench. We can keep the creations contained with caged bars and force fields, however the darkness and dread always leak out. Please, you will see it is not as bad once we enter the containment area."

The group was very surprised to find themselves led into a brightly lit, neutral smelling area, a long room with large, opaque preservation tubes on one side, and a bank of desks and displays, scientists at tables with data pads and notebooks on the other. Elund led them to the first large tube. At his beckoning the Lords crowded closer to see what it contained as he touched the surface of the tube, turning it completely transparent.

The tube held a creature, standing upright on two legs, so motionless that it was unclear if it was deceased or merely in stasis. There were no gasps of surprise or recoils of horror at the sight of this hideous creature. The Lords merely observed as Elund spoke. "Lycans were the first species used by the invaders to attack us. Fortunately, we discovered very early on that a heart shot or decapitation were efficient ways to dispatch these things. Our warriors had at first taken many hits, as these things are night creatures, and were sent to our planets as we rested. They seemed impervious to all defenses, healing almost instantly when shot or cut anywhere but the heart. Because of this, we only used them as a partial base DNA for their ability to heal as well as assimilate other life forms. Made a more cohesive bond, if you will, for the other beings we are using."

"Will there be any trace of this filth in the finished subjects?" the senior Lord queried.

"No. No visual or characteristics of the lycanthrope will persist in the finished creatures. Base DNA only."

"That is good to hear. Werewolves are such vile, dirty creatures."

Elund turned, leading the party past the next tube, touching it to illuminate it as he kept walking, continuing his narrative. "Similarly, the Vampiri, the Satyr, and the ghoul, all of these creatures were used as weapons against us. All were defeated. We used the parts of their DNA, again for their strong abilities to heal, adapt and assimilate other species.

This was imperative in melding all of the different creatures together."

Elund continued walking, touching each tube as he passed, and each tube cleared to show a creature of nightmares, each one more terrifying and grotesque than the one before.

"We decided to find creatures ourselves, rather than wait for attacks to collect the necessary materials. We started locally, in nearby systems that were located just outside our wormhole, then spread far and wide to find creatures with great power and abilities. Creatures both physical and magical, beings that we could harvest their physical and metaphysical powers to construct our warriors. Of course, we started with this one." Elund stopped in front of the last tube, one far larger than all of the others. The Lords, who were previously quietly talking amongst themselves, fell silent. Elund touched the final tube. The opacity took a little longer to clear on this one, but as it did there were audible gasps as the creature within was revealed.

Humanoid, but barely so, it looked to stand at least ten feet high. The creature's skin was a deep, dark red, almost black. From the waist down it was coated with rough fur, thick, wiry and a shade darker than the skin. The feet were hooves, cloven, like a pig's, and they were shiny black. It had large, muscular arms that ended in very large hands, each finger tipped with a sharp, black claw. The head was huge, a gnarled, evil looking mass of hate and malice, and each side of the forehead grew a large, curled horn, like that of a goat. The eyes were half open, and the Lords could see they were bright red, with slit pupils like a cat.

"The capture of the demon, and consequently the power it yielded, was not only our inspiration, but the very foundation, the first building block of our protectors."

Slowly, ever so slowly, the demon opened its eyes and turned its head to look at all of the people observing it. Lifting its chin, it smiled, then lunged at them, slamming into the side of the tube.

Chapter Fifteen
Gate Duty
Six Months Ago
Fire At Will

"Gate duty isn't what I expected, but I have to say I don't mind it at all," Ayden told Sarah as he sat down beside her at the forward console. "It kind of reminds me of space invaders, you know, the game they'd always have in the corner of the drugstore, or the pizza restaurant?"

Sarah ran her hand across her display screen, searching for any anomalies on the sensor grid.

"Yeah, I know the ones. Never was a big fan, but my son had one on a Nintendo when he was seven or eight, I think, and I played it a couple of times with him. Used to beat me pretty quickly, though."

"Ship approaching grid four, section seven over nine," a guard informed the captain from his console on the side of the bridge.

"Identify," the captain instructed.

"Requesting identity." Ayden tapped his screen. "It's the Hoya, returning from reconnaissance."

"Alert the quarantine team and inform the Hoya to prepare for inspection."

"Aye, cap." Ayden was smiling as he tapped his pad.

"You always do that," Sarah laughed.

"Do what?"

"You smile, no matter what ship it is, no matter whether it's one of ours, or a hostile, you smile when you make contact."

"It's the kid in me," Ayden told her. "I mean, this is every science fiction adventure I ever watched, and believe me, I watched a lot, and here I am, living it, every single day."

"We all felt that way when we first got here." The captain joined their conversation, her face a soft smile reflecting fond memories.

"Does it ever wear off?" Sarah asked.

"I will let you know," the captain smiled back.

"Hey, I have something here. Wyn, can you check grid thirteen, section… wait." Sarah tapped the screen on her console. "It's moving pretty fast. Section five over sixteen."

"I see it," the guard replied. "It's definitely a ship."

The Captain looked over at Ayden. "Identify."

"Requesting identity."

Ayden worked on his console, sliding his fingers across and tapping the smooth screen.

"No response. Unable to identify."

"Continue requesting identity. Wyn, track trajectory."

"Affirmative, captain. Tracking. They are coming in fast, headed for, uh, changing direction, there. They'll enter grid one, between section four and nine."

"Visual." The captain's smile had faded.

Sarah swept her hand over her console and the forest scene on the wall in front of them transformed into a view of space, blackness dotted with the pinpoint light of stars filling the entire wall.

Sarah tapped at the screen and a grid superimposed over the top, then she zoomed in on one square of the grid.

"Will they never give up?" muttered the captain as she swung a small data console up from beside the arm of her chair, positioning it in front of her.

"Is that who I think it is?" Ayden asked.

"If you are asking if that is the Clethora, then yes, it is who you think it is. Is this your first time against these vermin?"

Ayden continued working on his console. "If you don't count simulations, then yes, it's my first time."

"Mine too," Sarah added.

"Well then, my rookies, what's the first thing you should be doing?"

"Sound general alarm." Sarah touched her console and the light changed on the bridge from warm white to bright blue, and a soft alarm sounded, joined with a disembodied voice.

"*Alert. Current crew to engagement stations. Hostile detected. Alert. Current crew to engagement stations. Hostile detected.*"

"Bring us around, Ayden. Ready us to engage."

Several more black-uniformed guards joined the bridge crew, touching the walls on each side of the room which triggered consoles to appear. Chairs automatically rose from the floor, where previously there had been no indication of their existence.

"Ready to engage, captain."

"They are firing!" Wyn called out.

"Evasive action," answered Ayden as he

maneuvered his hands over the console, bringing the ship around to avoid enemy fire.

"The Iris has just joined us," Sarah reported.

"We will never refuse extra firepower." The captain touched her consol. "Syncing with the Iris. Prepare to fire."

"Ready, captain."

"Fire at will."

"Firing." Ayden's smile threatened to split his face. "Iris matching fire."

"They are firing again," one of the crew on the side called out as Ayden maneuvered the ship to avoid being hit.

"Targeting blasters, readying cannons." Sarah touched the side of her console and a second, smaller data screen lifted up.

"Firing." Ayden looked up at the viewer as the Clethoran ship exploded. "Score! I mean, Clethora destroyed, Captain."

"I would have thought a military man would be a little more subdued." Sarah touched the smaller pad and it returned to the side of her console.

"You think we didn't applaud a victory in the armed forces?"

"I know I did. Well done, Ayden. Let's scan around, see if there are any more of those filthy scum lurking in the distance."

"Aye, Captain."

Chapter Sixteen
Trauiss Outer
The Battlefields
A Long Time Ago
For the Sake of My Soul

"Are you okay?" The young warrior, a tall, black-haired, well-muscled young man, coughed and wiped the blood from his face. "Robert, are you okay?"

A groan escaped the fallen man at his feet. "Brother, answer me!"

The groaning man rolled onto his back as his brother leant over and grabbed his arm, lifting him to a sitting position.

"Robert? Are you injured?"

"For the sake of my soul, James, let me catch my breath!"

James exhaled a sigh of relief. He patted his brother over, checking for injuries. His brother was covered in more blood than he was, and not all of the blood was red. There were splashes of thick purple and black ooze, a stinking, viscous mess of creature blood that coated the young warrior, whose face was so similar to his own.

"I am fine, James. Nothing that will threaten my life. Just help me to my feet, please."

A painful hiss was all he allowed to escape as James heaved him to his feet. They were almost identical in features and stature, clearly brothers, clearly similar in age and physique. James kept his arm around his brother, supporting him, and turned them both to survey the landscape.

The view around them was almost more than a man could bear. All over was death and destruction. Men, warriors, all of their battalion, lay before them, most of them torn limb from limb. There was so much death, so much carnage. Viscera and body parts lay in a sea of blood, and James felt his heartbeat quicken at the realization that there were not just the bodies of his fallen comrades, but those of women, children, babies, innocent farmers and village folk. They had all been slaughtered and their blood now mingled with that of the warriors that fought to protect them.

The town was gone, razed, rubble and smoke were all that remained. All buildings, structures, and even the trees were flattened.

The silence was overwhelming, but short lived. From here, a groan and moan of the wounded. From there, a child's cry, a woman's sob, a mother's call.

Survivors.

Not many, but some.

Some had been spared.

Warriors climbed to their feet, they were covered in blood and gore, their leather attire torn and filthy.

With heavy feet and painful gasps, they made their way to the brothers, from several thousand, a motley few dozen that somehow survived, eventually drew a ragged circle around the men.

A clink and drag of heavy chains brought their attention to the creature that caused all this mayhem and slaughtered so many.

The chains were iron, hand wrought, thick, heavy, unpolished links, each one thicker than a man's wrist. It had taken thirteen men to wield the chain. Thirteen warriors.

Only one survived.

Robert looked at the vile creature that tore their planet apart over the last few weeks, the most powerful, evil thing they ever encountered in all the years their multiverse was under attack. This one came the closest to defeating them. It was sheer luck that they discovered it had an aversion to iron. More than an aversion, it rendered the thing powerless.

The chains clinked again as the thing desperately tried to move, to muster up enough strength to break free. All its efforts were in vain, it could barely move.

James lifted his blaster high as his warriors surrounded him, the remaining townsfolk nervously edging forward to catch a glimpse.

"Behold!" he cried, one arm held the raised blaster, the other supporting his injured brother. "Behold the filth that wrought havoc on our people! Behold as it writhes against the burn of pure iron! We have prevailed! We have defeated and captured the Demon!"

Chapter Seventeen
Gate Duty
Six Months Ago
The Three Amigos

"Well, I am not going to lie to you, that was awesome," Ayden told Sarah as she joined him in the dining hall. "I could do that any day."

"You didn't find it a little intimidating? You know, they could have actually destroyed us."

"It's unlikely, the Clethora haven't gotten lucky for a very long time. We had the Iris backing us up as well."

"He's right, you know." The captain sat down opposite them, placing her plate on the smoothly polished tabletop. "While we don't ever want to become complacent, it's unlikely that the Clethora had much of a chance against the Beta Squad, and both the Tulip and the Iris. The firepower from our two ships combined is enough to take out a dozen Clethoran vessels." She paused to take a forkful of food. "Your friend Peter has been directly responsible for our new weapons array, but I'm sure you are aware of that."

"No, I haven't actually spoken to Peter for a while. Have you, Ayden?"

"No, not me, but that's awesome to hear. We knew he was a bit of a genius, so I'm really not surprised."

"Feeling a bit guilty about not keeping in touch,

though. We should send him a com after shift tonight."

"He has come up with several new ideas for finding the Dahn, as well. The way he is going he'll end up on Alpha team with you two!"

"That'd be fantastic. The three amigos back together again."

"Is that what you call yourselves? The three amigos?"

"Nah," Ayden replied around a mouthful of food. "Sarah just came up with that now. But she's right, it would be great to have us all together on the Alpha team. It's unbelievable how far we have all come."

The captain nodded. "It is funny, you know, new people seem to have more drive, more ambition than people who have lived here for centuries, or those that were born here. I think it is because we still feel mortal, still have that drive to achieve something within our lifetime. Once people start to feel immortal, they tend to lose that drive, that burning ambition. They settle into the longer picture, like arts, philosophy, a more peaceful life. There is nothing wrong with that, and certainly not everyone feels that way, I just see the newer people burning a little brighter."

Sarah looked thoughtful, mulling over what the captain said. "How long have you been here?"

"Just on three hundred and fifty years since I officially died on Earth. I didn't enter the academy straight away, like you did. I took a few years to really adjust to being here, I was not happy at losing my life on Earth. Which is very silly, I did not have a very good life there. I had been raised as a warrior, to fight in the Emperor's army, never knowing my own family. They gave me up when I was three years old. It was unusual, but not unheard of, for women to become Samurai class warriors. I was good at being a soldier. Very good. I just wasn't so good at being a woman in a patriarchal society. I died a senseless death, an honorless death, murdered in my sleep by one of the men who served under me. He felt disgraced being ordered around by a woman, especially a woman who was a better warrior than he was."

"You actually died?" Sarah asked, the shock showing on her face. "We were taken before we died. I didn't know that people actually died!"

"As you know, there are several minutes where you have a chance to be resuscitated. Most of the time the rescue team can get in and grab you just before the actual death, but something happened moments before they got to me, and I died." She smiled at the two shocked faces opposite her. "It did not last very long."

"You seem to like your life here now, though, don't you?"

"Yes. I like my life here very much." The captain placed her utensils on her plate and stood up. "I got to fight bad guys in hand to hand combat. I got to travel to distant worlds, to see pink skies and purple stars. I've ridden a real unicorn and danced with butterflies the size of elephants. And I met the woman I will spend eternity with, so yes, I like my life here, and I am happy."

"I think I'm happy too." Sarah stood and picked up her plate. "I miss my kids, but the alternative is that I would be dead. Not much of an alternative."

***

"*Hey Peter, sorry I missed you, thought we'd leave you a message to let you know we're okay, having fun, and killing bad guys.*" Ayden's smile was genuine, and Peter almost smiled back at the vid-link recording.

"*We hear you are responsible for our Clethora-destroying weapons, so hey, fantastic job there!*" Sarah looked as happy as Ayden. "*Anyway, give us a yell when you can, be great to catch up on all you're doing there.*" The recording ended, and Peter pushed *decline* on the *reply now* tab.

"You don't think they'll get suspicious if you don't call them back?" Frank asked from over his shoulder.

"No, they'll just think I am busy. I'll leave them a message when I know they are on a shift. I just need to get all of my lines down pat. They know me better than anyone else, and I don't want them asking any questions I'm not one hundred percent sure how to answer."

"Good thinking, I suppose. Besides they're all shiny happy in their new life, damn irritating if you ask me."

"It's not so irritating. I don't mind my life here, it's exponentially better than my life on Earth was. I wasn't anyone there, just some pimply geek with no real friends and no family. At least here I'm somebody."

"That's right. And with our help you're becoming more of a somebody every day."

Peter pushed the vid screen aside and stood up. "I'm very grateful for that, though a lot of ideas were my own, too."

"We know that, Petie old boy, we wouldn't have brought you on board if you were not an absolute genius."

Chapter Eighteen
The Alcea (Angie's ship)
Present Day
A Sighting

"Finally! This is she!" Kyle exclaimed before he frowned, running his hand through his collar length hair. "I can hardly believe that we finally have a sighting of her. Brilliant work, Elyse."

The green-eyed woman shook her head. "The praise should go to Sarah. She is the one who found the images."

Sarah smiled a little, then cleared her throat nervously.

"I am justified in selecting you for the duty of guardian."

"Honestly sir, it was more chance than skill." Sarah cleared her throat again and shuffled her feet. "I was looking on social media and came across the pictures. They are causing quite a stir. Media outlets are running the story and interviewing the photographer."

Kyle's frown deepened. "Social media, Sarah?"

"Yes sir. I'm sorry. I just wanted to see if I could, um, you know, maybe see how my kids are doing. I know I'm not allowed, really, but I just thought, um, just a quick look, you know, maybe it wouldn't really hurt."

"I did not order you away from social media, per se, however I do hope that you did not do anything that could identify yourself. It would greatly hurt your family if they knew you were still alive."

"I was very careful, sir. I did not use any accounts of my own, and I made sure that all of my tracks were covered. Peter helped me."

Kyle looked up at the former technician.

"Way to throw me under the bus, Sarah!" Peter stood up from his station and joined the three at the viewer. "Actually, Sarah approached me with the thought that social media was an excellent place to search for a trace or sighting of Angie. I agreed, so I set up an algorithm that would allow a search of all social media platforms and sites without needing to sign in or create an account. While I didn't specifically rule out having a look at her family, I did make sure Sarah could not be identified."

"I actually found the picture and story of the Angie sighting because my daughter shared it to her account. I reported it to Elyse as soon as I found it."

Kyle turned from the viewer and addressed Peter. "We need to make sure these pictures, and the story, are stopped immediately." He tugged at the neck of his black uniform, as if it irritated him.

"All ready to go on your command, sir." Peter held up a data pad. "I also have all available pictures, and also the information on the photographer."

Kyle sighed and ran his hand across his forehead and through his fair hair again. "Remove all traces, immediately. I suppose this is why you are all feeling that Angie has been active, Elyse?"

"I cannot explain it, sir," Elyse shrugged and

smiled a little. "It is just a feeling, but I have to say the feeling grows stronger every day."

Kyle frowned. "You are not the only one to have told me this. Many have come to me to tell me the same thing."

"He is not happy that nearly everyone on board is feeling this, everyone except for him." Michael stood and walked over to the other side of the room and turned on the viewer beside Kyle's. "I do not find it strange."

"You do not?" Elyse asked, the surprise clear in her voice.

"No, Elyse, I do not," Michael answered. "If the Dahn is going to shield herself from anyone, it would be him. It makes sense, I feel."

Kyle grunted and turned back to his viewer. "I am glad you all feel amused by this."

"No, Kyle, we do not find this amusing. This actually concerns us greatly. Luke and I were discussing this earlier. This means that not only can she block people, she can also target one person in particular."

Luke nodded in agreement, his face reflecting his concern.

"It was always *I* that could feel where she was," Kyle acknowledged. "If all of you can feel her presence, she must be using her powers. You must all be sensing her through her powers."

"I believe they are, and even I am, a bit, but I'm a little confused about something." Sarah leaned on the console and tilted her head a little as she smoothed the collar of her black uniform, a habit that followed her from her former life. "If we're so far away, like barely in the same galaxy, why can we feel her, when Longstaff and Cotter are on the same planet and haven't noticed a thing?"

Michael nodded. "That is a valid point, but not very unusual. She would be able to block anyone on Earth, as they are so much closer to her. However, it does prove to us that she is not using all of her controls."

"Of course she is not using all of her controls, but we knew this, did we not?"

"Yes, Kyle, we knew this, I was merely explaining it to Sarah." Luke touched his own silver band on his wrist. "These types of controls can be fitted by the wearer, but most of the internal controls need to be inserted surgically and cannot be fitted in any other way. While we are fairly sure that she is using some internals, she could not possibly use all of them."

"It is time to contact Longstaff and Cotter. Now we have a definite sighting, it is time to involve the detectives," Kyle turned to Michael. "Prepare the controls we need to take, and make sure our team is at the ready."

"It seems that our detectives are with Sheriff Guard at this moment." Peter tapped a few instructions into his data pad. "They'll meet us in his house, if that's fine with you, sir?"

Kyle raised his brows. "I am assuming there is a reason they are all together?"

Peter shrugged. "They didn't say. I guess you'll find out."

"Yes, I suppose we will. Will you join us in the transport portal?"

"Hell yeah! I can't wait to see those guys again. I mean, yes sir, thank you sir."

Chapter Nineteen
Trauiss III
The Laboratory
A Long Time Ago
Demonic Base Materials

"The demon cannot escape. For four hundred years it has never managed to do more than lunge, but as you can see, that act has cost it dearly. The effort, and resulting pain of the controls we have installed, will ensure the demon takes decades to recover. If you look closely, you will see the external controls. They appear as iron bands on the hands, feet, and a thin band around the torso."

The Lords shuffled and murmured, embarrassed by their shock and fright at the demon's lunge. Clearing his throat, one of the younger Lords took a step towards the creature, who was now still as death. "Yes, I can see these controls you mention. External, you said, I take it that there are internal controls as well?"

Elund nodded and gestured for one of his assistants to join him. A slim young woman hurried to his side, a data pad in her grasp. "My first assistant, and chief researcher Xanya, has been leading this initiative."

Xanya nodded and touched a small panel on the side of the demon's containment tube. The illumination changed immediately to a more subdued hue, allowing an internal view of the creature. Another tap of the panel allowed the onlookers to see several twisting objects within the body of the demon.

"Each control is attached to a nerve cluster that, through experimentation and test applications, were established to be the most effective." Xanya tapped the panel again and the demon slowly rotated, giving the Lords a view of controls transferring the spinal column. "There are approximately seventy five percent more controls inserted than are required, we do prefer to err on the side of safety."

"Given the devastation caused when this thing was unleashed upon our universe, we would concur with that decision."

Elund motioned for the group to follow him as he led them through larger, heavily reinforced doors at the end of the room. The doors opened slowly, soundlessly, allowing the Lords to enter the darkened room. There were more tubes along the side of this room; though of similar construct, they were infinitely larger, and all were illuminated, albeit with a soft glow of muted light. The Lords were silent as Elund led them past these tubes, no explanation was needed for them to know that these were also demons, each one larger and more hideous than its predecessor. There were other creatures, very similar to the demons, however these were darker, covered in rougher fur, and they sported large, leathery wings, now held folded against their backs.

Elund led them forward, stopping at another heavy set of doors. Xanya stood by his side, her data pad raised as she tapped quickly onto it.

"This next containment area that we will now take you through shows what you have come to see, our failed experiments, the rejected output of our artificial breeding program." He turned and tipped his hand to signal Xanya to open the door, which she did by placing her palm against a sensor. These doors also were cumbersomely slow, opening for the Lords to step through a downdraft of air that rushed and hissed around them. As they stepped out of the downdraft their senses were once again assaulted with the rolling stench that greeted them when they first arrived. The stench was not the only thing that they had to deal with, once again the deep sense of foreboding and feelings of malice engulfed them, seeming to permeate their very souls.

"You have felt the insult to your various senses, my Lords, and for this I can only apologize. We have done all that we can to control this, however, as you have noticed, we have not been entirely successful."

The Lords nodded, unconsciously huddling together, taking some comfort from their peers. They moved slowly to follow the technicians as they made their way into the gloomy chamber, glancing at the barred stalls on either side as Elund led them forward.

"You'll notice the dimmed lights, this is necessary as all of the spawn, without exception, are photosensitive. Xanya will explain further."

The slim woman brushed a lock of her dark, short, straight hair behind her ear and gave the

Lords a grim smile. "We expected the aversion to light as this trait was carried by so many of the creatures that we used. We felt that this was not a worrisome issue."

"Unlike so many of the other, more worrisome issues you have been having?" one of the Lords interjected. "Do you not believe our creation would need to be utilized in the sunlight at any time?"

Xanya nodded. "Most certainly, and we have an efficient solution to that problem, so, for us, it was not an issue," she turned and led them past several of the caged creations, describing each monster, gesturing towards each one as she narrated the way. The Lords could see that there were heavy demon influences in each one, the dark, rough fur, wings, claws, and horns in varying and horrific manifestations on each. Most of the creatures seemed subdued, though an occasional one would growl, or lunge at the bars that contained them. The Lords did not flinch, they had full confidence in Elund's containment methods.

"As you know, my Lords, the amalgamation of creatures, while interesting and very often useful, was not culminating in the ultimate beings that we need to protect our multiverse. More often than not, we found our breeding resulted in creatures that were either not viable, or not satisfactorily controllable. Thus, the decision was made to include human DNA in the equation. We believed this would allow a better communication, a better temperament, in short, a more controllable and more successful product." Xanya turned and led the entourage to a new series of tubes, each one opaque. A touch on her data pad triggered the tubes to become transparent and illuminate. They contained grotesque cadavers that were human/creature hybrids.

"As you are aware, it was very much a trial and error process, with fewer errors as we progressed. The rejected products you see here were, unfortunately, extremely violent."

"Yes, as Elund's report informed us," the senior Lord gestured towards the cadavers. "We were curious as to your thoughts on the reason for this."

"Combining human DNA with the demonic base materials proved to be a toxic mix. Each one of these rejects, these failures, contained biological material from all of the creatures you saw in the first room. We took the capabilities, the powers, the gifts, if you will, from each of them, then combined them with the human-demon hybrid." Xanya touched the data pad again and the cadaver tubes became opaque. "After extensive experimentation and research, we concluded that no matter how much human DNA we included, it was not enough to overcome the evil from the creatures. Including the demon, though it gave us an exponentially more powerful outcome, it also gave us more destructive, and harder, often impossible to control, creatures." She smiled grimly before turning and leading the group through yet another door. This room was bright, impossibly so, the glare was so strong that the Lords lowered their heads, eyes half lidded.

"Could you turn that down?" the senior Lord

asked as she held a hand up to shield her eyes. "This is as bad as the gloom from the earlier chamber. Maybe worse."

Xanya was again joined by a goggle-wearing Elund, who handed the Lords eye protection. They were given the same dark goggles that protected him, and now Xanya, against the relentless light. "There are no illumination panels operating here, and this is just the ante chamber for the next room. You will need to wear the eye protection to enter," he said as he handed one to each Lord. "In the next room is what you have all been waiting to see."

Chapter Twenty
Earth
Present Day
Would I Lie to You?

Annette shivered and pulled her sweater tight around herself as she waited for her bus. She wished she'd grabbed her coat before she left for work this morning, the weather report had said it would be a cold, damp evening. She had even taken it out of her closet last night, ready to wear it the next day. Her alarm hadn't gone off on time and she had rushed around like a mad woman, it wasn't until she was locking the front door that Annette remembered her coat. She didn't really have time to rush back inside, and the sun was shining bright and warm, so she decided to forget the coat and hurry to catch the bus instead. She didn't give the coat another thought until she walked out of work, having been held up until it was nearly dark when some thoughtless parent had taken forever to pick up their snot nosed kid.

Annette was alone with the child as the last assistant had to go when her lift arrived, and once the child was picked up and signed out, the place seemed deserted. Annette hated locking up by herself, while the childcare center was a bright and cheery place in the daytime, filled with children and staff and music and laughter, it was a very different place with most of the rooms dark and closed. There were too many shadows, too many creaks and groans in the old building, and Annette had a quick and overactive imagination. She hurried to set the alarm and lock up, the hairs on the back of her neck standing up as she imagined some axe murderer watching her leave. She had a real creepy feeling that she was being watched and try as she might to tell herself that it was only her imagination, the feeling persisted.

The covered walkway to the childcare parking lot protected her from the early evening drizzle, it wasn't until she closed and locked the gate that the cold soft rain found its way onto her bare arms and tickled her neck and face. She had pulled the sweater that was tied around her waist and quickly put it on as she walked, arms folded, down the street to the bus stop. The streetlamps had already come on, it was so much later than she was used to leaving and wasn't sure how long it would be before the bus came along.

The creepy feeling lingered with her, she supposed it was just due to the late hour, or the misty arc from the streetlamps, or the way the light glowed and bounced off the falling rain. She pulled her sweater even tighter and walked as fast as she could without running towards the bus stop.

Now that she was here, waiting at the uncovered stop, the world seemed even darker and colder. The one light above the stop illuminated only her immediate area, turning the misted rain into a globe of golden sparks, but it also made the surrounding area invisible to her.

Annette was cold, but her shivering was for more than that, she was genuinely scared. Not a brave soul in the best of times, the creepy feeling of being stalked was almost overwhelming. She started to mentally tick through a list of people she could call to pick her up if the bus took any longer. Gawd, she'd even call Kevin, her creepy neighbor, rather than stand here in the cold and rain, waiting for a rapist axe murderer to grab her from behind.

A car pulled up to the curb and the passenger window opened.

"Hey, pretty lady, could you use a lift?" Annette couldn't see the guy properly, but he looked to be a typical middle-aged sleaze bag. She knew better than to get into a car with a stranger.

Somewhere behind her the bushes rustled, and she swore she could hear a low growl, a soft, animal like sound that was terrifying her more than the thought of getting in the car with Mr. Gropey.

"C'mon, girl, it's raining and cold, and I think you probably missed the last bus."

The bushes rustled again, and Annette felt her fear deepen.

"How do I know I can trust you?" Annette leaned to the window to get a better look at the guy. He looked harmless enough, cheap suit, balding head, but he had a nice smile.

"Hey, I'm safe. A lot safer than standing here in the cold waiting for some crazy person to come along and grab you, right?"

Annette chewed her lower lip. It was a fifty-fifty chance between him and whatever was stalking her from the bushes.

"Hey, look at me. I'm a nice guy, you can trust me." The guy leaned over and opened the door for her.

"I'm not sure, I mean, how do I know you'll take me home safely?"

He smiled even brighter, and he did look kind of friendly.

"Would I lie to you?"

Another rustle in the bushes and Annette made up her mind. She stepped off the curb as a blur and rush of brown on the other side of the car caught her attention.

"Hop in! It's freezing out there, honey, and nice and warm in here."

The driver's window exploded, the glass scattering over the driver and even hitting Annette. She froze in shock as something reached through the window to grab the driver.

Some*thing.*

It was dark, the thing. Dark, hairy, and its jaws were wide and cruel. There were teeth, *oh god*, so many teeth, dripping with saliva and something else she couldn't process. The man started to scream, a high pitched, feminine sound, his hands gripping on the wheel as if to save his life. The jaws closed around the driver's head; they were so big that they almost completely covered his whole head.

Annette was still holding the door, her mouth open, her eyes large, unable to move, the fear rooting her to the spot.

The thing didn't pull the driver out of the broken

window, instead it closed its jaws, snapping the skull of the driver and removing his entire face. It pulled back with its grizzly meal, the sinews and blood pulling from the sides of the skull as a piece of the lower jaw dropped onto the driver's chest. Annette watched the stump of the esophagus burble and gasp as blood flowed thickly out, so much blood, a flood of red and black and gore. The smell hit her then. A vile, filthy scent of dirt and wild animal and shit, of dead flesh and rot and garbage. The smell from the body was bad, but the stench from the thing was so much worse. Annette gagged, and this served to wake her from her stupor.

She fell backwards then onto the curb, unable to scream, unable to cry out, a gasp of unintelligible noise escaping her. The thing reached into the car again, this time a hairy arm grabbed the driver as the thing bit into his chest, ripping the ribs apart until the sticky insides were showing.

Annette scrambled backwards, her heels kicking the concrete curb to find purchase. Rolling over, she found her feet and got up, a stumbling run until she caught her balance and she ran. She ran for her very life, her purse forgotten, the cold forgotten, she just ran.

She kept running, her pulse drumming in her ears, her feet pounding the sidewalk, she ran until she thought her lungs would burst.

Looking up she saw a light, a blue light, it was the local hospital, she knew if she could get there, get through the doors of the emergency room, that she would be safe, that someone there would call the police and they would find the thing and they would keep her safe…

Stop it, she thought. *You are getting hysterical. Just run, just keep running, you'll be okay, you'll make it, you'll be fine...*

The stench hit her first.

She didn't have time to scream before the jaws closed around her head, cutting off her breath, her life, her escape. Her feet drummed a staccato beat on the pavement as the thing ripped off her head, then tore open her chest, tearing her lungs aside to close the dark, bloody jaws on her heart.

Chapter Twenty-One
Earth
Drew's Kitchen
Present Day
As I Live and Breathe

"So, they have cell phones? Really?" Sam accepted the proffered mug and frowned. "Not something I imagined spacemen to carry."

"They probably don't," Nick replied as Drew handed him a coffee as well. "They probably have some fandangled way to send messages onto our cells."

"Be my first guess," Drew agreed as he pulled out a chair to join the detectives at his kitchen table. "By the way, I'm getting reports here and there of kills that sound like werewolves. Unrelated to our fellows, I think, as they aren't local. We have a bit of work ahead of us, and I hope we can talk to the guardians about getting some help there."

He felt the guardians arrive before he saw them, the change in the room was subtle, but enough that he could feel them. He placed his coffee on the table and turned and smiled at the black clad men, offering his hand.

Kyle grasped the outstretched hand and shook it warmly. "It is very good to see you again, Sheriff!" he exclaimed, and he, Michael and Luke shook the hands of the detectives as they stood to greet the guardians.

"As I live and breathe, it's good to see you, Peter!" Drew grabbed the man in a bear hug. "How are these spacemen treating you?"

"Well, technically, I'm a spaceman, too, now." Peter's grin was so wide it threatened to split his face in two.

"Looks like you're having fun," Nick smiled at the young technician.

"Not gonna lie, it's awesome. It's every boyhood dream come true; I can't believe I get to live this life."

Drew laughed. "Good to know. Though I never doubted you'd be in your element. How is Ayden enjoying the spaceman life?"

Kyle picked up Drew's coffee and sipped it. "He is well. He is on the ship and may join us in the future."

"He is a brilliant soldier. A great strategist," Michael accepted a coffee from Drew with a nod of thanks.

"He is also an invaluable member of the Guard," Luke added. "I am proud to call him my friend, as well."

"So, my friends, you've found Angie on social media, is that right?" Nick asked.

"That is correct." Michael pulled a chair from the table and straddled it backwards. "There are posts about her."

"Oh, good, I thought maybe she had set up her own profile. I had duck-lip selfies in my imagination."

"Don't worry, I'll explain later," Peter smiled at

the guardians' confused expressions. "We found a picture of Angie taken by a wildlife photographer." Peter took a data pad from the bag he was carrying and tapped it a couple of times before handing it to Nick. Sam and Drew leaned forward to see the image of Angie with the wolves.

"As you can see, the Dahn has been sighted." Kyle pulled a chair over to sit beside Michael. "This is the first time in all these months of searching that we have any sightings, or any hint of her whereabouts."

"Well, we have some information, as well," Sam told them of the feelings of being watched, the werewolf deaths and the feather.

"Why did you not contact us?" Kyle ran a hand through his hair, his frustration beginning to show.

"We didn't think it was enough to go on," Sam explained. "We'd only just come to the conclusion ourselves, and really, there isn't anything that definitely proves it was her. It's just, I don't know, a hunch?"

"A hunch? A feeling?" Kyle stood and started to pace. "All three of you are having these hunches?"

"Yes, why? Aren't you? I mean, didn't you feel like you were being watched from the moment you zapped in here?" asked Nick.

"Not so much," Peter answered them. "Seems Kyle is being blocked somehow by the Dahn. We're not one hundred percent sure why."

"We have theories," Kyle explained. "However, there is no definitive answer as to why she has blocked me, and no one else."

A flutter of unseen wings, and there, in the corner of Drew's humble little kitchen, stood Angie, her head cocked to one side, a soft smile floating over her lips.

Chapter Twenty-Two
Trauiss Outer
The Battlefields.
A Long Time Ago
Today, We Die!

"Why do they keep coming? Why do they covet what is ours?" James shook his head, trying to find clarity and understanding.

"If they keep invading our world at this rate there will be nothing left to covet." Robert put a hand on James' shoulder. "Brother, it is up to us to prevail. We must protect our world and find a way to close the Gate to all that would invade and try to destroy us."

James stood; the long bank of rocks they were behind shielded him from the multitude of large craft that landed in the fields not ten minutes ago. He looked to his side, and behind, taking in the crouched readiness of his warriors. They were young, well rested, their black leather and silver studded uniforms clean and new.

He knew they would not stay this way, that it would not take long for the beasts that invaded this world to tear at them, to shed their blood, and to fight and rip and tear and die. Time after time they repelled the forces that invaded their Gate, that came into their universe through the black hole that previously hid their existence. These aliens, these creatures of nightmares, so many dark, disgusting, terrifying beasts. James was grateful that the scientists discovered the alien invaders enslaved the demon combatants with iron and silver, the controlling devices and implants easily replicated and then used to take down and control the demon that the aliens used to raze several worlds already.

They believed that war to be won, and celebrated the victory, only to be horrified with the emergence of this new fleet through the Gate. He moved to a crevice in a rock that would allow him a clear view of the invading craft and tapped his visor to allow a zoom image of the legion of craft that lay before him.

He almost wished he had not.

"What is happening?" hissed James. "What in hell's name is coming out of that craft?"

The warriors behind him looked at each other with trepidation. "Sir?" one called out as he nervously handed his weapon from one hand to the other. "Sir, is there something we should know?"

"By my soul's grace, this cannot be!" James felt the blood drain from his face, his heart pounding so hard he feared it would burst from his chest. "My soul's grace... Robert, we are doomed!"

Robert tapped his visor to zoom and leaned over to look through the space that James had been occupying. The sight that greeted him made his bowels feel as water. Emerging from each craft was a new type of demon, a large, evil creature, larger, much larger, and more vicious looking than anything they had battled previously. Following each demon was a horde of smaller, but no less terrifying, black, twisted creatures.

"It is a demon's army," gasped Robert. "There are so many, so many!"

The large field in front of them was now black with the teeming horde, they appeared to number in the thousands. The creatures surrounding the demons, while smaller, seemed to at least stand the span of a grown man. James looked again at his battalion. There were many, a number well over five thousand. This was the sum of all men and women of fighting age from every planet in their universe, every able-bodied human that could hold a weapon. They numbered many more than this before the attacks began, but three years and multiple onslaughts reduced them to this, to the last five thousand warriors who would sacrifice their souls to save their planets.

And sacrifice they would, James knew. Though they were brave, and most highly skilled and strong, they were no match for the demons and unholy creatures they were to face.

James again placed his hand on his brother's shoulder, and he turned to face the regiment. "Brother, you need to address the troops."

Robert nodded and took a steadying breath. "What we see is not encouraging. There are many demons." Gasps and groans greeted his proclamation. He raised a hand to silence them. "There are many demons, and each one has its own army. We face a multitude of horror when we take to the battlefield. Each of you are brave, strong, and trained to fight. There is no choice. There is no alternative. If we do not fight, we will be slaughtered anyway, our families enslaved, our planets lost. We must face this horde, and we must fight. We will die fighting to protect our planets. But make no mistake: today, we die!"

Chapter Twenty-Three
Earth
Drew's Kitchen
Present Day
No, Not You

The coffee mug emptied its contents as it hit the linoleum, bouncing once before shattering. Michael dropped it when he sprang to his feet, followed by Sam and Nick. Drew remained seated, though his face wore the same expression of shock and surprise that all the men in the kitchen displayed.

Angie stood there, seemingly calm, and watched them. She was dressed in blue jeans, leather boots, and a flannel button down shirt with the sleeves rolled up. Her long, white hair fell to her waist in a tumble of curls, with dreadlocks dispersed through the silvery locks.

She was tanned, her skin a healthy olive, and she wore dark sunglasses. On each arm the bottom of her tattoos could be seen, but they had faded a little from when the detectives had first rescued her from the hospital.

On each wrist she had several silver bands, and each of her fingers bore several plain silver rings.

No one spoke, the surprise of seeing the woman appear before them rendered them speechless.

Angie cocked her head from one side to the other, she seemed to be appraising the seven men that crowded into Drew's kitchen.

"Angie!" Nick finally broke the silence. "It's really you!" He cleared his throat and shook his head to clear his thoughts. "I mean, of course it's you. After all this time, you finally show yourself."

A hint of a smile fluttered across her full lips, but she didn't respond.

"Why? I mean, why now, why here?" Sam asked her.

"We have all been looking for you for so long, we have searched the entire planet," Luke added.

Michael took a step towards the woman who stepped back, her brows scrunched with concern. Kyle raised a hand and Michael stopped. "Caution, we do not want her to flee."

"Angie, I cannot believe that you have finally appeared!" Kyle opened his hands in supplication. "We will not harm you."

Angie took another small step back, her brow furrowing, her expression reflecting her concern.

"Can you tell us where you have been?" Kyle asked, but again, she did not answer.

"You have been watching us, haven't you?" Nick asked.

Angie looked at him but gave no response. Nick took a step towards her and she again stepped back, this time her back touched the wall. She looked nervous, the smile was gone, replaced with a worried frown. To the men, she looked as if she was about to flee.

Drew stood, his look of surprise now changed for one of thoughtfulness. He walked to the icebox and opened it, taking out a casserole dish. He placed it on the table and grabbed a loaf of bread from the counter. A few bowls joined the food, and he sat back down. "Let's eat something. This is a sweet potato casserole, baked by my neighbor Janice, a devout vegan. Everyone sit down and eat."

No one moved, so Drew placed the bowls around the table, and sat down. He took a large spoon and served himself some casserole, then placed some in a second bowl. He placed a slice of bread near the bowl, tossed a short nod at Angie and he patted the seat beside him. Without waiting for Angie to respond, he dipped his bread into the cold stew and bit off a mouthful, chewing as slowly and calmly as he could.

"What are you doing?" hissed Nick.

"Chill, dude and follow my lead," Drew whispered back through a mouthful of food.

One by one the men sat at the table, ladling themselves some stew and commenced eating, dipping their bread the same as Drew.

Kyle remained standing, he was at the opposite corner of the kitchen to Angie and did not move from there.

After a few moments Angie moved forward, she stood behind the chair Drew had invited her to, tentatively, unsure, before the sheriff pulled the chair out and tapped the seat again. She slid into the seat, her movements sinuous, graceful, and silent. She looked at each of the men at the table, then picked up the bread, dipping it the same way as everyone else. She sniffed it before taking a bite, then started shoveling the food into her mouth, using the bread as a spoon.

They ate silently and awkwardly for a few moments; the only sound was the chewing of food. When Angie had emptied her bowl, she served herself some more, and took more bread, eating and refilling her bowl until all of the casserole and bread were finished. The men had long since eaten their share and sat quietly watching the woman eat far more than she should be able to.

Drew got up from the table and took a bowl of fruit from the counter, placing it in front of Angie. She took an apple, sniffed, then bit it, eating the entire piece of fruit, even the core. The men watched as she proceeded to eat every piece of fruit in the bowl. Once the fruit was gone, she looked around, seeming to search for something else to eat.

"Are you still hungry?" Sam asked her. She looked at him, head tipped to one side, but didn't answer.

"Maybe thirsty?" Drew asked, and Angie smiled, but shook her head.

"For many millennia I have known what you wanted, what you needed." Kyle spoke, his voice soft, almost a whisper. "I knew your every desire, your cravings, when you were hungry, when you were tired. When you angered, or laughed, when you needed company or desired to be alone. I knew when you needed to fly, or swim, or just walk alone. I have always known what it was that you needed." He paused, his face troubled, his eyes searching, his breath ragged. "And you, you knew the same of me. But now, I cannot feel you. I cannot sense you, even sitting so close to me, I cannot feel your presence. Why is this, Angie? Why have you cut me off so completely?" He took three steps and went down to one knee in front of her, reaching out to take her hand. Angie pulled her hand back before Kyle could touch her. He recoiled at this gesture like he had been hit.

"Why have you cut Kyle off, Angie?" Michael asked her. "We can all feel you, though not as much as before, but you have cut Kyle off completely."

Angie frowned, her face troubled.

"Can you tell us why?" Michael leaned forward, his hands flat on the table. "Please, Angie, let us know why?"

She turned her head and looked at the man, on one knee he was at eye level with the diminutive woman. "Not you," she said. "No, not you."

Kyle looked at her, confusion clouding his features. "I do not understand, girl. You are not making sense."

Angie pushed herself back a little from the table and took off her glasses. The light in the kitchen was too bright for her, and she squinted. Luke stood and closed the blinds, allowing her to open her eyes all the way. Sam and Nick gasped in unison at the bright green glow of those eyes, framed with thick, black lashes. She blinked slowly and smiled at Kyle.

"You can find. Always. You can find where I hide. Others can feel, but, ah." She paused, seeking the right word. "See! You, um, you see, you the only one, um, that can see me, see where I am. That is not good."

"Why, girl? Why is that not good?"

She reached out to touch his face but pulled her hand back before making contact. "They follow. They follow, to find me. You would lead the way."

Kyle was shocked. "Who do you think follows me, girl?"

"Not think. Know. I know."

"We are the Guardians of the Gate. We make sure that no one could ever possibly follow us. You should have remembered that."

Angie's frown grew deeper. "There is someone. Someone. They can see... They can see you."

"Are you sure, man, that no one has managed to find a way around your secret agent stealth?" Nick pushed his chair back from the table and stood. "Those pretzel guys seemed to have a pretty strong bead on searching for all things Angie."

"Do you mean the Presas? No, I don't believe they can follow us when we are on our ship. It has a shield that renders us completely invisible."

"A genuine cloaking device." Peter couldn't help but smile. "It works the same as the Star Trek ones, too, it's how they stay around with no one on Earth being able to detect them."

"Us, Peter," Michael corrected him. "You are a Guardian too, now."

Angie watched the men talk, her frown deepening. Drew noticed her expression and touched her hand. She didn't pull back from his touch, instead she looked at him, her brows raised in a question. Kyle could not hide his shock and hurt.

"Do you know who is following the Guardians?" Drew asked.

"Guardian."

"Yes, do you know who is following the Guardians?" he repeated.

"Guardian," she repeated.

"Wait." Sam leaned forward. "Angie, do you mean just one Guardian is being followed? Like maybe just Kyle?"

"Yes. No."

"Well, that's not helpful." Nick started to pace, the small kitchen allowing only a couple of strides each way, back and forth. "Are any of us here on Earth being followed? Sam, Drew and me?"

She tipped her head to the side as if she was listening to some distant sound, and blinked very slowly, her gaze on the table. She looked up at Nick and nodded, then placed her sunglasses back on her face, and disappeared.

Chapter Twenty-Four
Trauiss III
The Laboratory
A Long Time Ago
Surely You Jest?

The Lords murmured in anticipation. The air crackled with static electricity as Elund approached the heavy, enormous iron door. Both he and Xanya touched the door, palms to the sensor panel, fingers spread, so the panel could read their biological signature.

The doors shuddered and moved slowly, so very slowly, opening outward and spilling even brighter light into the ante chamber. The static increased, and even though the Lords wore long robes, their heads covered with heavy cowls, they could feel their hair prickle and stand on end, goose-fleshed skin under crackling, static-ridden cloth.

The maudlin feeling that washed over them in the previous rooms was gone, replaced with a joyous elation. Coupled with the bright light, the Lords were struck by the stark contrast this room provided.

The uplifting feeling became stronger, to the point of feeling overwhelming. The Lords were quiet, even their footfalls seemed silent, hushed, reverent. Elund and Xanya stopped in front of a very large tube, this one was covered with a heavy cloth that did nothing to hold back the relentless, bright light.

"This is it?"

"Yes," Elund nodded. "This is, indeed, *it.*" Xanya touched her data pad and the heavy cloth lifted, revealing the containment tube and the creature it held.

As one, the Lords gasped in awe. They had been expecting to see this creature, however, to be in its actual presence was more than they imagined.

"My Lords, it is with great pleasure that I present to you," Elund paused for dramatic effect, "one of the angels of light, our greatest and most important treasure."

The angel was pure light. So much light flowed from it, through it, all around it, that even with the protective goggles the Lords still needed to squeeze their eyes to a barest slit to even look close to the creature.

They stood in awe before the containment tube. The creature was tall, perhaps twice the height of a tall man. It had the body of a man, strong, muscular, and covered head to toe in a delicate white fur, or perhaps downy feathers. The brightness made it difficult to determine exactly which. Its head was bowed, no hair covered the skull and the face was not very visible. From its back, near the shoulder blades, two large, white, feathered wings lay folded against its back.

The angel was beautiful, strange and alien, deadly still, and frighteningly powerful. Along with the static, the feeling of hope, the uplifting sensation, radiated an atmosphere of great strength and power.

"It is beautiful!" breathed one of the Lords.

"Indeed," another gasped. "I am overcome with pure joy; I weep before this creature."

"You may also feel something else." Xanya moved away from the tube. "The power this creature holds is exponentially more than any of the other creatures, in fact more than all of them put together. When it was discovered it had put down several demons and their army. We were only able to capture it as it was exhausted." With a touch to her data pad she lowered the cover back over the angel's containment tube. The light dimmed, allowing the Lords to see a little better, though the goggles were still required. "The angel has more controls than the demon, there are *so many* needed to subdue it, and we did not want any risk of it regaining consciousness. This containment cylinder is also the most powerful we could build, and we actually tap into the angel's own power to help operate it."

"This was our breakthrough, the one creature that not only would allow us to move towards creating our ultimate warrior but would generate enough power to ensure our very survival." Elund smiled and took the data pad from Xanya. "The 'something else' you are feeling is that. Being close to the angel will cure anything that ails you. You will feel not only elated, yes, joyous, but also fitter and healthier than ever before. Stand here long enough and your age will actually stop, even reverse."

The Lords reeled back, incredulous. "Surely you jest?"

Xanya nodded at Elund, then turned back to the Lords. "It is indeed true. You are aware I have been the leading researcher working with the angel. What you are not aware is that I have *always* been the leading researcher. For over seventy years! I am older than I look. A great deal older. Elund is my granddaughter's son. I am his great grandmother." With her proclamation, Elund turned the data pad to show them an image of a young infant sitting on the knee of an elderly lady. The resemblance to the young woman was undeniable. "I did not just stop aging, I actually became younger, physically. I have been the equivalent of a twenty, maybe twenty-five-year-old, for over fifty years. And it is not just I. You may have noticed that every researcher you passed by was a young person, however that is true in their appearance only. The youngest is, like Elund, over forty years old."

"I am aware that I do not look my age," Elund smiled. "And I am happy to tell you that it is not just the people who work here that are affected. Slowly the angel's influence has spread over the entire planet. As you were landing, you may have noticed the beautiful gardens? This was not much more than a rock when the facility was set up. Now, all of the planet, the people, even the animals, are young, healthy, and thriving."

As one, the Lords nodded. "We were aware of the transformation of this planet," one Lord moved forward, closer to the angel's tube. "We were not aware of the effect the angel was having on the people, and the lifeforms here. We have many questions."

"Yes," another Lord agreed. "How do we spread this good fortune amongst the rest of our universe? Do we move the angel around? Will it also have the same effect on the other creatures, specifically, the demon? Will it recover and escape?"

"The controls we have placed on, and in, the demon will stop it from ever escaping. The same with all of these creatures, including the angel. Xanya and myself have had extensive discussions and tests on the effectiveness of the angel on the surrounding worlds, and we have a few useful hypotheses. The belief is that the world the angel resides on will be the world that most benefits. The power of the angel does seem to traverse beyond the atmosphere, albeit slowly. We are concerned with moving the angel to other worlds, as we do not want to risk awakening it, but believe that our home world should be the place that the angel is kept, as it is the most central to our universe. And, of course, holds the most citizens."

"Yes, the home world would be the most appropriate place," the senior Lord tipped her head in query. "When can this be arranged? And what of the breeding program? Do you not need biological material from the angel?"

"We have taken the angel's blood, tissue, and, most fortunately, his seed."

This proclamation drew murmurs of approval from the Lords.

"Seed? The angel has sperm?" The senior Lord smiled. "You can now breed our own angel, our own world savers?"

Elund matched her smile. "Yes, my Lords. We believe we can."

Chapter Twenty-Five
Earth
Drew's Kitchen
Present Day
In Theory, Anyway

Kyle leapt to his feet, and Sam slammed a fist onto the table.

"What did I say?" Nick exclaimed. "I just asked her a question, that's all!"

"I do not know." Michael shook his head, disbelief and confusion clouding his features. "I am as bewildered as you. I am also concerned with her speech; she should have recovered completely by now. A great deal of time has passed."

"Now I'm confused." Drew stood and started to gather up the bowls. "I thought she had a traumatic brain injury, I mean I know she heals quickly, but there has to be a point that she can't heal any further."

"No, there is no point, no injury, that she cannot recover from," said Luke.

Kyle nodded. "Well, at this time, we have not seen her injured to that point. She was once incinerated. Her body did heal. Her mind healed. That injury was far worse than this one."

"Her head was cut clean in two, right down to her chin," Nick said. "Surely it would take her a little time to grow back all the cognitive parts of her brain?"

"When she was incinerated, her brain was burned almost completely away. She was speaking much better within six months than what she is now. Her brain heals much quicker than the rest of her," Kyle explained.

"Even if it healed at the same rate as her body, she should be fine by now. Her body seems to be perfectly healed. She seems to be completely sound," Michael added.

"Yes, you're right," Nick agreed. "She was down to just scars within days of the crash. She broke her own plaster casts off."

"Those, um, what did you call them? The silver bands?" Drew asked.

"Controls," answered Luke. "They are controls. They stop her from transforming."

"Into what?" asked Sam. "What do they stop her from transforming into?"

"That would be a discussion for another time," Kyle answered. "Why do you ask about the controls, Sheriff?"

Drew put the bowls he had been holding in the sink and turned back to the group. "When she sat, her shirt lifted a little. Just at the back, a bit. She had those bands, those controls, around her waist. There was more than one, I think, and they looked pretty thick. Could she maybe be wearing too many? Or maybe the wrong ones?"

"I believe you have a valid theory!" exclaimed Kyle. "That would explain much. Her controls, if placed incorrectly, or even if too many are placed, do slow down, and also stop her healing."

"Why would she do that to herself? Surely she would want to heal all the way?" Nick questioned.

"Maybe she doesn't realize that she hasn't healed all the way." Drew held up a hand "Hear me out, guys. What if she doesn't realize she isn't healed? You guys said she had a traumatic brain injury, what if she put those controls on and stopped herself healing all the way, before she healed enough to know that she wasn't ready to stop healing?"

Michael and Luke nodded, digesting the theory, but Kyle did not look convinced.

Peter cleared his throat to get the attention of the others. "I haven't seen a lot of information on the controls, so it's hard to comment, but I think, if you're right, I might be able to help. In theory, anyway."

Kyle turned to the young man. "I do not see how anything can help, unless we are able to get close to the Dahn."

"I think I can track the controls, and if I can, I should be able to modify, or maybe deactivate them from a distance."

"How much of a distance?" Kyle looked, for once, hopeful.

"Not a large one, maybe only a few kilometers. Or less. Hard to say." Peter frowned. "Maybe only a few feet. Point is, at least we wouldn't have to touch her. If she popped in once, there isn't anything to say she won't pop in again."

As if on cue, a rustle of unseen feathers preceded Angie's sudden appearance.

Chapter Twenty-Six
Trauiss Outer
The Battlefields
A Long Time Ago
Prepare for Battle!

The demon nearest the edge of the field sniffed the air. It was a grotesque creature, tall, at least two or three spans that of a man, with shoulders wide and well-muscled. It was covered in a rough black fur that bore a tinge of red here and there. On its head were horn-like protrusions, twisted and stubby, like a malformed goat. As it turned its head this way and that, sniffing the air, James could see that it had almost no neck, the thing needed to twist its entire torso to turn its head. He was astonished to see deformed, leathery wings on its back, small, twisted knobs of useless, dried flesh that would not be able to lift the hideous creature.

On each of its well-muscled, thick arms, just above the clawed and taloned hands it wore bands of silvery iron, the same style around its waist and each cloven hoof. James knew that the bands served to control the creature, put there by the aliens that sought to take over his universe. How they originally discovered the demons, let alone learned how to control them, was not something he knew. The aliens wore suits that contained some failsafe unit that terminated their life by incineration when they were captured, and none of the scientists found a way to circumvent this.

They were not able to identify these aliens, such was the efficiency of their incineration. To this day, through many invasions, many battles, countless deaths and destruction, no one was the wiser as to who was infiltrating the Gate and wrestling for control of the peaceful universe within.

James thought of them as cowards. Spineless cowards that did not fight their own battles but sent the harnessed power of their demon slaves to massacre the peaceful people within the Gate. The invaders they captured had been from the few upper atmosphere battles that occurred prior to the demon attacks. The invaders never made any approach, any contact, any requests nor demands at any time. They launched straight into attack, and those attacks were relentless.

They used weapons, then the vile creatures such as those circling their demon lieutenants in the battlefield. Then they sent demons, but one at a time, and to James' reckoning, it was, perhaps, the same demon each time. They fought hard to subdue the monster, to no avail. It was only the dissection of the smaller creatures that led to the discovery of the controls, and the aversion to iron. Trial and error led to the development of iron swords, bullets, and iron chains. These led to the eventual capture of the demon, and the vain hope that perhaps the war had been won.

The dark battlefield below showed the hope was, indeed, in vain. The demon turned to face the rocks, still sniffing the air. His blunt features were twisted in a frown and his scrunched, bat-like nose twitched. He grunted, then howled out to his fellow demons, gesturing towards the rocks.

"We have been discovered." Robert unsheathed his sword. "It seems the battle will now begin."

James took a deep breath and lowered his visor. His battalion followed suit, their visors were part of their full-face helmets, specially designed to filter the air.

This became necessary after it was discovered that riding on the terrible stench emitted from the demons came a feeling of malaise, of loss and hopelessness, something that cost many lives in early battles when the warriors gave up hope.

"We need to move back from the rocks, or they will jump right on top of us." James stepped back as he spoke and raised his sword. "Prepare for battle!" he ordered, and his men unsheathed their swords and stood at the ready.

Flanking the swordsmen were warriors with projectile firing weapons, iron bullets loaded and ready to subdue the horde. The battalion moved back about a hundred steps, with James and Robert at their front. The two were the most senior ranked warriors, and they commanded the army. They were promoted through necessity, after all of their superiors were killed in previous battles. The brothers knew, in their hearts, that this would be their final battle. The horde that they now heard racing towards them, battle cries flowing over the rocky wall, was a voice of legion.

There was no possibility of survival.

Chapter Twenty-Seven
Earth
Drew's Kitchen
Present Day
Let's All Talk

Everyone was startled; Luke actually fell backwards off his chair with surprise. Angie frowned at him, then offered a hand to help him up. He looked shocked at the offer but accepted her hand and allowed her to lift him onto his feet. She let go of his hand immediately and stepped away.

"No," she said, unprompted.

"No?" Kyle reached a hand towards her, but she stepped back, avoiding his touch.

"You're answering my question, aren't you?" Nick deduced. "*No*, no one is following the guys here on Earth. Am I right?"

Angie nodded.

"And you went, um, somewhere, I guess, to check that?"

Angie nodded again.

"Can you tell me where?"

She didn't react to this question. Nick took a step towards her, just a small one, and was surprised that she didn't step back. He took another, putting him within arm's reach of her. "Maybe you can't tell me, or maybe, I think, you don't want to tell me?"

Still she did not react.

Nick moved a little closer, not quite a step,

acutely aware that all of the men in the room were focused on him, their breath stilled, their actions frozen, not wanting to spook the strange, white haired woman.

"We aren't being followed, or watched, though, right?"

She tipped her head, and Nick could see her eyebrows knit into a frown beneath the dark sunglasses.

He slowly reached a hand up, expecting her to step back, and when she didn't move, he touched her cheek, softly, his fingers brushing gently against her soft skin. "Kyle is being watched, though, am I right?"

She nodded, a short, sharp bob of her head, but it was an affirmation.

"Can you tell me who is following him?"

Again, a nod, but she did not speak.

"Wait...wait," Sam interrupted. "I think she told us who was watching, or following, or both, whatever." He ran a hand over his face, as if to draw clarity from the action. "Angie, is a Guardian watching Kyle?"

She nodded, her brows relaxing.

"A Guardian! Surely not!" Luke's outrage was clear, and it was felt by Angie, who stepped out of Nick's reach, her frown back in place.

"Wait, Angie, he isn't calling you a liar," assured Nick, his hand still outstretched. "He is just, well, shocked, I guess. As we all are."

"Yes, I am shocked. I am in disbelief, not that you are lying, as Sam has explained. I am wondering if perhaps you are confused?"

She shook her head.

Nick took her hand, half expecting the woman to resist, and when she didn't, he led her to the table and pulled out a chair. "Sit down, Angie, and let's all talk. We can do that without you disappearing again, right?"

She didn't answer, and Sam walked over to the table and sat down on the other side of Angie, the other men following suit. Kyle remained standing, opposite Angie, behind his fellow Guardians.

"Okay. Alright. Let's figure this out." Nick turned to Angie. "You believe a Guardian is watching Kyle, right?"

She nodded, her long hair falling forward over her shoulders.

"Is it anyone here?" Sam asked at the shocked gasp of the Guardians surrounding the table.

Angie shook her head. "No. Not these. No, never."

Kyle exhaled, a loud sound of relief.

"Do you know who it is?" Drew asked her.

Angie took off her sunglasses but didn't answer.

Chapter Twenty-Eight
Trauiss Outer
The Battlefields
A Long Time Ago
The Dark Was Gone

The darkness rolled over the rocks first, a thick cloud-like gloom boiled and rolled like it had a life of its own. The demons not only exuded the powerful feelings of dread, the dark was as much a part of them as the malaise.

James felt his heartbeat quicken, his breathing deepened, and he crouched a little, his knees bent, his sword held high, his other hand clutching a smaller iron blade. Robert's stance mirrored his brother's, the battalion behind them all standing the same.

He heard the warriors behind him murmur and curse as the dark raced towards them, the shouts and growls of the creatures assaulting their ears as the creatures clambered up the cliff face and began to traverse the rocks. The first of the creatures breached the rocky edge and fell upon the battalion, their fierce bloodlust was shocking to behold. They tore into warriors with their claws, their twisted teeth, their grotesque fangs rending flesh to the very bone.

Warriors fought back with skill and strength, hardly seeming a match for the vicious horde of evil. Their swords flashed and clanged against the heavy hides of the creatures, and they seemed to be winning, beating them back even as they themselves were attacked, torn limb from limb. Their stomachs were torn open and their flesh flayed from their bones.

Suddenly the dark stopped, recoiled, then folded back upon itself. The monsters stopped fighting, stunned, they stood blinking in confusion as the warriors continued to take them down. The dark retreated even further, the monsters falling back into the dark as it rolled into itself, then over the cliff face.

The dark was gone. A light, so bright, so all-encompassing and powerful took its place.

From all around the light glowed, James could not tell where it originated, but it pushed the gloom back and silenced the horde as they tumbled and clambered over the rocks. The creatures howled in pain, covering their eyes against the unrelenting glow, screaming and gnashing their teeth they turned back to throw themselves over the rocky cliff face. Still brighter, unbearably so, the light continued to glow and cover the high ground and rocks, the dark now wholly banished back to the battlefield. The visors on the soldiers' helmets automatically darkened against the brightness, but James felt the light was so bright that he could not keep his eyes open. Along with the light came a noise, a loud ringing, growing in intensity until it was painful, and warriors threw down their weapons as they made futile attempts to cover their ears, their helmets blocking their hands.

James felt Robert grab him and pull him backwards, he could hear that he was shouting but the ringing was so loud, so overwhelming, that he could not make out the words. He felt his brother slap the side of his helmet and he opened his eyes, just a slit, to see what Robert was trying to tell him. His brother's visor was darkened so much that he could not see his face, but he could see his hand gesturing him to look up, above them, into the sky. James tipped his head back to see what his brother was trying to show him.

The light was too bright. It burned his eyes, piercing them with a brightness so intense, like nothing he had ever experienced. James shut his eyes tight against the light, but the insistent sounds of his brother's voice made him force his eyes open, the barest of slits, more closed than before, his thick lashes helping to shield the assault on his pupils.

There was *something* ... he shook his head and squinted hard, trying to open his eyes a little more, trying to decipher the barest of shapes that ascended from on high. He could make out a shape, perhaps humanoid, a figure of some kind. It was large, at least twice the height of a demon, but the brightness prevented him from seeing any more.

The bright, radiant figure moved forwards and down, drawing closer to the cliff face. James gasped with the pain of the loud ringing, the light hurting his eyes. The figure drifted over the rocks and out of his line of sight, the intensity of the light now a little subdued with the rocks in between them.

Robert pulled him to his feet and they both

stumbled towards the rocks, flanked by many of their warriors, all floundering under the oppressive noise and light. Finding holes to view through or climbing to the top as James and Robert did, they looked over to see the floating, glowing creature descend onto the battlefield.

James realized it wasn't floating, with the grace of distance he saw that the figure was actually flying. It had very large, white wings that slowly flapped as it hovered toward the battlefield, the horde of demon creatures screaming in rage and terror.

"What is it?" hissed Robert.

"I do not know," answered James. "I have no clue as to what this creature may be."

"Could it be an angel?"

Chapter Twenty-Nine
Earth
Drew's Kitchen
Present Day
Not Good. Bad

"You have to try to talk to us. We need to figure this out, and we can't do that unless you tell us what you're thinking, okay?" Nick spoke gently, calmly, surprised that he felt so calm. The last time he had been around this woman he had been frantic, obsessed and stressed, not able to think or function on any rational level. Now, though, he felt in control, with a deep connection, that, this time, didn't threaten to overpower him.

"Okay." Angie spoke softly, almost a whisper.

"Good. Let's have a think about this. Do you know who the Guardian is that is following Kyle?"

She shook her head. "No."

"But you are sure it's a Guardian?" Sam asked.

"Yes. Sure. Yes."

Michael scrubbed at his rough, stubbled jaw and cleared his throat. "Do you know if it is anyone on the ship?"

"No," she whispered.

"No, you are not sure, or no, it is no one on the ship?" he prompted.

Angie frowned, and looked at the Guardian, her almost too large, bright green eyes shining in the dim kitchen light. "No, not sure."

"We are making some progress." Luke nodded at his companions. "But not enough to find who is watching Kyle, nor why."

"That's a good point, Luke," Drew agreed. "Angie, do you know why this Guardian is watching Kyle? Do you know if they mean to do you harm? Maybe they just want you found or are a bit over keen. Or there could be a simple explanation?"

Angie frowned again, her head tilting to one side in confusion.

"Too many questions, man. Just try one at a time," Nick instructed.

"Yeah. Yes. Okay, Angie, do you know *why* this Guardian is following Kyle?"

She nodded. "Me."

"You? They want to find you?"

"Yes. Find me."

Drew leaned forward and gave her a gentle smile. "Good. Next question. Do you know *why* they want to find you?"

"Yes. No. Bad. Not good. Bad."

"Do you mean that you know it is bad, but not exactly *what* they want?" Sam asked.

Angie nodded.

Nick chewed on his bottom lip, his expression worried. Drew noticed him and shot a questioning look to the tall detective.

"Okay, well, I am wondering if this rogue Guardian was around right from the start. You know, when she was first attacked. You said she was kidnapped, right? What if the kidnappers had inside help?"

"That is something we had considered," Kyle spoke for the first time. "However, it is very difficult for any of us to believe that a Guardian would, or could, betray the Dahn. We are all bound to her, as you are. Tell me, Detective Cotter, could you ever betray her? Can you even consider it without feeling great discomfort?"

Nick nodded. Kyle was right. Even though he no longer felt out of control around the Dahn, he could not even bring himself to think of doing anything to harm her. To entertain such a thought was not just uncomfortable, it was impossible.

"You understand why we dismissed this possibility, but now, it seems, perhaps we were right to question this. As impossible as it seems, it does become a viable theory. It would explain how the kidnappers discovered the Dahn in the first place. Also, how they were able to evade us for so long. A Guardian would know our plans and our actions and be able to thwart us at every turn."

"Yes!" Angie nodded emphatically. "Yes! Them! They!"

"Is it just me, or has her speech gotten worse since we last saw her?" Sam asked. "I mean she was giving us sentences before, now she can barely string two words together."

"Yes," Angie touched her head. "Hurt. They found me. Hurt me. Hurt me." She swept her hair up and bent her head to touch the table, the back of her head and neck exposed. Gasps of shock from the men greeted the sight of a ragged black wound, barely healing, and a bruise that covered her neck to below her shirt collar and extended up through her hairline.

Nick stood and gingerly touched the wound, moving her hair to follow the gash. "Angie girl, did they try to cut open your head?" he asked softly.

She let go of her hair and sat upright again. "Yes. Cut all here." She pointed behind one ear. "Cut all here," she traced across the back of her neck to her other ear. "Take skull off."

"Oh lord!" groaned Drew. "No wonder she can barely speak. Angie, when did this happen?"

Angie shrugged.

"I'm guessing not too long ago." Nick sat back down. "Angie, do you know who did this?"

She nodded, but then shook her head.

"Okay, easier question. Did you see who did this to you?"

She nodded.

"Can you tell us who did this to you?"

She shook her head.

"Let me try, Nick." Sam touched Angie's arm to get her attention. "Did they hide who they were?"

Angie shook her head.

"Was there more than one?"

She nodded.

"Was it the Presas?"

She nodded.

"She clearly knew who it was, why couldn't she tell us that?" Drew asked.

"The Presas are mercenaries, hired killers," Kyle explained. "I believe she is trying to tell us that she doesn't know who hired them."

"Yes," Angie nodded. "Yes. Right. Yes." Her brow furrowed, eyes darted back and forth, as she searched for a way to tell them what she knew. Her frustration creased her features as she struggled to find the right words. "Guardian. Was, um, yes. Guardian."

"The Guardian hired the Presas?" asked Drew.

"Yes! Guardian did!"

Michael pushed his chair from the table, his face dark with anger. Luke hung his head in his hands as Kyle turned away, his shoulders slumped in disappointment and betrayal. Peter watched them, his eyes large, and for a moment he looked as fearful and unsure as he was when he had first laid eyes on the Guardians.

"More," said Angie, her voice tinged with sadness as she saw her words hurt the Guardians.

"How can there be more?" The pain was clear in Kyle's voice as he turned to face her.

Angie blinked slowly.

"It is okay, you do not have to answer that."

"What is the *more*, Angie?" prompted Nick.

"Presas. Yes. Monsters."

"The Presas are monsters? Yes, we know that," Nick assured her.

"No! Make. Presas make. Um, you, um," she slapped her hands, palms down, on the table in frustration. "Make monsters! Presas make monsters!"

"How can they make monsters? They have no creation skills," Luke said.

"Blood. They have blood," Angie answered. "Make monsters with blood."

"They have your blood?" asked Nick.

"Yes. No. No. My first. They have blood from, um, the one."

"The one? What is the one?" Kyle asked her.

"Vampire," she answered.

Chapter Thirty
Trauiss Outer
The Battlefields
A Long Time Ago
Brother?

James scoffed incredulously. "Do not be ridiculous. There is no such creature as an angel!"

"If we have demons, then why can we not have angels? If one exists, then surely there must be the other?"

He had not considered that. But now was not the time for discussion, so he mentally pushed the idea aside and focused on the field below. If he kept his eyes squinted, he could make out more of the glowing figure, and the light it emitted pushed the demon's dark completely away.

The demons roared and screamed, their stubby wings pounding their backs as they raged at the white figure. The smaller creatures gathered around, leaping and clawing to try and reach it, the cacophony of horror assaulting the ears of those watching.

As the white figure drew closer to the demons, the ringing seemed to have an effect on the monsters, they grabbed their ears, some falling to the ground, others howling in pain as they thrashed about. The white figure was now at the edge of the battlefield, it descended low enough to be within reach of the closest demon.

James gasped as some of the smaller monsters exploded. The ringing rendered most of them completely incapacitated, the closest ones to the figure were now piles of steaming viscera.

Taking three quick strides, a demon reached up and grabbed the foot of the glowing figure and swung it around his head before crashing it to the ground. In a flash the horde was upon it, biting, thrashing, clawing at the creature as it struggled to get up.

James stood and raised his sword. "Attack!"

As one, his warriors leapt and ran around the wall, following the wide road onto the battlefield. The creatures were too distracted with their attack on the glowing being to notice the warriors' approach, they were taken by surprise. They were fierce fighters, these warriors, they knew that they had just this one chance to gain any headway.

James and Robert slashed and fought their way towards the glowing figure as it fought the demons, instinctively moving to free the creature that perhaps could help them with this battle.

The figure seemed to know they were approaching, the ringing quieted to a bearable level, though the unrelenting brightness did not change. The brothers were joined with more of their battalion and together they pushed back the demons just enough for the glowing figure to break free. With a mighty pull from its wings it flew just out of reach of the demons, then turned and pointed its hand back into the melee. A ball of pure light, a powerful burst of energy, exploded where the figure pointed. It continued to thrust the energy burst into the demons, exploding the beasts into pieces in a maelstrom of blood, chunks of flesh and burned fur.

"The angel is prevailing!" Robert exclaimed. "See how it decimates these demons!"

As the battle continued, the white angel fought the relentless horde, the energy balls were ripping through the monsters, taking out dozens at a time. The angel would swoop in here and there and smash into a demon, ripping it limb from limb before flying out of reach to shower more of its firepower into the army.

James could see the tide turning, his warriors, aided by the angel, were making headway, the battle was definitely turning in their favor. A mighty explosion ripped through the creatures, taking out several hundred when the angel's power ball hit one of the ships. Bolstered by this, the glowing creature turned its power to the other ships, taking out all but one, and each massive explosion decimated the crowd of demons and their monster army.

James could see his brother fighting a fierce battle with a demon, there were several warriors assisting him as they hacked into the wounded creature with iron swords and bullets. A mighty roar made him pause and he saw a demon jump high enough to grab the angel by the leg, then throat, and smash it into the ground. The force was terrible, the angel seemed to have been injured as the ringing abruptly stopped. The battle sounds now took over, and for the first time James heard the angel cry out, the demon was upon it and was tearing and ripping with all of its force.

He rushed to his brother, who hacked the head from the demon he was fighting and slapped him on the shoulder to get his attention, gesturing to where the angel lay.

The brothers made their way through the battle, killing as many of the monster army as they could as they drew up to the demon. It had its back turned to them as it tore into the angel, taking great mouthfuls of flesh from the being.

The bright light was fading, the creature was losing its fight against the evil being standing over it.

Robert ran to the front of the monster, his sword waving, his dagger bloody, and attacked the demon, drawing its fierce assault from the injured angel.

James did not have to communicate with his brother, their bond was close, they fought many, many battles together. They often worked as one and they both knew how the other thought, how the other moved, how the other planned and strategized. He knew Robert was taking the attention of the great beast so that he had a chance to come up behind it, to hopefully remove the head from this creature and release the glowing being from its relentless onslaught.

Stealth was not entirely possible, from all sides the smaller creatures attacked, and he fought his way closer to the demon, all the time with one eye on his brother, knowing one warrior, no matter how fierce or skilled, was no match for one of these nightmare creatures.

A smaller monster came at him, followed closely by another two. James swung his sword under the chin of the first monster, taking its head clean off, then leapt onto its falling back, not breaking stride as he beheaded the second monster while stabbing the third through the eye with his dagger. He then leapt onto these two, using them as a launching board to leap onto the back of the demon fighting his brother. The thing was huge, and even though the warrior's helmet filtered the air the acrid stench from the creature assaulted his nostrils and made his eyes sting. The thing reached up to grab James, giving Robert a chance to move in and plunge his sword deep into the chest of the thing. It howled in pain and James lifted his dagger and plunged it into the skull of the great beast, breaking it off at the hilt.

The thing was still fighting, it reached forward and grabbed Robert by the throat, its hand circling the warrior's neck in a death grip. James lifted himself onto the shoulder of the thing and heaved his sword with all of his strength, cleaving the demon's head clean off. It fell backwards as James jumped free, the demon falling forward onto the angel and Robert.

James threw himself onto his brother, checking that he was okay, checking he was alive.

A ragged groan answered him, and he dragged the fallen warrior from beneath the demon. "Brother, are you injured? Brother?"

Robert coughed and pulled himself to his knees. "I have lost my breath from the weight of that thing, but I am alright."

James allowed himself a half second of relief then turned his attention to the angel, now half hidden by the demon corpse. The glow stopped; no longer did it emit any bright light. Robert reached a hand for James' assistance to get to his feet, and they both looked at the being, now able to see it more clearly without the blinding light.

It appeared to be a man, but was covered with white downy feathers, though they were stained with not only its own red blood, but also the purplish black ooze of demon blood. The massive wings lay folded and broken, the long white feathers dirty and ragged. It seemed dead, the eyes closed, no breath lifted its chest.

Around them the battle was drawing to a close, the angel brought them the advantage before its fall, killing almost every demon and most of the smaller creatures. Robert coughed again and stood on his own, his sword still grasped in his hand.

James nodded to his brother and they both turned and continued to fight, helping their battalion defeat the army. A shout from one of his lieutenants alerted the brothers that the last surviving craft was powering up. The large ramp slid back into the ship and the door was closing, a straggle of creatures and a wounded demon struggled to climb in before they were abandoned.

Before the brothers had time to react, a power ball shot past them and hit the ship, exploding into a cloud of flames and debris. Turning, the brothers saw the angel drop its head back down and lower its arm. It coughed and looked at them with its large, bright purple eyes. It frowned, coughed again and closed its eyes, unconscious.

"Call for transport," James opened his visor, his face covered with sweat from exertion. "Tell them we have captured an angel."

Chapter Thirty-One
Trauiss III
The Laboratory.
A Long Time Ago
Such Brutal Creatures

"Welcome back, my Lords," Xanya bowed and stepped aside to allow them to enter the Atrium. "You will notice that we have been able to contain the feeling of dread that greeted you last time you were here."

"I would say assaulted, rather than greeted, but yes, I must say that it is a pleasant change," the most senior Lord answered. "We are eager to see the progress your breeding program has made. Three hundred years is not such a short time."

"I am sure you will be pleasantly surprised." Elund was beaming as he walked towards the black robed group.

He had changed in appearance, no longer portly, he looked lean and muscular. His head was no longer balding, instead he had a mop of thick black hair. He seemed taller, too, towering over the tallest of the Lords. His eyes had changed, as well. Previously a dark brown, they were now a light hazel, with streaks of bright green highlights. Xanya's eyes were the same.

"Your appearance is somewhat of a surprise."

Elund's smile grew even wider. "Yes, I am finding some of the side effects of working here to be extremely pleasing. Our work is not just satisfying, it also has enhanced our quality of life in so many ways. You reviewed our regular reports?"

All of the Lords nodded.

"I believe you do not require an in-depth tour, though we would be very happy to take you through our creatures and research again, should you wish?"

"That will not be necessary," the Senior Lord answered. "We do not need to go through all of the creatures again. We are here to see the breeding."

"Excellent!" exclaimed Elund, and he and Xanya led the Lords through to the brightly illuminated corridor leading to their breeding facility.

There was a quiet excitement among the group, they had been waiting for this day for a very long time.

The breeding facility was everything that the Lords had expected, the light was subdued, the atmosphere pleasant. No shocks to the system that the previous visit had afforded them, this time the easy comfort was welcomed with quiet murmurs of approval.

Xanya explained that the glass walls along the hallway in front of them had a one-way view, there were rooms that backed onto this glass hallway, and each one was occupied with a different being. She explained that all sounds, sights and events in the hallway were hidden from the occupants of those rooms, but the Lords would be able to see and hear unimpeded. She turned to the first room, letting the Lords move forward to view the occupant inside.

A massively proportioned mountain of a creature

lumbered around inside, he was bipedal, with long, hairy arms that hung low, so low that its knuckles were dragging on the ground. He had stubby horns on his head, a broad, muscled back, and was covered in wiry looking black hair. As he turned, the Lords were afforded a glimpse of his face, his features oversized, grotesque, and clearly influenced by the demon blood in his veins. He was obviously male, his genitalia oversized and repugnant.

"This creature was the first of our breeding that was, in some ways, controllable. Previously all progenies were too violent to be allowed to continue existing."

"What would you use this creature for?" queried a Lord.

"They make excellent soldiers once castrated, in fact we have trialed a regiment only recently on Trauiss Seven, they were efficient in destroying the demon army that had been invading."

"Yes, I do recall reading your report, watching the footage was, shall we say, alarming? They are such brutal creatures!"

"Indeed," agreed Xanya. "They are strong, violent, and physically intimidating. Without castration they are unable to be reined in once the battle is won, the bloodlust is too strong."

She turned and led them to the next room. The creature looked almost identical to the previous one, though this one had bright, blood red fur. The next two rooms held similar creatures, both with varying colored fur. "We were not making a great deal of progress, the demon DNA was overpowering, even when we have reduced the amount to a barest miniscule."

"The decision was made to increase the angel and human component," Elund explained as he led the team to the next room. "This led to a better creature, more visually acceptable, and, I must say, infinitely more controllable. However, they still needed to be castrated. Testosterone made the creatures violent and wild once they reached puberty. We kept them entire as long as we could, but soon found that it was better to remove the testicles soon after birth. Especially those that were born with multiple testicles."

"Multiple?" the senior Lord inquired.

"Yes, unfortunately. Anywhere from three, five, to sometimes up to twenty. And as the testosterone made these creatures more violent, we needed to remove them as soon as they were born. This breeding male was kept entire, and he has only two testicles."

The Lords peered into the room to see a tall creature, this one more like a man. He still had little nubs of horns on his head, and his features could never be described as pleasing to the eye, however he looked more human than the previous creatures they had seen. He was covered in soft, pale brown fur, his arms, while longer than a normal man's, were still nowhere near the proportions of the other creatures.

The next room held another creature, almost the same as the last, but this one had less fur. The creature in the following room had no fur on his torso, though his arms and legs had a good crop of soft beige down, and his head had actual hair. The Lords could not see any horns, though the eyes were still very large, the rest of the face looked almost human.

"The next room is one you will find more interesting," Xanya told them as she walked ahead. "Far closer to what you are waiting to see."

Inside the small room a man sat at a desk, a data pad in front of him, as he appeared to be studying, or perhaps researching. He was wearing clothes, a simple tunic and trousers, but he was the first one to be dressed out of all the creatures they had seen so far. He had no fur on his body that they could see, and had short brown hair on his head, with no horns showing through. His eyes still appeared a little bigger than normal, but otherwise would pass for a human.

"We have many varieties of this fellow now, enough to soon stop breeding the first creatures we showed you," Elund explained.

"Is that wise? Are they as powerful as the other brutes?"

"No, but they are easier to breed, and far easier to control. We will keep the others that we have created, and the breeders, but no more will be made unless we have a major war. The fellow you see in front of you is powerful, brutal, and easier to train. Not too bright, admittedly, but they also have a willingness to obey."

"He likes to look at pictures," Xanya explained.

"He cannot read, nor write, but he does like to draw. His talent is crude but drawing on the data pad keeps him happy."

"What about the testosterone problems you have with the other creatures?" asked the senior Lord. "Are these ones castrated, too?"

"Yes," Xanya answered. "We have not been able to overcome that problem, not with any of the creatures we have bred so far. However, we do not see castration as an issue. These creatures are unable to breed outside of the laboratory environment, and as they are only useful as soldiers, we do not need them wishing to copulate with anyone, or anything."

"They have certainly helped turn the tides in our war with the invaders. Together with our new weaponry we can continue to win battles and keep our multiverse safe," the Lord smiled, her colleagues nodding with approval. "This is very pleasing; your work is exemplary."

Xanya returned the Lord's smile, before making eye contact with Elund, who gave her a small nod, his face creased into a proud smile.

"My Lords, we now invite you to join us in our nursery. We have some wonderful things to show you, and some even more wonderful things to tell you."

Chapter Thirty-Two
Earth
Drew's Kitchen
Present Day
Not The First Time

"Well, I guess that explains why we've been hunting so many creatures lately." Sam seemed less surprised at Angie's declaration than the Guardians. "We were actually wondering why there were so many creatures, they seemed to be spreading without any contact with other monsters, you know, to spawn them, or whatever."

"Do you know how long the Presas have been making monsters, Angie?" Drew asked her.

She shook her head.

"Why would they do this?" Luke asked. "We were not even aware of these creatures, so they could not have been made as a distraction to stop us hunting them."

"They did it to catch you, didn't they?" Nick put his hand on Angie's. "They knew you were killing the creatures that had been made from your blood after the accident, so they made more, to trap you. I'm right, aren't I?"

Angie looked down at his hand that covered hers and nodded her head. "They catch me."

"When did they catch you, girl?" Kyle asked her.

She didn't look at him, just shrugged her shoulders, her gaze still on the hands.

"How many days ago did they catch you?" Nick asked her. "Was it one day?"

She looked up from the table and met his gaze.

"Was it two? Two days?"

"It was four days. Wasn't it?" Sam asked. "The werewolf, in Lowell County, right?"

She didn't answer.

"No, not four days ago. We saw the wound. It's barely healed. They caught you today, didn't they?" Nick squeezed her hand. "They caught you just before you came here. Am I right?"

This time Angie nodded.

"That's why you left a feather, wasn't it? It happened in the struggle?"

Another nod.

"Okay. That's why you can't speak properly. You haven't had time to heal."

Angie yawned. She smiled and nodded.

"She needs to sleep to heal properly. A day or two, at the least, of deep sleep, and she will be fully healed. We can take her to the ship to heal." Kyle reached up to touch the small communicator button on his collar.

"NO!" Angie leapt to her feet. "Not ship! NO!"

Nick stood and turned to Kyle. "She's right. If the traitor is on the ship, it's the last place she should be."

"She can stay here," Drew offered. "I can put her up in the spare room."

"Don't the Presas know about you?" Sam asked.

Drew shrugged, but then frowned as he realized that it was most likely true.

"Angie, do the Presas have any idea where you've been staying up until now?" Nick turned to her. "Do you have a safe place where they can't find you?"

Angie reached her hand to touch his cheek but disappeared before she made contact. Only the faint sound of wings reached the tall detective.

"I didn't expect her to leave straight away," Nick absent mindedly touched his cheek where Angie's hand would have made contact.

"We have no way to contact her," Kyle sounded defeated. "We can only wait until she contacts us, and we will not know if she is safe."

"She's been safe up until now, we've got to trust she found somewhere no one can find her." Drew stood and walked over to the coffee pot. "I think you have to figure out who amongst the ranks is not what they are supposed to be."

Kyle watched Drew fill the coffee pot and arrange seven cups on the bench. He seemed thoughtful but did not speak.

"It is almost impossible to understand why anyone would betray the Dahn Ah M'Rath. Let me help you with those cups." Luke stepped forward to take some of the filled cups to the table. Peter opened the fridge, searching for milk.

"Second shelf," Drew called out as he sat his cups down. "So, guys, how are you going to root out the enemy?"

"We did not get to ask Angie how she knew it was a Guardian. That would have been useful, it may have given us a clue as to how to find the perpetrator," Michael took a coffee and allowed Peter to pour him some milk. "I cannot imagine anyone betraying her."

"You guys need to get over that," Sam said. "I know it's a first time in history occurrence, but clearly someone has a reason for wanting Angie, or her brain, at least."

"It is not." Kyle took a coffee and leaned against the kitchen counter instead of sitting.

"I'm pretty sure they were trying to cut off the top of her skull, looking at that injury."

"Yes, I agree, that is not what I meant." Kyle sipped the hot coffee. "I was saying that it is not the first time that a Guardian has betrayed the Dahn."

Chapter Thirty-Three
Trauiss III
The Laboratory.
A Long Time Ago
We Never Give Up

The nursery was behind some very impressive security doors, with various levels of shields and force fields. This roused the curiosity of the Lords, and their murmurs of intrigue and excitement were growing in intensity. It took both Elund and Xanya touching their palms to a flat panel on the door in perfect unison to finally allow them entrance.

As the doors moved open, the Lords were afforded their first view into the laboratory nursery. It was as they had expected, incubators, test tubes, and many banks of gestational cylinders containing various fetuses in differing stages of development. The air was sterile, the lights harsh and bright, and the technicians clad in white attire.

"Interesting, however, not what I would call *wonderful*," the senior Lord commented. "We have viewed your report on the nursery and visited this previously."

Xanya waved a hand to the banks of growing fetuses. "You see the future army, growing here in their artificial wombs, each generation more refined than the last, as we grow our new warriors." She walked over to the long row of cylinders as the Lords followed her. "We have refined the product, as you saw in the adult specimen, and have the breeding process perfected. We are happy to say that each of these will grow to become stronger, fiercer, and more loyal than any man, each one programmed right from conception to obey, serve, and fight for our continued way of life. As you will notice in this bank of cylinders, these fetuses have wings. We will have our first flying soldiers very soon, courtesy of the angel DNA. We have also been able to incorporate the rapid healing of the Vampiri to ensure the sustainability and endurance of these warriors."

"Impressive. These soldiers will indeed be valuable in our ongoing fight."

"Of course, we have many warriors in varying levels of growth and development. The first of these new soldiers are due to be deployed within the year."

"This is indeed wonderful news. Absolutely a worthwhile visit," the senior Lord applauded. "Bravo to you both, and your research and development teams."

"This is not the climax of our tour, my Lords." Elund had not stopped smiling, in fact he was positively beaming. "If I may, please follow me now to a special wing, newly constructed, where we will show you just how I became taller, fitter, along with every single person on this planet." He turned and led them through the nursery to another door, this one with a similar bank of shielding and force fields as the nursery entrance.

The doors opened to reveal a small foyer with a

second set of doors that did not open until the first closed. The Lords did not comment, but shared questioning looks, brows raised, and lips pursed.

Leaving the foyer, the Lords entered a darkened room that was warm, softly furnished, the sound of orchestral music playing quietly in the background. It looked like a real nursery rather than a laboratory, with carpet, wall art, and music. Xanya led them to a small nook where a young nurse sat in a rocking chair, holding a baby in her arms. She stood as the group approached and smiled, offering the baby for all to see.

The infant was small, but not a newborn, perhaps only six or seven months old, with a tousle of pure white hair and pink round cheeks. A thumb was being sucked in the cupid's bow mouth and the baby's eyes were closed, perhaps in sleep.

"A whole nursery for just one child? What is so special about this one?" asked one Lord.

"Is this a new experiment to humanize him? Is he going to be a different type of warrior?" asked another.

"This, my Lords, is a very different child. This child was bred to be something a little different, merely an experiment, but we have found some amazing side effects since the conception, and they have multiplied after the birth." Elund put his hands out for the child, who woke as the nurse handed the child to him, the eyes opening slowly, blinking, long black eyelashes framing strange, bright purple eyes. Like the adult creatures in the windowed rooms, the eyes were larger than a normal human, and in the dim light they seemed to glow.

The thumb was removed from the baby's mouth as a yawn scrunched the pink features, before the thumb was firmly reinserted. Each chubby wrist was encircled with a silver band.

"With our challenge of excess testosterone, we made the decision to attempt to breed a female, however, after nine hundred thousand attempts we finally decided to give up on that strategy, just as this one came along. We added a little extra angel DNA, and were surprised with this single success, one we have not been able to duplicate. My Lords, I present to you our first, and it seems, our only, female born to the breeding program since our inception."

"A female! As surprising as that is, I fail to see the benefits. Won't you have to sterilize it, once it reaches puberty? Or are you planning to breed from it?" the senior Lord asked.

The baby cocked her little head to one side, as if trying to understand what the Lord was saying. She scrunched her little brows in a frown and turned to look at Elund.

"This baby is the reason I look like I do, why the whole planet looks like it does. Since she was created, right from the very first cell division, we all started to improve. The power this angel hybrid exudes is far beyond the original angel. Her power, at this stage, is almost immeasurable, the transformation she causes, vast! Even through the multiple layers of shielding and force fields, her effect is felt even in our skies, our polar regions, caverns, nothing is out of reach."

"Perhaps you are already feeling the power from this baby?" Xanya asked. "The angel we placed on our home world has afforded you longer lives and better health than ever before, but you still age, albeit slowly. We believe this child has not only stopped our aging process; it has reversed it. There is no one on this planet that is physically older than thirty. There is no illness, either. None."

"Surely this cannot be true?" The senior Lord threw back her cowl. "Though even as I say these words, I am feeling the effects of the child. Tell me, my fellow Lords, do I look changed to you?"

She shook her long white hair, but even as she did the white was no longer pristine, streaks of black now threaded through her locks.

"Your face, you look younger!" exclaimed a Lord standing next to her, and he threw his cowl back as well. His head was nearly bald, but even as the other Lords looked at him, they saw a fine fuzz of hair appearing on his shiny scalp.

Elund laughed. "It is true! Just standing near her accelerates the effects! Imagine how powerful she will be once she grows! We are amazed, in absolute awe of her powers. And it is not just health she gives us. As we benefit from her, as we become healthy, the demons and monsters that attack us are becoming weaker. Her power has the opposite effect on them. We believe it will be the turning point in our battles against the intruders."

"This is indeed wonderful! Such amazing news! However, why stop at one? You say you have tried to breed more, surely you will continue to try?"

Xanya nodded. "We never give up. We have managed to produce a handful of males using the same mix, however not one has gestated to full term. There have been no females at all. It seems our little girl is unique."

"If we use less angel product, we can generate female embryos, but they fail to survive any longer than two or three weeks," Elund added. "They also do not generate any special side effects. The effects from this child were felt immediately. We believe that any less angel product does not yield the same result, however the amount of angel also makes the embryos not viable. While we continue to experiment, we may have to resign ourselves to the fact that this child is truly unique."

"Why is she wearing control bands on her wrists?" the senior Lord asked as she moved her cowl back to cover her now darker locks. "Surely you would not want to limit the effects of her powers?"

Xanya held out her arms and the child leaned into them, clearly comfortable with the researcher. "While she was born looking humanoid, she did have a covering of white down. As she grew, she began to regress into a more animalistic shape. She also became uncontrollable, vicious. Let me demonstrate." She placed the child in its cradle and took off one of the bands. The baby immediately snarled at her, a feral hiss and growl replacing the pleasant demeanor.

As the Lords watched, the child began to change.

Wings sprouted from her back, unfolding and stretching, and her face changed from that of a baby to something from a nightmare. The room darkened, became colder, and a wind stirred from nowhere to whip the robes of the Lords. They could feel the malice, the power, the frightening strangeness of the child as her body sprouted a coating of feathers, her hands and feet grew sharp ugly claws, and her eyes became even larger, the purple now glowing like lightning.

Elund grabbed the child by the arm, struggling with the strength of it, as Xanya snapped the band back onto her wrist, and the wind died down immediately.

The child stopped hissing and snarling, and the wings shrunk and disappeared in mere seconds. The feathers withdrew back into the soft baby skin, and her eyes resumed their previous size. She looked up at Xanya and held out her arms to be picked up. When Xanya shook her head, the baby stuck her thumb back in her mouth and sat, content, looking at the people gathered around her cradle.

"As you can see, she reverts to a more primal, a more primitive state. The monsters that make up her base DNA start to surface," Elund explained. "We have never let her revert completely, as we do not know if she will permanently stay in that state once she reverts, and we do not know if we can control her. Certainly, the positive effects stop immediately, and we do not wish to see if they will be replaced by negative effects. I am sure you would concur that we need to keep her controlled."

"We absolutely concur." All of the Lords nodded their agreement.

"As she grows, we have continued to adjust the controls, and we will continue to do so, in order to maintain this humanoid shape. Her power grows as she does, and the reversion becomes stronger. We are constantly adjusting and testing new controls as we need them, we have also implanted several inside her body, along her spinal cord and nervous system. We provide this comforting, humanizing environment to nurture her softer, gentler side. As she grows, we will plan to educate her, both in our culture, beliefs, art, sciences, whatever she is capable of learning. Of course, we don't know if she will be able to learn much, and we will base her training on her capabilities. An educated, well raised, well-mannered creature will be far easier to control, and work with, than a savage." Elund nodded at the nurse as the baby began to fuss, though she made no noise she started to kick her feet and the thumb was withdrawn from her mouth as her hands waved in discontent.

The nurse handed her a baby feeder, and the child took it, hungrily sucking on the teat as she lay back in her cradle, the large eyes closing.

"Does it ever make a noise?" inquired a Lord.

"As yet, no, she does not," Xanya answered. "Apart from the growls when she reverts, she utters no sound. Of course, we do see to her every need."

"Spoiling her?"

"No, merely treating her kindly, and making sure her needs are met. And as long as her needs are met, she is content."

"This news, and this visit, has indeed been wonderful." The senior Lord turned to her colleagues, who all nodded at her, a silent communication and agreement. "We would like this child to be relocated to our home world, where all can benefit."

"This decision was anticipated." Elund gestured for the Lords to follow him as he led them out of the child's nursery. "We would restore the angel to this facility and upgrade the holding facility you have there in order to best contain the child. We would ask, though, that you leave her here a little longer, so we can continue studying, testing, and training her."

"Unacceptable. We wish the benefits of this child to be felt on our home world. Perhaps moving her to each world as required."

"Pardon me, my Lords, but I disagree," Elund said as he led them through the main nursery and back to the entrance of the facility. "We do not yet know, nor understand, how her power works, or even if we are able to continue to control it indefinitely. Should we lose control of her, then the effects on the home world would be devastating. We would not want to risk that. Once we have assured ourselves that we have complete control, and there is no risk to our home world, or any world, we would be more than agreeable to the exchange of this child and the angel."

"What, then, do you propose? That we leave it here, while we age and die? While our worlds are ravaged by sickness, pestilence, and disease, left by our invaders?"

"We believe that the effects of this child can spread throughout our multiverse, even to the farthest galaxy. Slowly, but surely, all will benefit from her gifts, as she grows."

The senior Lord was not convinced. "If this were true, would we not have already felt the benefits from off world? We have only felt the angel's influence, nothing more."

"We have her shielded with many layers of protection, not just in her rooms, but the entire nursery and laboratories. Her wing was built to allow a total separation from the main laboratory." Xanya touched a wall and a map of the facility glowed to life. "You see here, we have placed her on this far most edge. We feel that if we isolate her from the rest of the facility and then downgrade the shielding, her power will start to permeate the universe."

"This theory has been tested? Is it sure to work?"

"It is untested; however, we are very sure it will work. We will need a stronger guard, however, as once the heavier shielding is dropped, we will become vulnerable to detection, even given our distance from the Gate."

"We concur. Given the potential of this child we will send our best warriors, as well as a complete battalion to back them up. Is this acceptable?"

"Completely," Elund's wide smile was back. "We will continue to file regular reports on the facility and breeding program, and now you will have progress of the female child included."

"Indeed, this has been a wonderful visit," the Lords agreed.

Chapter Thirty-Four
Earth
Drew's Kitchen
Present Day
There Is Another Option

"Betrayed? By whom?" Sam looked at Kyle. "Was it a guardian? Was she betrayed in the past by one of her own?"

Kyle frowned. "Unfortunately, she has been betrayed many times over her lifetime. By those closest to her, by those that should have her best interests at heart, even those that created her. For the entirety of her existence, there has always been someone, or some faction, that seeks to control her, to possess her, or to destroy her. She has never been entirely safe." He paused, a sigh reflecting his sadness over Angie's situation. "The title of Guardian is not a ceremonial one. We are actual Guardians. Guardians of our worlds, of the gate that leads to our world, but most of all, we guard the Angel of White, our Angie. We have had to guard her many times, and against many foes, and have been very distressed that a great many of these foes were trusted comrades, leaders, and teachers of the girl."

"I have it," Peter interrupted.

"What? What do you have?" Kyle asked.

"You know the betrayer?" Michael grabbed Peer's arm. "Who is it?"

"Um, no, sorry, gosh no, not that." Peter cleared his throat and held up his data pad. "I have a way to disengage the controls. On Angie. You know, so she can heal quicker."

"Does that mean you can also find where she is located?" Kyle was hopeful. "Can you find her?"

Peter smiled at his commander. "Not exactly, I mean, I can locate the basic area, maybe to within about five hundred meters or so, and that should be enough for me to disable some of the controls. I'm still working on how many will be disabled, I'm not sure I can determine the amount of controls I can turn off, whether it will be enough, or too many. It's your call, I can keep working or we can go with what I have."

"The decision is not an easy one. If we lead the Presas to her location while she is sleeping, then her safety would be difficult to ensure. Though if we were able to close off the effect of some of the controls then she would heal faster and not be asleep for too long, making her able to move around and avoid the Presas."

"There is another option," Nick stood up. "Sam, Drew and I can accompany Peter. We aren't being watched. We can make sure he is safe, and also check that Angie is okay."

"Angie said Kyle is the only one being watched, it makes sense that we can all go, except for him." Michael turned to his commander. "I know this will be strange for you, however I feel it is the most logical decision."

"You are correct, it is the most logical decision

that I stay, though I do believe that six men are not required. Michael and Luke shall accompany Peter, though you should not go any closer to the Dahn than is necessary. Correct the level of controls as best you can, then return. We will watch you from here."

"I have some suggestions." Sam tapped a finger on the table for emphasis. "Don't let anyone on your ship know what you are doing. Tell them you're tracking a monster, or a Presas, or something. And maybe get one of those drone thingies you used last time, send it to have a peek at Angie and see that she is okay."

"Makes sense," Nick agreed. "We can monitor it all from here and keep the traitor in the dark."

***

Drew moved the clear viewing screen a little to allow him to share with Nick as they both practiced controlling the small drones, moving them around the kitchen, the silent craft flying back and forth near the ceiling. Beside them Kyle showed Sam how to operate another of the drones with another screen. Sam was able to control the small craft easily, a grin spreading across his features as he looped and swung the craft around the Guardians in the small kitchen.

"All those years of Mario Kart coming in handy?" Nick grinned at his partner.

"Dude, yes! This is actually fun!"

Nick moved his drone over to the Guardians, his

skills with the small craft, while not as flamboyant as Sam's, were adequate enough to maneuver it to hover directly over Michael's head. Drew flew his drone over to hover above Luke, and Sam followed suit with his drone floating a few inches above Peter's head.

Kyle nodded towards Peter. "Are you ready?"

"Yes, sir. All good here."

Kyle looked down at his hands. He took a long, slow breath then raised his head to his fellow Guardians. "Be quick. Be silent. Do not compromise her safety."

As one, Michael, Luke and Peter gave a short nod of their heads, then they disappeared, along with the drones.

The screens immediately showed a different landscape, the small craft picking up a long beach, pristine white sand stretched along from horizon to horizon, with azure blue water lapping at it from one side, and a rocky outcrop filling the screens from the other. Sam immediately flew his craft to the coordinates Peter was feeding him through the data pad, the location of Angie pinpointed exactly.

The drone swiftly found its way to the rocky outcrop, then continued up and over, the landscape blurring as it continued on its way.

"I didn't think they would be that far away from Angie," remarked Nick. "You sure you're flying it right?"

"I'm not controlling it; the coordinates took over once Peter put them in. I take over when it reaches its destination."

"Which should have happened long before now." Kyle looked concerned. "If they are too far away, the adjustments for the controls will not work." He tapped the small pin on his collar. "Peter. Are you certain the location for Angie is correct? Module one has far exceeded the distance you estimated prior to leaving. It is still travelling; it has passed the rocks and continues."

"I am reading Angie's coordinates at exactly four hundred and seventy-three meters from where we stand. Let me check, one moment." Peter could be seen from the two remaining drones as he tapped on his data pad. *"Confirmed, four hundred and seventy-three meters, and the exact coordinates were entered into module one."*

"Are you able to extrapolate the destination of the module?" asked Luke.

Kyle touched the screen in front of Sam and then tapped a few information panels that were highlighted. "Module one has not malfunctioned. It is not operating under its own volition." He looked up at the three law men. "It is being controlled."

"By whom?" Sam tapped his screen controller, trying to make the drone respond. "I can't get anything from it."

"Unclear. There is no direct signature. It will not respond to any order from us. All we are able to do is observe and record what is happening." Kyle tapped his communicator button on his collar again. "Peter, please direct module two to Angie's location."

"Affirmative. Sending instructions. Module two

deployed." The drone Nick had been controlling turned and flew to the rocky outcrop, hovering in front of a small cave. *"Manual control now required. The rocks are too full of quartz and iron ore for automated navigation."*

Nick bit his lip as he concentrated on navigating the drone through the cave entrance. The dark, tiny entrance was not big enough for anything larger than the drone to enter, and it twisted and turned throughout the rocky outcrop. The drone automatically adjusted its recording to a night/dark vision mode, though the twisting tunnel was difficult to navigate even with a clear view.

White sparkling quartz veins streaked here and there, contrasting with the rust red ore deposits.

"She has chosen a cave that has no real access, and those veins of ore and minerals would severely hamper, perhaps even prevent, any transport beam." Kyle smiled, just a little, pleased that no one could take the woman by surprise.

A dark, very cramped turn scraped at the sides of the drone before it opened up to a larger chamber. The drone silently rotated as Nick searched the chamber for any signs of Angie. The chamber was empty, however there was a second opening, larger than the first, towards one corner. Nick piloted the drone to the opening, his breath shallow as he concentrated. No one spoke as they watched the screens, the view was direct feed from the drone, showing everything as clear as daylight.

The opening led to a second, slightly larger chamber. This one was different to the first, where the first chamber had a few veins of crystal and ore this one looked to be made purely of crystal quartz, the walls gleamed and sparkled in a pearlescent glow of mauve, pale pink and white. Leaning against the walls were long shards of stalactites that had been snapped off and leaned out of the way.

The floor of the chamber, not much larger than a broom closet, was covered with afghans and heavy blankets. Here and there were strewn rough, hand sewn cushions, and in the middle of the disarray lay a small figure, sleeping softly, her hair gently swirled about her pale face.

"Angie," Kyle sighed, his face showing both relief and concern. "Dahn M'Rath confirmed. Peter, disengage the excess controls."

"Affirmative." Drew's drone showed Peter again tapping on his data pad, while the drone Nick controlled hovered silently over Angie. There were no signs of any change in the sleeping woman, her breath, slow and steady, gently moved her chest, the only movement showing she was alive.

"I think it's arrived," Sam said.

Nick, Drew and Kyle looked up from the screen showing Angie, a puzzled expression mirrored on all three faces. "The drone gone wild? It's arrived wherever it was going. It's stopped," Sam explained.

The screen showed a stand of tall trees, planted in rows and surrounded by overgrown gardens, unkempt and weed filled. Behind the trees, barely seen through a break in the foliage, was a dilapidated mansion.

"Move it a little closer, Sam," Kyle spoke softly.

Module one moved silently through the break in the trees and approached the mansion. The doors and windows were boarded shut, the cladding on the house was grayed, peeling, the guttering rusted and hanging, the shingles lifted, and moss covered. Vines grew up the verandah posts, weeds peered through the broken decking, and several seasons of dead leaves and plants piled up against the steps. It had clearly been abandoned for an extensive period of time, no signs of life or recent access were to be seen.

"Take it around the back," Nick said.

"Wait. Peter, are you finished?" Kyle didn't look away from the feed from module one.

"Yes, sir. I have disengaged several controls, I have left enough, I believe, to allow her to function correctly."

"Return as soon as module two is recovered," Kyle nodded to Sam. "Move it around the building, slowly. Keep it high, away from the eyeline. Stealth is now required."

"If they brought it here, whoever *they* are, wouldn't they already be aware that it's here?" Nick pointed at the screen for emphasis. "They'd be expecting it, right?"

"We don't know that," Drew answered. "We can't even be sure who actually overrode the drone, can we?"

"No, we cannot." Kyle frowned as the drone moved around the building, his brows furrowed, the bright green eyes dark.

The side of the building was much the same as the front, windows boarded, cladding cracked and hanging off in sheets. The back was no different, so Sam moved the drone around the last side of the old mansion.

"There!" Drew tapped the screen. "Move it in there, Sam!"

The drone moved over the spot Drew indicated and the other three could see what had excited the sheriff. A path had been trampled through the overgrown grass, clearly many feet had beaten a track to the one unboarded door.

The drone moved closer, though there was nothing else to see.

"Take it to the next floor, perhaps there are windows that are not boarded," Kyle suggested.

The second floor of the rectangular building was in no better repair than the first, the windows were boarded as well, though a few had boards that were either hanging loose, or had come away altogether. Sam moved the drone to one of these windows and let it peer inside.

The interior was dark, the shielded windows did not allow much in the way of light to enter. There were no furnishings in this particular room, just some old newspapers stacked in one corner. Sam moved it to the next window, here there were less boards intact and the view was a little better. This room had a bed, though it consisted of only a rusted metal frame and a stained, torn mattress. A small wooden chair adorned a corner, where the peeling, faded wallpaper had drooped to almost cover the chair completely. The door to the room was open, and Sam gasped as a figure passed by the door.

"What was that? Could you make out anything?" Nick asked.

Kyle tapped the view screen and opened a new information box; he moved his finger back over it to reverse the view of the doorway. He stopped when he came to the figure. It had moved fast, and the hallway was dark, though the picture could not be mistaken.

"Presas." Michael spoke from behind Sam's shoulder and the detective started, the return of the Guardians had been silent and took him by surprise.

"Move to the next window," Nick prompted.

The drone moved quickly, the next window could not be accessed as all the boards were still in place, so Sam moved it around the corner of the house to the next window. This one must have been a bathroom, though the boards were haphazard and had plenty of gaps to look between, the glass on the window was semi opaque and held its secrets from their eyes. With a grunt of disappointment Sam moved the drone to the next window. This one had only one board left on the window, and he was careful to bring the drone in slowly, to one side, keeping it as hidden as possible. Though it was made for stealth with a reflective skin that made the module almost impossible to see unless you were specifically looking for it, the detective did not want to risk detection if it could be at all helped.

The afternoon sun reflected off the glass making the first glance a screen full of bright glare, but the drone adjusted its lens to reveal the interior of the room, dirty glass and reflected sunlight filtered away as much as possible.

The room had once been a sitting room, or perhaps a study, there was a very old, overstuffed sofa, now leaning crookedly on a broken leg, and small table and desk had been pulled to the middle of the room and were now covered in a multitude of screens and equipment that was clearly live, lights flickering as data scrolled across the screen.

The room was devoid of any beings, only the equipment could be seen. The data on the screen was in a language that could not be read by the detectives, the characters were complex and intricate, and flashed by far too quickly for the human eye to take in more than the barest glimpse.

"Are you reading that, Kyle?" Peter asked.

"Some," the tall man answered. "It is faster than I can read, however. I do not understand what it is saying, but I will be able to review the recording to see what it is later."

A man dressed entirely in black entered the room and Nick had to resist the urge to duck as a first reflex. The man walked over to the screen and stood in front of it. If he was reading the screen the watchers could not tell, he wore dark sunglasses, so his eyes could not be seen, but his head did not move side to side, it did not bow to see the screen, he merely stood motionless, his shoulder to the door, his back straight, his arms by his side. The Presas turned away from the screen and left the room, and Sam moved the drone to get a better glimpse.

The room held nothing else and the data screen was now blank, so Sam directed the drone to another window. This one was well boarded, only a sliver of a gap, though Sam kept the tiny craft there, in front of the gap, instead of moving it on.

"Next window?" prompted Drew.

"Move along, dude," Nick agreed.

"Can't you see it?" Sam asked, and Luke leaned in and pointed at the screen.

"Enhance," Kyle touched the spot Luke was pointing to and they all could see what Sam had noticed.

An eye.

A dark, evil eye, deep and mysterious, with a small glint of green, peered out of the slit between the boards. Sam moved the drone a little and the eye tracked the movement.

"The Presas see us!" Michael exclaimed.

"No, I do not believe it is the Presas," Kyle answered. "They always cover their eyes, even in the dark, and this one wears no glasses. It also has not raised an alarm. See, it watches, but it does not react."

"Perhaps it is the one who commandeered the module?" suggested Luke.

"Angie said they have a vampire." Nick leaned forward and nodded towards the screen. "What's the bet that's the vamp?"

"I believe you may be right, Detective," Kyle agreed. "Though I did not think it would have the ability to control a module. I have not had very much to do with these creatures, though what I know does not lead me to believe that this thing could bring the module to it."

"Agreed." Drew rested his chin in his hands, elbows on the kitchen table. "I've seen a couple, and while there may be some prescience, they seem to be rather a base lot, not much of the technical skills there."

"So, who brought the module to the house?" Sam moved the drone back a little, then forward, and the eye tracked its every movement.

"Move to the next window, Sam." Kyle leaned back. "We will ponder the module's route later."

Sam moved the drone along to the next window, only to find it tightly boarded. The next window was close, perhaps to the same room, and this one had a board that had slipped a little, allowing the men to see inside.

From one wall to the other, shoulder to shoulder, stood the Presas, their black suits, their slightly too long hair, their shoes, all exactly the same. They were close together, row after row, tightly packed with no room between them.

"Fuck!" Nick ran a hand through his hair. "There's got to be at least fifty of those things."

"Sixty-six," Peter touched the screen and the picture enlarged. "Thankfully they are facing the door, not the window. They appear to be dormant, but I don't know if that means they can't see us, though I'd rather not test that theory."

"I agree." Kyle put a hand on Sam's shoulder. "Please move to the next window."

The drone moved across. The next window had shed most of its boards, so Sam stopped the drone at the frame, sliding it over slowly in case there was anything, or anyone, in the room that may see it.

This room was also full of Presas, all stacked in as tightly as the previous room. Sam moved the drone away, and around the corner of the house to the back.

A third room revealed more Presas, also sixty-six, also standing shoulder to shoulder.

Drew cleared his throat. "Is there any significance to that number, sixty-six?"

"Not that we are aware," answered Kyle. "Though they have far more Presas than one would deem necessary to capture the Dahn in her present state."

"Maybe they know you are close by?" suggested Nick.

"Perhaps, if what Angie was saying about a traitor on board is correct."

Sam moved the drone to the last window, this one was fairly well boarded, and he had to move the small craft quite a bit until he found a crack to peer through. What he saw made him gasp in shock, and it was echoed by everyone in the room.

There were two Presas there, both standing as still as statues, and facing them, with his back to the window, was a black uniformed Guardian.

Chapter Thirty-Five
Trauiss III
The Laboratory
A Long Time Ago
We Fight Demons

"A child? We are being redeployed from the war to babysit a child?" Robert's disdain was clear in his voice as he walked away from the barracks with his brother. "You explained that we are the most senior warriors in this fight against the invaders? That we are responsible for the triumph of all battalions in all battles in the last three hundred years?"

"Yes, brother, I explained this. I vehemently explained this. I categorically explained this, in full volume. Would you like to know how they answered me?"

"Yes, James, I would be delighted to know how they replied to you," the sarcasm dripped from Robert's reply.

"They were very descriptive in the issues of the demons not being as fierce, or as strong, as they used to be," James shook his head. "And that is not all. They pointed to the scars on my face, and the grey in my hair. They told me we are becoming too old to fight in battles. *Old*. I was lost for words!"

Robert grunted. They had fought and won so many battles, they were directly responsible for capturing the first demon, and the only angel, and here they were, being retired to the farthest, no account planet in the multiverse. He shouldered his pack and climbed aboard the transport. He didn't need to look at his brother to know that his face reflected the same anger and disappointment that he was feeling.

They were silent for the entire trip to Trauiss Three, glaring at anyone that was unfortunate enough to make eye contact with them.

Elund met them at the entrance of the laboratory and gave them a grand tour; his joyful enthusiasm unable to be quelled by their abrupt answers and angry scowls. He showed them the guards' barracks, introduced them to the entire squadron of guards, the total personnel of the laboratory, including all of the maintenance and service staff, his smile never leaving his face. When he finally took them to see the child they were in charge of guarding, his excitement was uncontainable.

Elund lifted the child from her bed, though she had been asleep she did not complain at the intrusion to her slumber. She rested her sleepy head on Elund's shoulder, her thumb firmly planted in her mouth. She wore a simple linen garment, and her arms and fingers were adorned with silver bands. She wore silver dots on her earlobes, and a thin band encircled her neck. Her hair was a tumble of soft white curls, and her half-lidded eyes were bright purple in color.

"This tiny child is whom we are to guard?" James asked, his irritation clear. "She could not be more than two years old!"

"She is seven years old, and more precious than you could imagine," Elund answered.

Robert stared at the child, his irritation fading the longer he looked at her. Instead he felt a warmth, almost happiness, wash over him and fill his soul. His aching shoulder, something that had been with him for more than a century was forgotten, his back felt straighter and his eyesight seemed clearer. He turned to his brother and gasped. James had lost all grey streaks from his hair, and when he turned to see what his brother had gasped at Robert could see the many scars that crisscrossed his brother's face had softened, some seemed to have disappeared completely.

"Brother, your face!" exclaimed James, and Robert lifted his hand to feel his own scars softening away

"What witchcraft is this?" Robert could no longer maintain his scowl, he felt jubilation flowing through him. "Have you caught another angel?"

"No, my fine friends, no we have not. What you feel now are the effects from this wondrous child. The child you have come here to protect as we unleash her power into the 'verse!"

The child lifted her head from Elund's shoulder and looked at James, up and down she studied him before turning her attention to Robert. She also studied him from head to toe, then turned her gaze to Elund, her eyebrows arched in silent query.

"Yes, child, they are here to protect you. Not like the other guards, these men will live here with you, in your chambers, and tend to your needs."

"Nursemaids? We were not ordered to be nursemaids to this child!" James let his outrage taint his voice.

"No, my good sirs, not nursemaids," Elund assured them. "We feel it better that you behave as a family. We have nursemaids, and many instructors; we now feel that the child would benefit from a family environment. We understand that a normal family is not possible, and we also need to ensure her safety. This is why the Lords have chosen you two, as brothers, to protect her. The Lords informed me that you were the most trusted and skilled warriors in the entire 'verse, that no one comes close to your loyalty and skill. They wanted only the very best to protect this child." Elund explained to them how the child came to be, and the powers that she possessed. He outlined the future they planned for her, for her powers to infiltrate the multiverse and benefit every system, every person and ecology, every environment on every planet.

The brothers' skepticism, while strong at first, faded as the man spoke, for they were continuously feeling the effects of the child before them.

The child watched the brothers as they listened to Elund. She was perfectly still, seemingly content to be held on Elund's hip as he explained her story. When he finished talking, he looked expectantly at the warriors, awaiting their response.

Neither brother spoke for a moment, digesting all that had been laid out before them.

Finally, Robert broke the silence. "This is a great deal for us to take in. Of course, we have no choice but to do as you ask, as we have been ordered to do. It will be strange, this family, strange for us to live in such a place, to not fight every day, to be with a child. Surely you understand that we have no experience with children? Since we were young ourselves, we have had no contact with children."

"We do not know how to behave around children," James added. "We will make our best effort; however, I feel you should not leave us unsupervised with this one."

Elund laughed. "Do not be afraid of such a child, you will do her no harm. A nursemaid will attend to her needs during the day, and at night she sleeps soundly. You have nothing to fear."

Robert cleared his throat. "We fight demons, monsters, every day. We do not fear a small child."

"Of course you do! The one thing all men fear is holding a small child, hurting them, breaking them. Children are resilient, and this one more so. You will be awkward, that is for sure, until you become accustomed to your new roles." Elund lowered the child to stand on her feet. She stood beside him, quietly, no movement. "You have rooms here, at the end of this hall," Elund turned and walked to the hallway, leaving the child standing where he had placed her. Robert turned to look at her as he followed the researcher, intrigued that she had not moved at all. He knew little about children, but those that he had observed had rarely been able to stand still for long, and never stayed quiet for more than a few moments.

Their rooms were large, spacious, and fully

furnished. "This luxury is not necessary for us," James commented, unsure how he would feel living in such surroundings. A large bed, soft cushions, their own facilities, all of this something they had never experienced before.

"It is already provided; I trust you will become accustomed before long."

"We will become soft," Robert said.

"I do not believe that, however through here you will see you have extensive training facilities, and you will also have the rest of the guard to train with. They are not as skilled nor well trained as yourselves and will need you both to bring them up to your standard." He showed the men through the training room, and for once the men seemed pleased. "We made sure to not only duplicate your previous training facilities, but to improve them. You have the finest equipment, the best of the very best. The Lords were most insistent that you were to be given only the finest of everything. Your position here is extremely important, and we are more than grateful to have you here. This child is the most monumental thing we are in possession of and will change all of our lives. You two warriors have one of the most important positions in the entire multiverse. You were chosen because you are the best. We expect much of you, and we know you will live up to our expectations. I leave you now to your first day of guardianship, the nursemaid shall be along shortly to feed and clothe the child. Enjoy your day! I shall come by later to see how you fare. Do you have any questions before I leave?"

Robert shrugged; he could think of nothing.

"I have a question," James pointed at the child. "What is her name?"

"Oh, we haven't given her one," Elund smiled as he left.

The brothers turned to look at the child, who had remained standing where Elund had placed her.

"What do we do now?" whispered James.

"I do not know," Robert answered. "Do we touch it?"

"Do not touch it!" James sounded, for the first time that Robert could remember, as if he was frightened.

Robert walked over to the child and squatted down in front of her. "Girl? What do we do now?"

She didn't answer; she just blinked very slowly, thick black lashes framing her bright purple eyes, her thumb still firmly planted in her mouth.

He stood and felt panic threaten to take him. "I do not know what to do!"

The door opened to a nursemaid and relief replaced his panic.

"This is the most unusual assignment," he whispered to his brother as they watched the nursemaid take the child by the hand and lead her away.

"Most unusual," agreed James.

Chapter Thirty-Six
Earth
Drew's Kitchen
Present Day
It Is Unthinkable

"Who is it?" Drew leaned forward, squinting at the screen. "Can you tell who it is?"

The Guardians did not answer. All four men wore the same look of shock and despair.

"You were hoping she was wrong, weren't you?" Sam asked them. "You didn't really believe one of you could betray her."

Kyle shook his head. "We believed her, to some extent. She has been betrayed by Guardians before, though it was many eons ago. It is just that we did not think that anyone in the Alpha squad would do this."

"Never," agreed Michael. "It is unthinkable."

"Is it possible to ask the ship who is missing? Like on Star Trek, can you ask the computer who isn't there?" Sam looked hopefully at Peter.

"We need to decide if that is prudent." Kyle stood and began to pace the floor. "If that should trigger the traitor in any way, then any accomplice may not be revealed. I feel we need to be strategic here. We need to have a definite plan of action."

"You don't know if the person we ask to check will be in on it and lie. Or manipulate the answer. I don't think we should ask." Peter frowned. "I don't have any other ideas, though."

"I feel you need to know who that is," Nick suggested. "If you can figure out who the traitor is, then you can work out what to do next. I mean, you'd know who he has been hanging with, or who his confidante is. We just need him to turn around."

"I could tap the window with the drone?" Sam moved the drone a little as he spoke.

"No, I don't think so, whoever it is will see the drone and then the jig is up." Drew stood and refilled his coffee. "We need some other distraction, or some other way to get a glimpse of his face."

"Too late." Sam moved the drone over to give the men a better view of the room. "He beamed out."

"Peter, are you able to tell who used the transport last, without anyone on the ship knowing what you are doing?" Kyle stopped his pacing. "That would at least tell us who this betrayer is."

Peter chewed his lip, his brow knotted in thought. "I could, it wouldn't be easy, but yeah, I could. I would need to be on the ship, though. I can't do it from here. What excuse can I use to ask why I need to get back so soon?"

"Tell them the calibration of the controls was not successful and you need to configure another set?" Drew suggested.

"Excellent idea. Once you have the identity of the traitor, you need to let me know on a secure channel. Then, if it is safe to do so, extrapolate who may have been helping them, if anyone at all has. You will need to be formulating another calibration for the controls at the same time, lest you let the traitors discover you are on to them." Kyle sighed. "It is still difficult for me to imagine anyone betraying Angie this way."

Peter nodded, then tapped the communicator on his collar, disappearing almost immediately.

"Is there any way for someone on board to know, to figure out, say, where Angie is?" Nick leaned back in his seat. "Could the traitor have her position, right now, and that's why he beamed out from the house?"

The Guardians looked at the detective in complete shock. "We had not considered this, but, yes, they perhaps could." Kyle shook his head, as if to clear it. "If that is the case, then we would expect to see the Presas on the move."

"Um, guys?" Sam called out. "They *are* moving."

"The Presas?" Kyle rushed to the viewer, closely followed by everyone else.

The screen showed the Presas moving out of the rooms, moving in a single file, as orderly as robots. They formed lines once they were outside, waiting for all of the Presas to join them.

"What do we do? We only have a couple of hours, at most, once those things start marching. They don't stop for anything, guys, remember?" Nick looked at the Guardians, worry creasing his face. "We still have the coordinates for the cave, we could go in and grab her, maybe? Or beam her out?"

"The cave she is in is filled with ore and other

minerals that impair the transport beam. We would have to physically move her, however as we cannot access the cave through the entrance, we would have to drill, or dig, perhaps, our way down." Kyle looked at Michael. "Can you calculate how long it would take to manually excavate a path to Angie?"

"Why don't we just send the drone back and use that to wake her up?" Sam suggested. "We could bang it into her until she is awake?"

"That will not work. Once she is asleep it is impossible to wake her," Michael explained. "It is how they kidnapped her in the first place."

"Unless she is gravely injured while sleeping, but I will not do that to her." Kyle tugged at his collar. "She is not badly injured, and I did not feel she was at the end of her wake cycle, so perhaps your idea would work."

"Awesome! I had an actual workable idea! Can you talk to her through the drone?"

"No, we cannot speak to her, but your idea of bumping her until she wakes enough to change locations is absolutely worth trying. Luke, how long will it take for the flyer to reach Angie? And Michael, please continue to work out the time for excavation, just in case Sam's idea does not work."

"It'll work," Sam muttered. "I am a friggin' genius."

"One half hour," Luke announced.

"I have worked out that it'd take those Presas approximately three and a half hours to get to the cave, not counting how long it would take for all of them to get out of the house," Drew informed the men.

"They are all out," Nick added. "I would send your drone out quick smart."

"Make it so." Kyle handed a data pad to Luke. "Send both, we need to ensure we are successful."

Luke busied himself sending the drones on their journey, their path dizzyingly broadcast on the viewer.

"What will the Presas do once they reach Angie, Kyle?" Sam asked. "I mean, they can't fit in the cave, either, so are they just going to burrow down to her? Looking at the monitor, I don't see any drilling equipment, or anything."

"While I cannot answer that question, I must say I would rather not find out. They are ingenious, and there is no physical restraint on their stamina."

The men watched the viewing screen for a while in silence, the three feeds all showing at the same time. Two were of the modules travelling impossibly fast, skimming the tops of trees, speeding over highways, racing to the cave that held Angie. The other showed the Presas lining up in perfectly even rows, shoulder to shoulder, unmoving.

"Why aren't they moving?" Nick asked. "What are they waiting for?"

"I don't know, but at least it's giving us more time. We may need it," Drew suggested. "It's going to take a half hour for the drones to get to the cave, would anyone like anything to eat? Another coffee?"

"I don't like it," Nick answered.

"Bullshit. You live on the stuff," Sam chided.

"No, not coffee, dipshit. The enemies, the Presas. What are they waiting for? I mean, they don't know how long she will be asleep, how long she'll stay in the cave. They know it'll take them hours to get to the cave, and when they get there, more hours to dig down to her, all the while knowing she could wake up any minute, so why are they not moving?"

"You are right. They are not going to the cave, they are waiting for us to move her, I would surmise, somewhere she will be easier to access." Kyle slammed his hand on the table. "They know what we are doing. They know exactly what we are doing, the whole time we are doing it."

"How? Is my house bugged? The viewer? Your communicators?" Drew shook his head. "How can we figure this out?"

"We need Peter back here; he can figure out who has done this. Luke, disengage the flyers that are on their way to Angie."

Drew cleared his throat, trying to draw everyone's attention, but they failed to pick up on the clue. He cleared it again, louder this time, and everyone turned to face him. He winked then tipped his head just a little, in the direction of the door leading to the garden. Standing, he pulled his communication button off his shirt and placed it on the table, then without turning around to check, he walked out the kitchen door. In a moment he was joined by the two detectives and the three Guardians, all without their communication buttons.

"I think we can talk here, away from your spaceship tech, without being overheard. At least I hope so," Drew explained. "Whoever the traitor is, guys, he's clever enough to tap into all of your tech, as well as warn the accomplice while he was in the house with the enemies."

"I agree," Nick added. "They knew, real time, what was happening. I think they were seeing exactly what we were seeing, at the same time as us. Is this something that anyone could do, or would you need more of a technical upgrade?"

"Our technology is very defined, extremely safe and impossible to interfere with without triggering alarms and safeguards," Kyle explained. "While most of us would be able to piggyback the feeds, it would be almost impossible to do so without being noticed. There are many different safeguards that I would have said cannot be circumvented."

"Clearly someone has, though. Who's got that kind of skill set?" Drew asked.

"Hey guys, go with me a minute, here," Sam interjected. "This guy Peter, your new recruit. He has the skills, right? And he was right with us the whole time, always with one of those pads."

"No," Drew shook his head. "Peter was with me, right at the start. He's one of the good guys."

"Here's the thing, though." Sam scratched at his close-cropped beard, an unconscious action as he put his train of thought into words. "He moved up the ranks pretty damn quickly, for some tech geek from next door to nowhere, to being on the exclusive list on the Alpha team. How did he get

VIP access so quickly? I know you guys have an advanced training program and all that, but seriously, who else could possibly hack into the feeds without you guys knowing, and also send the heads up to his co-conspirators?"

"He has had five years of training on our home world," Luke spoke softly. "We sent him, Ayden and Sarah there. Time moves differently through the Gate. They were able to successfully train and move through the ranks, just as any Guardian on our home world would. We have not had any reason to ever doubt Peter's loyalty."

"They may be right." Kyle was frowning. "It is very difficult to be loyal to a being you have never met. He may seem loyal to us, or to Trauiss, but how can he feel loyal to The Dahn? And they are also right, he is the only one that has the ability and opportunity to instigate this level of espionage."

"I find this all very hard to believe. I mean, seriously, the boy fainted when he first met you guys," Drew protested. "And who is his co-conspirator? Sarah? Jacobs?"

"Sarah did find Angie on social media," Michael said.

"With Peter's help," Luke added.

"I do not know if Sarah and Ayden are involved, and I am still not completely convinced that Peter is the culprit. I trust Michael and Luke with more than my life, and though I would have said this of everyone on the ship, now I can only say these two men are the two Guardians that I am sure are not traitors."

"Do you still trust us?" Drew asked. "Sam, Nick and me?"

"Of course. Nick and Sam have spent much time with Angie, they will be loyal to the end."

"And me?"

Kyle smiled at him. "It was your idea to come outside to speak. Also, you do not have the skills to manipulate the feeds from the modules."

"Thanks for that, I think. Well, now we have to figure out if it really is Peter, without him knowing that we suspect him, as well as figure out who his accomplice is."

"There may well be more than one." Everyone turned to look at Nick. "Remember, Peter only came to you guys after Angie had already been kidnapped. Someone was working from the inside way before you met any of us."

"Go with us, guys, we are detectives. We do this for a living."

"Sam's right. In this case, we're the professionals. So, here's what I suggest we do. We think of a reason why we didn't have any communication buttons etcetera, and then we head back inside and act normal. If we are right, Peter is going to think of an excuse to get back here as soon as he can to figure out what is going on. If that happens, what do we do?"

"How will that implicate Peter?" Michael asked.

"Because he beamed up before the Presas came out of the house. He didn't know," Drew explained.

"What would stop the communicators from working?" Sam asked.

"I can say I set the signal in case the traitor was listening, but then reset it so they wouldn't suspect anything," Luke suggested. "However, I believe he will not be able to ask as it will show that he was listening in."

"Agreed," Kyle said. "Do not say anything unless he questions us, as he could say he tried to contact us and we did not answer. All of this now makes me start to question everything we have said and done with him. Even to question how and why he was selected for Alpha duty. Initially he was not even considered for a place in the Squad. In six months, he came up with so many inventions, and showed more promise than anyone has previously, even finding new and more inventive ways to search for Angie. It seems likely now, given what I am thinking, that he may have had many helping him. They would have collaborated, lending him their ideas and working to groom him for suitability to work with the Alpha team."

"Did the same thing happen with Sarah and Ayden?" Nick asked.

"No. They had been chosen after their graduation and had no contact with Peter for six months."

"Do you have any idea of how he could have been turned?" Drew asked.

"None at all."

"Well, that's something we can figure out later. What do we do if Peter gives himself away?" Nick asked.

"I have an idea." Drew reached into his pocket.

Chapter Thirty-Seven
Trauiss III
The Nursery
A Long Time Ago
Someone Was Watching

The brothers spent their days avoiding the child. They trained their garrison, they trained each other, they toured the laboratory and grounds to ensure all was well and secure, anything to avoid the strange child who stared at them without speaking.

They knew she didn't talk, they had been told as much, and this was a relief to the brothers, as they did not have to hear the child speak.

They passed their time quietly and efficiently, not interacting with any of the staff that looked after the child or maintained the nursery, other than a nod of the head or quick acknowledgement.

Elund came to visit almost every day, bringing Xanya with him occasionally to check on the child, to draw blood, or to weigh and measure her. She accepted all of their attention without a word, and to Robert she seemed to have no will of her own. James felt that she was well trained, he had watched some of her instructors and noticed everyone was firm and abrupt with the little girl. She endured her lessons with no change in her demeanor, whether it be music, art, arithmetic or dance. She seemed to be competent in all of her lessons, as far as one could tell without the child verbalizing anything.

The child slept through the night, every night, never disturbing the sleep of the brothers. Initially Robert would get up several times a night, unable to sleep in his new soft bed, and he would check on the child to see if she was sleeping. While she was more often than not asleep, there were nights where he found her awake, staring at the ceiling, lying motionless in her bed. Occasionally she would turn her head to glance at him, her thumb in her mouth, her eyes glowing softly in the darkness. She would then look back at the ceiling, leaving Robert feeling a little disturbed at the lack of emotion in one so young.

He took some time to grow accustomed to the bed, longer than his snoring brother, it seemed, who had learned to sleep anywhere and everywhere. It was a skill that Robert always envied.

Accustomed or no, he still slept very lightly, years of resting on the battlefields made him able to awaken at the slightest disturbance, and he would be ready to fight in the blink of an eye.

This night, as was his routine, he had locked every door, checked every shield, activated every force field, those inside and out, and patrolled every room in the nursery before taking to his shower, then bed. He had been asleep, dreaming, for several hours when something awoke him.

Robert's eyes snapped open, his heart rate increased, he felt ready to spring, lying there, waiting for his brain to catch up and tell him why he had awakened.

Someone was watching him.

He lifted his head, just a fraction, to look around the room.

There, beside the bed, stood the child. Her thumb was in her mouth and she wore the simple linen garment the nursemaid dressed her in for sleep. Robert sat up in bed, wondering why the child had come to him. She cocked her head to one side, her eyes glowing in the darkness of his room, as if expecting him to do something.

"What do you want? Do you need something?" he asked, at once realizing she was not able to answer.

He reached over and turned on his bedside lamp. "Are you ill?"

Slowly she removed her thumb, and extended her arm over her head, pointing to the ceiling.

"You want me to pick you up?"

She shook her head, curls bouncing in the dim light, and raised both hands, pointing at the ceiling. "I know not what you need, child." Robert got out of bed and reached down to pick up the child, but she moved back, her arms still pointing to the ceiling.

Robert looked up to where she was pointing and felt his heart start to beat faster. There was a noise, a sound, almost imperceptible, but it was there. Something was there. Something was on the roof.

He grabbed up the child and rushed to his brother's room. James had the same ability to snap to attention as soon as he was awakened, though he initially seemed very confused to see his brother standing there, holding the little girl.

"There is something on the roof. Call the guard!"

James sprang into action, racing to the main room where their communication station was located. The guards on duty were stationed in another wing, the main garrison in an entirely different building close by. James summoned them all, then dressed with the efficiency of a well-trained soldier. He held his arms out for the child so that Robert could dress, and she allowed him to take her, the thumb once again in place in her mouth.

The sound on the roof had ceased by the time Robert had dressed. The guards were already at the door, and James handed the child back so that he could allow them entrance. Robert followed them, hoping they had not called a false alarm. A tiny hand touched his face, turning his head to face her, the child then pointed at the ceiling again.

"The sound has stopped. I can hear no noise," he told her. She blinked slowly and shook her head, her arm still extended, her finger pointing at the ceiling. Robert frowned, wondering why he was even talking to the child.

"The guards can find nothing on the roof," James told him as he joined his brother in the main room. "I have sent some up to look to be sure, as just a visual through screens may not be sufficient."

The child took her thumb out from her mouth and used both hands to point at the ceiling. She looked worried, turning her face from James, to Robert, to the guards, and back again.

"The child looks concerned," one of the guards stepped forward. "Sir, we will stay here to help you protect it. There are several men on the roof, and the rest of the squad are searching the perimeter of the building."

"I cannot hear anything anymore," James put his arms out to take the child, but she shook her head. Her fingers were still pointing to the ceiling, and she looked up, then back at James, as if trying to communicate with him. She looked back at the ceiling, her hands moved, as if tracing a path of something. She pointed along the ceiling, then down the side of the building, towards the utilities shaft.

The men looked at each other, the guards and the brothers not willing to dismiss what the child seemed to know.

"Brother," whispered Robert. "Take the guards and check the service panels. I will stay with the child."

A guard handed him a blaster and stood at his side, his own blaster drawn, as the rest of the men quickly made their way to the other room, the services and panels all located in the kitchen.

Robert moved back with the child; her hands now dropped to her side. The guard was ready, alert, and stood in front of them, prepared to give his life to protect the child, should that be required.

A commotion on the roof could be heard, and at the same time the sound of a melee could be heard in the kitchen. Robert shifted the child to his other hip, leaving his right hand free to grip the blaster. He would have preferred to fight with the child in a safe place, not perched on his side, and decided at that moment to have a secure enclosure designed for times such as these.

The fight was quick, brutal, and efficient. Robert heard his brother bark commands, heard the squeal of beasts quickly dispatched, and from the roof he could hear the guards taking care of any escapees.

It took less than ten minutes; all invaders were destroyed and the pod that had brought them to the planet was seized for examination. The mess in the kitchen was cleared and the guards left the brothers with the child. There would be inquiries, meetings and debriefings in the morning, but for now the threat appeared to be thwarted.

"How did they get past the alarms, past the force fields?" James was angry, he started to pace the room, his dagger still gripped tight in one hand. "We check everything, every day. This security system is the finest in all of the multiverse. How did they break through?"

"The child was right. She heard the sounds and woke me, she allowed us to prepare." Robert held the child in front of him, both arms holding her by the waist as her little legs dangled. "She knew, and she woke me in time. Somehow, she must have sensed them, as well as hearing them."

"You should put her back in her bed, the child should be asleep now."

Robert nodded. "I shall. You performed well, small child. You need to sleep now. I shall put you to bed."

"Okay," she whispered. The child stuck her thumb in her mouth and watched Robert stare at her in surprise.

"She spoke! She can speak!" he exclaimed.

"We were told she did not speak!" James took the child from his brother, holding her high, though the thumb kept its place firmly on her tongue. "Say something, small child. Speak again!"

"We cannot make her perform for us, James," Robert took the child back, slinging her onto his hip. "She has given us two gifts tonight; I believe that is more than should be expected from such a tiny child. I shall place her in her chambers, in bed, then you and I will discuss this invasion."

The child yawned again, and her eyes were already closed as Robert lowered her into her bed. As he pulled the blankets around her, she sleepily opened her eyes and reached a small hand out and touched his face, a smile flitted across her features before she closed her eyes again, sleep quickly claiming her.

Robert frowned. He felt strange, protective, something that he had never felt for anyone other than his brother. He touched her curls, the hair so soft and silken that it surprised him.

"She likes you." His brother's voice startled him. "I believe you may be getting a little soft spot for her, too."

"Nonsense!" Robert straightened and strode out of the room. "That is not possible."

James smiled, then reached down and smoothed the child's soft curls. "Sleep well, little one," he whispered, and left the room.

Chapter Thirty-Eight
Earth
Drew's Kitchen.
Present Day
There's Something Weird Going On

Luke had disengaged the flyers that were on their way to Angie, and the view screen showed them still, just hanging in the air.

"Bring the flyers back, Luke. Let's see what happens when you do."

"You don't want to send maybe one there to keep an eye on what's happening?" Sam asked.

"No, I feel Angie is safe. She chose a perfect hiding spot. This is the discussed plan, and it is the one that has the best chance of yielding a result," Kyle answered.

"No change in the Presas. They're all still standing like statues," Sam informed the men standing around.

"What do we do now?" Michael asked.

"I don't know about you, but I need a distraction. I'm hungry. Anyone else? I could make us something to eat?"

"I could eat." Nick looked at Sam. "What about you? You're always hungry."

"Absolutely. I'm a growing boy. Got to keep my carbs up," Sam joked.

"Well, mighty Guardians, who is going to help me make some sandwiches?"

"There's something weird going on." Sam looked up at the others from his seat at the table, the view screen in front of him. "I'm not a hundred percent sure, but I think there's someone in the room with the vampire."

They all rushed to the table and leaned over Sam to see what the module was showing. Sam had steered it to the tiny hole in the window boards, this time no eye greeted them. The room now had a light source, though a very dim one, that could not be seen through the tiny hole, but it did allow the module to get a better vision of the room.

"You can enhance, here, I shall show you." Michael reached over but Sam swatted his hand away.

"I know, I figured that out already." He zoomed the picture as much as he could, maneuvering the drone to get the best angle. There was a Presas in the room, another man also dressed in dark clothing, and a Guardian. The Guardian had his back to the window, the other two men facing him. The Guardian nodded and the Presas grabbed the man from behind, holding his arms tight as the Guardian cut his throat, a slash that was deep and harsh, but not enough to kill him. It was clear now that this was no ordinary man as he snarled in anger and pain, his lips drawn back showing bright, long, sharp white fangs. The Guardian held up a container that caught a great deal of the blood, before the flow stopped, the skin already starting to close over.

He closed the container and placed it inside his uniform and nodded at the Presas again. "Destroy this filthy thing. I will be back as soon as I can." The Guardian disappeared and the Presas grabbed the vampire by the head, twisting it violently, attempting to rip it off. The vampire knew what the man was trying to do, and instead of struggling against the grasp he threw himself in the same direction as the twist, sending the Presas off balance for a second. That second was all that the dark creature needed, he flipped over the man, pulling his own head free with the movement. Grabbing the Presas from behind, he tore the man's head off and tossed it on the floor, stamping on it hard enough to squash it flat.

He grabbed up the dark glasses that had fallen from the Presas in the brief battle and put them on his face.

"Move the drone!" Nick yelled and Sam swung the flyer out wide as the vampire threw himself against the window, shattering the boards as he jumped through. The vampire landed on his feet, he glanced quickly at the drone then turned and ran off into the woods.

"Should I follow him?" Sam asked, hand at the ready.

"No, let him run, for now. We need to keep the module there so we can see what is happening," Kyle told him.

"I can take it into the building, have a look around?"

"Probably not a good idea. Someone may notice. Just keep it on the Presas, we need to see if anything changes there. And Kyle," Nick looked at the

Guardian as he took his communicate button from his collar. The others did the same and followed him outside.

"Did you recognize the voice of that guy? The traitor?" Nick asked.

"I did. It pains me a great deal to think this way, but to me it sounded like someone you met when we first came to you in this little food room. Someone I trusted almost as much as these men beside me." Kyle turned to his fellow Guardians and they both nodded.

"Simon," Michael said.

"I agree," Luke added.

"Simon? Isn't he one of your inner circle?"

"He is one of the highest-ranking officers in the Alpha Squadron. Only myself, then Michael, are above him. Luke is actually just one rank below him. Though as of this minute, Luke, please consider yourself promoted to the same rank as Michael. However, we will have to keep this secret until the entirety of this betrayal is thwarted, and all parties brought to justice. You will have to act like he is your superior officer until we can find all involved."

"Understood, and I am grateful for your trust. I am also feeling quite shocked, even devastated, as I am sure you are as well. As far as I can tell, only those of us here know of the betrayal, and that Simon is the perpetrator."

"As much as the three of you need to come to terms with this, I suggest you put your personal feelings aside. We obviously have a conspiracy here, and if someone so high up in your ranks has been corrupted, there will be no telling how far this goes, and, I'd guess, how many are involved." Nick sighed. "I'm aware that sounds harsh, but clearly Angie is in as much danger as when she first crashed on Earth. We need to figure things out, get a plan happening, and get it done fast."

"Nick, you are right." Kyle sounded defeated, but took a deep, steadying breath and stood a little straighter. "If only we could confirm if Peter was actually involved."

"I was wondering if he did more than just deactivate some of her controls," Drew said. "He may have done something else, maybe put a tracker on her?"

"It is possible that instead of deactivating some controls he actually strengthened them, that would make her sleep longer, and heal a lot slower," Michael suggested.

"Is there any way to find out, like check the controls, or check what he's done?" Sam asked.

"I would need Peter's data pad."

"Well it's going to be a little hard to get that without giving ourselves away." Drew looked at his watch. "Though the drones would have arrived at the cave about ten minutes ago, had we let them continue, so I'm guessing we will see Peter soon, if he is a part of all this."

"You ready if he pops in?" Sam asked Drew.

"He won't suspect we're onto him, and he won't think that we don't trust him. I'm pretty sure we'll have the element of surprise. Let's all get back inside and see what happens next."

As if on cue, Peter appeared in the kitchen as soon as all the buttons were firmly back on collars. He held his data pad in one hand. "Kyle! I know I shouldn't be here, but I just thought I'd check with you about the transport log."

Kyle looked the young man up and down and sighed. "I had been hoping that you would not come, but I knew that you would. I am disappointed."

Peter frowned. "What? Disappointed? I don't get it."

Drew pulled a taser out of his jacket pocket and fired it at Peter, dropping him to the floor. Instantly the three Guardians leapt forward and grabbed him, lifting him up and removing his communication button and holding his arms back for Nick to handcuff him. Drew patted Peter down as Luke scanned him, taking a second communication button hidden inside his suit.

"Make sure he is hiding nothing else!" Kyle ordered as the men started to remove the black Guardian uniform from the tech. Quickly the handcuffs were removed and replaced as they took off Peter's jacket, closely watching the groggy man as he regained his senses. Then Michael and Luke removed all but the young man's underwear before Drew and Nick cable tied him to a chair, his arms cuffed behind the chair back and each ankle restrained.

Peter didn't speak as the men undressed and restrained him, his eyes just got wider and wider, and his forehead was beaded with sweat. He looked at each man as they stood before him, his face flushing red and the sweat beginning to drip down his face.

Michael started to work on the data pad, his face expressionless. Peter could only look on, his panicked face drawn, his eyes darting from one person to another, but no one acknowledged him.

Michael handed the data pad to Kyle, who looked at the screen for a moment before walking behind Peter and roughly pulling the man's hand into the pad for identification. He then walked back in front of him, holding it before his face for a second level of confirmed identity. Peter had started to breathe fast, his skin turning paler with each shallow, rapid breath.

Nick walked over and slapped him on the back. "Slow breaths, old mate, we don't want you passing out. At least, not yet, anyway."

Peter gulped. "I think I'm going to throw up," he squeaked.

Nick lifted his leg and pushed the chair off the small kitchen rug with his foot. "You should be right to go now. Try to get most of it on yourself, though. Less for us to clean up."

Peter swallowed hard and looked up at the detective as he made an effort to breathe slower.

Nick smiled at him. "That's the way. Now you just sit tight while we explore the hidden levels in your little iPad-thingy. If you think of something we may need, just holler. Okay, Petey old boy?"

Peter swallowed again, hard, his Adam's apple

bobbing with the effort, and he nodded.

Kyle returned the data pad to Michael and watched as the Guardian tapped it, then scrolled through screen after screen, searching the information held there. Drew handed Michael a small device he had in his pocket, and Michael attached it to the pad. He kept scrolling the information, as fast as he could, while Peter looked on.

"See that thing there?" Nick asked him, walking in front of the young tech and then leaning back against the kitchen counter, a coffee mug in one hand, the other hooked into his front pocket, a veritable picture of relaxation. "You should recognize it. You gave that little scrap of a thing to Drew quite some time ago. Remember?"

Peter nodded.

"You are a very smart man, Peter. One could even call you a genius. You were clever enough to design your very own little thumb drive type of attachment to download and keep all the files from your first encounter with the Guardians. See, Drew kept that little piece of tech, not knowing if he would ever have to use it, but thinking it wouldn't hurt to be safe, rather than sorry. Didn't you, Andrew?"

"That I did Nick. That I did." Drew looked back at the data pad Michael was holding.

"See, Drew thought you would have some kind of fail-safe on your iPad-thingy to protect those toxic bilge of traitors that were working with you, so he and Michael came up with a way to extricate all of your information before the failsafe takes place. Clever, don't you think? I know you do, because it's exactly what you would do. You were just a little too smart for your own sake, there Pete."

"I'm willing to help. I will. Just please don't hurt me!" Peter yelped.

No one said anything to him, Michael, Kyle, and Drew still huddled around the data pad, Luke and Sam were at the table monitoring the viewer, and Nick just stood where he was, sipping his coffee.

"You need to listen to me!" Peter started to squirm against his restraints. "Seriously, we could all be killed!"

Nick sat his coffee down on the bench. "What's that, Pete?" His calm demeanor did not falter, he just folded his arms and regarded the panicked tech.

"The pad is set to blow up if anyone other than me goes through it. It's going to figure out that my hand isn't the one touching it and it launches a timer. If I don't enter the code it explodes! It'll blow up half the block! Now please, guys, I don't want to die, please let me have the pad!"

"What do you think?" Nick looked over at the others.

"How do we know he won't alert any of his conspirators if we let him have the pad?" Michael asked.

"Oh my god, I won't, I promise! Just give me the pad, we can't have very long left! Please, *give me the pad*!" He was screaming now and squirming so hard the chair threatened to fall over.

Nick calmly undid the handcuffs and Michael

handed the pad to Peter.

Nick took his police issue revolver from the holster under his jacket and held it to Peter's temple. "If I even think for half a second that you've tipped anyone off a bullet goes straight through your brain. Capiche?" He cocked the weapon, the click filling the silence like a thunderclap.

Peter nodded, his eyes now so large that they looked as if they would roll right out of his head. He held the pad out in front of him so everyone could see what he was doing as he applied his palm to the screen, then entered in a complex equation.

"Is that it?" Michael demanded.

Peter nodded his head furiously, the sweat flying off him like rain. "It's all done, it's safe now. It won't delete anything, either. Or it shouldn't. I don't know if the others put any safeguards in there, so, um, I guess the backup is a good idea. I can help you with that, if you want?"

"No thanks, we got it. Not that we don't trust you, Petey old man, it's just that you're a lying piece of shit and a low-class weasel coward, so no, we won't be asking for your help." Nick leaned back against the counter, his weapon still in his hand. "What you are going to do, however, is start talking. Talk like your life depended on it. Because, well, it absolutely does."

"Yeah, okay, anything. It's not like I owe them any loyalty or anything."

"Then why?" Kyle looked away from the pad, his face still showing no emotion. "If you owe them no allegiance, why did you betray our leader? It was her power that saves lives, and gives you this existence that you say you are grateful for?"

"This power she has, I've been told it comes from a demon, is that right? You guys are worshipping an actual demon?" Peter was blinking rapidly, his eyes still darting around each of their faces.

"The Dahn is no demon." Kyle spoke firmly, his eyes narrowed a little, the expressionless facade dropping.

"But she is made from a demon. I mean, you even said it yourself, the other monsters that these guys have been killing are all from her blood, right? So, she is made from demons, and monsters, and if you didn't fill her full of controls, she would turn into something even worse than those things she is made from?"

Kyle took two steps to the restrained man and grabbed him by the neck, picking him, and the chair, up until he was face to face with the Guardian. Peter was gasping for breath, the vice-like grip on his neck cutting off his air supply. Kyle just held him there, no signs of strain on his face as he held the man and the chair in front of him. "*The Dahn is no demon.*"

"Okay, let's put the weasel down, shall we?" Nick placed a hand on the Guardian's arm. "He can't spill the beans if you rip his throat out."

Kyle lowered Peter gently but dropped him when he was a couple of inches off the floor, allowing the jar of the fall to further unnerve the terrified man.

Peter began to cough, the red marks on his neck already starting to bruise.

"The Dahn is no demon," Kyle repeated.

"Okay big guy, we got it." Nick kicked the chair to straighten it and Peter squealed, triggering another coughing fit.

"I just wanted you to understand where I'm coming from," Peter croaked, before coughing again. "They're worshipping a monster, a thing that should be put down. It makes people sterile! How is that a good thing?"

"What about the health, long life, in fact a second chance at life for many, the paradise we live in?" Kyle stood and started to pace in the small room. "You even said you are living the dream, that it is everything you could ever wish for!"

"There is another way. We can still have most of that without the side effects, if you give her heavier controls and return her to the exile planet."

Kyle stopped his pacing and turned to look at Peter. Nick looked at Michael and Luke, both men were staring at Peter, their faces wearing the same shocked expression that Kyle now wore.

"That is the agenda?" Kyle ran both his hands through his hair. "You want to turn her into a base creature, barely existing in a fortified stone dungeon? All for what, so you may have a child one day?"

"You know there is more to it than that. You know her blood makes monsters. Every evil creature, every monster on Earth, all of those from legends and folklore, every scary story and nightmare through the ages, are from her! She is the origin of evil on Earth! We don't need her running around making monsters whenever someone decides to grab a piece of her. That's why we are trying to stop her. They told me that they have been trying to do this for centuries."

"Well, Peter, that's just what I want to hear." Nick redirected the conversation. "Care to let us know who 'they' are? Just how many 'theys' are there?"

Peter shrugged. "I don't know exactly. A lot."

"Well, let's start simply. Apart from you and Simon, who else on the ship is in on it?"

"You know about Simon?" Peter looked shocked.

"So far, yes, we know about him. You are going to tell my good friend Kyle here all the names of those that you're certain are involved. Starting now. Don't leave a single person out."

"Okay. I'll tell you everyone, I promise. There aren't many on the ship, just seven of us. I can also tell you everyone I know about through the Gate, as well. There's just one thing I want."

"I do not care what you want. You will tell us everything or I shall tear you limb from limb, and make sure those limbs stay apart, and your wounds stay open. As an immortal you will writhe in pain for all eternity." Kyle spoke menacingly, and convincingly enough for Peter to turn even whiter than before.

Chapter Thirty-Nine
Earth
The Vampire Artu
Present Day
In The Daylight

Artu ran swiftly from the house, from his captors, from the thing that had watched him from the window. He didn't stop running, even as he ran deep into the woods. He glanced back every now and then, but the thing, the drone-thing, had not followed him. He wasn't sure where it had come from, and did not know who sent it, but he had an idea. It had very little scent, but Artu was more than a man, more than even a normal vampire. He was the first, the strongest, and the one chosen to protect his maker.

The scent was the same as those men that had nearly taken his head off one time, the ones that had come to take his maker away. All he needed was to catch that scent again and he would find them. He slowed his retreat and left the path he had been following. He needed to take a moment to gather his thoughts, to decide his next course of action.

He found a small cabin in a clearing, the trees trimmed back around it, but there was enough shadow for him to rush to the door. A small sign advised that it was solely for the use of the forestry rangers and had a bar and lock on the timber door. Artu broke the padlock easily and dashed inside, slamming the door behind him. The sun would not be the end of him, not like in the fairytales, but he found it very uncomfortable. It did burn his skin, it felt like a thousand suns bore down on him and would very likely hurt him gravely if he stood out in the full sun for too long.

He ran a hand through his slick black hair and took in his surroundings. The cabin was not much more than a storage shed, various maintenance equipment and gardening implements were piled up against one wall, and against another an old sofa and table with a chair were pushed. Somewhere, he supposed, the rangers ate a meal or filled in their reports. He didn't care, as long as there was no one here right now.

Not that he would mind biting into the warm flesh of a human, he was starving and desperate to feed, but would have preferred not to kill anyone right at this point in time.

He didn't stay undiscovered for so long by indiscriminate killing, he had been very careful, very discrete, planning his kills and taking only those that were sure not to be missed, or those already injured or fallen, where he could feed quietly without raising any suspicion. The two detectives that were hunting his kind, that had taken out so many of his brethren, would be on his trail if he slipped up, and so far, he had managed to avoid those two. It was something he intended to continue.

He paced the small cabin, his mind racing, torn between his base desire to kill and feed, his need for self-preservation, and his directive to protect and defend his maker. He felt his fangs slip from his gums, his need for sustenance was great. He had been imprisoned before he had been able to feed and had been given nothing the whole time he was held prisoner. He had expended great energy to heal himself, then to escape, and he was finding himself feeling weak and unable to make a coherent thread from his thoughts.

He would need to hunt.

Now.

In the daylight.

He would need to seek out someone, something, anything with a blood supply, and feed enough to keep his mind clear and his body strong.

Feeding in the daylight was not just difficult, with the burning sun beating down, it was highly dangerous, with usually only the fit and strong out and about. Any decent sized animals would usually be hidden, sleeping the warmer hours away until the relative safety of the night. While he was perfectly capable of following a scent and finding the sleeping place of any larger creature, he would be limited in his ability to travel during the day.

He stopped pacing; head cocked to one side. He heard something. Something other than the normal rustle of leaves and call of insects and birds. Something running, and running fast. He moved to the door and opened it, just a sliver. It was enough for him to catch the scent, the overwhelming odor, of a warm-blooded animal.

He could tell by the scent and the sound of paws

that it was a large dog, young, fast, and coming his way. Pursing his lips, he whistled, a high pitch, unheard by any human ears, but one that caught the attention of the young dog and brought him bowling up to the cabin, leash trailing behind him. Before the dog even had a chance to sniff the door Artu grabbed it and pulled it inside, his hand closing around the canine's muzzle to keep it from crying out.

The dog didn't struggle, it was young, and playful, and thought this was just another game. It looked up at the vampire, the big, soft brown eyes of the young golden retriever were full of trust and love for humans, but then it realized it was being held by something other than a kind, gentle human. The eyes widened and the dog snorted in fear, trying to struggle free from the iron grip that held it tight, but to no avail.

Artu grabbed a handful of thick golden fur and ripped it back, skin and flesh, from the side of the dog's neck and plunged his face into the bloody mess, drinking deep as the dog struggled for life, digging with all four paws into the bare wooden floor, desperate for purchase, desperate to escape the pain and the creature holding him.

Artu ignored the dog's pain and distress, he just fed hungrily, the dog held tight with strength that was growing with every mouthful of warm, coppery dark blood. In less than a minute the dog was drained, its lifeless body, still warm, hung limply in the vampire's arms. He moved to the door, listening for the dog's owners. They were still a way off, calling desperately for their escaped pet. Artu opened the door and flung the dog's body up on the roof, the beautiful young pet, once a happy, bounding, bundle of fur and love and exuberance, was now nothing more than a bloody carcass, destined to remain on the high roof, undiscovered, until its rotting, putrid body fluids dripped through and befouled the cabin.

Chapter Forty
Earth's Far Outer Orbit
The Alcea (Angie's ship)
Present Day
Please Explain, Leo

Simon touched the console in front of him, scrolling through information and checking the boundaries around the ship. He was part of the Alpha Squad Guardian team, but also took shifts on the bridge, as did most of the Alpha Team. Technically he outranked even the captain but had asked to be treated like any other bridge staff and acted accordingly. Simon enjoyed his time on duty, kept his knowledge up to date with ship's procedures, and it was a welcome distraction when on a long mission. He did not like waiting, the often-extended times they had to stay on the ship, just waiting, passing the time, until they were ready to deploy on whatever their latest mission required. He knew some of the Alpha Team felt bridge duty was below them, though he knew Michael helped in the engine section. Luke and Bardi took shifts on the bridge, with Bardi often sitting in for the Captain.

This mission, the search for their all-powerful leader, had to be one of the worst. He had only one decent battle with the Presas, then the occasional hunt for a repulsive beast here and there. Small stuff, all below his status as an Alpha, but an easy distraction against the boredom.

This particular shift had been a long, uneventful one. He was nearing the end of his shift and was looking forward to a tough workout session in the training room. Sitting idle for several hours, while better than sitting in his room, always made him feel like he would bubble over with excess energy.

A security team entering the bridge caught all those on duty by surprise, Simon turning to see what they were doing. Elyse and Bardi were with them, standing to one side as the team of seven moved closer to Simon.

"Simon, would you sign your station over to Elyse and come with us?" Saskia, the Team Senior, asked.

Simon frowned. "Is there an issue that cannot wait until I have finished my shift?"

The Captain turned her chair to look at the team. "Is he needed on Earth? We have no communication from them indicating this."

"Captain, I would also ask you to sign over your station to Bardi. Please do so immediately and accompany us."

She looked confused, turning to look at the rest of her bridge staff, before making eye contact with Simon. There was a brief flicker of understanding shared between the two, but the security team was prepared. They drew weapons and aimed them at the two traitors, supervising closely as they signed over their stations.

"This is ridiculous!" the Captain protested as the team led her from the bridge.

"I would advise silence," Simon hissed as he followed her, a security guard to each side of him and one behind.

"You would be wise to follow his advice," Saskia cautioned as she led them away.

"These are the final two, please let Kyle know when they are secured in the holding cells," Bardi instructed Saskia, who nodded and closed the exit door behind them.

The rest of the bridge crew looked at Bardi and Elyse, but said nothing as the pair took their seats, Bardi quickly scanning the Captain's data screens to check for any problems, Elyse doing the same.

Bardi pulled up the smaller tactical screen from beside the Captain's chair. He punched the screen and a ship-wide tone sounded.

"Attention all crew. Effective immediately I have been appointed Captain of the ship. This is a direct order from Alpha Squad Team Leader," Bardi announced. The bridge crew turned back to their stations; they knew they would be told more when it was appropriate.

One man turned back and looked at Bardi.

"Sir, Captain, are there any new orders for us?"

Bardi smiled in a way that he hoped would be reassuring. "Just continue as you were. Simon and the Captain will be confined until we return to Trauiss. When the rest of the Alpha team return you will be briefed in full."

The man nodded and returned to his station but turned back to Bardi. "I think maybe you need to take me to the holding cells as well."

Bardi frowned. "Please explain, Leo?"

Leo stood and moved away from his station. "I knew what they were doing. While I was not a part of it, not directly, I also did not say anything when I found out. I should be there as well. I have already signed off at my station. That is all. I did not do anything untoward."

Bardi touched his data screen. "Saskia, please report to the bridge." Tapping it again to turn it off, Bardi let the screen fold back beside the chair before turning back to see Saskia entering the bridge. Bardi gestured towards the man. "Please place Leo in a separate holding cell, away from the others. He is to have no contact with any of the other detainees."

Saskia nodded and took Leo away as Elyse called for a replacement to take his station on the bridge.

"I am not sure if I admire his honesty or am distressed at his complacency," Elyse sighed as she returned to her station. "I think I am mainly distressed."

"As am I," Bardi agreed. "If Kyle can get to the bottom of everything then it will bring great relief."

Chapter Forty-One
Trauiss III
The Nursery
A Long Time Ago
A Word

The brothers worked tirelessly over the next several days, supervising the reinforcement of the roof, the installation of newer, stronger force fields and a newly developed dampening field that covered the entire facility. The creatures they had killed were the lesser demons that they had met many times on the battlefields, so they knew that this was perhaps nothing more than a random scouting mission that almost yielded an unexpected victory for their enemies.

The remote pod that had brought the creatures was the same type used in many such scouting attacks, usually targeting factories, schools, and military facilities. As best as they could tell the creatures had been drawn to the child's energy once they broke through the force field.

They worked from dawn to well after night fell, leaving before the child woke and returning long after she had gone to bed, the nursing staff attending and covering the absence of the warriors. They checked everything time and again, over and over, until they were satisfied that the nursery and laboratory could not be breached again.

They reported the completion of their work and

returned to the nursery earlier than they had in weeks, hungry and ready for an evening off.

Robert groaned quietly and elbowed his brother as they entered the main room. Elund was sitting there, waiting for them.

"So much for our night of leisure," whispered James.

The child stood at the entrance to her room, thumb in mouth, watching the brothers as they entered and greeted Elund, before they sat on the large, comfortable sofa in front of him.

She watched as they discussed the new security arrangements, the upgraded guard schedules and as Elund explained the impending arrival of another squadron. The brothers seemed satisfied, as did Elund, then came the discussion of the one word spoken by the child. Elund explained he had tried to get her to repeat the word, as had all of her instructors and nursemaid, however no one had been successful.

Elund looked over at the child and patted his knee.

"Come here, child, and sit on my lap."

She shook her head and pointed to Robert. The warrior frowned, unsure if the child was asking him to do something or if she wanted him to leave.

"Come, child," Elund repeated, and the child walked closer to him, but turned and moved closer to Robert, lifting her arms for him to place her on his knee.

Elund seemed very pleased. "She is bonding to you! This is good, as I explained when you first arrived, we did want a family environment for her."

"I am not sure she is bonding." Robert seemed uncomfortable. "We rarely interacted prior to the invasion, and since then we have not seen the child awake until today."

"Can you make her talk?" Elund asked, and Robert frowned.

"We did not make her talk the first time." James ran a hand through his hair, unsure what Elund thought they could do. "We merely asked her if she was tired or wanted to go to bed."

"Ask her again!" Elund wore his usual wide smile.

"Okay." Robert turned his head to face the child. "Child, do you wish to go to bed?"

She smiled around her thumb, her brows raised in amusement.

"Are you tired?" he tried again, and this only elicited a shake of her head, the curls tumbling about her shoulders.

"Are you hungry?" James asked, and again, she shook her head.

The nursemaid, who had been standing back, out of the way, stepped forward. "If I may?" she asked, and kneeled in front of Robert, her hand on the child's knee. "Do you like these men?" This brought a wider smile, and the girl nodded.

"Do you like one more than the other, maybe a little bit?"

Again, a nod, and the bemused smile.

"Which one, child? Which one do you like better?"

The child pointed at Robert, her grin as wide as Elund's.

"Do you know his name?" the girl nodded again.

"This is not working." James stood, his agitation barely controlled. "Child, if you were going to call us, if you were in danger and had to call out, what would you say?"

Her smile wavered, but she didn't answer.

"You try, Robert."

"Okay. Child, would you please say a word for these people to hear, so they do not believe we imagined it?"

"Okay," the child spoke so softly that they almost missed it.

"She speaks!" Elund leapt to his feet, his excitement giving them all a start. "Seven years! Seven years she has been silent! I knew this was the right thing!"

Robert frowned at the researcher's exuberance before turning his attention back to the child. "Why did you not speak before now, child?"

She shrugged.

"Try a different question," prompted James, and Robert lifted a hand to silence him.

"Can you tell me why you did not speak before now?"

"Yes," the voice was soft, baby-like, fitting to her tiny stature. "Did not need to talk."

Elund was beside himself, almost jiggling, until Robert shot him a stern look that had him quickly sitting back down.

"Why did you start talking now?" She shrugged

again. "You no longer want to stay silent?" Robert looked up at James for inspiration.

"Is Robert the only one you will speak to, now?" James asked.

She shook her head.

"Can you tell me who else you will speak to, child?" She nodded again and pointed at him.

"You." James smiled at that.

"And everyone?" asked Elund. She looked over at the researcher and nodded her head, sending her curls bouncing.

Robert gave her a little squeeze, and she giggled. This made Elund laugh, which made the child giggle even more, as she rested her head on his chest. Despite his earlier protestations Robert felt himself warming to this strange little creature, and affection was filling his chest and forcing a smile from his serious features. Elund laughed harder and the child giggled even more, her baby voice making the sound all the more charming. She yawned and the nursemaid stood and reached out her hands for the child.

"It is time for me to put this one to bed."

"Okay," the child said, and giggled through another yawn.

"This had been a fine day. Most fine!" Elund slapped his knee with joy.

Chapter Forty-Two
Earth
Present Day
The Vampire Artu

Artu pulled the cabin door closed tightly behind him, fastening it from the inside. While the dog's blood had taken the edge off his hunger it was far from a desirable meal, a filthy animal might suffice in desperate circumstances, but it would not maintain him long term. Should the canine's owners come stumbling into the cabin he was not sure he could control himself. He leaned against the door, listening to the young dog's owners calling for him as they stopped at the cabin, tried the door, then moved on, calling and whistling for their dog. It seemed he was safe, for now, and perhaps he could rest, perhaps just until dark. The one room cabin had no windows, nowhere for the sun to leak in and torment him, and with the door fastened from the inside he could rest for a while. If anyone tried to open the door he could be up and alert before they had a chance to know what hit them.

He lay on the sofa, the musty odor that spoke of the advanced age of the overstuffed leather and fabric sofa assaulting his nostrils, so he lay still as to not disturb the dust and staleness any further. He did not intend to sleep, there would be time for that later, he just needed to lay there for a while, at least until the sun went down, and then he could be on his way.

He needed to think as he rested, needed to come up with a plan, a strategy, he needed to know where he would go and what he was to do once he left this little wooden structure. Artu knew he would have to avoid the things that had captured him. He didn't know what they were, but they were not human. They looked like humans, but that was as far as the comparison went. They didn't smell like humans; they didn't have a living scent at all. Their strength was at least equal to his own, though he suspected that they would not tire should he engage one in any combat. While he had destroyed one, it was, he knew, purely due to the element of surprise.

He knew they were looking for his maker. They had not spoken of it; they had not spoken at all. When the men in the black leather uniforms had appeared, Artu had been shocked but hid his surprise. He had been aware, in the past, of these fierce soldiers fighting the strange speechless men, he did not know why, he did not care. He did know that these men were aligned somehow with his maker, they all bore her scent and her power could be felt radiating from them.

The ones that he saw in the silent men's house were traitors, of that he was sure, for although the silent men did not utter a single word, the traitors did speak, and they spoke of finding the Dahn, his master, and they spoke of keeping their intentions secret from the rest of their kind. From what Artu could ascertain, the traitors had been working against his maker for some time. Artu believed that the silent men communicated telepathically, he could almost hear what they were saying, could feel that there were words, that there was some sort of language he could not quite grasp, but it was there.

Every time the silent men faced one of the traitors, he could feel his skin prickle, his hair stand on end, and he knew they were communicating. He had tried to listen in, he had even tried to communicate with them, but to no avail. They either could not hear his thoughts, or they ignored them.

Artu was sure if they found him, they would kill him, but he didn't think they were after him. He knew he was no longer of use to them by the assassination attempt but did not want to appear on their radar any time soon, and preferably not at all. He did know that he would not be able to battle them on his own, so his missive to protect his master would be very short lived should he try to take on the silent men, and adding the traitors to the mix made the enormous odds against him even greater.

He needed help. He needed an army of his own, but to try and pull together the rabble of creatures created by the master's blood, and now his own blood at the hands of one of the traitors, was an impossible task. Artu did not always have control over his own thoughts and could often find it difficult being rational, especially if he had not fed, and he seemed so much more evolved than the other creatures. The others were not much more than animals, base creatures that were solely driven by their basic needs. They had no loyalty to their creator and felt no affiliation with himself.

He needed to find another way, he needed to find someone, or something, with enough strength and resources to take on these strange creatures and actually defeat them.

Artu smiled, his sharp white fangs slipping a little from his gums as he did so. The other black uniformed men, he would find them. He knew the hunters would be with them, the detectives that were taking it upon themselves to rid the world of his fellow creatures, but that was a risk he would have to take. He could think of no other way he could be remotely successful than pitting his enemies against each other. Enemies of my enemies and all that, he was sure that it was the only way to move forward and protect his fragile white-haired creator.

What better way to not only fight the silent men and the traitors, but to enlist the very beings they were betraying?

Chapter Forty-Three
Earth
Drew's Kitchen
Present Day
Who Did This?

"All traitors are secured" Michael reported. "And a few of the crew have come forward admitting complicity and have been secured away from the others."

"Well, Peter, so far so good. I just wonder if you told us about everybody." Nick was straddling a backwards facing kitchen chair, his arms folded atop the backrest. "Maybe I should get Kyle to start interrogating you, he seems pretty keen to make sure you're telling us everything you know."

Peter gulped, his eyes wide, and his bottom lip started to quiver. "I am! I swear, you gotta believe me, please, don't let him hurt me, Nick, please!" Kyle cracked his knuckles and Peter squealed. "Oh god, I swear on my life I have told you everything. I wish I knew more so I could tell you. Please, Nick, please!"

"I cannot believe this worm was an acting member of the Alpha Guards," Luke growled. "He is spineless, a coward. You should crush him, dispose of this piece of filth."

Peter was now openly sobbing, his snot and tears running down his chin. Sam looked over at the crying mess and shook his head. "To think you didn't even lay a finger on him. What a loser."

"I have to admit, I knew he wasn't much of a brave soul, but I seriously didn't take him for a screamer." Drew moved to fill up his well-used coffee pot. "Was it worth it, Peter? Were the risks involved betraying those who helped you with this, worth what you are going through now, and, I hate to think about what you'll go through in the future?"

"W... what? In the future? What?" Peter's wide greenish eyes looked from Drew to Nick, and back, his fear still too great to look at Kyle. "W... what?"

Kyle had been sitting beside Nick, he now stood, unfolding his tall, well-muscled body with a deliberate slowness, stretching his arms until they strained against his leather-look uniform before cracking his neck, this way, then that, then turning his chair around and sitting back in a mirror of Nick's position.

"There are horrors worse than all you can imagine," he said, his voice quiet, emotionless, but the foreboding in his sentence left the room silent.

Peter turned to look at the Guard for the first time since he was restrained. "I can't. I just can't. I'll do anything, literally *anything*, for you to let me go. I'll disappear, I can do that, you'll never see me again."

Kyle sighed. "You are correct in saying that I will never see you again. This is true. But to let you go, after what you have done? I do not think there is anything you can do that would make me even consider this."

Peter looked at his lap, his lips silently moving as he desperately sought a reason to give Kyle. After a few minutes he looked back at the Guardian, defeat finally showing in the man's face.

"Well, Petey old boy, seems you've finally run out of steam, hey?" Nick's sunny demeanor only highlighted the distress of the young man. "It's time for this big fella and I to pop outside and have a little chat. Sam and Luke are going to keep an eye on you while the rest of us have a bit of a think about what happens next. You okay with that, Petey?"

Tears started to flow again, Peter just nodded, his quivering bottom lip clamping tighter to control the shaking.

Sam stood up from the kitchen table, touching Luke on the shoulder as he did so, a silent communication to take over monitoring the drones. He walked over to Nick's chair and sat, also straddling it as the others had done.

"I don't get it, Pete. I mean, seriously, these guys gave you the fantasy life you always wanted. I can't believe that it's all because Angie may, or may not, have demon in her? Man, I have been with her for days, right next to her, she isn't evil. What you see is what she is, and I really can't figure out why you'd betray everyone. I mean, seriously, is their home world so bad?"

Peter barked a short derisive laugh and shook his head. "Bad? No, Sam, it's completely awesome! It's like every paradise you could ever imagine, with the most beautiful people you could imagine. And they have the most amazing creatures, like, real unicorns, and fairies."

Sam snorted in disbelief, but Peter just shook his head. "It's like living in a fairytale. And one of the best things is that they have all these people, these legends, that they snatched from Earth. I am talking music and movie legends, war heroes, even ancient Romans and Greeks. They have a way to sort of go back in time, by using their gate and different dimensions, and they take people at the instant they were going to die. They replace them with a copy, like they did with Sarah."

"What, like Elvis and Bowie?" Sam whistled through his teeth. "I so don't believe you."

"Tell him, Luke." Peter looked over to the Guardian. "Am I lying?"

"No, he is not. All that he says is true."

Sam turned his head to look at Luke. "You've gotta be shitting me. Seriously?"

"I am serious. It is how we three Guardians came to Trauiss. Kyle is the oldest, he was a Viking. Michael walked the Earth before men drove vehicles, and I was taken before my death in a battle in what you call ancient Egypt. All three of us were chosen by the Dahn herself, along with most of those on the Alpha Squadron. Our halls of music are graced by Earth's finest musicians from throughout history, our builders, our scientists, our scholars, so many of them are rescued from an early, or untimely death. Or even a timely death from advanced age, once on our home world the Dahn's power takes over to heal everyone, and even those who could survive no other way are made whole and live with us."

"What if they don't want to go, if they don't want to live there?" Sam asked.

"If they truly do not want that life, if they truly want to return to their deaths, then they are granted that wish. I can assure you, it happens very rarely."

Sam turned back to Peter. "So that makes me even more confused, man. It sounds like a perfect world! Why would you want to give all that up?"

Peter sighed. "I don't. I absolutely don't. It's a perfect place, and there are so many more worlds that I haven't even seen yet, places where dragons, mermaids, dinosaurs, all sorts of fantastical creatures live. I want to see them, I want to live forever and explore the universes, the different gates and dimensions." He paused, shifting as best as he could against his restraints to try and get a little more comfortable. "The thing is, it's so perfect that everyone else wants it. They have to fight constantly to stop all sorts of evil things from ripping it from them. I mean, they do welcome peaceful people, from what I'm told, but they are few and far between. I know they needed to do something to protect themselves, I do. I know it had to be something drastic, I've read a lot of their history, and I get it. The people who decided to breed that thing, Angie, they tried to do the best they could. Sam, they bred her to destroy things, they used the most vile creatures for a reason. They wanted something strong enough, not just to defeat things on the battle ground, but to destroy whole worlds. The long lives and healing and all that was a bonus, something added to her ability to wipe out everyone that didn't agree with the overlords. She has the ability, if she doesn't wear a massive amount of controls, to actually destroy whole planets."

Sam looked back at Luke, but the Guardian just raised an eyebrow, he didn't say anything. He turned to face Peter again. "Go on."

"Not everyone was happy with what they were doing, even some of those that were responsible for creating that thing started to have doubts. Sam, they started to lose control of her, even with all of the things they put on her to stop her reverting, and everyone that made her, all of the rulers at the time, decided she was far too dangerous to let run loose. Jeez, from what I'm told, she even started to eat people. Like literally tearing them limb from limb and chowing down on them!"

"That is enough!" Luke looked up from the viewer. "I know you feel you wish to justify your actions, but this slander of our God is too much."

"You know they locked her up, Luke. You know they kept her locked away for centuries, just to keep people safe. You're all so blind to what she is and what she's done, and what she will do again!"

Luke stood, anger reflecting in his face. "I told you, that is enough!"

With no warning a Guardian appeared behind Peter, in his black, leather-like uniform with the helmet closed, visor darkened, so his face could not be seen. He held a weapon ready and shot Peter in the back of the head, dissolving most of the skull down to the jawline. Sam jumped backwards off his chair, swiftly retrieving his weapon from the holster under his jacket as Luke fired, his weapon drawn fast, but not fast enough to hit the Guardian who disappeared as quickly and silently as he appeared.

Sam ran to the door to shout for the others as Luke stepped forward, looking at the ruined brain stump of the hapless technician.

Kyle, Michael, Nick and Drew came bursting through the door, their faces reflecting the shock found on Sam's.

"Who was it? Who did this?" Kyle demanded.

Luke looked up at his leader and shook his head. "It was a Guardian; however, I did not see any identification. His suit was clean. His visor was closed."

"Another Guardian? Another traitor that we missed out on?" Nick ran his hand from his hairline to his jaw, scrubbing it across his close-cropped beard. "Do you think he came from the ship?"

"Bardi would report if anyone was transported, but he has the ship in complete lockdown. No one, except we three, can come or go, not from the time we seized the traitors." Kyle tugged at his collar, his frustration overtaking his shock.

"There has to be another ship. Or another way they can beam out," Drew suggested.

"We would detect another ship. We have been monitoring the area very closely. I do not believe another ship could escape our notice," Kyle answered.

"That might be the case, exactly. With Simon

and your captain both traitors, maybe they were hiding something else, covering up for a ship, perhaps?" Drew glanced at Peter's body, grimaced, then turned away, opening a drawer and taking out a hand towel before draping it over the bloody ruin that had been a head. "Maybe, instead of a ship, they found another way to transport off your ship that bypasses your security? Like from a shuttle or something?"

Kyle turned to Luke. "Return to the ship. Find out. Do everything that you need to but find out who this was and how they did this."

Luke gave a short nod and touched his communication button on his collar, disappearing instantly.

"What do we do with him?" Nick pointed to Peter's corpse. "I don't think we can bury him in the garden."

Kyle pulled out his weapon from a concealed pocket on his leather-like jacket and touched a button on the side. He fired it at the corpse, and it disappeared, shimmering out of existence in a blast of yellow-white light. He turned the blast onto the blood and gore that had dripped and splattered around the kitchen, and it, too, disappeared. The chair, handcuffs and cable tie restraints remained, but the body was gone, all biological traces removed.

"That'll do it. Ah Peter, you silly boy. He was so scared of dying, and he didn't even see this coming." Nick looked over at Kyle as he returned his weapon to his jacket. "I guess you have quite a few of those types of gadgets to clean up all sorts of messes."

Kyle nodded, as Sam slapped his hand on the table.

"Guys! Look here at the viewer! The enemies are gone!" He sat in front of the viewer as the men gathered around him. Sam started moving the drone around, looking for the many black suited men. "They couldn't have gotten too far; we weren't away from the screen for that long."

Nick pulled the chair out beside Sam and sat down. "Clearly killing Peter was more than just a move to keep his mouth shut, they were trying to distract us as well."

"Move the module closer to the ground, check for footmarks, there are too many Presas to walk off without leaving any trace," Kyle instructed.

"There, you see that?" Nick pointed to the viewer. "There's the tracks, leading off that way."

Sam swung the drone closer and hovered it over the beaten track the Presas had left.

"Follow the tracks. See if you can find them." Kyle moved directly behind Sam to see the viewer better.

Within moments he found the army of black suited men marching in perfect rows, keeping perfect time with each other, arms close by their sides, not swinging with their movement as a normal man would walk.

"Where are they going?" Michael asked. "They are not headed to the caves, nor are they headed here."

"Thank god for that," Drew said. "Is there a way this thing can extrapolate their possible destination?"

Michael touched the viewer and a smaller panel opened on the bottom, showing a red dotted line leading towards the highway. "The line predicts where they may go, however they could change direction at any time. I see the highway; however, I cannot see where they may be headed."

"Is Angie still in her little cave, I wonder? Should I send the other drones to check?" Sam asked.

"We can now transport a viewer there, now that we have found who was tracing them." Kyle nodded to Michael, and Nick vacated the chair next to Sam so the Guardian could sit. Within moments he had transported a flyer to the little cave opening and sent the other drone to the house the Presas had just vacated. Using both hands he maneuvered one flyer into the cave where Angie had been and moved the other around the house to peer into the various rooms, checking for any movement, and perhaps the rogue Guardian.

The module at the cave flew quickly through until it reached the chamber where the woman had been asleep earlier, but now seemed to be empty. Michael moved it all around until they could see a person size mound in the rugs, and a twist around of the module showed a mop of blind curly hair poking out from one end of the rugs.

"I have considered that the adjustments made to the controls by Peter may be detrimental to Angie's well-being," Kyle said. "Now that the module is in such close proximity, can you tell if they are functioning correctly, or if there is some action that we need to take?"

Michael reached over for Peter's data pad and tapped on it. Frowning, he handed it to Kyle and moved the module a little closer to the Dahn, from this angle the top of her face could be seen, her eyes closed, her hair twirled around and over the blanket.

"Peter increased the controls; he has more than doubled their output. Instead of closing some down, he has increased them to the point that Angie will not heal for some time, these will have her healing slower than a human." Kyle frowned and tapped on the pad. "I am reversing the command. It seems I can use his same program to take them down to their previous level, then I shall lower them until they are at a better rate for her to heal. I feel it would be better if she was up and around, rather than asleep and therefore vulnerable."

"It's starting to get dark; I wonder where these Presas are headed? Don't they need some kind of light to see where they are going?" Sam asked.

"They do not need any illumination, and will continue regardless of weather or temperature, until they reach their destination," Michael explained. "They are relentless and impervious to any discomfort a normal living being would experience."

"The levels are at the lowest I feel comfortable having them." Kyle sat the data pad down and looked back at the viewer. There was no change in Angie, it was only the slow movement of her breathing that showed she was alive. "Leave the flyer where it is for now, and we can monitor if anything changes with her."

Drew's cell phone rang, making him jump at the sudden unexpected sound. He answered the phone, moving to the next room to speak. He talked for a few minutes before returning to his small kitchen. "It seems the vampire we saw escape has been busy. That was my office, they've found two bodies that have extensive neck trauma and exsanguination behind the local high school. I need to attend, being the sheriff. Nick, Sam, both, or either of you like to ride along?"

"We have more pressing things here to attend to than a vampire attack, Sheriff. Perhaps someone else could look into what is going on?" Kyle asked. "I can organize a clean-up team to remove all traces of the vampire and the victims if required."

"I want to confirm that it is a vampire, and if it is, I want to know if it's the one that we let out, or if it's a new one. We saw the blood being taken from the vampire the rogue Guardian was holding in that house. If he is making more monsters, we need to know were, and when. It may help us figure out who the traitor is. Maybe even find some CCTV footage. I can be there and back within a half hour, an hour at the most," Drew explained. "I can go alone, or I can take the detectives with me and speed things up a bit."

"Or you could ask me to help you." An oily

smooth voice spoke from behind the men, causing them all to turn, with Drew, Kyle and Nick drawing their weapons as they turned.

There, at the kitchen door, stood the vampire that had fled the Presas' house. He was standing in the shadow of the alcove, his eyes half lidded against the harsh kitchen lights. He was wearing a long black coat that was buttoned from his waist to high at the neck and wore black jeans and shoes underneath.

"No need for weapons, gentlemen. I am not here to harm any of you."

No one lowered their weapons.

"I assure you, there will be no need for your weapons. I have no intentions of attempting to hurt anyone."

Nick looked at the vampire, his calm demeanor and human-like, casual pose was unlike any vampire he had seen.

"You're different to the blood suckers we normally dispose of."

"Yes, that's right. I am not like any other of the creatures you have murdered. I was like them, at the start, but I have matured, evolved, if you will. I am the first, *her* first. I guess it makes me superior to all of the others."

"Why are you here?" Nick asked, his police issue revolver pointed at the creature's head. "You could have just run and hid, so why here, with the people who take great joy in destroying all of your kind that we can find?"

The vampire tilted his head a little, a move very

similar to that of Angie's. "I am here to help you."

"Why would you help us?" Drew demanded. "It's not like you owe us for your escape."

"No, that was something I managed all by myself, though it did take some time before I was able to execute my plan."

"From what I saw that was a bit of a pantser, there was no plan, you just acted when you saw the opportunity." Nick gave a short nod to his gun. "So, I'm asking you again, slime ball, why are you here?"

The creature sighed. "I am going to help you. All of you are fighting to protect the one who made me, the one I am beholden to. I cannot defeat the silent men, nor the traitors who help them, on my own. I need your help, and in turn, you need mine."

"*Beholden to*? What is this, a crummy romance novel? Seriously, no one talks like that." Nick took a step forward, his gun now much closer to the vampire's temple.

"I do, occasionally, though I never quite fancied myself the romantic in my life before. Now, I find that the word suits the life I have now. Or unlife, if you will. But I digress. I *am* here to help you, and I can tell you where the thing that took my blood has been. I can smell him, and my blood. I also have a connection to anyone that has been turned, whether they are a vampire or something else. You could use my help. And by helping you, I am keeping the one who made me safe."

Nick looked back at Drew and Kyle. He raised an eyebrow in query, and both Kyle and Drew nodded. He turned back to the vampire and holstered his gun.

"Okay, we work together, but let me tell you, if you so much as sniff our necks I will end you. Understand?"

The vampire smiled, a wide, cold, reptilian gesture that revealed his whiter than white teeth, the tips of his fangs spilling just below his lips before he closed his mouth. "That will not happen, Detective Cotter. Or should I call you Nick?"

"How do you know my name?"

"Know thine enemy. I know all of your names, the humans, at least. I do not know the names of the leather clad men, though they do present the same scent as the one who captured me. I am Artu, the first."

"The first? What do you mean by that? You said it before, *her first*," Kyle asked, his weapon still drawn.

"I am the first one to be touched by her blood that did not die, instead I not only survived, I changed. Others were changed after me, or made, but I am her first. She trusts me. She relies on me. In turn, she protects me. Now it is up to me to protect her."

Drew put his gun in his holster and grabbed his jacket from the back of one of the chairs. "Okay, I think, if you really can help us and sniff out the other vampires, and the Guardian who is making them, then we can use that kind of help. If everyone agrees with me, let's go. I'm driving."

"Fine by me," Nick looked back at Sam. "You

hold down the fort with Kyle and Michael, we'll be back as soon as possible."

Drew followed Artu outside and unlocked the car.

"You sit in the passenger seat," Nick told the vampire. "I'll be sitting behind you with my gun at your head. One wrong move and it's over."

"Of course. However, you will find that I am no threat to you. At least, not right now."

True to his word, Nick held his gun at the base of Artu's neck for the short journey to the back of the high school.

"What's with the black clothes?" Nick asked as Drew drove the car. "First the Guardians, and those Presas, now you, all clad head to toe in black. I'm feeling like there is some weird dress code that someone forgot to tell me about."

Artu didn't answer, and they drove the rest of the way in silence. The daylight had completely faded, and in the darkness the flashing lights from the patrol cars lit up the street and reflected off the school buildings. There were three portable flood lights set up around the crime scene, and Drew pulled up beside the police tape and turned off his motor. "Listen to me, vampire," he said as he turned to the creature. "You will stay right by Detective Cotter's side. You will not speak, you will not touch anything, you will not engage with anyone in any way."

Artu nodded, a smile dancing across his thin lips. "Aye aye, sir."

Artu walked beside Nick as instructed, his long

black coat flowing in the cold night air, lending him an air of an old-world movie villain. Drew approached his fellow officers as Nick walked over to the victims, Artu by his side.

The bodies of two high school aged kids lay on the cold asphalt, their heads twisted at strange angles from their bodies. There was no blood around them, none other than a small stain around their torn throats, their skin pale and lifeless under the bright lights. Nick turned to the vampire.

"Can you smell anything?"

"Detective, I can smell literally everything. However, to distinguish the individual signature of these kills I need to get a little closer. May I?"

Nick looked around, then placed a hand under his jacket, fingers resting on his revolver. "Okay, make it fast. And like the sheriff said, do not touch *anything*."

Artu dropped to one knee and leaned over the bodies, his head almost touching them. He sniffed one, then the other, before standing again.

"I have the scent. This was done by one vampire, a new creature, I have not felt this one before."

"Can you track it?"

"Of course I can. I can also feel what it is feeling, and a little of what it is thinking."

"If you could do that why did you need to sniff them?"

Artu snarled, a low growl emitting from his throat. Nick took a step back, the malevolence of that growl sent shivers up his spine and prickled cold sweat in his armpits. His fingers clutched his revolver, one finger on the trigger. "Back off, Dracula. I know bullets won't kill you, but they'll slow you down enough for me to take off your head, and I think a shot through the temple will hurt like hell."

Artu closed his eyes for a moment, as if regaining his composure. "I am not like a vampire from fiction, Detective. I have not been in close contact with humans since I became what I am. At least, none that I left standing. I am fighting my natural instincts every moment you are near me. Making irrelevant or sarcastic comments irritates me and makes it more difficult to refrain from tearing your throat out."

"If you try anything, at least one of us will bring you down before you so much as twitch." Drew stepped away from his officers after seeing Nick's reaction. "We are not like normal humans; I can assure you."

The vampire tipped his head to one side, his nostrils flared. "I can sense that. You smell like *her*. I can sense her strength in you, too." He shook his head, as if to gain clarity. "I can track the thing that took my blood, that made the new vampires, by this scent. I assumed you understood that's why I came here with you."

"So, what now? We put a leash on you like a bloodhound and follow you to the things?" Nick had not taken his hand off his gun.

"That may not be the best possible option. Enhanced or not, you would not be able to keep up with me. I will be in contact when I can tell you something."

"Hold on there a minute. I'm not sure we want to let you off and running without supervision. It's not like we allow vampires free range amongst the population." Drew felt his hands creeping towards his own gun, noticing that Nick was still clutching his. "Also, how will you get in touch with us if you find anything?"

"There is a secret vampire method, one known only to those of great power, this ancient wisdom. It's called a cell phone. If you give me your number, I can call you when I find something."

Nick snorted derisively and pulled out his phone. "Give me your number and I'll message you ours."

Artu gave Nick the number then tipped his head slightly, almost with respect. "If I find him first, I may just take my pleasure before calling you."

"That's fine with us, and let me assure you, this will be the only time we give you free reign on attacking anyone or anything, but don't kill him. We need him alive if we're to get to the bottom of all this." Drew leaned forward a little to emphasize his words. "Only him, Artu. No one else. Understand?"

The vampire opened his mouth wide, showing off his white, perfect teeth. A set of slim, wickedly sharp fangs lipped out of his gums, overlaying the teeth and extending at least an inch and a half from both the top and bottom of his mouth. Both men took a step back, the malevolence radiating from the monster was palpable, they could feel the evil almost dripping from him.

Shutting his mouth closed with an audible snap he grinned, a dark, mocking grimace, and was gone. He moved so quickly that he blurred into the night, the action silent, and so much faster than any other vampire they had hunted.

"Fuck me. If he wanted to take one, or both of us down, there isn't a thing we could've done," Nick gasped.

"I think I nearly soiled my boxers," Drew agreed. "The guys here have everything under control, let's get back to my place."

Chapter Forty-Four
Trauiss III
The Nursery
A Long Time Ago
Bountiful, Stable, and Safe

As the days passed the child did not speak very much, only doing so when she needed to. As soon as the brothers would return to the nursery of an evening, she would excitedly greet them, and either Robert or James would swing her up on their shoulders, a giggle their reward. Elund would come by most evenings on his way home, just to observe the little family he had put together. He was pleased with the bond they were forming; the progress that they were making to bring the child out of her shell was what he had hoped for, and what they were achieving.

They took the child with them into the training rooms, teaching her simple fighting styles and weapon use. Her formal training in dance and acrobatics helped her with her fighting skills, and as the weeks turned to months she became as skilled as a child her size could become.

There were no more attacks on the facility, though the brothers never grew complacent. They continued to train every day, both themselves and their garrison, keeping their fitness levels at a premium.

They also grew younger, physically, more

muscular, and quite a bit taller. Living so close to the child afforded them all the benefits of her gifts, and in turn the child thrived on the attention. She spoke a little more, and after listening to Robert sing a rousing bar ditty one night she had also begun to sing. Her voice amazed the brothers, it was clear, pitched perfectly, and mesmerizingly beautiful. Elund immediately arranged for an instructor to bring out the best in the songbird.

Robert and James continued to live with the girl, watching her learn, develop and grow, and though everyone around her grew taller, she did not. Her strength did, though, and her powers became, at times, frightening. Each time she became more powerful, Elund would place more controls on her, and also inside her. To do this he would take her away to another part of the laboratory, the brothers guarding her every step. Elund would make them hold her down as he inserted the controls. It was a painful procedure that would see the happy child become withdrawn for several days as she recovered.

She matured slowly, very slowly, and it was not known if this was because of the controls, however it was not of any concern. There was no hurry, no agenda to the child maturing, and the time allowed not only the study of her powers, but the fine-tuning of the controls as well. The brothers had lived with her for nearly two centuries, and in that time, it was estimated that she had reached the equivalent of a twelve or thirteen-year-old human.

It was obvious to everyone that she was very

attached to the brothers, she called them by name, and at times had long conversations with them, discussing strategies and war craft, battles won and lost, the creatures they had fought, and the aliens who had been trying to defeat them for a millennia. The brothers told her about the wormhole that was at the entrance of their multiverse, and the black hole that formed the gate to the wormhole. They told her of the many smaller wormholes that were spread about the multiverse, how there were different universes through them that had very different beings, different timelines, places that lived a century their time, though no more than a year would pass outside of that universe.

They told her that her power had not only travelled throughout the universe they were in, allowing everyone who lived here to benefit from her special gifts, now the other universes were reporting the same wonderful effects. Their people lived longer, healthier; their planets became bountiful, stable, and safe.

They did not tell her that the one downside of these gifts was that no one had borne a child since she was born.

The only way any children were created was with the help of Elund, and his laboratory. This wasn't very successful, and for all of the inhabited worlds, all the many universes, there were only a handful of children created every year.

The child was smart, her intelligence assisted by a photographic and eidetic memory. She never forgot anything and could recall even the day of her birth. Everything she was taught, everything she heard, read, or experienced, were captured in her mind and never forgotten.

She enjoyed the stories the brothers told her, and before too long she started to ask the brothers about the other worlds and universes they had visited. While not expressing any desire to visit these far-off worlds, the brothers knew that a continued interest might soon spark a desire to do so.

She watched the brothers leave the nursery to patrol the grounds, though she had not asked to join them. As far as the brothers knew, she had not left the building before they were assigned here, and they were certain she had not left since they arrived. Elund had never spoken of the child ever leaving the facility, nor had her nursemaids or attending staff. It seemed that she had lived her entire life in the laboratory nursery, with occasional visits to the main part of the laboratory to manage her controls.

It was James that finally suggested that they take the child on one of their patrols around the outside of the building, and Robert agreed. Together they approached Elund with their idea, and the researcher seemed surprised at the thought of letting his little experiment leave the confines of her nursery.

It did not take much to convince Elund, after so much time together he trusted the brothers implicitly. Never one to allow fate to take a hand, he did double up on the normal patrols from the laboratory guards as a precaution.

Chapter Forty-Five
Earth
Drew's Kitchen
Present Day
Absolutely Yes

"So, we're trusting vampires now?" Sam shook his head at Nick and Drew. "I get why you went with him, but really, we have no guarantee he'll contact us if he finds the Guardian involved."

"He didn't have to come to us at all, Sam," Nick pulled a chair from the table and sat down. "Trust me, he could have killed us at any time and there isn't a thing we could have done about it. This monster isn't like anything we've seen before, he's faster, and a lot smarter. Once this is all over, we are going to need some serious help in getting rid of it."

"Getting rid of it will be our responsibility." Kyle looked grim. "All of the creatures that are created, and being created, will be taken care of. That one will be the first, and as soon as we are able to do so, it will be taken care of."

"Any change in the Presas?" Nick asked.

"They stopped about twenty minutes ago and are holding steady. I mean, literally stopped. Not a movement from them at all. Freaky bastards, these Presas," Sam shrugged. "I'm sure they're more robot than people, even though they kind of bleed."

"So now we wait." Kyle was standing, hands on

his hips, his large frame making the kitchen appear even smaller.

"Perhaps we can take care of the creature that killed the two people tonight?" Michael asked. "I am growing increasingly impatient, the longer I am inactive."

"Agreed, take out that one, and the others, they need to be cleared out immediately," Kyle said. "Take a team and report back once it is done. It will also be good to have the team on Earth ready in case these Presas make their move, or we hear back from the vampire."

Michael stood, then turned to Nick and Drew. "Would you like to accompany us? You would have to be in uniform, if you did."

Nick stood so fast he sent his chair tumbling. "Absolutely, yes! I mean, sure, that would be fine."

Drew shook his head. "Not me, maybe Sam could use a turn at getting out from my humble kitchen?"

Sam's grin threatened to spit his face in half. "Yes! Same as Nick, except with no unbridled excitement. I am in!" He jumped up and handed the seat over to Drew to monitor the viewers.

"We will hold down the fort until you get back." Drew gestured towards Kyle. "The boss and I will take care of business till then."

Kyle nodded, his face still displaying his grim expression. "If there are any changes, we will inform you."

Michael tapped his communications button and the three men disappeared.

Chapter Forty-Six
Trauiss III
The Nursery
A Long Time Ago
I Should Be Dead

"You are finished eating, child?" Robert fastened the collar of his uniform as the blonde-haired girl walked into the room.

She nodded, her expression turning to one of puzzlement as James walked in and handed her a cloak. "No training this morning," he told her as she pulled the cloak over her bare shoulders, he just walked past her to the exit door at the far end of the training room. The puzzled expression became complete confusion, though she turned to leave the brothers to their usual rounds.

"Girl, you have your cloak, do not dally!" James called to her, and she stopped, looking to Robert for direction.

"Are you coming?" Robert didn't smile, he just turned and walked to the door.

She stared at the men, open mouthed, not sure how to proceed.

James frowned at her. "Move, child! You are to follow direction when you are told."

They walked out of the door and stood to one side, waiting to see the child react as she entered the garden for the first time. They kept their expressions neutral, not wanting to influence her first reaction.

The day was warm, soft white clouds so high in the pale blue sky that they cast no shadow, the perfume of many flowers carried by the breeze to caress their senses.

She stood at the door, her eyes wide until they touched the brightness, this causing her to shrink back inside, eyes squinting closed. The nursemaid was right there, waiting with a pair of dark glasses to shield the sensitive purple eyes.

So adorned she moved forward, out of the door, stepping down to the smooth path, though one hand stayed on the door frame as if hesitant to let go of her sanctuary.

"Come," Robert prompted, and she stepped towards him. James turned to lead her along the path, through the gardens that surrounded the building and walked around the corner. He walked slowly, allowing her to take in her surroundings, as Robert followed her close behind. They took her around the building and up to the guards' quarters, and then showed her the lake, the parade grounds, the barracks and the armory. She walked with them, overwhelmed with the many sights, sounds, colors and textures of the outdoors.

"You may ask any questions you may have inside that head of yours," Robert spoke softly. "We will answer anything you want to know."

She looked up at him and nodded but did not speak.

They continued the patrol around the building, letting the child set the pace as she looked at everything, touched flowers, dangled her fingers in the waters of the ornamental ponds, and gasped as birds flew overhead.

As they drew close to the end of their patrol, having circumnavigated the entire building, they came upon a patrol of guards. The patrol team drew close to them and stopped to greet the brothers, formally, with a salute, as was the procedure.

James touched the child on her shoulder to bring her closer.

"This is Howell, Pater and Mollis, they are part of the battalion of guards that help to protect the laboratory."

Each man nodded at her as their name was spoken. James led the child on as Robert checked in with the men.

"Did Elund protest at your decision to bring her outside?" Howell asked him.

"Not at all," Robert replied. "He knows that we will keep her safe. We have the strongest and most highly trained guards in all the 'verse."

"That is correct!" laughed Pater. "How is the excursion going?"

"She has not spoken, but I believe that is because she is overwhelmed. If she were not wearing the dark glasses, I am sure her eyes would be the size of a cannon ball!"

"I have never seen her up close before, sir. She is so tiny." Mollis watched the girl lift a butterfly onto her finger. "What is her name?"

"She has not been given a name." Robert frowned at the man.

"You must call her something, do you not? Have you not called her a name just for you and James to use?"

"Mollis, mind your place," Pater cautioned. "Apologies, sir, we shall leave you to your patrol."

Pater turned to leave, but Mollis and Howell didn't follow. Mollis and Howell were moving towards the child, casually, slowly, not causing any alarm to the brothers. The guards wore full uniforms and carried all their regulation weapons, including a sword, a blaster, and a dagger.

Howell drew his dagger and plunged it into James' back as Mollis grabbed the child, his dagger dragging across her throat in a split second. Robert lunged at the men, one hand grabbing Mollis by the shirt as his other reached for Howell, but the man was too quick. Robert pulled Mollis hard and slammed his head into the path, taking a step towards Howell to chase him as a blaster fired, hitting the guard in the middle of the chest. Pater leapt onto Mollis as the guard struggled to get to his feet, Pater's hand at the guard's throat, holding him down as he pointed his blaster at the man's forehead.

Guards came running, before he could blink Robert was surrounded with guards that were lifting Mollis to his feet to strip him of his weapons, others called for help as they reached over James to render assistance and try to stem the bleeding.

Robert picked up the child, her throat so deeply cut that her head had nearly been severed. Her blood splashed over him as he held her close, knowing he had failed, knowing that the child he had grown so fond of was dead, the men that should have protected her had let her down.

He moved his arm to let her head fall back onto her neck and clutched her to his chest, nearly dropping her as she moved in his arms. One of her arms reached up and touched his face before dropping back, and Robert fell to his knees.

Medics rushed to him and grabbed the child, running with her to the laboratory. Robert couldn't think; this was all happening too fast. He stood and turned to his brother and was shocked to see him trying to struggle to his feet. He had seen the dagger slice deep into James' back; he couldn't understand how his brother was conscious, let alone attempting to stand.

Medics carefully transferred his brother to a stretcher and raced him to the laboratory, and Robert turned his attention to the traitorous guard. He was now shackled, his uniform torn open in places to check for any hidden threats. His arms were cuffed behind his back and guards stood at his sides, each holding an arm. Blood dripped down his forehead from where it had impacted the path.

Robert snarled. "Why? Why would you do this? You were trusted to protect her, this was the one thing you were charged to do, above all else, your main directive! Why? Answer me this before I tear your head from your shoulders!"

Mollis sneered at the warrior and spat a mouthful of blood at Robert's feet. "You near cracked my skull."

Robert stepped closer, his face almost touching the guard's. "Answer me, traitor."

Mollis grinned. "You did your job well. It has taken many decades for us to even see the child, let alone touch her. You kept her so close."

Robert gripped the front of Mollis' uniform and slammed his head into the guard's, sending his head backwards and splattering blood from a smashed nose. He would have fallen if he was not held so tightly by the guards at his side.

"Why did you do it?" Robert growled.

Mollis coughed, the rattle turning into a laugh. "You are all fools. All you see is the longer life, thinking you have it all. What's the use of living, no matter how long, if we cannot have children?" He spat a mouthful of blood onto the warrior's shirt. "My wife, my brothers' wives, all barren. All of us, all of the planets, are barren. Howell and I are not the only ones who feel this way. There are many. A great deal of us are not happy. We were not given a choice. No one thought to ask us if we were willing to pay such a high price for the chance to live longer."

Robert let go of the guard's shirt and turned away. "Take him to the main office. We need to find out who else is complicit."

"Will you be accompanying us, sir?" asked Pater.

"Not yet. I must go to see my brother first. Make sure this filth is secured. Make sure he cannot harm himself."

Robert ran to the infirmary, his concern for his

brother and the girl overwhelming. So many years, so many battles, and no one, no *thing*, had been able to strike his brother down.

And now, on this soft home world, to die at the hands of a traitor!

He slammed through the doors of the tall building, demanding to see his brother immediately. A young attendant led him quickly to a room and held the door as he rushed inside. His relief at seeing his brother alive caused him to pause, his face showing his confusion.

"I cannot believe it, brother! I should be dead, that fool cut my spine. I should be dead, or at least paralyzed, but look at me!" James was sitting up, his color was good, he looked as if he had not been injured at all. Apart from his anger at being taken unawares he was fine, and the treating physician said his injury was healing at an expediential rate.

Robert asked if the child had survived, but his request was met with silence. No one would comment, no one was willing to tell him anything about the child at all.

He sat by his brother's bed and waited until he was deemed well enough to be released from the medical ward, and they were told to wait in their rooms until further notice.

Chapter Forty-Seven
Earth's Orbit
The Alcea
Present Day
Pretending To Be Spacemen

Nick smiled at Sam. His partner had not been able to wipe the grin off his face since they had arrived on the ship, his excitement at being suited up in a Guardian's uniform clear for all to see. Elyse and Bardi had greeted them when they arrived, and Elyse helped fit them into their uniforms, making sure they remembered how to use the various functions.

"What do you think?" Sam turned to Nick and opened his arms to show off the tight-fitting black uniform. It fitted him as if it had been tailored especially for him, the matte black, leather like fabric did not reflect the light, only the dull silver studs and plates contrasting against the fabric. The mid-calf length boots were heavily buckled and plated with silver panels along the sides, heel and front, and matched the gloves that also had the dull plating over the knuckles. When Sam flexed his fingers, the plates split to show overlapping blades, a vicious fighting accessory. The high collar bore a communications button on one side, and a button on the other that allowed the helmet and visor to slide up from its hidden position on the back of the collar.

"I think you look the same as I do," Nick smiled.

"You mean like a spaceman?"

"I mean like two city cops, pretending to be spacemen."

"And doing a fantastic job of it!" A beaming dark-haired Guardian stepped into the room, his bright green eyes lighting up at the sight of his friends.

"Major Ayden Jacobs, it's very good to see you!" Nick exclaimed as the man grabbed him in a bear hug.

"We wondered where they were hiding you!" Sam added, as Ayden released Nick and grabbed the taller man.

"Good to see you both as well! And it's just Ayden now, guys. How's Drew? How's the sheriff holding up with everything that's been happening today?" Ayden let Sam go and stepped back.

"As well as can be expected. He knew Peter from the start, and I guess he feels his betrayal rather personally," Nick told him.

"As we all do, I guess." Ayden's grin had faded. "We were recruited at the same time; I can't believe that no one could see what was going on with him. I can't believe that I couldn't see it."

"Nor I," Sarah joined them, her Guardian uniform was grey, and had less silver plating. "Hi fellows, it's really good to see you both."

"Hi Sarah! You'll be joining us on the hunt? Fantastic!" Sam enthused.

"No, not me. I'm on ship's crew, bridge duty. I

love it, perfect assignment for me." She smiled fondly at both the detectives. "We are all feeling what Peter did rather personally. It's making us think about everything he said, everything he did, and worry about everyone he was hanging out with."

"Did you guys get any heat?" Nick asked.

Ayden shook his head. "No, thankfully they took us at our word. I think our absolute shock and dismay convinced them that we were both not complicit."

"I haven't been able to talk to Simon yet. I don't know if I can," Sarah added. "I guess I'll have to, at some stage, but right now I feel too much anger towards him to have any real conversation with him."

"I hear you." Nick hitched at the crotch of his suit. "Do you think this is a little tight?"

Elyse laughed and helped Nick adjust his suit until he was comfortable. Sam continued to smile as the group were joined by several more Guardians, all outfitted the same. Sam and Nick were handed weapons, and the group stood ready, waiting for Michael to rejoin them.

Sarah waited with them and chatted, filling the detectives in on her life at the academy and how much things had changed for her since they last saw her. Ayden joined in the conversation, impressing the men with his sightings of famous people that had been lost on Earth, but their deaths had been circumvented as they were taken to Trauiss.

Michael walked in, Luke by his side. The rest of

the Guardians, along with Ayden and Sarah, stood to attention, the detectives merely turned and faced them.

"Luke has not had any progress in identifying the final traitor," Michael announced. "Though, we are fairly sure that there is only one left to be found, we all need to remain vigilant. This betrayal needs to be stopped; this mutiny of our forces is completely unacceptable."

"The interrogations are continuing, and Trauiss has been contacted and advised of our progress," Luke added. "Even now they are rounding up the traitors that Peter was able to name, though he did not know many. We can only hope that they have success in their interrogations. I wish you all great success as you hunt the vermin on Earth and make ready to take on the Presas."

With a nod Michael took his place in front of his team, touching his collar to activate transport and they all vanished, leaving Sarah, Bardi and Luke alone in the bare white room.

Chapter Forty-Eight
Trauiss III
The Nursery
A Long Time Ago
It Is Decided

They waited a full day, then were summoned to the main laboratory. The brothers were surprised to find the Lords there waiting for them, both dropping to one knee in supplication as befitted their roles.

"Stand, fine warriors, and be not alarmed," the most senior Lord addressed them. "We have summoned you here to tell you of your new orders."

Elund and Xanya entered the room, and for once Elund looked grim.

"We will be transferring you back to the home world, and you will continue guard duties there," the Lord told them. "This is to happen immediately."

Robert looked at the Lord addressing them, his confusion showing on his face.

"You have a question, fine warrior?"

"If you would forgive me, Lord, I do."

"Please do go ahead."

"Who are we to guard, Lord?"

A murmur rippled through the gathering of robed Lords.

"Why were they not informed that the child survived?" one of the Lords addressed Elund.

"We had thought it best, my Lords, to discuss

things with yourselves before involving the warriors."

"The child survives?" James was astounded, his shock clear to the others in the room.

"I felt her move, though her head was near severed," Robert told them. "I did not believe anyone could survive, though my heart is gladdened to be told this."

"She has indeed survived, and is healing well," Elund informed them. "She has not spoken yet, but we feel that it will not be long before she can."

"We no longer feel she can be contained safely here on Trauiss Three, so we shall be moving her to the home world, and you will continue to perform your duties as you have been doing here," the senior Lord explained. "We will trial housing her in the same manner as she is accustomed, and that requires for you both to continue cohabitating with her." She nodded to one of her companions to continue the narrative.

"We have been very pleased with her containment, and her living arrangements. She has been very docile and controllable, and we believe that is because of the bond she has formed with the two of you. For a being as powerful as she, this is of the utmost importance," the Lord explained. "May we inquire as to what you call her?"

"She has no name," James answered.

"We are aware of this, however we wanted to know how you address her, by what name have you been calling her?"

"We do not have any name for her," Robert told

them. "We call her 'girl', or 'child', but not by any name."

The Lords spoke in hushed tones amongst themselves, then turned back to the brothers. "We would like you to choose a name for her, we feel this will strengthen the bond between you. She should also call you by name, and you will treat her as family. You will accompany her to the home world, and reside there in a purpose-built structure, currently under construction. There she will continue her education, her training, and though we will observe her, she will no longer be subject to intense study such as she has been until now."

Elund looked unhappy at this but did not protest. As far as Robert could tell, there had already been discussion, and Elund had not been pleased at the loss of his prized experiment.

"When will we be leaving?" Robert asked them.

"As soon as the child has healed sufficiently to travel. Elund?"

"At the rate she is recovering, I would estimate two to three days. Four at the very most."

"The structure we will be housing you in is not going to be completed for some weeks, however part of it will be habitable in less than a week. We can house you in the palace until the completion of the accommodation."

"So, it is decided," the senior lord continued. "You will accompany the girl to the home world as soon as she is well enough to travel. Until then, I want both of you to stand a bedside watch, make sure the child is safe until transfer. Understood?"

Chapter Forty-Nine
Earth
Present Day
Vampire Hunt

The woods around the town were thick, tall trees too close together with bracken and woody undergrowth preventing any sunlight during the day, and even less moonlight in the evening. It was a dark place, rich with heady, earthy scents, quiet songs from various insects and the occasional call from a night bird. The undergrowth rustled and moved, allowing a small family of rabbits to make their way through as they sought greener forage.

The night was cold, much colder here in the forest than the town, the canopy so dense that it prevented any warmth during the day to linger and warm the damp, dark places. Moss covered the tree trunks and various fungi scattered here and there over the fallen leaves and branches that covered the forest floor. There were paths through the forest, places that had been trampled down by forest creatures over many years as their hooves, pads or feet tracked a way to water, grazing, or a place to hunt.

It was this path that the vampire hurried down, though he didn't quite know where he was going. He was confused, his ears were ringing, his head thumping, and his heart, well, it didn't seem to be doing very much at all. He knew that what he was now was not what he was yesterday, and he knew it had something to do with the man in the leather looking outfit that grabbed him and forced that vile liquid, *was it blood? He thought it must have been blood,* down his throat.

He remembered falling to the ground, though he seemed to keep falling, falling so far, and so fast, for what seemed like a very long time. He didn't remember blacking out, didn't remember losing consciousness at all, but he remembered waking up in the forest and he was hungry. *So hungry.* It was like nothing he had ever felt before. His ears were ringing, the same as now, and his head was playing a drum beat so hard he felt it would soon split open, but that was nothing compared to the hunger. He was laying on his back in the dark forest, yet he could see everything as clear as day. Not only could he see everything, he could hear everything, the creeping insects on the ground, the rodents scurrying about, even the birds that slept in the trees. And smell… he could quite literally smell *everything*. Everything had its own scent, and he knew them all. From the smallest fungi to the largest tree, from the insect crawling on his leg to the owl far above him on the highest branch. He smelled it all.

He could even smell the people that were walking to their cars, opening the car doors and stepping inside. He had stood, slowly, unsteady at first, and took a moment to clear his head. He was maybe a half mile from the edge of town, and he knew the people were maybe another half mile in, but he could smell them, even hear them. He started for the town, running swiftly, knowing exactly where he was going. He had not remembered his own name, but he remembered the town, he remembered the high school, and he knew that's where the people were.

He did not think rationally anymore, he just knew the hunger.

Nothing but the hunger.

He had found the school, found the people, instinctively crouching low, hiding, until there was only one person left. The second person came running as he tore out the throat of the first and he had held that man down with one hand as he drained the first person, then turned to the second and tore the throat out of that one. He heard a third person, another potential meal, but his hunger, for now, was sated. He turned and melted off into the street as the other person approached, the screams piercing his sensitive ears and making him run.

Running was good, he was swift, he was fast, and he was very quiet. The blood he had just consumed had made him stronger, warmer, more vibrant. He felt like he could run all night.

He had made it back into the forest, but then became confused. He sat down for a little while, trying to get his thoughts in order, trying to stop his head spinning and thumping, trying to remember who he was.

Who he was.

That was the question that he couldn't answer. He had no memory of himself before the man grabbing him, oh, there were vague, shadowy images, a half-formed thought and an almost spoken phrase, but that was all. He tried to think about it for a while, but only became more confused as any last rational thought danced far away from his grasp.

He heard the sirens, the people talking, though they were too far away for him to understand what they were saying. He didn't know if he would understand them if he could hear them, but he did know he didn't care.

He started walking then, just slowly, trying to fight through the confusion that jumbled his thoughts and twisted his brain into a miasmic mess.

The forest was large, it led right up to the mountains ahead, not that he could see them, but he could smell them. He knew what they were, he knew how high they reached, and how many people lived between here and there. He knew exactly how to track them, and how to rip them apart and devour their fleshy parts. His mouth watered at the thought of it and he felt his new, sharp, deadly fangs slip from their slits in his gums at the thought of warm flesh to tear.

He started to walk faster, even though he wasn't as hungry, he could not think of anything other than tasting some hapless human, or perhaps many humans. If he could remember how to whistle, he would have, his mood lightened at the thought of his future carnage, the confusion that had concerned him so greatly earlier disappeared.

He could hear the stream that trickled beside the path as it meandered down to the larger lake on the other side of the town, he could even hear the fish that swam along with the current. He knew, if he was ever hungry enough, that he could catch these fish and make a small, though unsatisfying, meal. Right now, though, he could only think of the scent of humans that drifted towards him upon the smoke of their wood fueled fires. He would eat again, tonight, and he would eat well. He would enjoy every scream, every panicked grasp for life, and he would revel in the panic, and would dine in ecstasy.

He didn't remember what had made him happy before he was changed into this creature, but he knew exactly what would make him happy now, and he could barely wait. His strode quickly along the path, his nostrils constantly testing the air for the tantalizing scent of his next meal.

As he rounded a bend on the damp, mossy park he was shocked at a group of people standing there, he had not picked up their scent before now, but his confusion over that faded quickly. He stopped and looked at the people who stood facing him. The night was very dark, the rain had stopped but the heavy cloud cover kept any moonlight from filtering through the heavy forest canopy, and the path was completely shrouded within shrubs and trees. There was no light at all, but that didn't hinder his vampire eyes, their ability to cut through the darkness something that he accepted without question. The people could not possibly see him even though they were all facing his way.

No person could see in this total blackness.

He felt his face smile, and the new, sharp fangs slid down from his gums. This would be fun. There were several men standing there, *wait a minute*, several men and *women*. He was salivating, already feeling how their flesh would taste. A low growl escaped him, and he paused to see how they reacted to the menacing noise.

They didn't move. They didn't speak. He thought they were frozen in terror, though he could not smell the fear on them. He didn't stop to think about that, though it would make killing them more enjoyable, he didn't really care what they felt. He just wanted to kill them all, tear them apart and eat and drink as much as he could. It was only when one of the men lifted his arm and pointed a weapon at him that he realized they were all wearing the same clothes.

That would not have been so unusual, he did remember uniforms for certain factions of the public, but these outfits were not sporting or school uniforms. He tilted his head a little. The people were wearing exactly the same black leather outfit as the man who had forced him to swallow that stuff that had made him this way, that had turned him into a vampire.

He didn't have time for any thought after that.

The weapon discharged.

The bolt of light was silent, the burning, bright light flashed quickly, too fast for him to react. The beam disintegrated his flesh on contact, but only his flesh. His clothes hovered for a moment, empty, still holding the shape of the vampire that had worn them.

Within a split second a body appeared, an exact

copy of the vampire, filling his clothes before they hit the ground. The blood and gore that coated the clothes was intact, all the evidence the police would need to solve the bloody murders, though a motive would be lacking.

"That was kind of awesome!" Sam's grin couldn't be seen through his helmet, but it was obvious in his enthusiastic declaration.

"I never tire of it." Michael nodded to the body lying on the path. "That is an exact replica of the vampire before he turned, while he was still human. We need to find the rest. This one was exactly where the vampire said he would be. Has he checked in again?"

Nick pulled his cell from a concealed pocket on his tight-fitting uniform and checked it. "He sure has. He's found another vampire over on the other side of town. He's even given us the coordinates."

"Then let us be away. This does make hunting these filthy creatures so much easier, but I am still uncomfortable working with the vampire," Michael sighed.

"If it finds the traitor Guardian, it'll be worth it," Sam assured him. "Then we can take him out in a little cloud of dust like this one."

"Yes, you can, Detective, yes you can." Michael touched his collar and the team disappeared.

Chapter Fifty
Trauiss Prime
The Nursery
A Long Time Ago
She Is So Smart!

Jasmine scented breeze wafted through the marble columns as the last purple and red fingers of the sunset caressed the ornate carvings that adorned the palace walls. Bird song graced the ears of the brothers as they walked the gardens, shoulder to shoulder, the warmth of the setting sun no longer warming them as they completed their rounds.

Pinks, purples and brilliant golds of many flowers graced the edges of the stone paths, though Robert appreciated their beauty he had no idea of their names, or even how many different varieties were planted there. His expression, mirrored by his brother, was stoic, and his stride purposeful. They maintained an air of strength and discipline, an intimidating visage that deterred any of the palace staff from approaching them. A squeal of delight from the child they were following did not make them smile, they did not break their stride nor acknowledge her joy in any way.

"Did you see, Robert, James, did you see?" Her white hair reflected the sunset in a tousle of purple curls as she scooped up the black cat in her arms. "I taught her that trick, and you saw, did you? She did it! She caught the little branch I threw and came back with it in her mouth! She is so smart!"

The warriors stopped before the girl, and Robert snarled as the lithe feline climbed on the girl's shoulder, its tail circling her neck.

"You did see it, did you not?"

"Yes, Faer, we saw the trick. Again. Your animal is very clever." James motioned the girl to continue on the path towards her quarters. "The night is attempting to beat us to our door, let the cat take her leave as we return to your chambers."

She turned and walked ahead of them, the cat still perched on her shoulder. It looked back at the brothers as they followed, and Robert was sure it was mocking them as it peered at them, the bright green of its eyes half lidded as if in contempt. He had not been in favor of the girl adopting the cat, the first thing he thought of when the scrawny black fluff of a kitten was handed to the girl was to take that thing to the stables and give it a quick end. James was supportive of the thought of a pet, and the two of them wore him down very quickly. He was no longer against the cat, in fact he found it gave the girl a sense of connection, a grounding, that she did not have before.

The cat often rode on the girl's shoulders, it slept with her, bathed with her, and even rode upon horses with her. Robert had not seen the cat leave her side since it was placed in her hands. He knew there would be an issue when they attended the reception for the Lords of the Many Planets but trusted the girl's obedience when he would tell her that the cat was unable to accompany them.

Chapter Fifty-One
Earth
Present Day
Sue and the Girls

Sue pulled at the collar of her jacket to pop it up, hoping it would stop the rain from seeping down her neck. Bobby was such a douche bag! She couldn't believe he had dumped her out of his car just because she wouldn't go all the way with him! For god's sake it was only their third date. And she knew that most girls gave in on the third date, but not her.

No way, Sue had decided to wait until at least the fifth date.

She wanted a decent present, maybe flowers and chocolates, and a meal at a good restaurant. Not Bugsy's, or Burger Palace, or a diner where you ordered at the counter, she wanted a real sit-down nice place with a menu and a waiter. And cutlery already on the table, and real fabric napkins.

If Bobby had just taken her to a nice place tonight, he may have gotten a bit luckier, but a drive through burger and coke meant he wasn't getting past second base.

Now here she was, turfed out into the freezing night, ankle deep in last fall's autumn leaves and the rain deciding to pick this very minute to start drizzling down. This sucked. This sucked big time.

She already called Margaret to come and get her,

and thankfully she had agreed. Sue wasn't real happy that Sandy and Linda would be in the car as well, she thought maybe they'd have a good laugh at her predicament, but if she had to put up with a few jibes it would still be better than walking through these cold dark woods in the rain, in the dark, and on her own!

The path was covered in leaves, and in the darkness, it was hard to see where the path led. She was using her cell phone as a light, worried that it would die before the girls got here, but too scared to turn it off and save the battery.

Bobby had chosen a dark corner of the park to turn his car down, then drove further into the woods so they would not be disturbed. She hadn't minded at the time, but now that she was forced to walk back Sue wished she'd told him to stop at the edge of the woods, at least there were some streetlamps around the park, and no deep soggy leaves to trudge through.

Her new suede wedges would be totally ruined.

She stopped to tug at her collar again when she heard a noise. It wasn't much of a noise, but it sounded louder than the rain hitting the wet leaves.

Well, it is the forest, anything could be lurking around, she thought.

She started walking again and was sure this time that she could hear something, someone, maybe, following her. The steps were almost in time with hers, and even though she was sure that whatever or whoever it was tried to be quiet, she could still hear the occasional crunch as the drier leaves underneath the wet ones gave way.

Her heart started to thrum in her chest, and she walked faster, much faster, until she was almost running. It was too dark and too slippery to go too fast, but she still near jogged towards the park. The steps behind her kept pace, and Sue felt the cold grip of fear tighten inside of her.

Then a growl, soft, very quiet and low, then she heard another growl.

She started to run, her high wedge soled shoes no match for the slippery path, the fall rain making it an even more difficult surface to traverse.

She slipped.

Sue went head first, screaming as she slipped, her hands out in front of herself like a superman trying to take off, and for a moment she thought she could escape landing on the ground, but her feet failed to gain purchase and she fell, slapping down into the piles of mud and wet leaves, her phone flying off to the side of the path.

For a moment she lay still, stunned, then rolled to her side and spat out a mouthful of putrid wet leaves.

I'm going to throw up, she thought, and scrubbed a hand across her muddy face.

The sound of the footsteps following her stopped, and for a moment Sue forgot about them as she lifted herself up, brushing the mud and muck from her clothes, gently picking twigs and leaves from her bloodied, scraped knees.

The sound of a crunched twig made her gasp and jump to her feet, nearly stumbling again as her shoe, broken at the heel strap, twisted and bounced as she ran.

Sue ran fast, her shoe flapping from the ankle strap on one foot, the other lost altogether, as something chased her from behind.

It got closer, she could hear the crunch and slap of the steps from whoever followed her as a light from in front suddenly blinded her.

Margaret's car!

Sue ran into the headlights as the car stopped, her friends stunned at the sight of Sue, soaking wet, covered in mud and blood dripping from her chin and knees, her face contorted in fear racing towards them.

"Is that Sue? WTF!" Margie gasped. "Grab something to wrap her in, I don't want that crap in my car!"

"OMG, what the heck happened?" Sandy grabbed a blanket from the back seat, Linda sitting there with her mouth open, her eyes wide and fearful.

"Look!" Linda squealed. "There's something behind her!"

The three girls could see something come up behind Sue, something large.

Sue still stumbled towards the car, her tears streaming down her face with relief. Sandy grabbed her door handle to open it as Margie placed a hand on her knee.

"Wait, Sandy, there's something weird happening."

Sandy leaned forward, trying to get a better view

of the thing behind her friend. "It's a dog, Margie. Just a dog!"

"Didn't the Butlers lose their golden retriever in the woods this morning?" Linda asked. "I bet it's just their dog!"

"That's not a dog," Margie gulped.

The thing behind Sue had moved a little closer, and as Sue stumbled to one side the three girls in the car could see it clearly.

It was no dog.

It was large, much larger than a golden retriever pup, and it was dark. The sleek, almost black, wet fur glistened in the light from the car, as the thing stepped closer to Sue. The body rippled with lithe muscles, and the head was weaving, a heavy, cruelly fanged wedge of a wolf like snout swaying back and forth in the light as it walked. It snarled; a growl so loud that the girls in the car could hear it.

Sue turned to face the creature and froze at the sight of it. The deep-set green eyes glowed and it growled louder, saliva dripping from the sharp fangs.

Sue's bladder released, and she screamed.

The three girls in the car screamed too as the wolf creature rocked back on its haunches, poised to strike.

"*RUN*!" Linda had opened her door and stepped from the car. "Run, Sue, run!"

Sue ran.

She made it to the front of the car when the creature leapt, and the girls watched in horror as it seemed to sail in slow motion, legs stretched out in front as it flew through the air, turning its head to one side, jaws agape.

Those jaws clamped down on Sue's shoulder, and it carried her with it as it crashed into the car, the huge paws denting the hood as its claws dug deep furrows in the metal. The girls screamed, Linda falling backwards onto the ground as the car jolted, and the thing, the wolf creature, tore Sue's shoulder away, her arm hanging loose in the thing's mouth.

Linda scrambled to her feet and joined her friends' screams as Sue somehow sat up, blood spurting from the gaping hole in her body, her eyes wide, and her mouth moving, but no sound came out. The wolf thing shook the shoulder from its mouth and grabbed Sue again, slamming her down onto the hood and holding her there with one paw as it ripped her chest open, the cruel fangs tearing through her clothes, her skin, her ribs. The thing looked up then, turning its head to the girls in the car.

They screamed louder, Linda climbing back into the car as she screamed, slamming the door behind her.

The wolf thing threw its head back and howled. A long, loud, and blood curdling sound that made the girls scream even more.

Incredibly, Sue was moving, her free arm beat weakly at the paw holding her down, her heels drumming on the hood of the car as her mouth still moved, as if she were trying to speak. The thing finished its howl and stared at the three girls in the car, then turned and bit into Sue, into her chest, and grabbed a mouthful of her organs. The girls could see her blood spouting forth, her sinews and muscles still attached to her chest as the wolf thing chewed and bit into her again.

Sue stopped moving, her body only jerking as the creature burrowed inside her, his bloodied snout seeking her fleshy insides to devour.

"Start the car!" Sandy slapped Margie on the arm. "Start the fucking car! Reverse, Margie, *get us the fuck out of here!*"

Margie was frozen in her seat, her hands gripping the wheel, her eyes rooted on the thing on the front of her car as it tore chunks out of her friend and ate them.

"Start the fucking car!" Sandy was frantic, but she couldn't get through to her friend.

Linda leaned forward and slapped the side of Margie's face as hard as she could, breaking the girl from her stupor.

Margaret pressed the ignition button and the car started; she slammed it into reverse, gunning the accelerator. She didn't look back as the car jumped into motion.

The wolf thing slipped from the hood, Sue's body still underneath it.

The car didn't travel far, without looking behind her Margie had sent them speeding rearward into the path of a tree and the car hit with a spectacular crash.

All three girls were flung through the back window, the broken glass cutting and slicing their flesh, the landing breaking their bones.

The wolf had regained his feet and the crash startled him a little, he cautiously moved forward to see where the tantalizing scent of blood was originating from. He sniffed the air as he moved towards the back of the car, Sue's body discarded as the scent of warm flesh drew him close.

Margie had been thrown to the rear of the car, her legs tangled in the thick underbrush of the forest, her vision obscured by the blood that poured from a gash on her head. She was momentarily confused, unsure of where she was, of what was happening.

She heard a crunch of twigs, and a frightening growl, and everything came flooding back to her in a rush. Margaret gasped and wiped her eyes, the darkness complete, the headlights of the car no longer illuminating the night.

She felt hot breath on the back of her neck, a stinking, fetid smell of blood and death, and closed her eyes as the creature's jaws closed around her head, and she knew no more.

The air crackled and zapped with static electricity as several leather clad men appeared, their helmets drawn and visors closed. The wolf had enough time to leap over the car and face the men, a growl escaping his rough snout as one man raised his weapon and fired at the creature.

The shot hit the animal in the head, and it dropped him, stone dead, in an instant.

The scruffy wolf carcass devolved from its shape, transforming back into the body of a young man, naked, his skin wet and pale.

The men walked over to the creature, making sure it was dead, before checking Sue's body.

"Poor girl did suffer before dying," Michael said and he used his bio blaster to disintegrate her remains, another body reappearing almost instantly, with arm intact.

"We will have to make it look like she was killed in the crash," Ayden explained to the detectives as he opened his visor. "Same with the boy. You two check if anyone else was hurt."

Nick moved to the back of the car.

"Hey guys, I got two bodies here."

Sam leant down to check each one. "These two are dead. Nick, check that girl, there, see? There's another body."

The girl groaned as Nick touched her but did not regain consciousness.

Ayden hurried over and scanned her with his small data pad.

"She's hurt, but not so badly that she'll lose her life. We can make a call to emergency services and get her help."

"Won't she say something about wolfie boy there?" Sam gestured towards the dead body the Guardians had placed with the other deceased women.

"You think anyone will believe a woman that survived a tragic car accident that killed all of her friends and left her with a severe concussion?" Nick asked him, then pulled out his cell as it pinged an announcement of a new message.

"We are done here," Michael said as he moved closer to the detectives. "Do you have news from the vampire?"

"Looks like. Seems there is another vampire sighting. He's given me the coordinates." Nick put his cell phone back into his jacket and closed his visor. He joined the Guardians, Sam by his side.

Behind the car, over on the side, where she had been thrown, Linda gasped and rubbed her eyes as the men in the black leather uniforms disappeared.

Chapter Fifty-Two
Trauiss Prime
The Nursery
A Long Time Ago
I Said No

"I despise these formal functions." James tugged at the collar of his dress uniform. "We should have been informed that we would be obliged to attend many of these such occasions before we accepted this duty."

"It would make no difference." Robert reached over and straightened his brother's collar. "We would do as we were ordered, regardless of how many functions we were to attend."

"You like to look at the ladies." The girl bounced ahead of them, her formal gown, while made of the most luxurious fabric available, was a simple design, and unadorned with embellishments. Her white hair was twisted into a simple knot at her neck, and she wore no adornment in the modest coiffure. "And they like to look at you, too."

James tugged at her hair in a mock reprimand and she giggled, her bright green eyes dancing from one brother to the other. They had been pleasantly surprised that she had accepted their order to leave the cat at home, and they didn't question where the cat was now. It was unusual for it to not be at her side or riding her shoulders. Robert smiled and draped a cloak over her shoulders and opened the heavy doors, the night greeting them with brightly colored lights and lanterns, festive music and distant voices filled the air, the brothers nodded at the guards that waited to escort them to the main palace. The long hall between the child's quarters and main building would normally be used, but for this occasion they were required to walk around the outside to the main entrance.

The girl smiled at the guards, but they remained stony faced, falling into line in front, beside, and behind the trio as they led them to the front of the Glass Palace of the Trauiss empire. The girl had been very well schooled on how to behave, her excitable nature was now tempered, and she seemed calm as she walked serenely along the path with her guards. Robert knew she would be bursting with the desire to skip along the path, to sing with joy and marvel at the lights, the music, the performers, and the many dignitaries and royalty that now milled about the lavish front entrance to the palace.

Her tutors had been stringent in their lessons with the girl, ensuring she followed the strict etiquette and customs of the empire. She understood duty and obligation from living with the brothers, never questioning why she lived the way she did, nor why she was expected to attend these formal functions. She behaved exactly as she was expected to, every time, every day, every function, every occasion. She never rebelled, was never willful, never rude, never disobedient. The brothers would like to have taken credit for her behavior, but they knew that the girl could have acted like any other teenager, should she wish to.

The music grew louder as they approached the main entrance, and the guards in front of the trio parted to let Robert and James lead the girl towards the crowd. Their approach triggered a change in the music, becoming more formal, a military style march trumpeting the arrival of the girl.

The crowd parted to let them through, the performers stilled their dancing and juggling, the fire breathers doused their flames as people stood with reverence to watch the special girl enter the palace. The girl walked serenely, head high, her faithful warrior guardians to each side.

As she stepped into the grand entrance the guards that had accompanied her fell back, lining each side of the opulent foyer. Robert and James stayed by her side, as they would the entire evening. The trio entered the grand ballroom, the most luxurious room in the palace, though the lavish decor was not new to the trio as this was not their first formal function. They walked across the marble floor, the gold inlays reflecting the many chandeliers, the crystals throwing their sprays of iridescent rainbows around the room like dazzling fireflies.

When she reached the far end of the massive ballroom the girl paused and turned, facing the crowd that had followed her at a respectful distance. An aide moved forward to remove the Faer's cloak, slipping it off and retreating quietly.

A gasp from the aide caused Robert to glance sideways, and he groaned.

"What is that?" hissed James from the other side.

"This is totally unacceptable!" Robert hissed back as the girl stood, stately and silent, completely ignoring the lithe black cat that was draped over her shoulders, its long tail gently weaving back and forth across the girl's chest.

The music changed tempo and the crowd again parted, letting the procession of Lords enter the ballroom. The Senior Lord led the way, her thick black cowl draped over her head, the other Lords attired in deep red robes, their cowls also drawn over their heads. They made their way to the end of the room, passing the girl and her guardians and stepping up to their seats, the long table on the dais decorated with draped silks, flowers and foliage.

The Lords stood in front of their banquet table and the music ceased.

"My esteemed guests," the Senior Lord addressed the crowd. "We wish, firstly, to thank you, not only for accepting our invitation for our Futures conference, but to travel from your worlds and 'verses to grace us with your venerable company. Over the next three days we will explore all of our options, plan our future, and engineer a future for our multiverse. Together we will move into that future with a clear and fruitful plan, ensuring our utilization of our most valuable asset.

"Before we feast and celebrate, I would like to introduce the asset, the product of many millennia of research, trials and hard work. I present to you The Dahn Ah M'Hoth, the future of the Trauiss multiverse."

As she had rehearsed, the girl stepped forward and curtseyed low, her head bowed, her hands spread wide, palms down. The crowd applauded, then a murmur and gasps as the cat stood up, stretched, and wrapped itself back around the shoulders of the girl.

Faer stood and turned to face the Lords, again curtseying, the cat again standing as its host moved beneath it. Robert knew the Lords noticed the feline, and though they didn't react he could feel the hairs on the back of his neck rise as he felt their gaze upon him.

The child turned and stood, dignified, the cat draped over her shoulders like a fur stole.

"My esteemed guests, please, take your seats and enjoy the feast that our bountiful harvest has produced. We shall have music, and entertainment, as you eat. Tonight is a celebration, tomorrow we begin our deliberations!" The Senior Lord turned, led the rest of the Lords around the table and they sat, their cowls lifted and dropped to reveal their faces. The crowd made their way to the tables that lined each side of the ballroom.

Robert and James turned and flanked the girl as she moved to her place, standing behind the Senior Lord as the food was served.

The warriors stood, arms behind their backs, faces stern, their black uniforms adorned with their many medals and accreditations.

"May I ask you, boy, to explain what the hell that is on the girl?"

The Senior Lord did not turn, but it was clear she was talking to the guardians.

James cleared his throat, but Robert was the one to answer.

"It was not there when I put the cloak on her."

"*It was not there when I put the cloak on her.* What is that to do with anything? It is clearly there now. Remove it. At once."

"No." The girl spoke quietly, but the word stopped the Lords instantly. The Senior Lord turned her head to look at the girl.

"What do you mean?"

The girl blinked, slowly, her face expressionless. "I wish the cat to stay."

The Senior Lord turned back to her meal. "Take the creature. Now."

"I said no." The girl still spoke quietly, but this time her tone was more determined.

"Girl, this is not the time to choose defiance." Robert spoke in a hushed tone, desperate to diffuse the situation. "I will have an aide take the cat to your chambers. We can discuss this later."

"No." She reached up and caressed the cat's head. "The cat stays with me."

"Take it." The Senior Lord waved her fork at Robert. "Take the damn thing out of here."

Robert stepped in front of the girl and reached for the cat, but something in her face stilled his hands midair. Her eyes, always larger than normal, seemed to grow in size. The green lenses that protected her sensitive purple eyes from light now sparkled with violet streaks, bright and dangerous.

Robert felt his skin prickle with static electricity and could tell James felt it too. Though they had faced many dangers in their lives, fought many creatures, won many battles, both men felt the visceral grip of fear at the power starting to radiate from this little girl. The Lords had stopped eating, though had not turned to see what was happening.

"I must take the cat, child, but I will not harm it. I will ensure it is safe and sound, waiting for you in your chamber."

"I said NO." The girl's hair was now loose from its restraint, the soft curls were moving as if they were alive, and her hands were clenched in fists. The cat started to react to the moment, standing up and hissing at the warrior.

"Stop!" The Senior Lord tried to keep her voice low, she did not want to alarm the guests. "Take the girl and return to your chambers. We will discuss this tomorrow. Leave now and take the internal passageway. I will not have her paraded in front of everyone in this state."

Chapter Fifty-Three
Earth
Present Day
A Girl

The cave was warm, silent, and completely safe. She would not have chosen it if it was not safe. The second opening was small, so small that she had to wriggle to get in, and she had carefully placed lots of twigs, rustly dry leaves and broken seashells in the larger opening chamber so that anyone trying to climb in would be heard long before they got to the second, smaller opening. She found the cave ages ago, not the first time Mom had dropped her at aunty Vikki's, not the second, not even the third. She hadn't needed them then; she hadn't needed to run and hide and find a place to be safe at first.

In fact, coming to aunty Vikki's had been safer than when she stayed with Mom, and she had enjoyed coming there. No need to worry about any of Mom's new boyfriends wanting to play with a pretty little girl, no need to escape their slimy grasp, no need to hide from their stinky breath and groping advances.

Aunty Vikki wasn't very good at being a responsible adult, but she was kind, and she didn't ever beat her when she ran out of alcohol, or even when she'd had too much alcohol. Aunty Vikki didn't mind if she was gone all day and didn't nag her to take a bath or clean the house.

There was always food in the icebox and clean sheets on the bed, and her fluffy old cat, while he could be mean, liked the occasional cuddle, and he slept on her bed at night, his loud purr a calming and comforting sound.

No, she hadn't needed the cave then, hadn't needed to escape, hadn't needed to keep herself safe. Life had been very good then, well, as good as she had ever known. She had been happy and exploring the local beaches with the fluffy cat following her was about as good a life as she needed.

She had never been to school, never been to a doctor, or dentist. Born on the rug on her grandmother's floor, she had been raised by the old woman, with the occasional ministrations of her mom, until the old lady drank herself to death. That's when Mom took over her full-time care but being a full-time mom was more work than the woman was capable of, and it interfered with her drinking and partying lifestyle.

Having a child around did get her sympathy, though, and when the time came for handouts and grifting, the child with the large, sad eyes could be quite an asset.

When her mom needed a break from her barest amount of responsibility, she dumped the hapless child on Aunty Vikki, sometimes not picking her up for many months. The girl didn't mind. She liked it here. She even liked Aunty Vikki, just a little.

But then her mom had been in a car accident. Knowing her mom, she had probably been driving drunk, or a passenger with someone who was driving drunk, the girl didn't know, and didn't really care. She just knew her life had turned bad then, and bad had then turned to worse. Mom may be in a wheelchair, but that didn't stop her partying, drugs or drinking, only now she had Aunty Vikki joining her. Once again, the girl had to fight to survive, had to dodge the groping hands, the spiked drinks, the sleazy attentions of the many men that graced the lives of her mom and Vikki.

The cave had been a lucky find, though she often wondered if maybe the day she followed the fluffy cat onto the sandstone cliff face the cat knew exactly what it was doing as it led her around the boulders and prickly tufted grasses into the dark opening of the cave. The cat seemed to be very comfortable in the caves and the girl was sure he had been there before.

Every time she escaped to the safe haven the cat followed her, and it stayed with her until she decided to go back to Aunty Vikki's. She never called it home. The girl had never had a home. Even Grandma's place had not been a home, and Mom never stayed anywhere long enough to feel like it was somewhere she belonged. The cave was probably the closest thing to somewhere she could feel at home, but it was just a cave.

A cave stocked with plenty of water and what food she could find, a warm blanket and a few pillows, and things that meant something to her. A picture book, though she had never learned to read, a stuffed toy or two, a few empty bottles that had a pleasing shape or color, and an old, shabby brooch that her grandma had owned. She kept that, not because it reminded her of her grandma, but because it was shaped like an angel. She had never been to church, had never read the bible, but she was fascinated by the little winged woman on the brooch. Grandma had once told her that an angel watched over her, and not really understanding the metaphor she believed there was an actual angel, and that it looked exactly like the shabby dime store brooch.

She didn't understand why the angel watched, though, and why it didn't do anything. All this time it watched as she was hit, kicked, had cigarettes burned into her, starved, ridiculed, abused and molested, this angel had watched. Grandma had never explained why the angel watched, but the girl could not wait until she finally met the angel to ask her.

Stretching, the girl yawned and ruffled the cat's fur, the feline turned and hissed at her before escaping through the small opening. The girl pulled her blanket up to cover her pillow and pulled on her shoes. She was out of food and needed to pee, and maybe a change of clothes was a good idea. She sniffed her underarm.

Definitely a good idea.

She moved to the narrow entrance and wriggled through, surprised that the cat was still waiting for her. Normally it would meet her outside the cave, especially when he was in a bad mood. This time he sat and looked at the tiny opening on the other side of the entrance chamber, a hole high up in the side of the cave, and so small that the girl didn't think even the cat could fit through. That cat looked at the girl then leapt up to the hole, slipping his lithe body through with a bit of a twist and turn.

The girl was confused, the cat had never gone into that tiny cave before, and there was no way she could follow him. Her need to pee turned her back to the other entrance and she climbed through, lifting herself onto the ledge then onto the top of the cliff, the tough grass giving her plenty of purchase to make the rather scary reach a lot safer than it looked.

It was getting dark outside, the girl felt her stomach growl and figured it must be around dinner time, though she had been in the cave since the night before and knew that she had not been missed. She was never missed.

She moved herself across until she was a good arm's reach from the cliff, squatting to relieve herself, then started her traverse towards Aunt Vikki's house. She stopped when she got to the rickety front gate. The white picket fence had seen better days, and those better days would have been many years ago. The paint had peeled, and a lot of the pickets had split in the harsh ocean air, but the gate always worked, the rusty spring snapping it shut behind everyone who walked through it.

Today, though, the gate lay in a pile of broken pickets and torn wire on the ground, half the picket fence had been pushed over, and it was splashed with something that looked an awful lot like blood.

The girl felt her heart beat a little faster, she couldn't hear anything coming from inside the house, and with the trashed front fence she could only imagine that something bad had happened. The cottage was set far back off the road, so she couldn't imagine that a car had driven through the front, and there were no tire marks anywhere. Her underarms prickled with a frightened sweat when she noticed that the cottage was dark and silent. Even when the power went out, and it often went out, the house was never dark, and absolutely never silent. There were always dozens of candles and hurricane lamps around to light the darkness when the power blew, and Aunty Vikki had more than one battery operated radio. She liked to have music playing all day long, even after she went to bed.

Her mom and Vikki both had loud voices, and they were always talking, singing to the radio, or arguing with each other. If they had company, and more often than not they had company, there would be loud, usually drunk, masculine voices added to the cacophony. Tonight, though, tonight it was silent.

She stepped over the broken fence and tiptoed towards the front door, her heart beating so loud that she could hear nothing else.

The screen door had been torn from its hinges, it lay to one side of the door in a twisted heap. The front door was not completely ajar, but it was open just a little, the darkness inside velvety black. The girl's heart was racing now, she was close to panic as she stepped closer to the door.

"Aunty Vikki? Mom?" Her voice was hoarse, shaken, like she was in a dream and couldn't yell for help. "Mom? Mommy?"

The door creaked as it opened a little, though she could not see the hand that pushed the door.

"Mommy? Are you inside?" Her voice was small, and she felt like a little child, much smaller than she was. Her mother had never been one for comforting the girl if she was sick, scared or sad, that had been Grandma's job, but right now the girl would have been happy for a slap over the face and a scolding for being emotional. She felt a hot tear fall from her eye as she reached to push the door over enough to enter.

The fluffy cat jumped up on the step that was in front of her and hissed at the open door. The girl had not realized that the cat had caught up to her, but instead of feeling comforted by his presence, his arched back and growling hiss was raising her fear levels even more. There was a sound, a strange sound, suddenly behind her. It was almost like the ruffle of a bird's wings. The girl didn't turn, instead she took another step close to the door.

"Stop."

The voice came from behind her, and she started at the sudden voice. It was a woman's voice, but not her mom's, and not Aunty Vikki's.

"Stop," the voice repeated, and the girl took a step backwards and turned to see who was behind her. As she turned, a hand snaked out from the darkened house and grabbed her outstretched arm by the wrist, the grip tight, hard, and it jerked her towards the house. The cat screamed and backed up, its fearful yowls and screams frightening the girl to a blind panic. She lost her footing and would have been pulled inside had not the woman stepped forward and taken hold of the hand that grasped her. The hand was strong, so strong, and it hurt. It hurt so bad! The girl cried out, and this seemed to spur the woman to hasty action. She grabbed the strong arm further down the wrist with her other arm and snapped it with an audible crack, the hand immediately released the girl and she stumbled, falling towards the path.

Quicker than anything the girl had ever witnessed, the woman caught her, lifting her and holding her up as the other pulled the offending arm, bringing its owner out of the house and flinging them on the ground, but not letting go of the arm she held. The girl started to cry as the woman placed a foot on the back of the person on the ground, holding the squirming man down, but he swiveled his head sideways allowing the girl to see his face.

Maybe it was the failing daylight, maybe it was her fear and shock, but he looked like he had fangs, like a dog, or like the cat, but not like a normal man. His face was covered with something, maybe ketchup, and he was hissing and growling like a crazy thing.

The woman let go of the girl and pressed harder with her foot, the sound of cracking and crunching bones was a sickening sound, and the man started to scream. His scream was guttural, more angry than painful, and the girl clamped her hands to her ears, her breath rapid and light, she was going into shock.

The woman still had hold of the man's arm, it was bent back at a strange angle, one that the girl was sure a normal arm should not be able to bend, and when the woman let it go she realized it was broken, flopping loosely as it fell to the ground.

Before she had a chance to think, a group of people appeared like some kind of strange magic, where there had been no one, now there were all these people wearing black shiny clothes, all dressed the same, all wearing helmets with black visors. The girl wanted to scream, wanted to scream so loud, but she couldn't, she felt lightheaded and cold, and had started to shake.

The distraction of the people appearing had allowed the man to scramble to his knees, but the woman didn't let him go, she grabbed his head and twisted it, hard, all the way around like an owl. The girl stared at the woman, this woman who saved her, who was so strong she could twist people's heads near all the way off, and sat down abruptly, her legs giving way, and spots started to appear in front of her eyes.

"The girl is going into shock," she heard someone say, and a person stepped over to her, and bent down to one knee. With a touch to the side of their head the girl saw the helmet fold back into itself and vanish into the back collar of the shiny black jacket, revealing a pretty lady.

"Hi, I'm Sarah. What's your name?"

The girl looked at her, her wide eyes blinking rapidly.

"I need to give you something to stop you breathing so fast. It's like medicine. You've had medicine before, right?"

The girl shook her head.

"Well, this won't hurt. I just need to touch your arm with it." The lady had a shiny pen thing and she touched it to the girl's arm. She was right, it didn't hurt, but within seconds she felt her breath slow down, and the spots disappeared from her vision. Her heart was calming, and the lady, Sarah, helped her to her feet. She looked around at everyone, they were all watching her, and she felt her fear returning. Sarah still had one hand on her shoulder and gave it a reassuring squeeze.

"What is your name, honey?" she asked again.

"G... Girl."

"Your name is Girl?"

The girl nodded.

The man on the ground growled and started to move. One of the people in the black clothes gave a signal to the others, and someone aimed a gun at the man and shot him. Only it wasn't a gun, not really, it shot bright blue light, and the man disappeared. As quickly as he disappeared, he reappeared, this time he was still, quiet, and his head wasn't bent at a strange angle anymore.

The man in a black suit, that was at the front of the others, turned and looked at the woman who had saved the girl.

He touched his helmet and it all folded up the

same way that Sarah's did.

"Angie," he said, and the woman gave a tiny nod. "You saved the girl."

The girl looked at the woman as she disappeared, this time there was no mistaking the sound of ruffled feathers. The girl turned to look up at Sarah.

"I know her!" she gasped.

"You do, honey?" Sarah frowned. "How do you know her, Girl?"

Girl smiled. "She is my angel, the one who watches over me."

Chapter Fifty-Four
Trauiss Prime
The Nursery
A Long Time Ago
His Brother Was Right

No one spoke as they walked briskly through the long hallway that led to their quarters. Robert was relieved that the static had dissipated, the girl's eyes no longer flashed with violet light, and the cat had gone back to sleep on her master's shoulders. They walked silently, swiftly, not speaking until the door to their accommodation was closed and bolted behind them.

"What, in my soul's name, was that?" demanded James, his anger tempered a little by the fear he had experienced in the great hall. "If you felt the need to defy us, why would you choose a night such as this to do it? I am at a loss, Faer, a loss!"

The girl stood before the warriors, her head bowed in supplication. Gone was the defiance, though the cat still wrapped itself around her shoulders.

"My girl, can you not explain yourself?" Robert spoke softer than his brother, while he felt as angry as James, he felt it best to hold his temper in check while he tried to discover the reasoning behind the girl's behavior.

She didn't answer, and after a moment Robert realized that he could see her tears falling to the floor. Her shoulders moved in a silent sob, so he stepped forward and scooped her into his arms. "Now, girl, do not cry. Do not be distressed. Do not cry."

James looked at him, one brow raised in query, but Robert shook his head as answer. He lifted the girl gently in his arms and carried her to her chamber, instructing her to take her gown off and go to bed. Kissing her on the top of the head he closed the door, leaving her to her cat and her own thoughts.

"Why did you not admonish her?" James threw his hands up in frustration. "Are you not setting a dangerous precedent?"

"I do not think so, brother. In my heart, I do not think she meant to defy us. I believe she was not able to control her emotions."

"You are being serious with me?"

Robert nodded. "Yes, I am. I feel she is changing, I can feel it, and I am sure you do, too. I think she is entering puberty."

"Oh," James frowned. "Oh.'

"She may need her controls adjusted, or something to help her with the transition. What she does not need is those that she loves the most making her feel she is wrong."

"Or dangerous. Because she is, isn't she, Robert?" James unbuttoned his stiff dress jacket. "I felt it, and so did you. That power was unlike anything she has ever displayed before. There is a very real, and very dangerous power in that girl, and we do not know what will happen should she lose her temper."

Robert met James' eyes and knew that his brother was right.

Chapter Fifty-Five
Earth
Present Day
Zoey Grace

"This is a mess. Poor women didn't stand a chance, one morbidly obese and the other wheelchair bound. Man, I hate vampires." Sam turned to Ayden. "I'm just glad this one is gone. Seems whoever is the asshat that is making all these extra monsters knew it would keep us distracted."

"I wonder if they knew it would also bring Angie out of hiding?" Ayden looked thoughtful. "This could be exactly what they had planned."

Nick joined the two men in the darkened house, the bodies of the women left exactly where the vampire had killed them, though their wounds had been altered so as not to look like they had been bitten by an evil creature. He carefully stepped over the blood and broken glass, and handed his cell to Sam.

"The girl's birth was never recorded. She has no history of schooling, no medical records, nothing. Looks like the kid was dragged up, not raised, and as far as Drew can find she has no living relatives apart from an elderly great uncle, who has dementia, and lives in specialized aged care."

Michael leaned in the front door. "We are finished here. We need to do something with the child."

The detectives followed Ayden out to the front of the small bungalow, the darkness had engulfed the day and everything that the tiny porch light didn't reach was pitch black. The girl stood by Sarah, her eyes still large with fear, but she was calmer than before, and no longer looked like she would pass out.

Sam filled Michael in on the girl's status, then turned his attention back to the child.

She was frail looking, pale, skinny, very unkempt. It was hard to tell how old she was, her face looked wise, but her stature was tiny, not much bigger than maybe a five or six-year-old.

"Girl, that's your name, right, it's Girl?" he asked her, as he squatted down so as not to be so intimidating. The girl moved behind Sarah, clearly not trusting him at all.

"Girl, this is Sam. He's my friend, and he's also a police officer, a detective. Do you know what that is?" Sarah asked her.

The girl shook her head.

"It means he is a special policeman, a very important one. He is a good man, and you can trust him, okay?"

Girl nodded.

"I wondered, um, Girl, do you know how old you are? Or when your birthday is?"

Girl shook her head.

"I'd bet she doesn't even know *what* a birthday is." Nick joined the trio. "Poor kid doesn't look like she's ever had anything nice in her life, let alone a birthday party."

"Grandma said I came from the Easter Bunny." The girl looked up to Sarah for assurance.

"Grandma? You have a grandmother?" Sarah asked.

"She died." The small voice grew even softer.

"Drew said the maternal grandmother passed away three years ago. Liver failure. There's nothing else much on her." Nick gave a grim smile. "I can get him to call child services."

The girl reached into her pocket and pulled out the angel brooch, holding it out for them to see. Sarah took it and smiled reassuringly at the girl before turning it over. "It has an engraving. Zoey Grace, March twenty fifth, and a year. It makes her six years old, if this is Zoey. Girl, did your grandma ever call you Zoey?"

The waif nodded, tears forming in the big brown eyes.

"Not allowed," she said.

"You're not allowed to say? Or you are not allowed to tell anyone your name?" Nick stood and shook his head. "You weren't allowed to have a name, is that right?"

The girl nodded, tears now falling freely down her face. Sarah bent now and handed her back the brooch. She gave the child a hug, though the child stiffened, unsure, clearly not used to the affection.

The ruffle of unseen wings behind them made everyone turn, the Guardians standing to attention, their right fist thumping their left shoulder in salute.

Angie stood there, a cotton sack in her hand, her head tipped to one side as she looked at the child.

"You came back!" exclaimed the girl, her face lighting up.

Angie nodded, then looked up at Sarah, then Michael.

"The child is alone." She spoke quietly, though her voice was clear, strong, the soft accent lilting her words.

"Yes, she is alone," Michael confirmed. "The detectives will arrange for care."

Angie shook her head. "No. Take her. I will take her."

Michael opened his mouth to reply, but Angie raised her hand to silence him. She reached over and placed her hand on the child's head and they both disappeared, the rush of the unseen wings the only sound that heralded their departure.

"I hate it when she does that," Sam muttered behind them, and Nick couldn't help but smile. Just seeing his Angie, even for such a short amount of time, lifted his spirits and sent his soul soaring with joy.

Chapter Fifty-Six
Trauiss Prime
The Nursery
A Long Time Ago
Now We Worry

The Lords had summoned the brothers to their informal room early, before dawn, and listened as Robert explained his theory. They didn't speak, but clearly were worried by what they had just heard. They dismissed the warriors to wait in the ante room as they discussed their plans, then summoned the brothers to return.

The Senior Lord spread her fingers on the long tabletop and leaned forward to emphasize her words. Robert and James stood at attention in front of the Lords as was befitting their status, and they looked alert and stern, as they had been trained to do so many years ago.

"We have decided, for the duration of the conference, that the Dahn shall stay confined to her chambers. She is not to leave for any reason, unless accompanied by yourselves and only for assessment. We have decided that we shall have her assessed by Elund and his team, who are, as we speak, on their way here. If they can treat her and improve her controls, the matter may end there. If they cannot, then we will have to explore ways to contain and control her, so that we remain safe while still receiving the rewards her powers have afforded us. For now, at least, you are to remain with her as she is assessed and treated. Should we need to alter these arrangements, we trust you will be cooperative, and that you have not grown too fond of this girl to ignore our instructions?"

Robert and James snapped their heels together and gave a short nod, the military movement for acquiesce.

"At any time should you see her display any atypical behavior, or any displays of defiance, power, or anything you deem to be out of the ordinary, you are to report it to us immediately. Is that understood?"

"Yes, My Lords." The brothers spoke as one.

"Elund will attend your quarters within the hour. You are dismissed."

The girl was finishing her morning meal when the brothers returned. She no longer required a nursemaid, and often made her own meals in the mornings as the brothers prepared for the day. The cat was nowhere to be seen, and no one mentioned the feline, nor its absence.

Faer looked up at the men as they entered the room, her expression worried, as she dropped her food back onto the plate.

"You have a music lesson this morning, is that correct?" Robert picked up a piece of bread and took a large bite.

Faer nodded. "Yes, in an hour and a half."

"Get changed. There is time for fitness training. James and I will tutor you. Be prepared to work hard!"

She nodded, hurrying off obediently. James raised a brow to his brother in query but didn't voice his concern.

The brothers did indeed work the girl hard, and she took it all without complaint. She was strong, much more so than both the brothers combined, and she rarely tired. James made her lift heavy weights, Robert concentrating more on her suppleness and balance. The girl was lithe, nimble, she could effortlessly cartwheel and backflip across the large training room, stopping on one hand, her feet stretched towards the ceiling as she maintained the single handstand, her balance perfect. From this position she triple-flipped and landed on the other hand, then leapt backwards onto her feet as the sound of applause startled the trio.

Elund and his team were standing on the mezzanine viewing platform.

"How long have they been observing us?" hissed Robert.

"I am not aware, but it matters not." James gave the team a short nod. "They will do what they do, regardless of our actions."

"This I believe." Robert offered a nod to Elund as well. He turned to the girl. "Faer, please go and make yourself ready for your lesson."

She ran to the door, not acknowledging the researchers in any way. Robert knew she must be confused and worried, they had not discussed any consequences as yet for her behavior the night before. The girl was not stupid, she would realize that such defiance would carry severe consequences.

"You may join us, if you please, in the main room?" Robert called up to the team as he and his brother made their way through the same door as the girl had taken.

"Now we worry." James voiced Robert's thoughts exactly.

Freshly showered, hair still damp, the girl sat at the piano with her music teacher, as she played the most intricate symphony. She played well, her fingers dancing over the keys, her tempo and timing expressing the emotion and depth of the symphony, her skill on the keyboard clearly impressing all those watching her.

Elund and the four researchers that accompanied him stood back, silently watching, occasionally one or the other would tap into a data pad.

The researchers followed the trio around for the entire day, watching them as they guarded Faer at her strategy lesson, weapons training, and her formal literacy and scholarly lessons. They stood back, quiet and unobtrusive, but their presence was nonetheless felt. The girl was perfectly behaved, no signs of defiance, no signs of her previous anger, and no signs of the cat. Occasionally Robert and James exchanged worried glances, but they did not voice their concerns out loud.

The team followed the girl and her guardians for the entire day, not taking a break to eat or rest. It was only at the time for their evening meal that the team stepped forward, informing the brothers that they would join them to eat.

"You are aware we prepare our own meals?" James asked them.

Elund smiled. "We would be honored to partake of your efforts."

"You may not feel such a way once you have partaken," James told them, and Elund laughed as James turned to busy himself with helping Robert and Faer as they prepared a meal for everyone.

Chapter Fifty-Seven
Earth
Drew's Kitchen
Present Day
She Is My Angel

Drew nearly fell from his chair as Angie appeared in his small kitchen, her customary feathery announcement adding to his fright.

"Angie!" Kyle leapt to his feet, his face beaming with excitement. "We did not expect you to wake this soon!"

Angie looked at him, no emotion showing on her face, her larger than normal bright green eyes glowing in the dark kitchen.

"It is very good that you came back. The Presas are here, not too far away. We need to get you home, where you are safe."

She blinked, very slowly, and tilted her head to one side, as if trying to understand what he was saying. Kyle sighed, his frustration at the change and distance in his leader was beginning to get to him.

"I guess this is the girl Nick told us about?" Drew was trying to help but didn't want to scare the strange woman away again. He stood but stayed on his side of the table.

Angie nodded, not speaking.

"She has no family, Angie, no one to look after her." Drew opened his hands, trying to show he was no threat, nothing to spook her. "We can find her a place to live, someone to look after her."

Angie shook her head. "No."

Kyle frowned. "No?"

"We can have her." Angie moved behind the child, her hands now on the tiny girl's shoulders. "We can look after her."

"What do you mean?" Drew asked, and Kyle raised his hand a little behind him, signaling to Drew that he understood what was implied here.

"Yes, we can, Angie. We can take the girl…"

"Zoey," Angie corrected, the name sounding exotic with her accent accentuating the syllables.

"Zoey, okay, I understand. We can take the girl with us to Trauiss. You can take her there, and make sure she is safe."

"She is my angel!" Zoey spoke, her face animated at the proclamation. "She watches over me and keeps me safe!"

The men looked at the little girl, their surprise at the child's certainty clear in their expressions.

"Yes, I guess she must seem that way," Drew agreed.

"She really is. I know it! My grandma said an angel is watching over me, and she was! She saved me today when the bad man grabbed me. She saved me!"

Angie lifted the child onto her hip, the grubby little girl clinging close to the diminutive woman, seeking safety and solace in the protective grasp of her savior.

"We can all go to the ship now, where you both

will be safe. Is that okay, Angie? Will you come with me?"

Angie nodded, but did not speak. Kyle turned to Drew.

"Please inform the others of this situation," he said, before turning back to face Angie as he touched his collar. "Saskia, the Dahn and I are ready to be transported. There is also a female minor accompanying us."

Kyle and Angie disappeared without any noise, without any of the characteristic sound of rustling feathers that usually accompanied the departure of the white-haired woman. Drew stood for a moment, stunned by the sudden turn of events, before he picked up his cell and called the detectives.

Chapter Fifty-Eight
Trauiss Prime
The Nursery
A Long Time Ago
That May Change

"This is a very tasty meal, I must say," one of Elund's team commented. None of the researchers had been introduced to the brothers or the girl, and Robert did not ask her name now.

"Thank you. We have improved our cuisine immensely since Faer had lessons with the palace chefs."

"Wonderful!" Elund exclaimed. "It seems her education is extensive and well rounded. Tell me, girl, do you enjoy cooking?"

Faer's hand stopped, her fork poised in front of her mouth. She looked frightened, unsure what to do or say. She looked at Robert, and he gave her a reassuring smile.

"You should answer, Faer, it is okay. Please be honest in what you say, you may answer exactly how you feel."

The girl nodded. "I make sure every meal is prepared exactly as I was taught."

"Every time?" the researcher asked. "You prepare every meal exactly the same way, every single time?"

"Yes, as I have been instructed."

"What about when you play music, or dance, or

do acrobatics? Do you ever deviate from what you have been shown?" Elund asked, his eyebrows raised with curiosity.

"I do exactly as I have been shown." Faer's eyes flicked to her guardian brothers, then back to the researcher. "I do only what is asked of me. I do not deviate, I do not exceed, unless it is asked of me."

Elund looked at each of his team, making brief eye contact with each before putting his fork down and pushing his plate aside. He tented his fingers in front of him, elbows resting on the table.

"I feel we should perhaps change that." His expression was neutral, his voice even. "Starting tomorrow, I would like you to use some initiative. Be creative. Exceed. Do more than is asked. Also," he placed his hands flat on the table, palms down, "I believe you have a pet. A cat, I am told. Where is this creature?"

Faer looked at her guardians, her expression openly fearful and worried. Both the brothers maintained their neutral expression, not wanting to frighten the girl, or worse, trigger another incident.

"That sounds like an excellent idea." James stood and began to gather the plates. "Robert and I will clear up here, and girl, you should prepare for bed."

"The cat? I trust you are not avoiding the question?"

Robert cleared his throat. "The cat comes and goes as it pleases, as cats do. I am sure you will see it when it is hungry. Or when it pleases."

"Indeed. We will see you all in the morning."

Elund beckoned his team to follow him. "I, for one, am looking forward to seeing how creative the girl can be." He smiled at the brothers, then followed his team to the door.

"Oh, before I forget," Elund turned back to the brothers, "the name you gave her, *Faer*, is rather unusual. May I ask why you named her that?"

Robert sighed and looked at his feet for a moment, before looking back at the team.

"It was our mother's name. Her given name, before she came here."

"Perhaps a little sentimental, however I do not have any issues with your choice." Elund turned back to the door before pausing, turning back to face Robert. "I do not have any issues, for now. That may change."

James waited until the door closed behind the team before turning to his brother. "For now? What do you suppose that means? And why do they want her to show more initiative? Are we not meant to keep her under control?"

"I feel they want to see just how much control we can maintain once Faer starts to test her boundaries. Perhaps they are trying to trigger her reactions."

James looked thoughtful. "We cannot warn the girl, can we?"

"No brother, we cannot. We can only pray that she keeps a level head about her and does not lose control."

Chapter Fifty-Nine
Earth
Drew's Kitchen
Present Day
Precious Treasures

"The child will be very loved; she will never want for anything again," Michael assured the detectives. "As Peter told you, we cannot bear children, so any child that comes to our world is greatly appreciated and treated as the precious treasures that they are."

"That's reassuring, I guess. And in some ways, rather worrying. Do you take children from Earth very often?" Nick asked.

Michael sighed. "No, we don't. This is a very different circumstance than we normally discover, as you can imagine. Our directive is to keep children where they belong, where they are with their culture and species. It is a very complicated process, and is, of course, a highly emotional one."

"I get that, but can't you just, like, do that body swapping thing with sick babies?" Sam asked.

"There are more than enough people to populate our worlds, and as we have such a long life, not everyone wants to have children," Michael explained. "Some are happy to pursue their life's dreams, a career, or their artistic desires. Myself, I have no desire for children. I do not know anyone from my home world that does."

Nick nodded, but Sam seemed unconvinced.

"From what Peter was saying, it seems like a big thing. I mean, if they take the risk of trying to catch Angie and overthrow your government, all to have a baby, then I kind of think it's a big deal."

Michael looked uncomfortable.

"To be honest with you, I do not believe that is the real reason for this betrayal. Perhaps it was what Peter was doing, however I feel there is a greater plan behind all of this."

"Do the other Guardians think the same way you do?" Nick asked.

Michael shrugged.

"I believe Kyle does; I cannot speak for anyone else."

"I know this is probably just speculation, but who do you think it could be?" Sam asked.

Nick's cell rang, saving Michael from answering Sam's query.

"That's Artu, he's sending us to a whole nest of vampires. He believes there are at least a dozen of them, newly turned." Nick frowned, the cell still at his ear. "Okay, Artu's found the scent of the traitor. He's closing in on him now. He said that the traitor is near the nest."

Michael touched his collar and the squadron disappeared, along with the two detectives.

Chapter Sixty
Trauiss Prime
The Nursery
A Long Time Ago
It Is for You to Choose

The team arrived as the brothers were training Faer in self-defense and fitness. They watched again from the mezzanine level as they had the day before, quietly taking in all that was happening, tapping into their data pads or whispering to each other. After a while, Elund came down to join the trio.

"Faer, I see no difference in your performance today than I did yesterday." He pointed to the weights the girl had been lifting. "Are you holding back? We have requested that you exceed and be creative. This is something we need to see in order to make a fair and reasoned judgement."

Faer nodded and moved back to the weights. She nodded at the brothers, and they loaded up her weights with heavier discs.

"More," she spoke softly, nodding towards the discs stacked against the wall.

Robert loaded more heavy discs onto the lifting bar. With some effort he fastened them securely.

"More," she spoke softly, her voice tinged with certainty.

"The bar is at the limit," James told her. "Should I place any more on the bar it would break, if you were even able to pick it up."

She gave the brothers a tight smile and picked up the bar with one hand, holding it with no visible effort. She transferred it to the other hand and lifted it, then tossed it high above her head, catching it with her empty hand. Walking to the wall, she placed it down as if it were a feather, no effort required on her part.

"How heavy was that?" Elund asked.

"More than ten men could lift," Robert answered, his brow furrowed with worry.

James frowned. The brothers knew they could not control what the girl may do but were fearful of the consequences should she fail to keep her emotions restrained. He gestured towards the gymnastic area. "Shall we see what you can do with your athletics workout when you do not restrain yourself?"

Faer looked at the brothers, then tipped her head to one side, quizzically, a gesture the brothers had not seen since she was very young. She raised one brow, smiled, and ran to the padded floor. Her spins, leaps, lifts and twirls were unbelievable. She almost flew, her agility and grace taking each and every person watching by surprise.

She did not seem to tire, her amazing workout continued with as much energy as when she first started, and when she decided she was finished, she landed lightly, almost soundlessly, in front of the brothers. She again tipped her head to one side, then the other, her smile drifting across her lips in an almost mocking gesture.

"Well done. There is time before we partake of our mid-day meal, perhaps you want to choose what to do next?" Robert kept his voice neutral, he wanted to show no signs of amazement. "Or are you hungry now?"

Faer looked momentarily confused, her brow scrunched as she looked up at the tall guardian. "You have never asked me this before."

"It is the day where you choose, remember, child?"

She nodded. "Are you hungry now?"

Robert smiled. "It is for you to choose, not me."

"I choose to let you decide."

Elund cleared his throat to make his presence known. "Today is the day where you need to choose what you do. It is vitally important that we see you make your own decisions, and how you react to those choices."

Faer nodded. "I understand." She pulled the tie from her long hair and ran a hand through it. "I think I would like to have a shower first, then I would like to ride the horses, if that is okay?"

"Excellent!" Elund exclaimed. "This is perfect!"

Chapter Sixty-One
Earth
Present Day
Artu's Favor

Michael motioned to his team to surround the building, gesturing for the detectives to stay behind him. The building was a disused drive-in theatre snack bar, the floor to ceiling windows were covered in sheets of plywood, protecting them from breakage. There were two doors on either side that would have normally led to the snack bar, and a rear loading bay door. The projection room was on top of the snack bar, but had seen better days, now it was only an empty shell, no walls covered the skeleton of the framework. Two Guardians were on the roof, ready to access from the projection room. Sam felt his heart beat a little faster.

If there were twelve vampires in the empty snack bar then the fight could be a little more difficult than picking off a single newly turned monster, but he didn't think they would be overpowered, the Guardians were too powerful for that, but it could be a lot more interesting than the previous encounters. With a nod from Michael, the two Guardians in front kicked in the door, Sam could hear the same thing happening from the rear, and the other side. He knew the Guardians on the roof would be doing the same thing, and he waited, knees slightly bent and his hand on his weapon, until Michael gave the all-clear to enter.

It was Ayden who stepped into the doorway to call the detectives inside, his helmet folded away. He looked grim, and the detectives followed him into the darkened space.

The vampires were young. They could not have been out of their teens, most wearing their track uniforms, with a few cheerleaders mixed in.

They were all dead.

Their heads had been ripped off, the blood from the wounds splattering the ceiling and walls, and pooling around the bodies. The Guardians were matching heads to bodies, arranging them so they looked intact. As the detectives watched, they fired short bursts at each one, their weapons giving off a reddish light this time.

"What are they doing?" Nick asked as his helmet folded back into his collar.

"They were all deceased when we entered, it looks like they were killed literally moments before we arrived," Ayden told them. "The Guardians are making them look like they died from smoke inhalation. They're going to burn the building down, cover up this mess."

"Do you think Artu did this?" Sam asked.

"Most definitely." Ayden looked around at the carnage. "The swiftness and power displayed here could only be a vampire."

"Why?" Sam asked. "I mean, these are clearly kids, newly turned, how on earth could they be any kind of threat?"

"Even newly turned vampires are dangerous."

Michael joined the trio. "If the vampire was hungry, he could feed from these newly turned children, the rest may have died simply because of the bloodlust."

"I don't get it. Why did he call us if he'd already killed them?" Sam pondered.

"When he called me, he was still watching them from the outside. Maybe his hunger got the better of him, who knows?" Nick sighed, the loss of so many young lives was a deeply felt tragedy. "I'm thinking he got here just after they were turned. I don't see any fangs on these kids."

Michael nodded in agreement. "If he arrived just after they turned then he may well know who the last traitor is. We need him to contact us about who it is, and where they are."

"We hope it's the last traitor. How will we know if that's really the case?" Ayden looked grim. "Anyway, these guys are ready to light it up, we need to be out of here."

"If he had a bead on the traitor, why would he stop to kill these vampires? That's wasting valuable time letting the traitor get away," Sam said as he followed the others outside.

The flames took hold of the building very quickly, the heat oppressive and forcing the Guardians to step back. Nick felt his cell vibrate and pulled it out of his uniform, surprised that he had a message from Artu.

Michael noticed the detective reading his phone.

"What does it say?"

Nick shook his head, his face reflecting his

disbelief. "He says he killed the vamps to feed, and as a favor to us. The traitor has 'beamed out', and he doesn't know where, but that he has something interesting to show us. He didn't say what, but he has given me coordinates."

"I do not understand this vampire's definition of a favor," Michael frowned. "However, I feel he did have his reasons, and I am intrigued by what he feels we should find interesting. We shall make our way there, with haste."

"Haste being the key word, I hear sirens." Ayden touched the side of his collar to activate his helmet, the others following suit before Michael tapped his communication button on his collar and the group disappeared.

Chapter Sixty-Two
Trauiss Prime
The Nursery
A Long Time Ago
I Have Always Known

Faer had dressed in her usual riding attire, something that was clearly observed by Elund's team as they whispered amongst themselves and tapped on their data pads. The team followed a few dozen steps behind the girl and her guards, far enough not to intrude, but close enough to hear and observe what she was doing.

The palace stables were large and extensive, and contained many breeds of horses. Prior to today, Robert and James had always delivered the child to Patrick, the stable master, never questioning his decision as to which pony, or horse, she should be schooled on. Faer had never asked to ride any other equine, as with all things she had quietly accepted what she was handed and performed exactly as required.

Today they walked to the stables but did not go inside. Instead the girl veered to the left, leading her entourage around the back and into the larger fields. They walked past the riding horses, the plough horses, and the military war horses. James gave a nod to these horses and Robert smiled at him. They had fought many a campaign, side by side, mounted on magnificent beasts such as these.

Still they walked, the lane between fields a long and winding one, taking them quite some distance from the stables, and the palace. Faer led them even further, past the brood mares and foals, past the yearlings, past the retired older horses. No one questioned the girl, no one tried to stop her. Occasionally Robert and James shared a worried glance with each other but followed the girl silently. The path entered a small wooded area, flowing willows waved their emerald green fronds over the wooden fences that enclosed the yellow graveled path. Small birds flitted about in the foliage, their bright colored wings flashing like jewels in the late morning sun.

The path opened up then split into two separate lanes, Faer chose the one to the right, walking confidently, as if she had been here before. Robert would bet his life that the girl had never been this far away from the palace since she arrived. A quick glance at James confirmed that he was also confused about the girl's choice of paths, but they said nothing.

The trees cleared a little and the path came to an end, a gate to a field blocking their way.

Faer walked up to the gate and hesitated briefly, then vaulted over the gate, walking through the long grass a few steps until she stopped.

"Danger. Do not enter."

Robert started at the voice behind him.

"I apologize, it was not my intention to startle you." Elund moved up to the brother's side and pointed to the sign beside the gate. "Stallion paddock. Danger. Do not enter."

Robert grabbed the gate to leap over it, but James grabbed his arm, stilling his action. He pointed to the far end of the field where several white horses had emerged from the trees. They cantered up to the girl as if called, though she has done nothing to summon the beautiful stallions.

Their necks were arched, tails held high like flags, they surrounded the girl as they snorted and puffed, nostrils flared and long manes flying.

Robert held his breath; one wrong move could see these creatures trample the diminutive girl to death. James had not let go of his arm and he could feel his grip becoming tighter and tighter as the stallions drew closer to the girl.

"What shall we do?" squeaked Elund, his voice shrill with panic.

"Hush," Robert admonished. "This is your doing, so now hush, and watch. What happens, happens, and we shall be ready to spring into action should we be needed. For now, hush and observe."

One stallion stopped in front of Faer and bowed his majestic head to sniff her. He snuffled her hair, then stood still as she moved to his side, mounting him in one quick leap.

"Do you see that?" whispered James as a small black thing streaked across the field and leapt onto the girl's shoulders. "The cat, it is back!"

Elund gasped as the stallion reared, kicking his forelegs high. Faer did not fall, she held a handful of hair from the horse's mane and smoothly rode out the rear, then rode the horse expertly around the field, the other stallions following her, the cat firmly wrapped around her shoulders.

She rode like she was born on a horse; her seat was perfect; she was at one with the creature.

James' death grip relaxed. Robert let his hand fall from the gate as they watched the girl, the research team and the brothers in awe of the sight before them.

"Has she ridden this horse before?" Elund asked, his voice hushed.

"I do not believe she has ever seen this horse before." Robert did not take his eyes off his charge.

"I do not believe she has ever seen this part of the palace grounds before," James added.

"That is not the most surprising thing." A voice behind them made everyone turn briefly to see who had spoken. The stable manager, Patrick, stood there, his face reflecting the shock that the others wore. "That stallion has never been trained to take a rider. He has only ever lived as a breeding stud."

"Are you certain?" Elund pointed to the girl. "Clearly he is allowing her to ride him!"

"I am absolutely certain. I came to find out why you had walked right past the stable instead of bringing Faer for her lesson. I had her horse ready to go."

"Today the girl makes her own choices," Robert explained. "This was her choice."

"Why did you allow her to do such a thing?" Patrick sounded outraged.

"She did not speak of her intentions, there was no opportunity to dissuade her."

Faer rode the horse around the field, then brought it to face her audience. She started to take the animal through complicated moves, riding as an expert horsewoman.

The other stallions fell back, standing quietly as the girl took her stallion through his paces. She had him doing some very intricate and difficult moves, making them seem effortless.

"She is certainly a talented rider," Elund commented.

"She exceeds my talent." The stable manager sounded surprised. "I was not aware she could ride to such a high level of skill such as this!"

"You have been her instructor since she was a small child, how could you not be aware of her level of skill?" James asked, but Patrick did not answer.

Faer steered the horse close to the gate and slipped off, turning to kiss the horse on the nose before he cantered away, back to his companions, back into the wooded area. The girl watched them go, then turned to her watchers, a shy smile flitting across her face.

"Faer, have you ever ridden that horse before?" Robert asked her.

She leapt over the gate and faced him, her head tipped to one side.

"No, I have not."

"May I ask, child, have you ever seen this horse, or this field, before?"

Faer looked worried. She looked from one brother to the other, her eyes starting to fill with tears.

"Have I done the wrong thing? I only sought to do as I was instructed, to choose what I wanted to do, to exceed what I have been taught?"

"You have not done the wrong thing, girl," Robert assured her. "We were merely curious as to how you knew these horses were here?"

She shrugged, lifting the cat in her gesture as her shoulders moved.

"I just knew. I have always known." She brushed an errant tear away and sniffed. "I am hungry now. Could we take our mid-day meal now, if that would be okay?"

"Yes, child, I think that would be perfect," James told her, and she turned to make her way back along the path. This time, at every field they passed, at every yard and enclosure, each horse turned to watch the girl walk by them. Those that were eating stopped, those that were lying down stood up, and all of them, from the foals standing with their mothers right through to the older retired horses, all watched her go.

Everyone noticed this phenomenon, the researchers furiously tapping on their data pads as they followed the girl back to her quarters, the cat still calmly resting on her shoulders.

Chapter Sixty-Three
Earth
The Warehouse
Present Day
The Traitor Is Here

"Drew has just informed me that the Presas are moving. He will advise on their trajectory once he has a firm idea." Michael turned to look around, taking in the abandoned warehouses around him. "I fail to see anything interesting here."

"You will." Everyone turned to see the vampire Artu standing at the edge of the woods that bordered the empty parking lot in front of the warehouses. "You must be very quiet, use the most stealth, and follow me."

Artu walked towards the furthest warehouse, identical to the others, the rundown, rusting metal walls with peeling paint, tatty signage and multiple broken windows. All of the structures had signs on the exterior doors advising against entry and the presence of asbestos, and most of these signs, along with everything else, were covered in vulgar graffiti.

Even the graffiti looked to be very old, the trash scattered about and blown into corners and archways was old, faded, and mixed with several seasons of fall leaves. This place had not seen any human life in a very long time, and with nothing for any forest creatures to scavenge, perhaps no nonhuman life, either.

Sam slapped Nick's arm as they walked towards the warehouse, and indicted ahead, to the windows that ran down one side of the building.

"See that? The last window, see? There's a faint glow, like a nightlight's on."

"You are correct, Detective Longstaff." Artu was at the front of the Guardians but had still heard the whispered comment. "There is a slight glow, an electric glow, in these buildings where electricity has not been connected for approximately twenty years."

Michael touched the side of his helmet and the visor closed, those that had opened their visors followed suit. Sam looked at Nick then back at the warehouse before also closing his visor. Artu slowed and crouched, walking much slower, carefully quiet.

The Guardians moved as one unit, drawing their weapons and mirroring the vampire's sideways crouching walk, their blasters held high, their faces masked by the dark visored helmets. Sam and Nick also drew their weapons, and Sam could feel his heart beat faster as he readied for action. He held his weapon the same way he would have held his police issue revolver, though this weapon was smaller, and so light it felt to be a cheap child's toy.

Far from any toy, Ayden had shown both he and Nick how to use the weapon, though there were many settings and uses, they had reset theirs on a stun blast, knowing it would take down pretty much anything they faced. With so many Guardians surrounding them, the two detectives had been confident they would not need kill force, at least, not straight away.

The group hunched low as they passed below the shoulder height windows, all of the men very tall, except the vampire. He was no more than five seven, five eight at a pinch, though still needed to crouch to escape being seen by anyone inside. As he drew closer to the faintly glowing window, he indicated for the group to stop, motioning them to wait as he moved around the back of the warehouse. The light from the window flickered gently, reflecting softly off the dull surface of the neighboring warehouse. It reminded Sam of the blue glow of a TV, though this glow was more of a whitish green.

The group waited silently for the vampire to return, no one moving, no one speaking. Sam's legs were not used to being crouched in this position for such a long period and he felt his knees start to ache. Nick gently moved his elbow to touch Sam, a reassuring gesture, and one of empathy. Sam nodded, a barely perceptible movement, but it acknowledged his partner's gesture.

Artu came back around the corner, no longer crouching. "You can all stand, gentlemen. Your traitor is no longer in the building; however, you will need to stay quiet. The room has some of those nonhuman men, the ones that dress in all black."

The Guardians stood and turned to look in the window. They saw a large table, with an electronic display screen that faced the window. On either side of the screen were various pieces of equipment, though Sam couldn't identify what it was, he did recognize that they were not something that could normally be found on this planet. The screen itself showed a slowly scrolling display of strange symbols, the greenish lettering unrecognizable to Sam. Behind the table, facing the far wall, were the Presas. There were nine of them, Sam counted, and they stood motionless. Like a lineup of mannequins.

"Get down! Now!" Artu hissed as he dropped to a crouch, and everyone did the same, instantly, working as a single, well trained unit. Artu snarled, his fangs sliding down from his gums and his dark eyes turning completely black.

"The traitor is here," he whispered. "I could feel him coming."

Sam gripped his weapon tighter. The moment that they had hoped for was here, and he felt the tension rise amongst the Guardians. It was all he could do to stop leaping to his feet and taking a shot at the man who threatened Angie, he didn't know how the Guardians could control themselves. They were all turned towards the vampire, awaiting his cue. He snarled again, then turned to Michael.

"Stay quiet, and I will lead some of you to the door. You can break through and confront this evil being."

Michael grabbed the vampire by his shoulder and the Guardians disappeared, reappearing in the warehouse, directly behind the Presas. Sam stood up as the Guardians fired on the back suited men, vaporizing them before they could react. Without a word they turned as Michael faced the traitor, who was standing at the table, his hands on the display screen. He touched his collar to transport out, but nothing happened. His shoulders dropped in defeat, and he pressed the side of his helmet to open the visor and folded down the helmet into the back of his collar.

"I have blocked all transport." Michael stepped forward. "I must say, I am shocked. I would never have suspected that the traitor could be you." Michael sounded defeated, his voice flat. Before the traitor could answer, Artu launched himself at the man, his movement faster than any human eye could follow.

Chapter Sixty-Four
Trauiss Prime
The Nursery
A Long Time Ago
Consequences

Robert and James prepared a quick meal while the girl showered, relieved to have a break from Elund and his team who had returned to the palace to take their meal, and most certainly to discuss what they had witnessed. The brothers busied themselves silently for a few minutes before Robert sighed and turned to his brother.

"The horses could feel the power coming from her as she moved before them. In my soul's name, *I* could feel the power! I believe it is what brought the damned cat running to her. Do you think that the team could feel it, brother?"

James placed the bowl he had been holding on the table and turned to face his brother, his face deeply lined with concern. "Yes, brother, I felt it. Just as you and the animals did. And, I believe, Patrick noticed. If the researchers had spent as much time as we have around the girl, they would have felt it as well."

"All of this freedom of choice has Faer letting go of her control. If this continues then I am unsure as to how far she will go. How far her powers may grow."

James sighed and ran a hand through his hair. "I

believe this is what they wanted, the researchers. They need to see her lose control."

"That is something I never want to see. For I believe if she ever loses control, we may never bring her back. Also, that she may destroy all of us before she is done."

The sound of the door to the shower closing silenced the men's conversation, and before too long Faer joined the brothers for a light meal, her black cat sleekly covering her shoulders as droplets of water bounced over its coat from Faer's damp curls.

While the brothers ate sparingly, they watched the girl eat with an appetite unseen previously, finishing off everything on the table, including all that Robert and James had not eaten. No one spoke until the girl finished, her gaze finally meeting Robert's eyes as she gulped down a huge glass of water.

"You seem particularly hungry today."

Faer nodded, wiping her mouth with the back of her hand. James raised his brows; such an uncouth mannerism had never been used by anyone at the table. "You cannot reach your napkin?"

She tipped her head to one side, considering his comment, then the realization crept across her face.

"I apologize. I was not thinking."

"Exactly." James handed the linen napkin to the girl. "You have not been thinking. That is very unlike you. Normally you think over things, sometimes extensively, and do not normally act without thinking."

"Today is not a normal day." Faer spoke softly, trying to understand what her guardian was inferring.

"The choices you make today could have consequences that dictate the entirety of our lives." Robert stood and started clearing the table. "Making your own choices also would suggest when to choose to exceed, as well as when to choose to be restrained."

Faer sat silent as James rose to help his brother. They exchanged a loaded look, each one knowing that they should not encourage or advise the child to act in any particular way, but both fearing the little they had said was not enough. Their thoughts were interrupted by the return of Elund and his team, this time they were joined by three extras. Again, there were no introductions, but the brothers did notice that Xanya was one of the three that had joined the observers. She nodded to each brother in recognition, a warm smile gracing her lips.

"Well, Faer, we are all eager to see what you have planned for this afternoon!" Elund clapped his hands together in eager anticipation.

Faer stood and gave him a respectful nod. "I have formal study today, mathematics, history, applied sciences and strategic planning."

"Is that what you choose to do?" Elund asked her.

"Yes. I enjoy my studies, and I feel they are important."

"Oh. Well. Of course! Yes, we shall keep back, observing quietly as before."

"It is a beautiful day. I think I will walk outside instead of using the internal walkway."

"Is that unusual, for you to walk outside?"

Faer nodded. "Yes, it is, but today is the day to choose some different paths."

The brothers took their accustomed places at her side as she walked the long path, halfway to the main entrance the cat jumped from her shoulder and walked for a little while by her side, slowly drifting further and further away until she had completely wandered off the path. As subtle as the movement was, it did not go unnoticed by the team, a casual glance over her shoulder revealed pointing towards the cat and a lot of tapping on the data pads.

Faer just continued on, walking lightly, acting as if nothing had occurred. The brothers stayed by her side as they made their way into the palace, accompanying the girl to her tuition rooms, and standing guard while she took her lessons. The girl took her lessons in the normal classrooms that the rest of the palace children were schooled, though she was always taught alone, scheduled to use the rooms when the other children had different activities.

The afternoon lessons passed as normal, the girl dutiful, polite, occasionally surprising her tutors with a burst of knowledge or intuition that was above her normal range of learning but was also nothing alarming. Robert felt that Faer must have understood his warning, but he still did not feel relaxed. He knew, without looking, that his brother felt the same way. Elund's team remained unobtrusive, the occasional hushed whisper all that could be heard, the silent tapping on their data pads at a minimum as Faer continued to be unremarkable, compared to earlier in the day. Robert feared they would soon begin to suspect the girl was holding back, and perhaps provoke her into action.

Once her lessons had finished, the team followed her as she accompanied the brothers on their rounds, as they checked the perimeter of the palace. Again, nothing out of the ordinary occurred, and the team again joined the girl and her guardians for their evening meal.

This time the brothers helped Faer prepare the meal, as there were so many mouths to feed. They ate outside, as the only area that would hold such an entourage was the large wooden table placed in the manicured gardens outside the music room.

The table was made from a large, single plank of wood, intricately carved on the sides and polished to perfection on the top. Robert had always admired the workmanship but had never inquired as to the table's creator. He again took a moment to appreciate the table when he saw the team doing the same, Xanya running her hands along the top as she made her way to her seat.

"It is beautiful, such workmanship," Xanya commented. "Who made it?"

"A man named Hooper Callum," Faer told her.

"Oh, have you met him?" Xanya asked.

"No, none of us have met him." Faer started to place the plates around the table. "He died many years ago."

"So how do you know he made it? Is his name on the table somewhere?"

Robert opened his mouth to answer but hesitated when he saw Faer place her hand on the table, palm down, and closed her eyes. "He carved it for the King, when there used to be a King on Trauiss, before this was even called Trauiss. He found the tree, an enormous, ancient tree, and cut it down with his own axe. It took him over a month to cut down the tree. Then another month to cut the branches and the top of the tree. He carved this table in one piece, the legs, the top, are all from one piece of wood. He polished the top until it was like a mirror and carved the story of the last four kings into the sides. It took him many years, working in between his job as a woodcutter, before the table was finished. He was very proud of his work, very proud of what he had achieved. He sent word to the King of his gift, but the King was unhappy that such a tree should have been cut down. The King felt it was a sin to have taken such an ancient tree from the forest, where it would have lived for many centuries, providing shelter and a home to the creatures of the forest.

"The King accepted the gift, but only after admonishing the woodcutter. He placed the table here, outside, so that the tree would never leave nature, never grace the walls of the palace, or a place that was built by man. Of course, there were no gardens here then, the palace was much smaller, the edge of the woods came all the way to here, and the table was placed in a clearing. Over time the palace was made larger, many wings and buildings added, and the gardens were established. The table still sits exactly where it was placed, right here, in this spot."

Silence greeted Faer's story, everyone looked at her with amazement across their features. She opened her eyes to see everyone staring at her.

"You could tell all that just by placing your hand on the table?" Xanya asked, her voice hushed in awe.

Faer looked each of them in the eye, moving only her head, as she did so. Suddenly she smiled, a childish giggle escaped her.

"No, I learned about it in my history lesson last week. The table is a famous part of the palace's history."

Laughter greeted her declaration, though Robert felt a nervous twist in his stomach. Never before had the girl joked like that, it was not in her nature. James glanced at him as he forced a chuckle, and Robert could tell he felt the same way.

The joke had relaxed the group, instead of eating in silence as they had the previous day, today they chatted, laughed, and told anecdotes of their families. Robert and James didn't join in but listened to the banter and felt themselves relax a little. Faer shared no more stories, though did encourage others to talk, her questions and responses brief, but correct, handling the social situation with grace.

"I have a question for you, Faer, if you will?"

Elund leaned forward. "What do you call your cat?"

It was an innocent question, but Robert felt that twinge in his stomach again.

"I don't call her anything," Faer replied, her voice soft.

"How do you call her? When you want her to come to you?"

The girl blinked, very slowly, then cocked her head to one side.

James kicked Robert's ankle under the table. Robert nodded, a short, sharp bob of his head, but he did not look at his brother.

"Faer, please, would you call her now?" Elund asked.

The banter at the table died down and all eyes were on the girl.

The girl did nothing that anyone could see, but within seconds the cat appeared, leaping onto the table and walking up to her mistress, purring so loud that all could hear her.

Robert saw a loaded glance between Elund and Xanya and he felt the twinge in his stomach take a full roll.

"Well, I think it would be time to make our way indoors, now, it is getting dark." James stood and began to clear the plates.

"Indulge us, a little, just for a moment longer." Elund leaned back in his seat. "We would like to ask the girl a few more questions."

James froze, his arm in midair, just for a second. He took a breath and continued to clear the table, stacking the dishes slowly, quietly, trying to remain as calm and act as normal as possible.

"Take a seat, brother, please." Robert spoke quietly, but his voice carried a command that could not be disobeyed.

James sat, his body rigid.

"If you wanted, could you call all of the cats?" Elund asked, his jovial smile in place.

Faer blinked, and within moments cats came from all around, jumping on the table, their tails high, all purring.

"What about sending them away?" asked Xanya.

Faer tipped her head and all the cats jumped down from the table, standing around, silent, waiting. She blinked, and all of them ran away.

All except her black cat, which calmly climbed upon her shoulders, settling into its usual spot.

She blinked again, her bright green eyes flashed briefly, and the brothers felt the hair on their arms prickle with goosebumps.

A loud squeal and a rush of wings heralded the arrival of an eagle, one so large that it towered over everyone as it landed on the table.

A low growl in the deepening dusk turned everyone's heads, and gasps of shock met the hot eyes of several wolves. Faer did not move or speak, but somehow the signal was given for the eagle to fly away, and the wolves to slink back into the growing darkness.

"Excellent!" Elund slapped the table with glee. "This is far better than I could have hoped!"

The team started to chatter with excitement, but

James gripped Robert's arm, the brothers pushing their chairs back from the table.

"Faer," Robert spoke steadily, but firmly. "Girl, it is time to stop now."

None of the researchers noticed the brothers' alarm, as they tapped into their data pads, excited at the display of power from the girl.

"Child, please. Take a breath," James prompted, but she did not respond.

The air crackled with static electricity and finally the researchers felt something was awry. Faer stood, and all chatter ceased. Her hair no longer fell in tumbling waves down her back, it now swirled and flowed with a life of its own, twisting corkscrews of curls writhing like the snakes of Medusa. Bright purple shards glowed through the green protective lenses, her eyes flashing the power that was now being felt by all.

"Was that a good performance?" Faer snarled. "Did the trained monster perform as required?"

Elund gulped. "No... No one called you a monster."

Faer tipped her head to one side. "But you did, did you not? Did you not whisper it amongst yourselves, and typed it into your recordings? Did you not think it, all of you, as you watched me ride a horse, or call the cats to the table?"

"I did not!" Xanya protested, and Faer turned to her.

"You were thinking about it just now. You thought, *By the name of my soul, how can we control the monster she will become?*"

Xanya gasped.

"The only ones who do not feel that way are my protectors, my guardians. Even now, the fear they feel is not *of* me, but *for* me. I am done with performing like a trained monkey."

Suddenly every researcher at the table started to claw at their throats, choking from an unseen force.

Robert jumped to his feet. "STOP!" He reached to touch her, his fingers stopping just before they made contact. "Girl, Faer, you must stop this right now!"

She turned her head to look at him, and sighed. The researchers gasped in lungfuls of air as their hands dropped, the force now gone.

"All of it, girl. You need to stop it all." James' quiet, calm voice stilling the wild hair, and the flashes of violet in the girl's eyes dimmed. She dropped her head, then fell back into her chair. No one spoke. No one moved. For a moment, there was silence.

Elund cleared his throat, then coughed. He looked around the table, taking in the wide eyes and fearful expressions on the faces of his researchers. Finally, his eyes landed on Xanya's, and she gave him a nod. He nodded back, then gestured for his team to stand. Standing himself, he turned to the brothers, his face grim.

"I trust we are now safe, and we can leave this table?"

Robert shrugged. "This is not a situation we have experienced before." Robert looked at the girl, the powerful creature she had been was gone, leaving a girl sitting with her head hanging low, her hair shielding her face. "However, I feel that we have passed the climax of the evening, and the child needs to sleep."

"I do find it hard to still think of her as a child." Elund shook his head. "If these are, indeed, the actions of a child, I do fear what will happen when she is an adult."

He turned to leave, following his team, when he stopped and turned back to the brothers.

"The way to proceed has not been something we desired, but we have planned for it for many years. Many, many years. Get some rest, now, and we will meet with the council of Lords in the morning. Be ready to be summoned to attend."

James and Robert looked at each other, faces worried, eyes dark.

"Faer, please take your shower and go to bed. You may keep the cat with you, if you wish."

The girl slinked off to her quarters, not speaking, nor turning to look at her guardians until she reached the door.

"I am sorry." Even though she spoke barely above a whisper, the brothers could hear her very clearly.

"My child, you never have to apologize to us. Do you hear me? Never!" Robert felt his throat catch with emotion.

"We are always your guardians. Never feel any different. Remember that, come what may tomorrow," James assured her.

She nodded and went inside.

James started to gather up the plates.

"Leave them, brother. Let them be taken care of by the staff tomorrow."

James sighed and sat the plates down. "What are we going to do?"

"Well, I think tonight we get that rather large bottle of liquor that we received last festive season and see which of us passes out first."

James gave his brother a weary smile. "I believe that is the best thing I have heard all day."

Chapter Sixty-Five
Earth
Present Day
He Is Not Dead

Artu pinned the man down and ripped his throat out. The man's blood sprayed in a wide arc, hitting the roof and splashing the windows as he thrashed and grabbed at the vampire attacking him. The traitor tried to fight back, his arms heavy with the sudden blood loss. Michael stepped forward and grabbed the vampire by the collar, lifting him high, away from the bleeding figure on the floor. The creature struggled against the grip, twisting and turning, before his shirt ripped and he dropped. He hit the floor running, faster than any creature should be able to move, he crashed through the window and was gone. No one moved to chase him, all eyes were on the figure on the floor, who, despite his injuries, was struggling to get up.

"Who is it?" Nick whispered to his partner.

"How the fuck would I know?" Sam whispered back.

"It's Frank." Ayden sounded disgusted. "He's also from Earth, a year before us. Didn't make Alpha squad, but somehow he got a place in the engine matrix section."

"Which I found strange, at the time, not having any real experience on a working ship." Michael stood over the fallen man. "I thought it was perhaps due to the fact that you had such high marks from the academy, and somehow managed to get recommendations from the Council of Lords. I speculated that perhaps you had favored someone there, perhaps they liked a young, fresh recruit. I was not right, was I, Frank?"

Frank was on his back, both hands trying to hold the ragged hole in his neck closed as the blood seeped out through his fingers. Blood also dripped from his mouth and one nostril, his eyes were red, bright red, and his skin deathly white. His mouth moved as he tried to speak, but the blood just bubbled and foamed at his mouth without giving any voice. As the rest of the Guardians approached, Frank's eyes fluttered and rolled back in his skull, and his chest lay still.

"Peter didn't name this one." Michael looked back at Ayden and the detectives. "That little worm managed to keep at least this name from us. How many more did he fail to mention?"

"Well, we can't question this guy now." Sam looked down on the body of the traitor.

"He is not dead." Michael kicked Frank hard in his side. "We are immortal, remember? He has just passed out from the shock and the blood loss. We will take this scum back to the ship and see what he has to say for himself once his neck heals over." He gestured to the equipment on the table. "Take that as well. Perhaps we can learn something from the Presas technology. I will send Sam and Nick back to Kyle."

"We can fill him in on what's happened here,"

Sam said.

"No need. He has been following everything through our feeds. We will need to find the vampire at some stage, but for now I feel he will lay low. He has amply fed."

"Sam and I can always hunt him down. It's what we do now."

"The detective monster hunters. It is not what I feel you would have expected from your lives."

"No, Michael, I can assure you it is not." Nick offered him a strained smile. "It is, however, something we've become rather good at, though."

"Why do I get the feeling that this all doesn't end here with Frank?" Sam looked down at the unconscious man. "He had help, and probably from people very high up. Peter obviously held back, but I'm betting he didn't know who was really behind everything."

"I completely agree with you. With some luck and much effort, I am sure we will find out more names." Michael nodded at the detectives and touched his collar, sending them back to Drew's house. The Guardians had gathered up all the equipment and Michael touched his collar again, and once more, the warehouse was empty and dark.

In one corner, at the far end of the long room, a pair of eyes glowed, soft and green, in the darkness of the night.

Chapter Sixty-Six
Trauiss Prime
The Nursery
A Long Time Ago
You Are Dismissed

Robert stood, then sat down, then stood again.

"Do you have the urge to make water, brother?" James chided, his nerves frayed beyond patience.

"I feel as if my legs are full of ants!" Robert sat down again, but almost immediately he started bouncing his knee. "Why are you not nervous, child?"

Faer looked up at her guardian from her seat on the floor. "I do not need to worry. There is enough between the two of you to last me a lifetime."

"Why did you decide to develop a sense of humor?" Robert stood and started to pace. "I care for it very little."

"My soul's grace, why are they taking so long?" James stood up and began to pace in the opposite direction to his brother. "They could have sent for us when they were ready, not three hours before."

"Our sincere apologies." An aide stood in the doorway. "The council was ready, but in the short time it took you to walk here there was another theory raised, and they needed to discuss that before coming to a conclusion."

"Have they come to that conclusion?" Robert asked.

"They have. You may follow me."

Faer stood, but the aide held up a hand. "You are to wait here."

"Why?" James looked troubled.

"While it is not for me to say, I would suggest that some of the Lords may be apprehensive about the thought of the girl losing her temper."

Faer nodded. "I understand. I also feel apprehensive about that."

"Be calm, be quiet, and wait for our return." Robert frowned at her, then let his features take the emotionless, professional expression he wore when official duties were required. James perfectly mirrored his brother, and they followed the aide into the Lords' minor council room. The Lords were seated at their council table, this time they were attired in their formal robes, their cowls drawn over their heads, their faces stern.

James and Robert stood to attention before them, then placed their arms behind their backs, their legs spread slightly, and gave a respectful nod to the Lords.

The aide hurried to her place in a corner, quiet and unobtrusive, she lowered her eyes respectfully, seeming to blend into the very wall itself. Robert could feel his heart racing, the anxiety making a prickling sweat moisten his armpits, but he stood, silent and stoic, as the Lords lowered their cowls and faced the brothers.

"The council thanks you for attending, and for bringing the Dahn here. The council would also like to thank you for your many years of service looking after the Dahn, keeping her safe, training her, teaching her the many things that you have." The Senior Lord looked to the Lords seated each side of her, then faced the brothers again. "I know you have observed all that has been happening with the Dahn, and of course are worried, just as we are. The reason we sent Elund, Xanya and the team to observe you with the Dahn during the normal course of her day was not just to watch her, but to test a few new control adjustments they were working on. They did not inform you at the time, but they turned on the adjustments, and then assessed how effective they were. As you may surmise, they had little to no effect. This is most disturbing. Xanya has confirmed your suspicions that the Dahn is entering puberty, and her power is growing exponentially as each day passes. Without the inability to curb her growing powers, and the clear signs of aggression she has exhibited, the decision has been made to incarcerate the Dahn in a secure, impenetrable location."

Robert tried to maintain his imperturbable demeanor, but the Senior Lord noticed his struggle. "Did you have a question, Robert?"

The warrior took a breath to calm his racing mind. "Incarcerated? You mean housed in a different facility?"

The Senior Lord raised her brows a little. "Housed? You are asking if she will have a home with the comforts she has been accustomed to? I am afraid it will be a little less opulent than she has experienced, however she will be safe, and more importantly, the Trauiss Multiverse will be safe."

"If you will pardon me, my Lord, for how long?" James asked.

"She will only need to be detained until Elund's team are able to manufacture an effective control. Once that happens, she can resume her life as before. We envision that this will not take very long at all."

Robert glanced quickly at James, then looked back at the Lords. "Are we still to serve our duties as guards over Faer?"

The Senior Lord gave him a forced smile. "For the time being the Dahn will not need bodyguards, the facility will be guarded, but by a regiment that will be housed there. You will return to your quarters for now, and with the morrow you will be reassigned to the training garrison. You will train new warriors, maintain fitness and battle readiness of existing guards, and when the Dahn has been effectively controlled we will assess the situation and determine if she should be placed back into the previous arrangement. Any further questions can be addressed to your commanding officer when you assume your new roles. For now, you are dismissed."

"Excuse me, my Lords, and please forgive my impudence." Robert bowed his head in supplication. "Are we to accompany Faer before we are reassigned?"

"The Dahn has already been transported to her new facility as we were speaking. Again, you are dismissed."

The brothers gave a short nod of their heads in salute and turned on their heels, marching out behind the aide who had shown them in. The girl was gone, all they could do was return to their quarters, walking silently until they were behind closed doors.

"They separated us so they could take her." Robert tugged his jacket off, leaving just his tunic and dress pants. "She will not understand what is happening, she will be frightened."

"She will think we have abandoned her." James opened his jacket and tugged at the collar of his tunic. "She will be scared, and this will trigger more of the behavior that got her there in the first place. This is a complete disaster!"

"Did you notice that the Senior Lord did not call her by her name, not once, nor did she refer to her as anything other than the Dahn. The creature offspring. They are not seeing her as we see her, as a young girl, a mere child, with hopes and dreams and fears, they see only power and problems. Nothing more."

"You are correct." James found the bottle of liquor they had been drinking the night before and poured two glasses of the dark liquid. "They see only what they have created, and not what she has become. To them she is a product that needs to be dealt with, not a person that can be taught and educated. I believe we could have helped her gain control of her abilities on her own, perhaps with the help of the researchers, but given time, I truly believe she could have gained control."

"I agree with you." Robert downed his glass and offered it up for a refill. "I cannot think that we have any option but to comply and hope that they let us visit with Faer sometime soon. Though, if they do not think of her as a person, they may not see the need for her to have visitors."

James looked at his brother, his face drawn and pained. He drained his glass and refilled both to the brim.

Chapter Sixty-Seven
Earth
Drew's Kitchen
Present Day
An Ambush

"Like you, I do not believe that we are finished with this. I believe there are more traitors, and we need to find them, and stop them, before Angie will be safe," Kyle sighed. "I am used to hunting fugitives and enemies, I did not ever believe that the enemies would be on my own ship."

Nick pulled a chair out from the small table and straddled it, his arms folded over the back rest.

"Just how far does this conspiracy go?" Nick asked as he stifled a yawn. "I wouldn't be surprised if someone high up is involved, especially as this Frank guy had recommendations from the council people."

"The Council of High Lords. They govern our multiverse. If this corruption is going through the Council, then we are truly in trouble." Kyle ran a hand through his hair. "It would not be the first time this has happened; however, I cannot believe it is all over a lack of reproductive abilities. There has to be some other reason for this."

"Why didn't Angie stay on the ship when you took the girl there? Surely it must be safe by now," Sam shook his head. "You've got to wonder why she still doesn't feel safe."

Nick yawned again and Kyle stood, moving his chair under the table.

"The two of you should get some sleep. The Presas are on the move, and it would be good for everyone to be rested and at full speed for whatever may eventuate."

Drew stood and Kyle took his place at the display screen, arranging the feeds to show the Presas on their endless march.

"Any idea where they are headed?" Sam leaned over to see the screen.

"Not yet." Drew tilted his head and cracked his neck, stiff from sitting at the screen for so long. "C'mon, guys, I'll show you where you can stretch out, we'll call you if anything happens."

As Drew led them away, Kyle focused back on the computer, plotting out the route of the Presas. He tapped a few screens, moving from one view to another, when a soft flutter of wings made him catch his breath, and he looked up to see Angie standing in the doorway. He didn't move or even breathe, fearful he would scare her away.

Angie just stood there, her back against the door, head cocked to one side. She was still wearing her dark sunglasses, but Kyle could tell she was looking around the room by the way she moved her head. She didn't speak, she just stood in the doorway.

"Angie! I'm glad to see you!" Drew walked into the room and flicked off the main lights, just leaving the light from the living room to filter into the kitchen. "Are you hungry? I can make you something to eat. I have some steaks in the freezer, maybe some chicken, if you prefer?"

"She doesn't eat meat," Kyle spoke softly, not wanting to alarm the woman.

"That's okay, I have other things. So, hungry?"

Angie took her glasses off and folded them before putting them in her breast pocket. Her green eyes glowed softly in the dull kitchen as she met Drew's gaze.

"No thank you." Her accent was the same as the Guardians, a gentle mix of many different inflections, and hard to place. "I am not hungry."

Drew smiled, genuinely happy with the reply.

"You spoke full sentences!" Nick exclaimed from behind Drew, making the sheriff start.

"I thought you were going to sleep?" Drew stepped aside to allow Nick to enter the kitchen.

"I was, but I felt Angie arrive. And here she is! Here you are! And talking, no less. How are you feeling?"

Angie cocked her head to the other side, a smile touching the corners of her lips.

"I am fine. I have healed."

"You're fully healed?" Nick grinned. "That's fantastic news!"

Angie blinked slowly. "Not fully healed. Not yet." She glanced over at Kyle before bringing her focus back to Nick. "I am more healed than before."

"Why are you here?" Kyle asked.

Angie turned to face the Guardian, her head tilted to one side.

"Do you have some more information on the traitors?" Kyle looked uncomfortable, clearly unsure of how to speak to Angie.

"The enemies are coming." She tipped her head to the other side. "They are coming for all of us."

"Here?" Drew looked over to Kyle as he checked the display screen.

"They are not heading this way, Angie. I fear you are mistaken."

"Where are they heading?" Drew asked. "Can you tell?"

Kyle concentrated on the display screen, his frown knitting across his brows. "They are definitely not coming this way. What makes you think they are coming for us?"

Angie looked back at Nick, the soft smile was gone.

Nick shrugged. "What does it matter? You can just blast them like we did in the warehouse."

"They were taken unawares. That is the only way our blasters work against them. They have some sort of protection when they are not dormant and can only be taken down with force. Traditional guns, knives, etcetera."

"Bummer. So, can you project where they are headed?"

"I do," Angie spoke. "I know where they are heading."

Kyle looked over at her, and the three men waited for her to continue.

"There is a trap for us. The traitors are trying to lure us."

"You are being a little cryptic, Angie." Drew moved over to the table and pulled out a chair.

"How are they making a trap?"

Angie disappeared. There was only the soft sound of wings, no other warning for the men that she was going to go.

"Well, I didn't see that coming!" Nick exclaimed.

"Really? She only ever disappears without warning, I've noticed."

"She will be back." Kyle seemed very sure. "You asked her a question that she couldn't answer. I believe she has gone to find the answer. It is what she did earlier."

Nick joined Drew at the table just as Angie reappeared.

"They have made more creatures," she informed them. "They have them near a school, a sleep school."

"A sleep school?" Drew looked confused.

"Where the children stay. Stay and sleep."

"A boarding school!" Drew smiled at her. "You are doing very well, Angie. Most articulate."

She smiled at him, her perfect, white teeth gleaming in the reflection of the living room lights. "Thank you. I am still, um, not right?"

"I think you are perfect," Nick gushed, and Drew cleared his throat.

"Oh, um, I think you are doing very well," Nick corrected, red-faced. "I mean, you are so much better than when you were here before, and it's only been such a short time. You should be really pleased with yourself. I am. Really pleased, that is."

Drew slapped Nick on the shoulder and grinned

at the man. "Okay Nicky boy, you need to stop gushing. Angie, I believe you were trying to tell us about the trap that was being laid for us?"

Kyle had been silent, his attention divided between the display screen and the white-haired woman. He didn't speak now, he just frowned a little, Drew noticing the worried expression that colored the Guardian's face.

"They march to the school. They know I will not like that. I will want to protect the children, so they march to the school. To lure us." Angie sighed, her frustration at her inability to properly explain herself evident. "They still try to catch me. So, they still have orders. Still have someone ordering them."

"How do you know that for sure?" Drew asked. "Maybe they just have a contract to fulfill whether the person ordering them has been captured by us or not?"

Angie tipped her head to one side and for a moment Drew was worried she would again disappear, though she just shook her head and scrunched her brow.

"Cannot tell you." She looked upset but didn't try to explain herself any further.

"So, you are just guessing, is that what you mean?" Drew gave her a reassuring smile.

"No." Kyle stood and stepped away from the screen. He approached Angie and opened his hands, palms up, and spoke to her in a language that he had not used before.

Drew couldn't place it, if he were to guess he

would say it sounded like Russian, French and Japanese all mixed into one, a little like the soft accents that all of the Guardians and Angie spoke with.

Angie listened and then nodded, before answering in the same language. She seemed to speak a little easier in this tongue, her sentences seemed more complex.

"She cannot tell you as she was not able to explain how she knew," Kyle translated. "She is certain that there is at least one more traitor on this planet, though she has not seen them."

Angie spoke again, a little more animated this time, her grasp of this foreign language much better than her use of English.

"She thinks that they did not come on the ship, she feels that they are travelling separately, but are also one of us." He stopped to listen to her a little more, nodding as she spoke.

"She can feel them, a little, though they are shielded. She needs the vampire; she says he will be able to find the traitor. You didn't kill him, did you?"

Nick smiled. "No, we would have, but we didn't get the chance. He took off. That sucker is fast. Like, superhero speed."

"Where did he go?" Drew asked.

Nick shrugged. "Beats me, but I bet she can find him."

"Yes. I can find him. I will go find him and I will tell him. I will instruct him."

"Do you need one of us to come with you?" Nick

asked.

She shook her head, but then looked up at the detective. She nodded, and grasped his arm before they both disappeared, the soft rustle of wings heralding her departure.

Chapter Sixty-Eight
Trauiss XXII
The Dungeon
A Long Time Ago
Waiting

The walls were stone, large, gray slabs of damp, cold stone that were crisscrossed with veins of rusty colored ore. On one wall a patch of slimy brownish green moss hung dankly across the stones, on another a constant drizzle of water fell, its path lined by more gelatinous moss and sticky ooze. There were no windows, no light source, no bed or chair, it was simply a cell, a cold, dark, damp cell, with only one barred cell door that ticked and crackled with the power running through it. The bars allowed a trickle of light that filtered through the dark corridor and reflected off the water flow, but it was barely enough to see anything. A frigid breeze crept into the cell, circling the damp walls and making the wet stone floor even colder. In the middle of the cell, shrouded by the darkness and embraced by the cold air huddled a single person, a small, fragile looking being that balanced on the balls of their feet to avoid the wet and cold floor.

A guard walked along the corridor, pausing to check the occupant. He shone a light at the feet of the huddled lump, marveling at the perfect balance of the being, the balls of their feet steady and stable. He turned and shone the light outside the cell, and as he did so the occupant raised their head. A glimpse of white hair, greyed by dirt and dampness, fell across her face as the girl lifted her head and stared into the darkness, eyes no longer protected by their bright green lenses, they now glowed with a fierce, purple fire. The guard felt a shiver writhe its way down his spine, and he backed up a step or two as the eyes brightened in their intensity, then closed, slowly, as the girl lowered her head.

"Good eve, Albert! How is the resident monster holding up tonight?" a gruff voice called out from further down the corridor.

"Argh, Tom, good eve to you, but that thing always makes me feel loose in my bowel, with those glowing eyes and standing on the toes." The guard moved down the corridor towards his next charge. "I have not seen that thing move from the spot in the twenty and two hundred years I have walked the corridors here."

"I have been here thrice that and more, and no, I have never seen it move more than its head, just to shine those purple eyes on you. I do not trust anything that does not eat or shit. Even the demons we used to have here ate and shat. Not that thing, no, it just sits there, on the balls of its feet, like it is waiting. Gives me the vapors."

The guards moved off together, and the huddled shape stayed still, poised on the balls of her feet, and waited. Always, endlessly waiting.

Chapter Sixty-Nine
Earth
Drew's Kitchen
Present Day
Like A Virus

Nick felt like his body had been both torn into a thousand pieces, and compressed into a small space, all at the same time. It wasn't particularly painful, but it was definitely uncomfortable. He couldn't breathe, he couldn't see, and he couldn't hear. It wasn't black. Or any color. It was just nothing.

A complete void, no sight, sound, only the weird physical sensation. It seemed to last for several seconds before the two of them appeared in a dark place, he stumbled for a second as Angie's iron-like grip steadied him, and she let go as he became stable.

His senses were assaulted with sounds and scents, it took a moment for him to realize that he was in a forest, the scent was from the trees and the humus, the dew and the dirt. There were no lights, and the canopy was thick enough to block out any beams from the moon.

Angie was looking at him, he could see the green glow of her eyes in the pitch darkness. It was the only thing he could see.

"Artu is near. He will sense I am here and will come."

"Okay. Sure. I understand. Um, it's, um…" Nick

struggled to pull his thoughts together. "You took me with you. It was weird. Strange. Not like the transporter from your ship, nothing like that."

"Shhh. You need to be quiet."

"But-"

"Now. Quiet."

"Yes, Detective, you need to be quiet. You do talk a little too much, at times." Nick couldn't see the vampire, but the voice was unmistakable.

"Artu." Angie spoke very softly, but it was a direct command. The vampire did not respond that Nick could tell, but the silence was almost overwhelming.

He felt Angie take his arm again, and then he could see. Not as clear as day, he could barely see, but he could make out objects, the trees, the path they were standing on, Angie's long white hair, and then, and only because it moved, a dark shape that was the vampire.

"Do you understand?" Angie still spoke softly.

"Yes, yes I do. I still have the cell phone; I can call you when I find them."

"Go then. Go now." Her grip tightened on Nick's arm and they disappeared, again the strange void and the simultaneous feelings of explosion and compression, and the detective was back in the small kitchen. Drew looked startled as he sat next to Kyle at the display screen.

"I went with Angie!" Nick exclaimed.

"Yes, we can see that," Kyle looked at Angie. "Did you find him? The vampire?"

She nodded, releasing Nick's arm, and

disappeared.

"What happened? Did she talk to him?" Drew asked.

Nick began to pace. "She did, I think, but I couldn't hear anything. She just asked him if he understood, he said he did and that he still had his cell, then we were back here. I think it was telepathy or something. Is that possible?"

"I'm sitting at my kitchen table with a spaceman, looking at his spaceman screen at dozens of robot-like men hunting a demon hybrid, and you ask me if telepathy is possible?"

"If she communicated with him like that then she has a strong link to the vampire. It would mean he is bound to her and would do anything to obey her." Kyle tugged at his collar. "That is good for us, at this moment. The vampire will be able to do something that we have been unable to do. The traitor will not expect a creature to be hunting them. It is a good plan. Did Angie say where she was going now?"

Nick shook his head. "No, just the usual wink out without notice. I guess we should be used to it by now."

Angie reappeared, her arms holding a large duffle bag. She placed it on the table and unzipped it. The men moved closer as Angie took out a large, rifle sized weapon. It looked like a bigger version of the handheld blasters the Guardians used.

She pulled out several more, placing each one on the table as she lifted them out. The last thing she removed was a data pad, identical to the one that

Peter had used.

"Where did you get all of this?" Kyle asked her.

She answered in her language, then frowned, shaking her head. "I am sorry. I will explain. I find these, found these, before I was attacked. Before they hurt me," she lifted her hand and touched the back of her head, indicating the earlier wound. "More, there were more, but I, um, I could not grab."

"They were with the pretzels?" Nick asked.

"Presas," Kyle corrected.

Angie nodded. "Where they were. Before." She touched her head again. "I felt, I could feel, someone. It was strange. I could feel but not feel. Like they were hiding, um, like, um, shield? Yes, like a shield. The shield was ours. Was Guardians."

"Do you have any hint at all who they could be? I mean, clearly they are a Guardian, and we have figured out they were not on the ship, but is there anything that would, or could, give us an idea of who it is?" Drew picked up the data pad, his brow furrowed as he spoke. "You maybe can tell who used this last?"

"Of course!" Kyle grabbed the pad from Drew and sat back behind the display screen. "We can tell who this was assigned to, or if that is blocked, when it was assigned, and from where. Peter will be able to…" Kyle realized what he said and shook his head. "I do not think Peter will be doing anything very much anymore."

"That's okay, we don't need him. Who would you normally use to look at this kind of thing?"

Drew looked at the data pad. "You would've had someone before him that could do all of this?"

Kyle grimaced. "The people with the skills we need all seem to be in our compromised group. I will get Michael to look at it when he returns, he has some skills in these things."

Angie looked at Kyle, her head cocked to one side. She held her hand out to him, and Kyle handed her the data pad. She placed her other hand on the pad, palm down, and closed her eyes.

Nothing happened. The data pad didn't spring to life, no lights or noise came from the unit.

"What's she doing?" Nick asked.

"Angie was able to access all units, all systems, everything. She only needs to speak or touch something and it can recognize her from then on."

"Everything from your home world?" Drew seemed impressed.

"Everything, everywhere. Any system that has heard her, or felt her, will be accessed by her. Her powers infiltrate them, and they are unlocked to her."

"Like a virus?" Nick asked, then saw the look Kyle shot him, one of horror and defensiveness. "I mean a computer virus, you know, like it infiltrates everything. I should shut up now."

"Yes, Detective, you should perhaps refrain on making judgements. However, in a way you are correct. If Angie has even scanned her insignia into anything, she will have access."

"So, can you see anything? Is it working?" Drew asked.

Angie opened her eyes, a frown darkening her face. "I can see."

"You know who the traitor is?" Kyle asked, hope in his voice.

Angie shook her head. "This pad has not been used. Not for a time. It was programmed by Peter but has not been used since then."

"Is there anything useful in it?" Nick indicated the pad. "Can you tell anything, or what they were planning?"

Angie nodded, but didn't speak.

"Angie, can you tell who the traitor is?" Kyle asked.

The woman looked at her Guardian, her face grim. "The program says it is you."

Chapter Seventy
Trauiss XXII
The Dungeon
A Long Time Ago
By My Soul

Albert moved back along the corridor, his first rounds done, his charges checked, fed, and all locks and doors secured. He looked in on each charge again as he walked back, he was always careful, always checked everyone twice, and had never had an incident in all of the years he had worked in the highest security dungeons. One could never be too careful with the creatures and beings that were housed here. Most were monsters captured from the battlefield, and were vile, vicious creatures, unfortunately blessed with a long life from living so close to the girl. The others were things that had been bred in the program looking for a replacement for the girl. Rejects, these ones, too evil to be controlled, but still containing valuable DNA that may be required by the scientists in the future. With nowhere else to keep them, the dank, dark cells of the abandoned fortress on Outer Trauiss Twenty-Two was the perfect place. It was not only built of solid ore, many feet thick, but electrified and fortified, virtually impenetrable. In all of his time there, Albert had never known of anything escaping. Tom had spun the tale of a time, many years before Albert arrived, that the creatures had banded together and broke free from their cells and made it almost to the entrance.

Since that time the fortress had been refortified, and there had been no further successful attempts since.

If Albert really put thought to it, he could recall no attempts at all, successful nor otherwise.

Rounding the dark hallway towards the brighter lit staff quarters Albert called out to his co-worker.

"Aye, Tom, will you be joining me for the meal of the eve?"

He wasn't overly concerned when there was no reply, the walls were thick, and sound did not travel very well. Should Tom be relieving himself, he would have no chance of hearing anything Albert said.

"Aye, Tom, where would you be?" he called as he opened the door to the staff area. "Tom?"

He frowned, but still did not worry. He didn't get an answer, so just started to spread his food out on the table. He always brought extra, Tom was a fan of Albert's wife's cooking, and Albert did not mind bringing an extra serve or two. Tom should be rounding the corner at any moment, stomach rumbling as he looked over the feast Albert provided.

He was nearly finished eating when he decided that he had better look for Tom, it was unusual for the man to be late for a meal. Tom may be late for many things, but never a meal. Albert was worried it would be something dirty, a broken sewage pipe or cleaning hose, so he donned his heavy gloves and stood from the table as Tom opened the door.

"I was starting to fear I would need a search party! What delayed you this eve, man?"

Tom looked sideways and gulped but did not answer. Immediately Albert felt his bones chill, he could see something was very wrong.

"Tom?"

A hand pushed Tom through the doorway, thick black gloves matching the black clad arm. Albert looked at the weapon he had lain on the table when he had started to eat, trying to calculate if he could leap for it before the owner of the hand rounded the doorway. He did not want to spook them and risk hurting his colleague.

The man entered, followed by another, almost identical man, both very tall, muscular, and angry looking. They wore warrior uniforms, complete with full shielding and weaponry.

Albert gulped and completely dismissed any thought of reaching for his weapon.

"A welcome to you, fine warriors, though our fortress did not record you entering. I do not believe I saw a request, either?

Tom's eyes widened and he shook his head, an almost imperceptible movement that only Albert picked up.

"Where is The Dahn?" demanded the first man as he pushed Tom towards the table.

Albert shook his head. "We don't keep any important people here, good sirs, this is a dungeon, a jail, not somewhere one would keep someone such as The Dahn."

The men looked at each other and the second man stepped forward.

"A girl. A smallish girl, with white hair, and very big eyes. Do you have a girl here?"

Albert looked to Tom, then back at the warrior.

"We do have a girl, but she is a dirty, strange creature. You would be mistaken to think that it is The Dahn!"

The warriors exchanged a quick glance and then looked back at Albert.

"Take us to her."

Albert took a step back, unsure of what he should do.

"*Now!*"

"We cannot, that is not allowed!" protested Tom.

The warriors drew their swords, their other hands firmly placed on the blasters on their hips.

"You will take us there, *now*, or you will die."

Tom started to visibly shake. Albert took a steadying breath and locked eyes with his colleague. No matter what beast they held in their dungeons, he had never seen Tom look fearful before. Tom winked, slowly, his eye away from the warriors, so they could not see the reassurance.

Albert let his breath release, knowing that Tom was putting on a show to fool the warriors. He would wait for his chance, and then the two jailors would show these warriors that they were not to be trifled with.

Albert nodded and grabbed his keys from the table. The warriors ushered both men out the door and followed them along the dark hallway, not seeming to notice the cold air, nor the damp walls.

Albert felt Tom at his side as he unlocked the gates leading to the next hall, and Tom let his shoulder touch Albert's for support. They both kept silent, not sure exactly what the warriors were expecting, but certain that the dirty creature they were leading them to was not what they were after.

The next set of gates had two locks, and Albert motioned Tom to help him open them. In truth they only needed one key to open them, but it gave the chance for both men to step together and hide their motions from the warriors as they slipped their long knives from their sheaths.

Both men felt the prickle of a sword at the back of their necks.

"My brother and I have fought in too many campaigns against too many enemies to be bested by a pair of dungeon guards."

Tom sighed and stepped back as Albert opened the gates, letting the warriors march behind them, together, stepping perfectly in time.

Albert stopped when he reached the far end of this dark corridor and stepped aside, motioning to the warriors to look inside the small viewing window. He caught Tom's eye, making sure that he would be ready in an instant if the opportunity arose to take on these foes.

One of the warriors stepped forward and looked into the window, then stepped back.

"Open the door," he ordered.

"I am not sure that I can. In all the time I have served here, that door has never opened." Albert opened his hands in supplication. "I do not even hold the key."

"How do you feed her?"

"We do not. She does not eat, nor drink. She does not sleep, nor wake, she does not change her clothes, nor bathe. She just is."

The brothers looked shocked, their stern faces showing emotion for the first time.

"You never feed her? Ever?"

Albert shook his head. "I was instructed to only check visually through the viewing window. That is all. I have never seen her move more than her head, in all these years."

"We need to open this door. If you do not have a key, then we will need to find another way."

"If you break the door it will interrupt the security fields to this whole wing. It will allow other creatures to escape, creatures that should never be set free!" Albert was genuinely concerned; he could see how determined these men were and did not want to risk unleashing the horrors they held in these dungeons onto the outside worlds.

"We have no choice, if you cannot open the door, we will have to take whatever action is required."

"I have a key." Tom spoke softly, but his words broke the silence like a shout. "I can open the door. I have never had any reason to open it, but I do have the key."

"Do not continue speaking, make haste, man, open the door!" The warrior motioned him towards the thick, roughhewn stone door.

"You must be sure this is the course you wish to take, sirs, as once this door is opened, we cannot make any claims as to your safety, nor as to ours."

The warriors just pushed him to the door. Tom put his hand down the neck of his tunic and pulled a chain up, a chain that Albert had always thought to be a decorative memento from Tom's father and had never questioned its existence.

The key was large, black, and seemed to be very heavy. In all the centuries Tom must have carted that thing around his neck, he never once complained about the weight, nor the reason he held it secret. Albert looked towards the door. If the key to the strange girl's cell had been a secret all of these years, then perhaps she was more than she seemed, more that Albert had known, or even guessed. Perhaps she *was* The Dahn. Perhaps she was here, alive, all these years, secret even from himself.

Tom turned the key and then pressed his pass into the slot, putting his code in, then another, then placing his palm on the reader. He turned the key another revolution and repeated the sequence, doing it three more times before the shielding shimmered off and the door creaked and moaned as it slowly swung open. He stepped back quickly, hand on his long blade, his face creased with concern. Seeing his fighting stance and hand on weapon, Albert turned toward the cell, his back against the corridor wall, and matched his colleague's stance.

The warriors stood at the door, one facing the guards, sword drawn, the other looking at the girl.

"My soul's sake, James, what have they done to her?"

The warrior facing the guards turned, and his sword arm dropped, the tip of the blade touching the ground.

"By my soul, Robert, by my soul," he responded, his voice breaking at the sight of the girl balancing on the balls of her feet, huddled, crouched low, as the water dripped behind her.

Chapter Seventy-One
Earth
Drew's Kitchen
Present Day
And Someone Is

Kyle stumbled backwards, his face pale and shocked. He grabbed the table to steady himself and looked towards the woman before him.

"Never! I would never, not ever. You must believe me, Angie. By my oath, by my life…"

She smiled, shaking her head. She spoke to him softly, using the strange language they had used before. Kyle fell to his knees, his head in his hands. Nick looked at Drew, an unspoken question in his eyes, unsure if they should do anything.

"She knows." It was a gasp, a genuine gasp of relief. "She knows I would never betray her; I would never do anything to hurt her. She knows."

"So, someone is trying to set you up, to turn her against you?" Drew nodded. "They clearly didn't realize the depth of her trust in you."

"Maybe they are trying to deflect the attention from themselves?" Nick suggested. "I mean clearly they would be someone that knows the way things work and have access to Angie to kidnap her in the first place."

Kyle rubbed his hands over his face and stood, his head bowed, and took a deep breath. Angie reached up and touched his face, then turned to

Nick, her brow furrowed.

"You thinking that, um, that maybe it is someone I trust?"

"Don't you? I mean, who else would know where you are kept when you sleep, or be able to infiltrate your closest Guardians?"

"I think Nick is right," Drew stepped closer to Angie. "I can't think that anyone who isn't a part of your inner circle, or at least high up in the hierarchy side of things could achieve this level of infiltration."

Kyle nodded. "I do agree, as well. However, I am lost to try and think who it could be. There is no one I could imagine that would do that."

"But all along —" Nick started, but Kyle waved him silent.

"I know that I did not want to believe that any of us could betray The Dahn, however Peter, Simon, so many others have proved that they can, and have, betrayed our leader, so I need to open my thoughts more to the truth. This clearly is the truth, that someone we know and trust is behind this."

"I think this too," Angie said. "I think that, hmm, um, I think that someone would love me, would have to love me, to hate me this much."

"That is all of us, Angie, but most especially me. I do not believe anyone loves you more than I." Kyle reached to take her hand but dropped his before he made contact.

"There are others. Others. And maybe not so much, um, so much love? But so much, yes, there are others. And someone is. Someone is here, and someone is doing things. Someone."

"I will search until my last breath to find them, and to stop them!" Kyle vowed.

"You aren't the only one who will do that," Nick agreed.

"I'm pretty sure that you two aren't the only ones, but the problem facing us now is figuring out how to move forward and find out who is behind this." Drew moved back to the table and the display screen. "We need to work out a strategy to move forward and find and defeat the traitor."

"Yes, we do. When Michael returns, we will discuss that." Kyle touched Nick on the shoulder. "You should get some sleep while you can. We will wake you when something happens."

Nick looked at Angie, and she nodded, then tilted her head to the other room. "Join Sam. Sleep. You will know if I need you."

Nick looked reluctant to acquiesce but turned and left the kitchen. Angie frowned, turning towards the display screen, then to the back door, then back to the screen.

"Something." She shrugged, then shook her head.

"Something? What do you mean?" Drew looked down at the screen. "Oh, definitely something."

Kyle joined Drew at the table and nodded. "Yes, I must agree. I will summon Michael and his team back."

Chapter Seventy-Two
Trauiss XXII
The Dungeon
A Long Time Ago
The Rescue

Robert felt like his heart was twisted in a vice grip, his breath caught in his throat. He knew that the girl had been imprisoned all of the centuries as he and his brother trained warriors and fought many battles, but all this time he had believed her to be living the same kind of life that she had always led, though with greater restrictions. They never, in all of those years, imagined that she would be treated so badly.

The hope of the multiverse, the savior of the realms, and here she was, squatting on a damp stone floor, with no food, only dirty water flowing down the wall, and nothing more than rags to cover her bones.

Robert could see her bones poking through those rags, though she was still, conserving her energy, she had not eaten in many years, possibly not since she sat at the table with his brother and himself. He felt sick at the thought of the pain and anguish, the confusion that she would have suffered. James placed a hand on his back to steady him.

"Faer?" He spoke softly, not sure if she could even hear him. The huddled shape did not move.

"Faer? Girl? Can you hear me?"

Slowly, so slowly, the dirty hair shifted as the head rose. Her eyes were closed as she faced them, her face covered in grime, her hair gray and matted. She opened her eyes, again, very slowly, the bright purple orbs much larger than a normal person's, and in the sunken cheeks and emaciated features, they looked even larger.

"Faer? It is Robert, and James, we have come to find you, to rescue you!"

The girl blinked, once, very slowly, though her face showed no signs of understanding or recognition.

Robert took a step forward, his boot splashing in the pooled water. A fetid stench of mold and decay assaulted his nostrils, but he tried to ignore it.

"Girl, it is Robert, with James, we have come to get you. We searched for many years to find you. We searched many years and many worlds, and we never gave up. We never gave up the thought that we would find you and save you."

The girl blinked again and tilted her head to one side, she looked owl-like, with her large glowing eyes and sunken face.

"You know us, girl, you know who we are. Do you remember us, Faer? Do you remember?"

James could feel the dungeon guards close behind him now, but he did not turn to warn them back. Their curiosity had beaten their sense of duty and they now wanted to witness the scene unfolding before them.

"I am going to pick you up, Faer. Will you let me pick you up and whisk you away from here?"

The girl tipped her head to the other side, her brow now creasing as she struggled to make her mind work. Her mouth opened, but no sound came out. Her silence over so many centuries had stilled her voice, her mouth parched and dry. Robert took three steps and scooped the girl up without hesitation, her weight nothing, she felt no more than a bundle of dry bones tied in a rag. He stepped to the cell door.

"Let us be away, brother, before the alarms are sounded."

He looked down on the guards, but they just looked confused.

"Is... is that really her? Really? The Dahn?" Albert gasped.

Robert nodded, his tears now falling freely as he felt how frail the girl had become.

"Our savior was here the whole time, all these years, in the worst cell in the dungeons?" Tom looked at his colleague, then the men parted to let the warriors through. "We will not try to stop you. We will not sound the alarms. We will not say anything at all until someone notices her to be gone."

"How long will that give us?" James asked.

"I cannot say, however we are the only two guards that ever walk these halls and have done so for a very long time. No one ever checks on the girl, or any of our charges. Occasionally someone will come for a sample from one of the breeders, but they never come down to these cells."

James gave them a rare smile and sighed as he

turned to leave.

"We thank you. This is not something we will ever forget," he told them as he hurried after Robert.

Tom locked up the cell before turning to Albert.

"Do you know how to clear all evidence of this occurrence from the databases?"

Albert smiled. "I will make sure all is done, while you eat. I do not believe you have had a chance to taste my wife's new recipe. She made it just for our meal, you know. I think she cares more about your diet than mine."

"It has been a strange eve, my friend, a very strange eve."

"Aye, Tom, that it has."

Chapter Seventy-Three
Earth
Drew's Kitchen
Present Day
Sandwiches It Is, Then

"They are nearing the school; they'll expect us to fight." Ayden was seated at the table, Sarah by his side as they monitored the screens.

"They will be ready for us, ready for Angie. We need to eliminate these things with as little impact to any surrounds." Michael looked over at Angie who was standing in a corner, looking thoughtful. "She cannot come with us, of course."

"Must come. Must stop these enemies!" Angie shook her head in frustration. "I not stay here while you fight. I not!"

"They are setting a trap for you girl, the last thing you should do is come with us," Kyle explained. "You can stay here and observe with Drew."

She shook her head, her brow furrowed, and her hands clenched in fists. "Must help. I *can* help."

"Why can't we just blast them from a distance?" Sam asked, his hair mussed from bed, and his black Guardian uniform opened at the waist. "Can't we just take them out with a shot from your ship, or those bioweapons you have?"

"They will be armed against our bio eliminators, those only work when they are dormant, and to fire from the ship would be inaccurate at best, and too hard to cover our presence to the rest of the planet." Kyle adjusted his jacket and checked his sword. Slipping it from the scabbard at his waist he held it high, the dim light in the kitchen reflecting off the wickedly sharp blade as he turned it around. All of the guardians had similar scabbards on their belts, they had the swords as a last resort weapon against the Presas. "We will need to take them on in close contact, as we have done in the past. I also feel it would be in poor judgement to take Angie with us, however I cannot see what we can do to stop her if she insists."

"How many Guardians do you have to meet these enemies?" Sam asked. "By our earlier count there are around two hundred of those creepy terminator guys, so we'd need a few Guardians to take them down."

"We have one hundred Guardians. That will be enough to fight them. We can defeat them comparatively easily; however, I cannot see how it will bring us any closer to finding the traitor."

"I agree Kyle, however we still do not know if there is only one traitor," Michael sighed, his frustration clear.

"I shall check." Angie stepped forward. "I shall check if things work."

"At the school?" Nick asked her. "It's nearly lunchtime, by my reckoning the kids will be about to go to lunch break."

"If children not open. Um… If children not see, then, um, we could, um…" Angie looked frustrated with her own inability to form a proper sentence and make her thoughts understood.

"Hey, it's okay, Angie," Nick soothed. "Take a breath and try again. We'll do our best to understand, okay?"

Angie nodded and took a deep breath, then exhaled it slowly. She took her sunglasses out of her top pocket and placed them on her face before she smiled at Nick, then disappeared.

The men looked at each other, unsure what to do, but Angie appeared seconds later.

"Flyer."

"You want a flyer?" asked Kyle.

She shook her head.

"No, need flyer. Flyer can shoot Presas. Flyer can take them. Flyer will be good. Is a space. Flyer and take them in the space."

"She's right, you know." Drew tapped the display screen. "The Presas are in a wooded area, but there is a clearing a few hundred meters in front of them. They'll hit the other side of the woods that open onto the school after that. If you can get a couple of flyers there quickly, they can help take them out. The Guardians can deal with any stragglers. No one will be able to see the fight."

"We have a plan, then." Kyle turned to Michael and spoke to him in their own language, clearly giving him orders, his voice stern as he spoke quickly, the authority clear in his tone.

Michael nodded and touched his collar, disappearing in a brief shimmer of transport beam. Drew and Sarah stood, with a nod they touched their collars and disappeared as well.

"Drew, Sam, would you please take over monitoring the display screen?" Kyle asked. "We have a feed to the ship, but it would be good to keep this one active as well. It will let Angie see what is happening."

Angie tipped her head to one side, her brows raised in query.

"Nick is here, he will be with you, as will Drew and Sam. Please, Angie, stay here with them, where you are safe. Do not let the Presas' plan have any chance of success."

Angie seemed to mull this over before she nodded. Kyle smiled at her, his relief at her agreement very clear on his features as he touched his collar before he, too, disappeared.

Angie pulled out a kitchen chair but didn't sit, instead she looked around the kitchen. Nick moved to her and took her sunglasses off.

"You are hungry." It wasn't a question, now that he was in such close contact with her, he could once again feel how she felt. He knew exactly what she wanted, and he was compelled to give her whatever she desired. The compulsion was not as strong as when he first met her, but it was there, the bond was unmistakable. The more time he spent with this white-haired woman, the stronger it grew.

Angie smiled at him and put her hand out for her glasses.

"What do we have that she can eat?" Nick asked Drew as he handed Angie her sunglasses. "Bear in mind that she doesn't eat any meat at all."

Drew looked up from the display screen.

"It's odd, you know, since I met her, I haven't wanted anything *but* meat. I'll have to look. I don't think I have too much. Wasn't expecting visitors, you know. Hey, you guys are probably starving, too. I know I am!"

Sam looked up from the screen.

"Whatever you are making, it'll have to be quick. The enemy guys are almost at the clearing."

"Sandwiches it is, then." Drew hurried to the fridge and Nick grabbed the bread from the bench and pulled out a few plates from the dishrack. Angie didn't help, she just stood and watched the men as they hurriedly made a stack of roast beef sandwiches, then a few peanut butter and jelly ones that they arranged on a separate plate. Nick carried them to the table as Drew grabbed four beers and joined him.

Angie looked at the sandwiches, her expression one of confusion. Nick handed her a peanut butter and jelly sandwich as he leaned over to watch the view screen, a roast beef sandwich clenched between his teeth. Sam grabbed at the plate as Drew opened a beer and handed one to him, his eyes not leaving the screen.

Angie took a beer and looked at it before placing it back on the table. She ate all of her sandwiches and then licked the plate, making sure every crumb was gone before she picked up the beer and twisted the top off. Nick stared at her as she drained the whole bottle without taking a breath, then belched loudly, a childish giggle following.

"Here we go!" Sam announced around a mouthful of sandwich.

They all looked at the screen as the Presas breached the edge of the clearing, walking in unison, their rows perfect, stepping in time. They didn't break step as they saw the Guardians appear before them at the other side of the grassy clearing, their helmets covering their faces, weapons drawn and black uniforms gleaming in the midday sun. Onwards they marched, ready to fight.

Chapter Seventy-Four
Trauiss XXII
Escaping the Dungeon
A Long Time Ago
Carrying a Corpse

Robert held the girl tight as James started the flyer, checking around them for anyone that may be following.

It seemed the dungeon guards were true to their words, the liftoff was uneventful, and James turned on the stealth shield as soon as they were in the air. They would leave them on the whole trip, not wanting anyone to see them or guess where they were heading.

Robert moved a little in his seat, trying to shift the bundle in his arms to a more comfortable position. It was hard to see that it was the same girl that had been whisked away from them in the hall of The Lords. Her hair hung in thick knotted matts, her skin was grey and cold. If it were not for the slow breaths and the soft beat of her heart, he would have believed he was carrying a corpse.

The girl turned her head and looked into Robert's face. Her eyes were slit against the bright visual displays, and James muted them to make the cabin more suited to her.

She opened her eyes fully now, the bright purple iris' glowing in the dark of space. She stared at Robert, her pupils narrowed, her brow scrunched.

"It is really me, girl. James and I found you and we are taking you somewhere safe."

The girl blinked, then smiled. Robert could not control himself, he started to cry. James wiped his eyes with the back of his hand and tried to concentrate on flying. He had never seen his brother cry before, not ever.

"Perhaps she may want something to eat, brother?" James suggested, noticing his voice sounded choked with his emotions.

Robert scrubbed a hand across his eyes. "I feel we should wait until we get her safe. You may need me if anyone follows us." He held the girl as tight as he could without feeling like he would snap her bones as they flew on.

Faer continued to stare into his eyes, not moving, not talking. After a while her eyes closed, and she drifted off to sleep. There was a third chair that could recline, Robert could lay her down and let her sleep while he helped his brother fly the craft, but he felt he could never let her go again. So, he sat there, in the second pilot seat, and held her as she slept.

As they approached the shimmering edges of the black hole that served as the gate to their multiverse, James looked over at him, indicating with his head to set the girl down on the empty seat. Robert frowned, then stood and carried the girl, sitting in the third seat himself. He arranged a heavy coat over the girl and reclined the seat to make it look like he was sleeping, with the coat bunched up on him for warmth.

The gate patrol didn't stop them, they didn't even acknowledge the craft going through, James read his clearance message on the display screen as he passed through. "They are not taking their duties seriously, I feel, brother. There should be a greater check of who would come and go through the Gate."

Robert uncovered the girl's head. "It is of more importance to worry about who would come in than who would go. They do not know that we have such precious cargo. Perhaps procedures will change once they discover that she is gone."

He stroked the dirty hair of the girl as she slept.

"They will know the day we choose to return, brother, and they shall rue that day."

Chapter Seventy-Five
Earth
Present Day
The Battle

The flyers zoomed from overhead, two sleek, silent, elongated craft that were a shimmering silver blue, a color that made them almost imperceptible against the clear sky. As they banked and turned, Nick realized they were exactly like the crashed vessel they had seen Angie first appear near, in the footage of a doomed cameraman.

The ships banked and moved downwards, then fired a bright beam of light on the black suited Presas, their beams cutting through the ranks and taking out at least twenty of the enemies before some kind of invisible shield stopped the weapons having any effect. The weapons then changed, blasts of bright blue plasma fired down and splattered the bodies of the men, ripping limbs and torsos apart. The Guardians in the clearing charged now, their weapons high as they fired identical plasma blasts, hitting many of the men before the shielding changed and repelled the shots. The flyers moved up and banked again, the sun barely glinting on the surface of the ships, the material that they were made of seemed to absorb the light rather than reflect it. They swooped low, this time a different weapon blasted a bright green that swept several Presas into oblivion. They managed a couple of passes before the shielding adapted and their weapons bounced off, the light dissipating immediately.

"They're pretty badass when it comes to fending off the Guardians' weapons," Sam commented as he grabbed another sandwich. "They've barely made an impact on them. If they don't come up with something soon, they will be fighting hand to hand, and are seriously outnumbered."

Drew touched the screen and brought up a closer view of the Guardians as they clashed with the Presas, their fighting skills second to none, they were vicious, fast, and fought with such vigor and fervor in a furious manner that it was hard to imagine anyone defeating them.

Angie was sitting in between Sam and Nick, watching the screen. Drew was to one side but could easily see and reach the large screen, he had elected to sit on the side as he could get up and keep them all fed and taken care of. He did this to try and occupy Angie and keep her from joining her Guardians at the battle ground, where the trap to capture her was surely playing out as they watched.

"Anyone want a beer? Or maybe some donuts? They're yesterday's but I'm sure they are still edible."

Drew got up and moved to the icebox, pausing as he heard a knock on his kitchen door.

Like most inhabitants of the small town he lived in, Drew's front door was rarely used, everyone came to his kitchen door at the side of his humble bungalow if they wanted to find the sheriff. He didn't find the knock unusual, more that it was just unexpected.

"You invite anyone to the party?" Nick asked, a half-eaten sandwich in his hand.

"I'm not expecting anyone, not that I can recall, anyway. It's probably my deputy, just stopping in on his way through."

"Should we take the screen into the other room?" Sam asked.

"No, I'll try to get rid of him. He's a good fellow, if I imply that I have feminine company he should leave pretty quickly."

Another knock and Drew started to the door before it flung wide, a large, black leather clad figure in the doorway. The Guardian's uniform was obvious, the helmet and visor drawn to conceal the identity of the person. Clearly male, the tall, strongly built man stepped into the kitchen, his head turned this way and that until he spotted Angie. He stood still, facing her, as the woman sat there, her head tipped to one side in confusion. Her brow was furrowed and her lips tight, she seemed to have no idea who it was.

"You're him!" Nick jumped to his feet, his hand reaching for his police issue weapon. "You're the traitor!"

Drew reacted instantly, also drawing his gun as Sam grabbed Angie and flung her behind him into the corner of the kitchen. All three men had their weapons drawn and faced the man as Angie scrambled to her feet, Sam's body shielding her from the Guardian.

"You're the traitor, aren't you?" Drew asked him, and he turned to face the sheriff. "No funny moves, there. Three of us have a weapon on you, at least one of us is going to get a shot off no matter how fast you go."

The Guardian didn't answer, but behind him Presas started to move into the room. There were a few of them, Nick counted four in the room and another three that stood behind the Guardian. All wore the severe black business style suits, dark glassed on their faces, hair just a little too long that brushed their back collars and shirts buttoned high on their throats.

Each one held a plasma weapon, all pointed at the men as they took their places to the side and behind the Guardian in the crowded small room.

None of the humans moved, their weapons still trained at the Guardian. For a moment no one moved, no one spoke, and the atmosphere was stifling.

Nick forced a smile onto his concerned face.

"You know, at least one of us will still get a shot off, at least one of us can kill you."

The Guardian faced the detective, then looked past him to Sam, and the woman behind him. Angie leaned around the policeman, her confused expression freezing and disappearing as she saw the Presas. She clutched Sam's arm, her grip hard, and she took a breath before stepping to one side so she could see the Guardian more clearly, and he could see her.

Her head tipped to the side, but she did not

speak, did not try to engage with this man at all. Nick could feel his heart hammering in his chest along with a kick of complete annoyance, he felt furious at himself for not realizing that the trap was right here, that the attempted attack on the school was just a ruse to get Angie alone, none of her Guardians around to protect her. A swift glance to the Sheriff and he could tell that Drew felt the same way, he didn't need to look at Sam to know that his partner would be feeling it, too. The traitor Guardian touched the side of his helmet and his visor opened, the helmet folding down into his collar.

Nick didn't recognize the face, it was no one that he had seen before. He met Drew's eyes and saw the same thing; this man was not known to them. Angie moved past Sam and stood next to Nick, her head no longer tilted, and her expression now one of surprise. She tried to move past Nick, but he held his ground, not letting her pass, not letting her near the traitor. She touched his arm, indicating he should let her through. Reluctantly, Nick stepped back.

She stepped very slowly towards the tall man, moving almost reluctantly. Drew took advantage of everyone's attention being on Angie and discreetly touched the small, round, brass colored button on his collar. He tapped it a few times, not sure of the protocol in the current situation, but aware he needed to alert Kyle and his team.

Angie moved close to the traitor, looking as small as a child next to the hulk of a man. He was taller than Kyle, and his shoulders were broader. His features were strong, handsome, and he was the first Guardian Drew had ever seen that had scars on his face. They were not disfiguring, in fact they seemed to add to the man's rugged good looks. Angie clearly knew him, she stood before him, her head tipped back to see his face. She reached up and touched his cheek with the tips of her fingers, letting them trace the strong jawline, the path of his scars and the bridge of his nose. The man cleared his throat to speak.

"Hello, Faer."

Chapter Seventy-Six
The Hideaway
A Long Time Ago
The Blue Planet

The bright blue planet rotated below them as James checked his coordinates. He adjusted a few calculations then looked over his shoulder at his brother.

"I am ready to take us down, now, it will be evening when we land, the sun has just set. I suggest strapping Faer into the seat and then you can join me at the controls."

Robert sighed and shifted himself from under the sleeping girl, carefully buckling the seat restraints before sitting beside his brother.

"Good?" James asked, not looking at Robert.

"I am fine," Robert replied before adjusting his restraints over his shoulders. He tapped the displays a couple of times as he checked his brother's calculations and confirmed the landing coordinates. James was an expert pilot, he slipped the ship in through the atmosphere quietly, gently, and then brought it into land on a rocky outcrop.

"This is a quiet area?" Robert asked as James maneuvered the ship into a large cave in a cliff face. It was very dark in the cave, a flick of the console display and James had the outer lights on, illuminating the vast interior of the cave.

"This is the cave I found on my last trip here. We

will be safe. There is a small tribe of people living on one side of the forest. They breed horses, so when the girl is feeling better, she will be able to play with them, should she wish. On the other side, past the forest, is a village, nice and quiet."

"That sounds like a perfect area. Let us get her out and into our new home."

"I am sure you will be happy with what I have provided, brother. The cavern is multi chambered, dry, and clean. I have hewn out some very good rooms for us to live in, and the ship will be well hidden here."

Robert gathered the girl into his arms and followed James out of the ship, marveling at his brother's ingenuity as a shield formed over the entrance to the part of the cave the ship was in, and it blended perfectly into the surrounding rock walls. The front entrance quickly transformed to a smaller entrance with a replicated door that resembled timber but would far exceed the strength of any natural materials.

James led them through a smaller opening into a living area, and Robert admired the warmth and luxuriousness of his brother's attempts at making a cave network their new home.

The roughhewn walls were covered with plush tapestries, and wall sconces held lights that looked exactly like burning torches, but with no smoke nor smell Robert knew they were merely a clever copy. There were ottomans and large woven blankets, timber tables and chairs, and soft furs and skins covering their beds.

"I cannot place her in a bed in this state, she needs to be cleaned." Robert looked down at the filthy bundle in his arms. "I think we will need to cut all of her hair off, this mess would not possibly be salvaged."

James smiled and nodded before leading his brother through a door into a very modern bathroom arrangement, with a large bath, shower and basins, electric light fittings and thick, plush towels.

"I decided to keep this room the same as what we are used to, the door will only open for us, so if any locals ever choose to visit, this will be hidden from them." James leaned over and started to fill the large bath.

"Good thinking, brother, though I do hope we will not be mixing with any locals much. A low profile is what will be most desirable, I feel."

The brothers gently undressed the girl, the ragged, torn clothes falling apart as the brothers removed them. They were shocked at the emaciated bundle that Robert still held in his arms, her ribs were clearly visible, along with every bone in her spine, and her arms and legs looked no thicker than sticks. Robert felt his heart would break at the sight, how this child survived so long in this condition was a testament to how strong her powers were. Still the planets that relied on her had prospered and grown, while the child withered away. Faer stayed asleep, even when James cut the heavy mats of hair from her head, even when he shaved her scalp, and even when he cut the last remnants of clothing that they had not been able to undo.

She finally woke when Robert lowered her into the warm bath, the water a little cooler than he would have liked but understood that James had not wanted to shock her body in this vulnerable condition.

A brief moment of panic flicked across her eyes before she recognized the brothers, and she relaxed against Robert's arm. He wasn't sure she could support herself so cradled her shoulders as James gently washed her, the soft cloth he was using infused with some sweet-smelling oils. Robert didn't ask what it was, or where he had obtained it, the urn that held the oil looked to be from an ancient bazaar.

Faer allowed herself to be cleansed, James gently unfolding her legs and arms, the warm water helping the stiffness that had settled in on her joints from centuries of not moving.

Draining the bath water, Robert wrapped the girl in a soft towel and carried her back into the main room, laying her on a pile of skins and blankets.

"We need to feed her. I have rations here, and there is food on the ship if you do not want to cook anything." James frowned. "I feel she could not process much more than a simple broth."

Robert tucked the soft towel around the girl's shaven head, her large eyes looking even larger now, the black smudges under her eyes emphasizing the bright purple glow.

"Could you eat something, girl? We need to nourish you back to health, James and I."

Faer blinked, very slowly, then smiled. She

didn't try to talk, and the brothers didn't mind that. They were more than happy that she was responding to them, even in such a limited way. After they had learned where she was being kept, and the conditions she was kept in, they had not held up much hope for any rational thought from the girl. To see her smile, and comfortable enough to sleep, warmed their hearts and gave them hope that they could bring her back to health before too long.

James made some simple vegetable broth for the girl and watched as Robert spooned it into her, the effort of eating was more than her wasted body could take and she fell asleep as she was eating.

James tucked another fur around her, and the men retreated to the table to eat something themselves, neither of them able to take their eyes off the girl.

Chapter Seventy-Seven
Earth
Present Day
No Detectives, No Sheriff, No Angie

Kyle severed the head of the last Presas, his sword heavy in his hands. His plasma weapon holstered, his own blood coating half his chest. He looked around at his men, at least half lay injured on the ground, some in very bad shape. They had fought long and hard, defeating the Presas was not easy, there were so many of them and they were brutal, dirty fighters. Their invisible shielding rendered their blasters useless after a few shots, they had to fight hand and knife, sword and fist. They had not doubted that they would defeat the enemies, but it was not an easy task.

Kyle reached up to tap his communication button when his visor readout came to life, the transparent letters scrolling across his field of vision. Michael stepped over the body of a Presas and touched his visor, opening it to face his commander.

"You saw that? Something is wrong at the house."

Kyle hit his collar.

"Transport the wounded back to the ship, and the rest of us to the house. Immediately."

Only forty-seven Guardians appeared at the house, and Kyle felt his alarm rise dramatically at the sight of the kitchen door hanging off its hinges.

He drew his sword and blaster, holding them high as he stepped into the house, closely followed by Michael and several other Guardians. There were signs of a struggle in the small room, the table was overturned, chairs smashed, the bright curtains pulled off their rail. The display screen was on its side on the floor, still showing the feed from the battlefield as the drones hovered overhead, the vision showing Guardians disposing of the Presas bodies and cleaning up the signs of any conflict.

Kyle ordered the Guardians to check every room, and they moved swiftly, but the house was empty.

No detectives, no sheriff, no Angie.

"Clean the mess. Get the screen up on the table and wipe all traces of our existence here." Kyle started to pace, his thoughts racing, his anger growing. Clearly, he had been fooled, the trap was not to get Angie to the school, the trap had been to get the Guardians away from Angie.

He had failed her again. Once more the traitor had her, and she was not at full strength, was not healed enough to take care of herself, nor protect the innocent men with her.

He had failed her.

His guilt felt like a knife to his stomach, cutting deep and hard.

He had no idea who the traitor was, and even less of an idea where to find him.

"Sir! Look at the screen!" a guardian exclaimed.

Kyle spun around to see Angie standing in the middle of the clearing where they had just fought the battle, Guardians surrounding her. Behind her stood Drew and the detectives, looking disheveled and confused.

"Fix the door." He pointed to two Guardians. "The rest with me." He touched his collar and they all disappeared, reappearing in the clearing. Kyle stepped forward three great strides and grabbed Angie by the shoulders.

"I thought they had you! I thought I had lost you again, that I had let you down once more!"

Angie shook her head and gave him a crooked grin, her eyes squinting in the bright light. Her sunglasses were no longer in her pocket, so Kyle grabbed up a discarded pair from the ground that a Presas had worn.

"What happened at the house?" Kyle asked as he handed the glasses to Angie.

"The traitor turned up with his Presas. Knocked on my kitchen door like he was an Avon lady."

"I do not understand what that is, but I could see that we fell for the trap. I feared you were all taken, or worse."

"He showed his face to us. I didn't recognize him, and I don't think you two did, either, did you?" Drew turned to the detectives who were shaking their heads.

"Did you recognize him, Angie?" Kyle asked.

She didn't answer, but instead looked around at the battlefield and the Guardians clearing any signs of the Presas, then turned back to Kyle. She touched his vest that was covered in blood, then touched the cut in the leather-like fabric, his blood still dripping from the gash.

"You are hurt." It was a simple statement but did not answer his question.

"She knew him, all right. He tried to take her arm and she dodged him, then smashed those Presas within a blink of an eye. I've never seen her fight, never seen anyone fight like that. It was insane. She was like something from a *Matrix* movie. Smashed them, then grabbed us and zapped us out of there." Sam was breathless in his explanation.

"The traitor just stood there and watched her rip those Presas apart, then he tried to grab her again," Drew added. "She literally just touched us all, as Sam said, and we winked out. Took us to some cliff by the ocean, then a forest, then here. I thought I would pass out; it was the weirdest feeling."

"Whoever it was, they took all of the Presas remains with them, the house was a mess but there was no sign of any intruder." Kyle turned back to Angie. "You saw him, you saw who it was. Who is it, Angie? Did they talk to you?"

Angie tipped her head to one side but did not answer.

"Let us go back to the ship, we can discuss this on board." Kyle gestured to the clean-up operation around them. "These Guardians will be finished soon, and I feel it would be safer there at this moment."

He looked down at Angie, and she nodded at him, the smile still in place.

"Drew, Detectives, you will join us as well. Are you ready, Angie?"

Angie nodded again and disappeared, the soft

sound of unseen wings taking her instead of a transport shimmer.

"I hope she went to the ship," Nick sighed. "He did talk to her, you know. Just for a moment."

"What did he say?"

"He said something in your language, he seemed really sad, I guess. She seemed shocked. Oh, before that, he called her something. Fur? Fay?"

"*Faer*," corrected Kyle, his face suddenly pale. "Are you sure?"

The three men all nodded, and Kyle's face turned a shade of gray.

"This cannot be."

Chapter Seventy-Eight
The Hideaway
A Long Time Ago
A Roast for Supper

The girl slept for several days, waking very briefly to take in small amounts of food before falling asleep again. The brothers were heartened in the improvement they could see, it was only small, a slow recovery, but her hair had started to grow back, and her skin had turned a healthier color. She wasn't taking in enough food to cover her bones, but they knew once she awoke, they could feed her and fatten her up to health.

The men passed the time by exploring the local area, always one at a time as the other watched over the girl, never leaving her to wake alone. James went first, having come to this planet to establish their new home and scouting the area, he was familiar with the surroundings and knew where to forage, hunt, and where the local indigenous tribes were located. Robert ventured out less, wanting to avoid any accidental meetings with the locals he only left to hunt and cut wood for the fire.

James had done a fine job converting the cliff face, it appeared as nothing more than a sturdy wood cabin set into a recess in the rock. It looked small, rustic, and not at all suspicious to any who would find it.

And find it they did.

Many a day James would find a local youth, or traveler, or village elder at their door, their curiosity over the tall strangers and the wooden cabin drawing them in. So far, he had managed to send them off with little explanation, but he knew it would not last long, and he didn't want to inflame the superstitious nature of these local people.

It was the evening after finding several men staring at the cabin from afar, making their signs to ward off evil, that he decided to discuss the issue with his brother. He had been hunting, successfully, and had a large deer straddled over his shoulders when his brother opened the door to him.

"Good eve, brother, I see you have venison for us this sup!"

James handed the kill over to Robert so he could skin and gut the carcass.

"That I have, Robert, but I also have concerns I wish to discuss with you."

Robert tossed the deer onto his roughhewn cleaning bench and turned back to James, a smile breaking through his features and lighting up his face.

"What cheers you so? I have not seen you look this pleased since you found that the tavern girl in Milnas had a twin sister."

"She awakens, brother! She has been awake for two and more hours, and has eaten, and even walked. I did have to help her to bathe, but she is awake!"

James felt his grin split his features as a small face peered through the darkness of the doorway, soft blond hair now long enough to tumble in a muss of curls across her scalp. James strode forward and grabbed her up in his arms, gently but exuberantly he twirled her around, his genuine, deep laughter eliciting a childish giggle from her. He lifted her away from himself so he could see her face, but her eyes were scrunched tight against the dim twilight.

"Let us move inside, I can prepare the deer in a moment. Come, both of you, into the warmth."

James carried the girl inside and Robert drew the door closed behind them. Once he set her down in the dim interior, Faer opened her eyes and smiled. She was still very frail, painfully thin, and very pale. Her hair had grown a half finger length but was not enough to cover the sharp cheek bones or jutting clavicle, her fingers looked like sticks. James tried to ignore her emaciated state and instead took comfort in her smile and her upright stance.

"Are you hungry, Faer?" Robert asked her, and she shook her head.

"How many times have you fed her since she woke, Robert? Leave her be, she can only fit so much into her shrunken stomach."

This made the girl giggle again, her very large eyes, now looking so much larger in her thin face, crinkled at the sides in delight.

"How are you feeling? Are you feeling better?" James mussed her hair and grinned down at her. "You certainly look much better!"

"Good." Her voice was soft, barely more than a whisper, but it made Robert grab her up and hug her before setting her down on the low seating at the side of the room.

"That was her first word, James, she has not spoken until now! What a good day, I am happy, brother, I am happy!"

"I can see that, brother," James laughed and pulled a wooden chair around, straddling it and smiling at his brother's excitement.

The girl yawned sleepily and leaned back, her eyelids drooping, but her smile still gracing her delicate features.

"I do have concerns I wished to talk to you about, Robert. As I came over the rise towards home, I found the local villagers making signs on themselves to protect from evil. Brother, I feel if we do not address this soon, we will have a few clans hunting us for witches or as some other evil creatures."

Robert sighed. "It was bound to happen, and be it sooner than we hoped, it is not unexpected. What do you think we should do? Invite them in to take a meal with us? Sup with the village leaders?"

James looked thoughtful. "No, not invite them in, as such, but let them see us as normal. They have a gathering of clans, an open marketplace, where they set up their goods and products and barter and sell them. I think we should take some of our skins and furs and trade them. Do something that makes us look no different to them."

"That is a good plan, brother," Robert nodded. "What do we do with Faer? I would not feel comfortable leaving her here alone. Maybe eventually, but not now. Not yet."

James looked at the girl, she had drifted off to sleep sitting up, her head slumped to one side on the soft cushions of the divan.

"I agree, it is too soon to leave her at home. They meet every twenty days, by my count, and we have five days until they meet again. Let us see how she is feeling then. She may be well enough to leave here, in the rear of the caverns, where the shielding can be turned on to keep her safe."

"Coming."

The brothers looked over to the girl, her head still lumped over, but her eyes were open, just a little.

"Coming," she repeated before yawning and curling up into a fetal position.

"Well, that settles it, I suppose. We can take her to the market with us," James smiled.

"I do not feel she could walk that far."

"We will have to build a cart. We will need to transport the goods to trade, and she can ride in the cart."

"Well, that will be something I can start tomorrow. For now, I shall clean the deer and set a nice haunch to roast for our supper." Robert slapped his thighs and walked to the door. "You can set the fire, James. I think your plan is a fine plan, now all you will need is a story to tell the people about who we are, who she is, and why we are here."

Chapter Seventy-Nine
Earth's Orbit
The Alcea
Present Day
That's The One

"Are you certain that is what he called her?" Kyle paced the floor, his head bowed, his fists clenched. "I find it very hard to comprehend this, very hard. I do believe you, but it seems impossible!"

Michael was sitting at the long oval table, the surface a translucent, opalized cream color, the same as the walls and the floor. One wall was transparent, it showed the stars and the distant moon, the Earth a brilliant blue orb in between them. Drew couldn't help but feel awed and humbled all at the same time, he had not been on the Guardian's ship and had to keep shutting his mouth that had hung agape more than once. Drew noticed Michael kept shaking his head, as if to clear it, his expression was as confused as Kyle's.

Around the table there were several Guardians that Drew had not met before. Sam and Nick sat opposite Drew, their Guardian outfits now swapped back for their normal clothes. They both looked a little confused, not privy to the possible identity of the traitor. Angie had not joined them in the ship, much to everyone's disappointment, in fact no one knew her location and they were all very worried about her.

Drew cleared his throat. "If I may ask, Kyle, who is it that you think is the traitor? It's got you very upset, and I can see everyone is just as outraged as you are. Sam, Nick and I are at a bit of a loss when it comes to the inside knowledge here."

Kyle stopped pacing and faced the sheriff. "My apologies, gentlemen, for this oversight. I shall get Elyse to explain, as briefly as possible, as to why we are so concerned."

Elyse stood and walked over to the window wall. She touched it and immediately the clear view changed to a plain wall, the same color as everything else in the room. She touched it again and a small touch panel showed, and she tapped this a few times until a picture filled the wall.

Angie stood center, smiling, her blonde hair swirling in soft curls to her waist. She was dressed in a dark blue velvet formal gown, it was adorned with jewels glistening and shining, a tiara on her head and chunky diamonds adorning her neck. On her shoulders lay a black, sleek cat, and to each side of her stood very tall, stern looking guards, dressed in very formal looking military uniforms. Swords in ornate scabbards hung from their sides, shorter daggers in similar scabbards hung beside the swords. They wore helmets that obscured most of their faces.

"This is a formal portrait taken many millennia ago when Angie ruled our multiverse, she was the supreme ruler and commander. At her sides you see her personal bodyguards that history buffs believe actually raised her."

"History buffs? Are there no records of this?" Sam asked.

"There were several coups and changes of government, prior to this image capture, and many records were lost or destroyed," Elyse explained.

"How long ago was this, if you have no reliable records?" Drew asked. "Is there no one surviving from that period?"

Elyse looked uncomfortable. "Certain events in our history meant that those in government and also those involved in the early years of Angie are no longer alive. There is no recorded history from that time, and those that are still alive from that period were not in a position of knowledge." The humans exchanged loaded glances, then looked back at the wall.

"Here is another picture of the three of them, we are not sure when this one was taken." The screen showed Angie on a white horse, her hair streaming out behind her as the horse galloped, her two companions were by her side, also on horses.

"The men that were purported to have raised her were instructed to give her a casual name, something to call her instead of her formal title. We believe they called her Faer."

"Have you asked Angie about any of this?" Nick asked.

"She does not talk about it. She flatly refuses to discuss it in any way," Kyle informed them.

Elyse tapped the screen again and this time the image was more casual, it showed Angie sitting on a log in the darkness, a fire burning in front of her. She was dirty, her hair pulled back from her face, and her guards again by her side, the darkness and the dirt on their faces obscuring her features.

Elyse indicated the men. "There is not a lot known about these guards, we know they were the first of the Guardians, of a sort, and it is thought that they were military, some kind of warriors, but little else is known. We don't know if they were brothers, lovers, or just two men put in charge of her. They are thought to have never married, nor did they bear any offspring, though that is not unusual. The images you see are all that we have of the three of them together. We have some other random images of guards from that time, though we don't know if it is of them, or just other guards."

Elyse let the images scroll now, there were military line ups, some of men standing with blasters in their hands, or a drink at some informal function. It was difficult to see if the faces were all the same, or of different men. In some scenes Angie would appear, dressed in uniform as well, or standing with weapons, or holding a beverage. One last picture filled the wall, that of Angie, looked a little wistful, with her two guards standing to each side, their stern, handsome faces no longer covered.

Nick gasped. "That's him! That's the guy that came for Angie!"

"Which one?" Kyle asked.

"It is Robert." Angie stood there, near the door. No one had heard her appear. "Robert is the one. He came to take me. Came to kill me."

Chapter Eighty
The Blue Planet
A Long Time Ago
What Fine Horses

"Hail Robert, hail James! A good day to you both. Where is that girl of yours?"

"Hail, Ulvert, and a good day to you. Our niece has run to see what fine horses the traders have today," Robert told him as he threw down a large rug onto the ground and started to unload the furs and leather hides to sell.

Ulvert turned and looked towards the far end of the market where the horse merchants corralled their livestock, then turned back to the brothers. He ran his hand through the thick fur that graced the top of the cart, a white spotted sable deer fur very pleasing to the touch.

"You find something you would like?" James asked him.

"To be very honest, every time you come to trade, I find something I like. This past half year has seen me take home a very many of your furs to my wives, and they were all very well received. This time I have been tasked with two errands by my wives. One is to buy some leather hides to make fine ladies' garments, and the other, well, that is something very different."

The brothers exchanged looks and then turned back to the older man. Ulvert had been their best customer and their much-appreciated spokesperson, taking to the two men as soon as he met them, including them in the feasts and gatherings that the village celebrated.

"What is the second task, my friend?" James pulled another fur from the cart and rolled it up, setting it on the rug on the ground. "You seem reluctant to share."

Ulvert scratched his beard and then patted his more than ample stomach.

"It is my wives, you see. Two of them are sisters. Fine women. Good cooks. Even better companions in the sleeping chamber, if you understand me."

"We understand you," Robert laughed as he tossed another fur to James.

"Well, my friends, they have given me some very fine children, these wives. And girls, my goodness, my friends, I have many daughters! These two wives once gave birth to daughters on the very same day. At the very same time, no less! These girls, well, they look very similar, often it is almost impossible to tell them apart. Beautiful girls, also very fine looks, and I am sure they would be very fine companions, as well!"

Robert looked at his brother, who was shaking his head.

"I also have sons. Not as many as daughters, but I have fine, strong sons. Much finer than myself, let me tell you! My youngest son, Ulhamen, he is a good boy. Tall, why, he would nearly be as tall as yourselves! He is of a good age, too, and will need a wife. A good wife, someone he can take care of. I think your niece would make such a wife, my friends. It is time for her to look past her grief of losing her parents and look to make a family of her own."

The brothers stopped what they were doing and looked at Ulvert. He took a step back, intimidated by their stern gaze as they towered over him.

Before they could say anything Faer came running up, her face bright with happiness. The brothers had rigged her a crude pair of dark glasses that allowed her to see in the bright winter sun, and while it was initially treated with suspicion, the happy, infectious nature of the girl won over the sceptics.

At first the brothers had been shocked that she had bounced back so well, after so long being incarcerated in such horrific surroundings, the girl was almost as happy and bright as she had been before she was taken from them. They had seen no outbursts of anger or strange powers, no resentment, and no fear. Occasionally she would fall quiet and want to be alone, but these times were few and far between, and the brothers were forever grateful to have the girl back the way she was.

"What is it, child? What has you so happy?" Robert asked.

"Can you see anything?" Faer turned around, spinning on one foot, her waist length hair shining in the sunlight.

"What is it you hold on your shoulders, Faer?" Ulvert asked, and the brothers leaned forward to catch what the portly man had seen.

A small brown face pushed through her long locks, sleek pointed ears and bright yellow eyes blinked fearfully at the tall men.

"A kitten! Hah! You have a new pet!" Ulvert laughed and patted his stomach. "Pierse was trying to get my girl to take one, as well!"

"Oh yes, Alcea has taken two! She said that you have mice in your storage house, and that they will come in handy!' Faer reached up and pulled the brown kitten from her shoulders. It was a straggly, mangy looking thing, James had no doubt it would have been the runt of the litter, more suited to having its neck rung than catching mice for anyone.

"We have no mice, Faer," Robert said, his voice, while soft, was very guarded. "Perhaps you should take that poor creature back to its mother. It looks like it needs to have her care for a few more weeks before it finds a new home."

"Oh, it cannot! The mother has passed, and all of the kittens have been given away. This is the last one, and she needed me. I could feel it. She came straight to me and climbed up on my shoulders."

A young man sauntered up, trying to look disinterested and tough, but his eyes gave him away when he looked at Faer.

"I like your kitten." He spoke shyly, his face coloring as he spoke.

"Let me guess, this is your son that you spoke about?" James asked.

"Oh yes, please, let me introduce you to my youngest son. Faer, Robert, James, this is Ulhamen."

Faer turned to look at the boy, her head tilted to one side. She looked him up and down as if assessing livestock.

"Ulhamen. I see. Do you know much about horses, Ulhamen? The trader from the east is arriving with some finely bred horses that I am eager to see. Alcea and I are going to have a look at them."

The boy nodded profusely and looked to his father for permission. Ulvert smiled and nodded, then laughed as the two young people ran off towards the livestock.

"It looks like we will not have to do very much matchmaking with these two."

"We will see, Ulvert. Now, how many leather hides were you looking for? James has found some very fine deer hides that are as soft as a baby's behind. Here, James, pass them up."

"I am thinking that you two could deliver the hides after the market. Stop and take a meal with us. You can meet my daughters, and your niece can spend a little more time with my son. Agreed?"

Robert smiled, but it was forced. He needed to think of an excuse, but James could see him struggling to think of something that would not insult Ulvert.

"We would be very pleased to drop the hides for you, Ulvert, but would prefer if we took a meal and met your daughters when we are not tired and dirty from the market. We would not, perhaps, make such a good impression."

Ulvert smiled at James and nodded.

"That sounds like a very good idea. Alhamen can bring the hides. I will speak to you at day's end to make a better time. Excellent! What a good day it is. Now, I can see that you are becoming busy with many souls eager for your wares, so I will go and supervise the young ones. We do not need them agreeing to purchase any horses today!"

Chapter Eighty-One
Earth's Orbit
The Alcea
Present Day
The Accident

"Where is he now, Angie?" Kyle asked.

Shaking her head, Angie walked to the wall, staring at her beloved guards. She reached up as if to touch him before letting her hand drop.

"Angie?" Kyle spoke very softly.

"I know not." She turned to face him, her expression sad. "Gone. Not anywhere."

"So, we hunt him, we find him. We know who it is now, so we have something to go on, right?" Sam asked.

"It is not that easy." Kyle pulled out a chair for Angie, but she didn't sit down. "This man was thought to be dead for many centuries. We have no way to track him, no way to know where he may be."

"But you know, don't you, Angie? You know where he might be?" Nick asked her.

Angie looked at Nick and tilted her head to one side. She shrugged.

"No, I do not know. Not, um, I am not sure? Artu will find him."

"That's where you were? With the vampire?" Nick frowned. "Well, I guess he's pretty good at finding people. Where does that leave us? What do we do now?"

"Wait." Angie touched her forehead and smiled. "Think. Plan. Get ready. Will be a battle. Will be trouble. Will be much trouble."

"How do you know this? What else did he tell you?" Kyle's hands were clenched in fists. "Did he say why he was back?"

Angie nodded.

"He said little. Not much. Said, um, said it is time. Time for me to um, to, ah…" She shook her head as if to clear it, frustrated, unable to form the words she needed to explain herself. "Said time to end. For me to end. For me to be no more. For killing James. Killing his brother. For being wrong. No, not wrong, um, for being, um, abnom? A bomb?"

"Abomination?" Michael offered, his voice nothing more than a whisper.

Angie nodded.

"Yes. I am an abomination. I will pay, and all who help me, um, all who help will die."

"He said that?" Nick jumped to his feet. "He threatened you, and us?"

Sam placed a hand on Nick's back, encouraging him to sit down.

"I'm sorry, it's just that he seems to have so much power. I mean, he got to her once, he's controlling all these enemies, and he knows everything the Guardians do. Also, where has he been all these years? I'm gathering you all thought he was dead, or something, so where has he been hiding, and why did he come back now?" Nick pulled Sam's hand away and sat. "If you knew where he's been hiding, maybe that's where you'll find him now?"

Kyle sighed.

"I can understand your frustration, Nick, but I am not sure there would be any way to find out where he has been hiding. If he is still alive, I wonder if he has been close enough to benefit from Angie's powers. How else could he survive without her?"

"Blood." Angie turned back to the picture on the wall. "He had blood. Blood lasts, um, a long time. Very long time. He lasts a very long time."

"He had your blood? But, Angie, that does not mean he could live this long. Most of us have had your blood at some time or another.' Michael gestured around the table. "It is what we use to save people when they have no other way to be saved."

Angie turned to him and nodded.

"Pure blood. Before. Long time before."

"Pure blood? What does that even mean?" Sam asked.

"Before. Before controls. Before these." She lifted her shirt and showed the silver bands around her waist. "Pure blood."

"That would have been a very long time ago." Kyle looked grim. "Do you know why he wants to destroy you? You said something about killing his brother? You killed James?"

She turned back to the wall and reached up, her finger outlining the face of her guard. She turned back to face the room, a tear trickling down her face.

"I did not. Um, I did not mean to. I did not mean to. Accident. It was an accident."

"An accident? Angie, how did he die? How did he not survive, especially as his brother survived? Did he not have blood, as well?" Kyle asked her.

Angie shook her head as another tear fell. She scrunched her eyes, then scrubbed them with her fists, an angry grunt escaping her.

"Could not! Could not! No blood. Accident. It was accident!" She looked up to Kyle, her eyes red, her face twisted with despair. "Accident," she said again, very softly, then disappeared.

Chapter Eighty-Two
The Blue Planet
A Long Time Ago
Be The Calm

"Are you sure we could not get out of this?" Robert asked as he adjusted his saddle. The horse shifted a little and nickered its concern.

"We have put them off for far too long, my brother. If we wish to keep all things peaceful then we need to appease the merchant and meet his daughters."

"I think you just want a wife, James," Faer teased as her white horse danced on the spot, its neck arched, and tail held high. "Come on, my stallion is anxious to move!"

"Do not forget, girl, that there is a fine husband waiting there for you as well!" James shot back as he mounted his horse, a heavy, black beast with a very long mane and feathers at his feet. Robert mounted as well, his horse an almost mirror image of his brother's. Only Faer rode a finer build of horse, a graceful, pure white steed with fire in his eyes.

"That horse is dangerous, Faer, I do not know how you talked us into trading for it." Robert pulled his cloak around himself and refastened the clasp. "Well, we cannot delay this any further. We must be off. James, you have the cask of wine?"

James nodded as he nudged his horse into

motion. Faer followed him, her stallion jig jogging behind, with Robert bringing up the rear. A blur caught his eye as a brown streak flashed past them. Faer's cat jumped up onto the stallion's rump and then onto her shoulder as they moved.

Robert had not been happy about the cat, he was worried about the potential to trigger an outburst, the likes of what happened in her past and caused her to be jailed. He had not spoken to James about his concerns but was sure his brother felt the same way. They had not said anything at all to Faer and she seemed happy, the cat was quiet, well behaved, and did indeed keep the mice and rats at bay. It slept in the stables, but Robert knew that it would slink in after they were all supposed to be in bed, Faer holding the door open quietly to allow it inside.

The brothers had managed to get their hands on quite a few of the controls that Elund and his team had made for Faer to wear, as well as the contact lenses that helped shield her eyes, and as a side effect, change them from purple to green. They did not know if they applied the controls correctly, or even if they had placed enough on her. They could only hope, and the verity that she had controlled her emotions and her powerful outburst led them to believe they were doing all the right things. James was building a workstation that could scan her, and them, to check on the efficacy of the controls, but it was still a few days off being complete.

The brothers had talked about what they would do if Faer's powers came back, if the uncontrollable force erupted again, and had not been able to think of a solution. They were pleased that, so far, it had not, though it was never far from their minds.

The ride to the village was uneventful, in fact Robert found it quite a pleasant ride, the scenery was beautiful, the skies clear, the midday sun was warm but not unbearable. Faer sang a little as they rode, a simple tune she had picked up from Ulvert's daughter Alcea. Robert loved to hear her sing, it was something he had always enjoyed, though she never sang any songs from Trauiss. Those songs, the tunes, the music and the dance were all gone, something that was never talked about, never brought up, and barely even thought about.

They rode through the wooded area, the road to the village, while rough, was easy enough to ride, and the woods were filled with the earthy scents of moss, leaves, detritus and softly petaled flowers. It was a soothing place, and a good place to hunt. It reminded Robert of the place he grew up, many years ago, before the wars, before he was a warrior, before he raised a little hybrid girl to become the savior of their multiverse.

"That horse has not settled the entire way," James noted. "It is not a wonder they accepted such a low price for him. I do not believe anyone else would ever be able to ride him."

"Perhaps, brother, but he does bring in a healthy price for his stallion services. All people can see is the beauty, not the fire." Robert scratched his horse's wither. "Me, I prefer my lumbering tank, here. What say you, Faer?"

The girl was quiet, causing James to turn and

look at her.

"Something is wrong. Something is very wrong," she said, her head tipped to one side.

"What is it, Faer? Is your horse ill?"

"No, not my horse. The village. Something is happening. People are screaming, people are dying. Something is very wrong!"

James kicked his horse into a gallop, Faer's horse needing no encouragement to race, and Robert's followed along obediently.

They broached the forest at a fast gallop, the village could be seen ahead and there were multiple columns of smoke rising. They could not get any more speed out of their heavy horses, but Faer's steed was swift and light and raced ahead. She slowed as she neared the village and let the brothers catch up, and what they saw caused James to reign his horse, it neighed as it stopped, heaving sweaty hot breaths.

"What are you doing? The village is under attack!" Faer cried.

"This is not our battle," Robert admonished her. "We do not know who is attacking them, we cannot risk exposing who we really are. It is not safe to enter the village or to help them."

"But my friends are dying! We have to help them!"

"Girl, we cannot. We must not."

Faer pursed her lips and frowned at the men. She kicked her horse and he jumped into a gallop as the girl raced into the village.

"Damn her. Damn her defiance," Robert growled

and kicked his horse to follow her.

As they drew closer to the village, they could hear the screams and the shouts, the sound of swords clashing against shields, men yelling and children crying. The village was being attacked by an army of men, they wore armor and rode heavy horses similar to the brothers. Faer was waiting for them at the outskirts of the village, her face red with anger. Her hair was full, high, and she crackled with power. The cat stood arched at her neck, hissing and spitting. She lifted the cat off her shoulder and dropped it to the ground where it immediately raced for home

"Faer! You need to take a breath; you cannot enter a battle in this state!" Robert yelled to her. "You need to be calm! Look at me, look at my brother. We never enter a battle angry. Faer, breathe! Take a deep breath, now!"

The girl whipped her horse to face Robert and he could feel her power slap him like a punch to the face. The dark glasses did not conceal the bright green flame of her eyes, but she was listening. She drew a ragged breath, then another. Her hair started to settle, and the fire left her eyes. She took another breath, then nodded.

"You should wait here," James told her.

"You know I will not."

"I know. You must fight to stay calm, though. Keep your head steady. Do not lose your nerve. You remember your training, do you not?"

She nodded.

"Then live it. Be it. Be the calm. You have never

fought a real battle. You have never killed a soul. It will change you, girl, remember that." James threw her a sword, both brothers carrying one on their waists as well as another on their horses.

"They are dying while we talk," Faer said as she caught the sword. "I am ready. I am calm. But I feel haste is required."

The warriors drew their swords, their training ingrained, their movements calm, steady, and their faces stoic.

Without a word they spurred their horses into the battle, clashing with the enemy within moments of entering the fray. Robert kept an eye on Faer as he fought the foes, while strong and good fighters, were no match for his skills and experience. He and his brother had met demons on the battlefield, no human foe had any chance against them.

Faer fought with all of the skills the brothers had taught her, and so much more. She seemed to grow in skill and power as she fought, her prowess with the sword impressive, her grit and determination admirable.

With the help of the girl and the brothers the battle turned, before much time passed the enemies were defeated, and the village people stood stunned, many dead and injured, many of the buildings burning. James and Robert were still mounted, they moved around the village checking for any stray combatants.

Faer was still on her horse, as well, and for once the stallion was standing quietly. Robert could see her talking to Ulvert, and her shoulders slumped as he spoke to her.

Riding over to her, he could feel his stomach clench with dread. While glad to see Ulvert had survived, he worried as to what news he would hear.

Faer turned to him as he dismounted, leaping from her horse to fall into his arms, sobbing.

"Ulvert, my friend, what ill has befallen you?"

James dismounted and strode over to the large man, the normally jovial face stained with tears.

"My children, oh James, it is beyond horror. They killed my daughters, the very ones you were coming to meet, and my dear Alcea. Alhamen is gravely wounded from trying to protect them. Oh, my friends, today is a bitter, terrible day!" Ulvert cried.

"But you three, you are our saviors!" A man Robert did not know stepped forward. "If not for your skills and fierce attack, we would be overcome! You have saved us! You have delivered us from these murderers!"

"Our heroes! Our saviors!" There were others, all coming forward to praise the brothers and their charge. Robert cast a worried glance to his brother, unsure of what to do or how to react.

"Oh yes, my friends, how fortunate for us to have retired soldiers in our midst! What good fortune that today was the day you accepted my invitation!" Ulvert fell to his knees. "My heart is torn from my chest with grief, but if not for you I may be mourning more than three children! Hail to our warriors! All hail our warriors!"

Despite their injuries and shock, the surviving villagers cheered and praised the trio, who took their applause with modest embarrassment.

"This is not the way we planned to live quietly in hiding on this planet, brother," James whispered.

"No, brother, that it is not," Robert answered, as Faer turned her tear-stained face to the crowd, her sobs still wracking her small body.

"I fear our lives here have changed, and I would not be sure that is a good thing." James looked around at the milling crowd.

"Time will tell, brother, and I hope that it will be sooner, rather than later, that we see what the next chapter of our lives will bring."

Chapter Eighty-Three
Earth's Orbit
The Alcea
Present Day
Farewell

Drew took a tentative bite of the food before him, then started to eat with more gusto. It was delicious, while he couldn't decide what it tasted like, it was the finest food he had ever tasted.

"Good, isn't it?" Sam asked around a mouthful. "I don't know what it is, but this is amazing!"

Nick grinned and continued to eat, shoveling his food in like a starving man.

"I am pleased you are enjoying this offering." Kyle sat at the table with the men, the large dining room empty except for them. "After you have fed us over the last few days, I felt it was only fitting."

"Much appreciated! This food is amazing. What is it?" Drew asked.

Kyle smiled. "It is all prepared here on the ship from vegetation grown in our home worlds. You are eating food that has never been seen on Earth. You are tasting something no one else on Earth has tasted."

"I feel special!" Sam laughed as he finished his last mouthful. "So, what now? What is next, not just for you, but for us?"

Kyle scrubbed a hand down his face, then scratched his short beard.

"We wait. We wait for Angie to come back with news. We wait to hear if the vampire contacts you. We wait to see if there are any reports or sightings of Presas. We wait. We have also organized for another ship to join us. There will be twice as many Guardians here, waiting with us." He placed his hands flat on the dining table, palms down. "You three should return to Earth and continue to fight the creatures that were created by these traitors. We do not know how many there are, or if they are multiplying on their own. It would be wise to proceed with the thought that they most likely are. We have heard multiple reports of attacks, and they are fitting the profile of creature attacks."

The three nodded, aware that Kyle spoke the truth.

"You may hear from Artu, and I know you will contact us as soon as this happens. You may also hear from Angie before we do. So, in a way, you will be waiting, as well."

"It will be reassuring knowing you guys are close if we need you." Nick pushed his empty plate aside. "I hope we can work together before too long."

The door to the dining room slid open and Michael entered, three police issue pistols in his hands.

"This will make things a lot easier for you to remove the remains of any creatures you have to dispose of. They are the bio eliminators, engineered to look like your weapons. They are the same as the ones that you have used when you accompanied the

Guardians. Drew, I will give you a quick rundown on how to use yours. It is not difficult." Michael handed the men the blasters.

Kyle shook hands with the men before standing.

"Michael will organize your transport back to Earth. We will meet again very soon."

"I hope so, Kyle, I really do." Drew stood, and the detectives joined him.

"We'll be in contact as soon as we hear anything," Sam said.

Kyle smiled, and raised a hand in farewell.

... to be continued ...

Acknowledgements:

As always, I thank my wonderful writing friends Vikki and Alison, and my reading friends Joan, Cassie & Julia, and all of you that read my books. I am humbly grateful for your interest, and your reviews mean more to me than just about anything.

To Helen, for being my dear friend and confidante, I treasure your support, encouragement, and love.

To Peter and Leanne Blakey-Novis for believing in me.

To Ayden, Elise and Zoey for asking me to tell them stories, and telling me theirs, too.

And lastly, to my unicorn, Todd, for being there when I need you.

Also from Red Cape Publishing

Anthologies:

Elements of Horror Book One: Earth
Elements of Horror Book Two: Air
Elements of Horror Book Three: Fire
Elements of Horror Book Four: Water
A is for Aliens: A to Z of Horror Book One
B is for Beasts: A to Z of Horror Book Two
C is for Cannibals: A to Z of Horror Book Three
D is for Demons: A to Z of Horror Book Four
E is for Exorcism: A to Z of Horror Book Five
F is for Fear: A to Z of Horror Book Six
G is for Genies: A to Z of Horror Book Seven
H is for Hell: A to Z of Horror Book Eight
I is for Internet: A to Z of Horror Book Nine
J is for Jack-o'-Lantern: A to Z of Horror Book Ten
K is for Kidnap: A to Z of Horror Book Eleven
It Came From The Darkness: A Charity Anthology
Castle Heights: 18 Stories, 18 Storeys
Sweet Little Chittering

Short Story Collections:

Embrace the Darkness by P.J. Blakey-Novis
Tunnels by P.J. Blakey-Novis
The Artist by P.J. Blakey-Novis
Karma by P.J. Blakey-Novis
The Place Between Worlds by P.J. Blakey-Novis
Home by P.J. Blakey-Novis
Short Horror Stories by P.J. Blakey-Novis
Short Horror Stories Vol. 2 by P.J. Blakey-Novis
Keep It Inside & Other Weird Tales by Mark Anthony Smith
Something Said by Mark Anthony Smith
Everything's Annoying by J.C. Michael
Six! by Mark Cassell

Monsters in the Dark by Donovan 'Monster' Smith

Novelettes:

The Ivory Tower by Antoinette Corvo

Novellas:

Four by P.J. Blakey-Novis
Dirges in the Dark by Antoinette Corvo
The Cat That Caught The Canary by Antoinette Corvo
Bow-Legged Buccaneers from Outer Space by David Owain Hughes
Spiffing by Tim Mendees

Novels:

Madman Across the Water by Caroline Angel
The Curse Awakens by Caroline Angel
Less by Caroline Angel
Where Shadows Move by Caroline Angel
Origin of Evil by Caroline Angel
Origin of Evil: Beginnings by Caroline Angel
The Broken Doll by P.J. Blakey-Novis
The Broken Doll: Shattered Pieces by P.J. Blakey-Novis
The Vegas Rift by David F. Gray
South by Southwest Wales by David Owain Hughes
Appletown by Antoinette Corvo

Art Books:

Demons Never Die by David Paul Harris & P.J. Blakey-Novis

Children's Books:

Grace & Bobo: The Trip to the Future by Peter Blakey-Novis
My Sister's from the Moon by Peter Blakey-Novis
Elvis the Elephant by Peter Blakey-Novis
The Little Bat That Could by Gemma Paul
The Mummy Walks At Midnight by Gemma Paul
A Very Zombie Christmas by Gemma Paul

Follow Red Cape Publishing

www.redcapepublishing.com
www.facebook.com/redcapepublishing
www.twitter.com/redcapepublish
www.instagram.com/redcapepublishing
www.pinterest.co.uk/redcapepublishing
www.patreon.com/redcapepublishing